Time-Crossed Love

Guardians of the Stones
Time Travel, Book 1

Jane DeGray

Leavesly Park Publishing

Cover design by: SelfPubBookCovers.com/Saphira
Library of Congress Control Number: 2020911482
Printed in the United States of America

To my husband, children, and family for their love, support, and assistance in helping me tell my stories. Thank you!

Contents

Chapter 1

Ashley Duvall stepped out into a foggy London morning, her heart sinking with each step she took leaving the midtown London flat. She had so hoped the visit to an old family friend would help them solve the mystery of her dad's disappearance from his worksite almost two years ago. It had not.

"It was worth a try," Uncle Zeek reassured her. She loved her uncle for caring enough to try to fill in for his absent brother. "It was nice to see Tom, anyway."

"Yeah, I remember when the whole Munroe family came to visit us one summer in Houston. Nice kids." She stopped in her tracks, stricken. "*Gah,* I forgot to even ask about them. Or their mom! How rude is that?"

"He knows why you were there, Ashley, so don't fret about it."

"Maybe, but it makes me feel bad not to have given them a thought. Claire and Jess were really nice."

They walked the rest of the way to Zeek's beat up silver Jeep Wrangler parked a block away without any further conversation, both deep in thought. As they crossed the street a cab driver honked at her for not moving faster to get to the other side. Feeling immense frustration at the moment, she was tempted to flip him off, but Uncle Zeek would not be happy, so she refrained.

When her uncle had offered her this trip to England as a high school graduation gift, she had accepted on the spot. Only afterwards did she think about the fact all the other students would be college upper classmen. That was classic Ashley--act first and think later. Those twenty-four other class-mates had respected her in a hands-off-the-professor's-niece kind of way. Most simply ignored her. That isolation had made for a long and lonely two weeks working at various dig sites around Stonehenge, so this day trip into London was more than welcome.

Catching up to her uncle at the car, she had difficulty sorting through all the questions flooding her mind. "Did you understand what Mr. Munroe said about the old lady who dressed in black like she was from another century?" Her uncle shook his head, frowning deeper as she continued, "He made her sound like a witch the way she appeared and disappeared in people's lives."

"I thought the same thing, which is strange because I wouldn't peg Tom as a person apt to believe in anything occult. If he knew more, he wasn't saying."

"What I don't understand is how she could be key to finding Dad if we don't know who she is or where to find her? We don't even know her name."

"True. I'll have to think about it, Ashley. I have a hazy memory of meeting someone rather odd like her years ago, but I can't quite recall the specifics. Maybe it'll come together for me once I sleep on it."

"It's just disappointing. I'll have to call Mom tonight and let her know. I was hoping to have something more exciting to share."

"When you do, give her my best. Josh, too." Zeek unlocked and opened the car door on the passenger side, ignoring the loud squeak of its rusted hinges. Ashley ducked inside, bumping the top of her head on the door rim. She was busy rubbing it when the slam of the door complained like old bones crunching. *How does this old car keep going? It must run on the fumes of rust and stinky shoes.* She rolled down the window a few inches with the hand crank for fresh air. Zeek was perfectly happy driving the iron beast, and while it rattled like it would fall apart at any moment, it kept rolling along with few repairs needed.

"We have a little extra time before my meeting at the university. Is there any place you'd like to go while I'm there?"

"No, Uncle Zeek. I'm not in the mood." He grinned at her, noting she was still rubbing her noggin. That made her smile and roll her eyes at her own clumsiness. "I'll go with you and find a place to wait until you're done."

"It might be safer," he chuckled, "but keep in mind I don't know how long this will take. You might be an artifact yourself by the time I get out of there."

$$\infty\infty\infty$$

The University College London campus buzzed with activity when they arrived at the Gordon Square office of the Institute of Archeology. Uncle Zeek insisted she meet his colleagues before the meeting even though she would rather have avoided it. The professors were waiting in Dr. Monica Wilson's office. The introductions went by quickly and Ashley missed the names of the two male professors because her attention had landed on Dr. Wilson.

An old saying of Grandma Jenny's came to mind as Ashley watched the tiny, bird-like woman. She sure had her "cap set" for Uncle Zeek.

"What a lovely niece you have, Professor Duvall." Her eyes never left Zeek when she asked, "Are you here for the summer, my dear?" Ashley explained she was in her uncle's archeology class, but she never managed to capture the attention of the little lady whose eyes remained lovingly on Zeek.

Declining the tea offered her, Ashley found herself grinning when Dr. Wilson proclaimed, *"Ah,* but I know precisely how you like your tea, Duvall. Very American. No milk, no sugar, simply blazing hot." She drew out the word "blazing" and her eyebrows waggled when she said the word "hot."

Ashley was happy she had not accepted any tea because she feared it would have spurted out her nose over that comment. If she was not mistaken, one of the other professors did exactly that but covered it with a cough and his napkin. The diminutive lady continued to flit and chirp around her *luv* in her very British way until everyone but Zeek was stifling a giggle.

Uncle Zeek did his best to ignore her machinations but wound up mumbling and blushing despite his efforts. This was a side of her uncle not seen before. How amusing to find her staid uncle was a lady-killer. His ability to flush a bright red was quite remarkable, too, so she couldn't wait to tease him on the way home. She had been the recipient of his merciless teasing often enough. Now was her chance to return the favor.

Excusing herself, she left Zeek to fend for himself, and went in search of a good spot to sit and wait until the meeting ended. She found the perfect place. Skylights and huge windows on either side of the main door of the outer commons allowed plenty of morning sunlight to stream in. Settling into a comfortable-looking brown leather chair in the center of a brilliant sunspot, she basked in its glow like a cat. Her dad had taught her a love of people-watching, so killing time here would not be a bother.

About ten minutes into her wait, a man caught her attention as he came through the door. Why, she wasn't sure. She must have been too obvious in eyeing him because he walked past her, stopped as if thinking, and backed up to speak to her.

Her pulse raced as he stood before her, a step too close to her. Something in the man's aura made her wish to be anywhere else but here, facing him. Who was he and why was he staring at her? She doubted he was a student, because he appeared to be in his forties. Was he a professor? She didn't think so.

The man sported a shiny black, three-piece, pinstriped suit, and had black hair pomaded straight back from his forehead. The word "slick" came to mind. *Decidedly unprofessorial.* When he opened his mouth to speak, he had an accent she couldn't place and a distinctive whistle when air escaped through the gap in his front teeth.

"Excus-s-se me. You are a relative of Profes-s-sor Zeek Duvall?

Who is this? She was shocked when her mouth dropped open, but no words came out. The man grinned at her confusion, enjoying it like a fox in a hen house. His brown eyes darkened to black as he turned more serious a moment later. "Such a pretty blush on such a charming child." She didn't know how to respond to that either, so she didn't.

The man's oily, ingratiating manner did not sit well with her. She gave him her wan, please-go-away-you're-making-me-uncomfortable smile. He didn't budge, although she suspected he knew what she was thinking.

"Have no fear, child, I mean you no harm. I did not wish to startle you." Why then did she feel that was exactly what he meant to do?

"Professor Duvall is a colleague of mine, and I knew a relative from America was with him this summer. You share a family resemblance, so I thought I would chance it to ask you and introduce myself, if s-s-so."

A family resemblance? Perhaps, but that was a stretch. Her dad and Zeek looked nothing alike, and she resembled her mom, not her dad. Besides, how did he know she was with Zeek when none of the other professors were aware of it until her uncle introduced her only minutes ago?

Choosing not to wait for her reply, the man lowered his head a notch as if bowing to her and said, "I am known as Abasi here in London. I deal in antiquities, so I know the university professors quite well. Since I am late for the consultation with your uncle I must take my leave. S-s-so nice to have met you--." He paused on an upward lilt with raised eyebrows, asking her to supply her name. Hypnotized by his basilisk stare, she froze and said nothing. To her consternation, with a slight sneer on his face at her unwillingness to oblige, he finished, "--Miss Ashley Duvall from Texas."

He took a long, unsmiling look at her from head to toe and back up again. Was he trying to creep her out? If so, he had succeeded. Then he turned and strode off, leaving her with her mouth wide open and a chill down her spine cold enough to make her wish for a sweater.

Unsettled by that exchange, she was thankful when her uncle completed his meeting and stood before her a short time later. She wanted to leave before that man appeared again. Zeek, however, insisted they buy sandwiches for the return trip at the snack bar on the lower level before heading to the car. Ashley, convinced Abasi would find them, was so preoccupied looking over her shoulder she wasn't sure what she ordered. Even though she should be plenty hungry by now, her stomach fluttered with nerves.

Once on the road, relieved at having avoided further association with Abasi, she wasted no time before telling Zeek all about her encounter with him.

He was not pleased.

"I'm sorry, Ashley. I should have told you about him, but I never thought you would meet him. He runs the largest antiquities business in London. We refer to him at the university as 'The Boss' because everything goes through him, whether lawful or unlawful." Zeek snorted his disdain for the man. "No one likes dealing with him, but it is all but unavoidable because he has his tentacles everywhere and in everything. Today we were there to authenticate an alabaster vase he is pitching to an important university donor."

"Is he as slick as he looks?"

"Absolutely. The man is pompous, pushy, and powerful, so no one chooses to tangle with him, knowing they'd probably lose." Zeek scratched his head and ran his stubby fingers through his hair, leaving it sticking straight up. "It is disturbing that he knows your name and where you're from. Why would he approach you while alone that way? I don't know what to make of that."

"Is the vase a real antiquity?"

"Yes."

That was the last word he spoke the entire ninety-some miles back to the worksite. Her usually chatty uncle unnerved her with his silence.

She passed him a roast beef sandwich, but he only grunted his acceptance before wolfing it down. She nibbled on hers, her favorite caprese sandwich, still not sure how well it would sit. Had she ordered it or had Uncle Zeek remembered it? Abasi had rattled her so much, she wasn't sure.

At last, their dust-covered SUV screeched to a stop next to an even dustier Jeep at her assigned archeology worksite. Ashley unbuckled her seat belt and leaned over to give her uncle a peck on the cheek. His frown lines had deepened in the last couple of hours, and his sandy hair now stuck out every which way, the result of too much brooding.

The chalky white cloud kicked up by their wheels on the bumpy, unpaved road, caught up with them, rolling over the small vehicle like an early morning fog. Hopefully, it was enough to shield her fellow students from seeing the kiss she probably should have skipped. Once again, a typical act first, think later move.

Zeek raised a professorial eyebrow as if to admonish her, but said nothing. She was allowed in his archeology class only because she was his niece, so it was poor form to make that connection so obvious in front of others. He had never married and had no children, yet she got the feeling he liked it when she did those daughterly things like kiss him goodbye.

She was busy gathering her stuff to get out of the car when Zeek decided to break his silence. "Why do you think Abasi spoke to you?"

With plenty of uninterrupted time to think about the man during the all-too-quiet ride back, she was quick to reply, "I think he works to unsettle people by doing or saying the unexpected. If you are thrown off-guard or intimidated, he finds out what he wants to know. You reveal your vulnerabilities, and he learns what he needs to know to win."

Her uncle's head whipped around, and he stared into her eyes, his surprise showing. "*Wow.* I think you nailed it, Ashley. You sound just as insightful as your dad." She bit her lip at the mention of her dad, and they both swallowed hard, but his praise made her happy. Zeek took a long look at her, his coffee-brown eyes troubled, and said, "It's probably time I told you about--." He interrupted himself by heaving a big sigh. "No, now is not the time. Remind me later."

What was she to make of that?

His demeanor changed a moment later as he looked away and slipped into professorial mode. "Try to forget about your dad and Abasi now. You have a job to do. We can talk later." He proceeded to open his work bible--a pocket notebook he kept on his person at all times--and found her name. "I have you scheduled with Alex and Tiffany today. Brett is sick, I believe. Alex is in charge, so listen to him. Tiffany is ... well, just keep your distance from her, if you can, and she won't bother you. Alex will make sure you get back to base camp. He is assigned to drive the Jeep."

"Got it. Thanks for taking me with you to see Mr. Munroe." She climbed out of the SUV and turned to close the door.

"We'll keep trying to find your dad, Ashley. I never know when or where Rick will show up, but he always has ... eventually."

She sighed and nodded, shutting the car door with a push from her hip. It groaned in answer and didn't quite close. She all but dropped everything in her arms as she threw herself against it one more time. Her efforts were met with screeching success, so Zeek hollered goodbye through the glass and drove off. She turned toward the worksite as anxious as a kindergartner on the first day of school.

∞∞∞

Ashley was searching the grassy area for her team members when a white haze off to her left drifted toward her. If they had been in the Scottish highlands, she would have said it was morning mist hanging in the shallows of a moor. Since the day was now into the heat of the afternoon, and they were on the Salisbury Plains with grassland all around them, this mist was out of place and time. Looking deeper into the vapor, she thought she saw movement within. It wasn't where her team was supposed to be, so who could be there?

As she stared, the silhouette of a person emerged. The mist swirled away for a moment, revealing a man who did not resemble Alex at all. A huge, broad-shouldered man dressed in a black tunic and black leather breeches appeared instead. He had a sword on his hip, a cap on his head, and tall boots on his feet ... like a medieval lord!

What was going on here? Was there some festival nearby she knew nothing about?

He was not alone. A feather in the man's cap bobbed up and down as he talked to a massive black horse in tones she thought she could hear. Was he real or was this her imagination making her see things in the white dust their car had stirred up? Could that be the source of the strange mist? The chalky stuff was unique to the area around Stonehenge. Maybe it was fairy dust and as mystical as the henge. She shook off that fanciful thought.

She was about to credit the mirage to a stressful day when the man swung his head as if she had called to him by name and looked directly at her. Somehow she felt those tawny eyes and the slow smile that spread across his face all the way to her toes. That intense look said he *knew* her. Intimately.

Shocked, she stepped forward trying to see him more clearly, but she blinked ... and he was gone. So was the horse.

The mist dissipated equally fast with a fresh breeze that rolled through, chasing the grass in ripples across the open grassland.

Her legs buckled and she sank to the ground. What on earth had she seen and why was her heart about to burst? Her mind reeled trying to make sense of this vision and how it made her feel. She would remember if she had ever met anyone like him. Of that she was sure. The way he looked at her ... *whew!*

She was sitting in the grass with her knees tucked under her chin staring into the distance when Alex found her.

"Hey, you okay? You haven't moved in like ten minutes."

She looked up at Alex Morse. His face showed true concern. Tall and tan, he was a good-looking guy by anyone's standards. How embarrassing that he now must think she was out of her mind. She would only confirm it if she told him what she thought she had seen. She needed to get control of herself.

"Ashley, is it?" She nodded, unable to form words for a second person, a second time, in a single day. She was never this tongue-tied. What was wrong with her? Her face heated from the neck up. When she sucked in a calming breath, it seemed to trigger uninvited words to fall from her mouth in a rush.

"Yeah, I'm fine. I get carsick and that bumpy road 'bout did me in. I'm always better if I sit for a few minutes once I'm out of the car." She had never been carsick in her whole life. Where had that lie come from?

Alex grinned. "Yeah, I've ridden in the professor's pile o' junk before. I think the only shocks in that thing expired about a dozen years ago."

"I'll tell him you said that," she answered with a straight face.

The smile fell from Alex's lips as he frowned down at her, questions in his bright blue eyes. Well, that joke fell flat. First, she was too uptight and then too loose. Was finding normal too much to ask?

She cocked her head and gave him an apologetic sideways

grin. "I'm teasing, Alex." He visibly relaxed. "Hey, it's not easy being the professor's niece. Everybody seems to be a tiny bit suspicious that everything they say around me gets reported back. I can assure you, it does not."

"Yeah, I see what you mean," he laughed and pulled her to her feet. "Tough spot to be in. I hadn't thought about that." He picked up her purse and her day bag from the ground, dusted them off, and handed them to her.

"Thanks! You're as nice as I heard you were." Now it was his turn to blush, which she rather enjoyed. Maybe she would take a page from Abasi's book and try throwing people off-guard. This was more of a response from anyone than she'd had since she arrived in England.

Alex ran a hand through his sun-kissed blond hair and cleared his throat, deciding to get down to the business of work. He shifted his stance and wiped a hand on his dirt-streaked pants before pointing to the field before them.

"That roped-off area over there is yours. It's next to mine, so if you need anything or have any questions, just ask. Tools are in the back of the Jeep. Help yourself." He started back towards his area and then turned to add one last thing. "Tiffany is way over there." He pointed to a roped-off area she had not noticed about half a football field away. "She's mad at me for something. Don't know what. Ignore her. That's what I do." He grimaced and shook his head before he sauntered over to his area to resume his work.

What an odd thing for him to say. Rumor had it the two were a couple. Still, back-to-back warnings about Tiffany meant she must really be a piece of work. Ashley decided she was fortunate never to have encountered the girl face-to-face in the time she had been here. If her new teammate were that much trouble, she would work to avoid provoking her.

Ashley changed out of her London clothes behind the Jeep with the hatch open, donning her field uniform of capris, a tank top, work socks and boots. She folded the skirt and blouse she had worn into the city and tried not to wrinkle them too much as she stowed them along with her flats in her day bag.

Laundry was not easy to do at base camp, so clothes were worn more than once. This Saturday the plan was to bus them to a local *laundrette*--something that would only happen every two weeks. All her work clothes were past needing a good washing, but then everyone had the same problem. This was her cleanest outfit and it still held the unmistakable stench of sunscreen, dirt, and sweat.

She grabbed one of the tool bags from the Jeep's storage compartment and slammed the tailgate. Throwing her day bag over her shoulder and clutching the tool bag, she hauled her possessions to the spot Alex had indicated was hers. She plopped down inside the ropes and sifted through her bag for sunscreen. It was hotter today than it had been, and she could feel her skin burning. She found the tube but stopped to pull her blonde hair off her shoulders and out of the way before she applied it.

The scent of coconut filled her nose, making her think of long, hot Texas summers. She missed the pool in her backyard and her little brother's swim challenges. Josh rarely beat her, but then he was three years younger. What she wouldn't give for a dip in the pool at the moment.

The sun that had felt so good this morning, now bordered on boil, shining so brightly she needed sunglasses. Hunting through her bag she couldn't find them. Where were they? She had them in London. Then she remembered taking them off in Zeek's SUV when cloud cover rolled in over the Salisbury Plains. Instead of returning them to her bag, she had tossed them down on the dash.

Sunglasses were impossible for her to keep up with. Knowing she had a talent for losing them, she had packed five cheap pairs for the trip. In two weeks she was down to a single pair. At least she knew what she'd done with these. If she were lucky, she would remember to retrieve them from Zeek's car tonight at base camp. In the meantime, she'd just have to squint. *Lovely.*

About an hour later, sweat rolled down her cheeks and her soaked hair stuck to her back. The same strand of hair fell in her eyes no matter how many times she shoved it behind her ear. *Ugh.* Uncle Zeek would have to suffer disappointment in her because she and archeology fieldwork were not a match.

Glancing over at Alex, hard at work in his area, she could see he was not the sweat-ball she was. You'd think being from Houston she would have a tolerance for heat, but honestly, she had none. At home summers were so hot everyone moved from their air-conditioned houses to their air-conditioned cars to their air-conditioned destinations. If she weren't at the beach or by the pool, she wasn't outside.

She got up and dug out a third bottle of water from her day bag. She might be well-hydrated, but the empty bottles were mounting. After taking a long swig, she wiped her mouth with the back of her hand. This bottle she capped and crammed into a side-pocket of her capris where it would be easier to grab.

Believing her last location a dud, she shifted to a place closer to Alex within her roped-off area. She sat down with her legs spread apart, so she could dig between her knees, too tired to sit on her haunches any longer. The hand trowel she had been using was behind her, so she scooted back like a land crab and snagged it. Back in place again, she jammed it into the earth to soften the area, but a few strikes later she hit something hard. A feeling not unlike that of hitting her crazy bone zinged up her arm from her fingertips. *Hmm,* interesting. Quickly, she shoveled several scoops of dirt away to reach the hard surface below.

Clearing the area of debris, she revealed the flat top of a stone about the size of a large paver. As she rubbed the top with her fingers she realized she needed a soft-bristled brush if she wanted to get a better look. Dumping out the contents of her tool bag, she came to the conclusion the one assigned to the bag was missing. Alex had told her to ask him if she needed anything, so this would be a good time to take him up on the offer.

"Hey, Alex!" He answered with a shouted *yeah* and turned to give her his attention. "Mind if I borrow your little soft-bristled brush? My bag doesn't have one."

"Sure thing." He scooped up a brush lying at his feet and tossed it to her with athletic ease. She fumbled the catch and it dropped in front of her. "You find somethin'?"

"Yeah, no, maybe, ... I dunno." What a decisive answer. She rolled her eyes in frustration.

Alex threw his head back and barked a laugh. "You'll be right with that answer every time." Heat filled her face again. He brushed the dirt off his hands and stepped over the rope separating their areas.

"What do you think it is?" Alex bent over to see what she worked on, but his eyes lingered a moment too long on the scoop neck of her tank top. Staring up into his handsome face, she wondered if he'd pressed her mute button. If not, why else would words refuse to come out? His eyes were smiling and non-judgmental.

What was it he asked? Her mind bounced around like a ping-pong ball in search of a net. She dropped her eyes to the rock in front of her and blinked hard in an attempt to order her thoughts.

That same wispy strand of damp hair that she had shoved repeatedly behind her ear, popped out again, just as a rivulet of perspiration trickled down her cheek. Distracted, she brushed the wetness away, wondering if her body was determined to embarrass her in front of this guy.

"Here," Alex chuckled, snagging a red bandanna from his back pocket. He knelt beside her and expertly whipped it into a cord before wrapping it Indian-style around her head. "You need this more than I do." He tucked the errant hairs under the scarf and tied it off on the back of her head with remarkable efficiency.

"Th-thanks, Alex." She could not hide her surprise at this

unexpected kindness as she all but stammered at him, "That's r-really ... n-nice of you."

"Well, you told me I was a nice guy. Remember?" Amusement twinkled in those blue eyes as he wiggled a finger at her smudged cheek. "Besides, you, *uh,* need it." Alex held the side of her face with one hand and wiped off what must have been a muddy smear with a swipe of his thumb. Mortified, she rolled her eyes up to his in apology, but once again she could think of nothing to say.

Alex tipped up her chin and gave her a quick kiss on her sunburned nose. A shiver rushed up her torso and fought its way out in a shake of her head. She grinned. Alex leaned back and winked at her. "You're cute when you get flustered."

And just like that, she found her mute off button. "Does that line actually work for you?"

"Hmm, you're flushed, short of breath, and your voice is fluttering. What do you think?"

"I think I retract nice for arrogant."

"Ah, come on, Ashley, admit you liked it. You're fun to tease."

Before she could launch a retort, he reached in and tickled her ribs. How did he know her ribs were her weak spot? Like a perfect idiot she shrieked and laughed uncontrollably until he deemed she'd had enough.

She was still gasping for breath when he got to his feet, smirking at his success, and strode off toward the Jeep. His backside, featuring wide shoulders and narrow hips, was a thing of beauty, so even though she felt miffed, she watched him saunter to the car, appreciating the view.

She hadn't been teased like that since Ryan Sanders stole a kiss in 7th grade. It made her a little homesick. She heaved a big sigh and picked up the little brush.

O-o-o-w-w-w!

Dirt and gravel avalanched down upon her head, knocking her flat with such force she couldn't catch her breath. For a moment, no part of her body responded to a command. Then she coughed, sputtered, and spit out mud, struggling to sit up.

Dragging her fingers over her eyelids, she swiped away the filth to reveal ... *Tiffany?* At least she thought it must be Tiffany because she was supposed to be the only other person out here. Blinking the crud from her eyes she got a better look at her. She was dark-haired and wore a black t-shirt, black jeans, and black work boots. It fit her mood, judging from the black look in her dark eyes.

"Why'd you do that? You don't even know me!"

"Keep your grubby little paws off Alex. He's mine." Tiffany glared daggers at her, the empty debris bucket resting on one hip.

"Fine! Ya' got him." She wanted to say Alex's grubby paws were on her, not the other way around.

"Hey! *He-e-ey!*" Alex trotted back toward them, a scowl marring his perfect features. "What have you done now, Tiff?" He stopped about an inch from her person and fisted his hands on his hips. "Huh, Tiff?"

She speared him with a glance hot enough to smelt iron. Slamming the bucket into his ribs, she took off at a run for the Jeep.

"Tiffany. Tiff!" Alex thrust the bucket aside as he tore off after her. It sailed past Ashley's face by a hair before skidding into the dirt beside her. Already halfway to the vehicle, Alex lunged and grabbed the girl's arm, jerking her around to face him.

"What is it this time? Remember you haven't spoken to me in two days."

Tiffany snatched her arm out of his hold and stomped off. "Leave me alone, Alex. You can just stay here with baby girl for all I care."

"What? You're jealous?" He enunciated his words with spitting precision. "Really, Tiff? You're upset over Ashley? I met her an hour ago! This is so beneath you."

Tiffany beat him to the Jeep and ducked inside. He caught the door a second before she slammed it in his face. Prying her out of the driver's seat, he pushed her over and into the passenger side. "No way are you driving, woman. Get. Over."

Their loud, angry voices were snuffed out by the slam of the car door. With a gear-grinding scrape, the battered Jeep jolted to life as if it were equally furious and peeled toward base camp, spewing out dirt chunks like nasty words.

Hey, what about me?

∞∞∞

Quiet rolled over the dig site along with a healthy dose of loneliness. *Wow. What a show.* She got to her feet, sending gravel trailing in streams down her front, and searched the landscape. No other worksite was visible. She was here by herself and stranded. What a fitting end to a weird day.

Alex was supposed to be responsible for getting her back to camp. Would he remember to come back for her? Would anyone tell Uncle Zeek she was missing? Would anyone care? Tears leaked from her eyes and sneaked down her cheeks.

In times like these, she missed the comfort of home. Deflated, Ashley snuffled as she thought about her mom, the one who bucked her up whenever life crushed her. She sighed deeply, then straightened her spine and pressed her shoulders back. Her mother was her rock, but the lady lived an ocean away in Texas, so Ashley would be bucking up herself this time. Her mom had enough on her plate caring for Josh as a single parent. She didn't need her daughter's problems compounding her own. The last promise she'd made to her mother was to do her best to be happy and stay safe this summer in England. She intended to keep that promise.

Shaking off self-pity, she forced herself to unwind, letting her eyes roam about for a moment. The events of the day had thrown her off more than she cared to admit, but she was strong. She could handle this.

She pulled out her smartphone and checked for coverage. None. No surprise there. She would find her way back to camp somehow. If no one showed up by dusk, she would get through to Uncle Zeek at some point by phone. Reception was sporadic, but it always got better toward evening. At the moment, she didn't want to talk to anyone anyway.

She might as well work in the meantime. It would make the wait go faster. Locating the brush Alex had tossed her, she sat down and started to dust the stone she hoped was worth all the trouble.

Minutes later, a faint roar in the distance made her glance toward the road where she saw a trail of dust kicked up and a black SUV coming toward her. *Yay!* Alex must have sent someone to rescue her. She jumped up, dusted herself off, and waited for the car to get closer. Her face turned as white as the dust on the road and her smile vanished when she recognized the driver was none other than Abasi.

Why was he here? Where was Uncle Zeek? The Boss was the last person she wanted to see out in the middle of nowhere with no one else around. The SUV turned in and stopped a few feet off the road. Abasi emerged a moment later, grinning ear to ear when he looked about and realized she was alone.

"Why if it isn't little Miss Duvall. How delightful to s-see you again so s-soon."

Ashley's heart was in her throat. Never had she felt so threatened. What did this man want? She summoned all her courage to respond with as much confidence as possible, but her legs shook along with her voice. "My uncle will be along soon to pick me up. Is there some message you want me to give him?"

Abasi took a step closer and his grin widened. "You as-s-sume I am here to find him? As you know, I deal in antiquities, so I thought I'd drop by and s-see what *you* are working on."

"Drop by? From London?" Ashley heard her voice rise to an uncomfortable height, revealing her concern.

"It pays in my field to be the first on the s-scene when someone finds an artifact. After all, it is my busines-s-s." His eyes traveled over the two worksites before him as if he expected an artifact to pop up and expose itself.

"Well, so far, nothing to report here." She strove for a carefree attitude with a little laugh at the end, but it was brittle sounding. Fear hung over her words like a wet blanket. "Perhaps you need to visit the next site a couple miles from here. Maybe their luck's been better today than mine."

"*Tsk, tsk!* You s-sound as if you do not enjoy my company, Mis-s-s Duvall. You do not wish me to stay and keep you company until your uncle comes?" Abasi threw his hand over his heart, mocking her. "You wound me." He was enjoying her discomfort way too much. She swallowed hard and attempted to look unconcerned, but his smirk told her he knew precisely how uncomfortable he made her. Well, she had had enough.

"Suit yourself. I have work to do." She turned on her heel and strode back to her roped off area, plopped down, and prayed he would leave. Picking up a trowel, she dug beside the stone she had been working on, dumping dirt on top of it. She didn't want him to see she had found something, or she'd never get rid of him.

Abasi whistled an eerie tune she didn't recognize as he took his time sauntering around Alex's work area, winding up directly behind her. Looming over her backside like a storm cloud, he did his best to intimidate her. It worked. She feared if she said anything at all to him, he would stay, so it turned into some kind of weird spitting match. He waited for her to speak, and she waited for him to speak. Neither would give in.

After what seemed like an eternity, he patted her on top of her head as if she were a small child and walked away. Without lifting her head she watched him get into his car, back out onto the road, and speed away in the direction of the next worksite.

It was several minutes before her breath evened out and her muscles could relax. She flopped back, folded her hands over her chest, mummy-style, and just breathed. A short time later, feeling somewhat better, she sat up and looked around to see if Abasi had disturbed anything. Everything appeared to be as Alex had left it.

E-e-e-o-o-w!

Without warning, her body neatly lifted off the ground by at least a foot before she was slapped back to earth with a thud.

Ashley scrambled to her feet as if the very devil himself had thumped her bottom. Wide-eyed, she stared down where she had been sitting in time to see the stone she had hidden from Abasi reveal itself.

About the size of a stepping-stone, the thing emitted a ghostly glow. As she bent for a better look, letters embedded on the face flamed to life like a fire had been stoked from within. Good sense and a shot of adrenaline told her to run for her life and not stop until she got back to Texas, never mind the ocean.

Inexplicably, she ignored both and dropped to her knees beside the stone. Every ounce of her pronounced it a dumb thing to do, but her body didn't listen as her trembling fingers reached out to touch the bright characters.

Then the command from her brain reached its destination and made her yank her hand back. Her act-first-think-later routine might be a real problem right now. She needed to be more careful, especially with Abasi skulking around. At least he wasn't here to witness this. Wouldn't he just love it.

The stone glowed eerily once the letters finished burning. Oddly, it did not smell hot. She tilted her head to better examine the crude writing and identified the characters, but they formed no words she knew. *Some ancient language?* These weren't English words. At least she didn't think so.

Twllyn amser.

Old English? Uncle Zeek would know. Sweat slid off her nose and dripped onto the stone, but no sizzle sounded as the moisture hit the fiery figures. How could they not be hot? *Amazing.* She tried to sound out the unfamiliar words, the tones trilling off her tongue.

Tuh-will-in-ahm-sir.

What did that mean?

Excitement coursed through her body as she played with the sound of the strange phrase, chanting it first high, then low, three times in succession. She shook her head to clear her mind. Was this really happening? Yes. Yes it was. Her mouth twitched up in sheer awe at the spellbinding stone before her.

A strong breeze startled her, whirling up and into her face, forcing her to rock back on her haunches. What was this? Standing, she frowned at the sudden change and looked around for the source. To her dismay, what she found instead was Abasi's black SUV parked right back where it had been only minutes before. *N-o-o-o-o-o!* Had he found no one to torment at the next worksite? What would it take to make that man go away?

As he stepped out of his car, the door slammed shut with the force of the wind, making him jump to get out of its way. He hollered something at her, his hands cupped around his lips, but the sound was carried away in the other direction.

Something wasn't right. Cool air that would have been a welcome relief from the heat only a few minutes ago triggered panic deep inside her. Where was this wind coming from? Dark storm clouds once lurking behind Stonehenge a short distance away were abruptly overhead. Lightning split the sky with whiplash speed.

Everything began to move at once. Tools shivered and skated away. Ropes split from their stakes, and her empty water bottles tipped, rolled, and became missiles. The last she saw of Abasi, he was sprinting toward her looking stricken, the whites of his eyes circling their black centers. She lost sight of him before he reached her when the swirling air turned into a whirlwind with her body at its vortex.

Terror-stricken, she threw her arms over the back of her head tornado drill style and flung her body over the glowing stone to protect it. She wouldn't give it up for Abasi to find.

Not now. Not without Uncle Zeek seeing it first.

Flying objects pinged into her bare arms and legs like shrapnel. A scream ripped out of her but was swallowed by violent gulps of wind. Horrified, Ashley felt her entire body lift into the darkness and spin out of control. Bone-deep fear sucked out the last thought she could form: *I'm sorry, Mom.*

Chapter 2

England, 1363

Horses thundered past him in the early morning light, their hooves sending dirt clods flying over the rutted trail like hailstones in a storm. Robert Spycer, heir to the Earl of Hertford, ducked on foot into the confines of the forest edge with only seconds to spare, expecting no friend and fearing foe.

He still held the game birds he had shot for breakfast as he crouched in foliage he hoped covered him well. More than a dozen men galloped by him heading in the direction of Hertford castle. Robert glared after them, alarm pinging through his body as he noted their formation meant the soldiers were holding someone in custody in their midst.

Whom they had arrested he could not tell for certain. He could not positively identify the standard they flew from his position in the ferns, but dread skittered across his being and panic pierced his heart. Deep down, he knew who it was.

Loud voices echoed in the morning air as he raced along the tree line toward the old hunting lodge. It appeared through the mist as if dropped in place before him by a magician. Those unhappy words confirmed his worst fear. His love, his life, his soon-to-be-wife was gone! A vision of her blonde loveliness and her sky-blue eyes shimmered before him and then melted into nothingness.

Robert awoke with a start in a full-body sweat that turned icy in the damp, nighttime air. Several frantic heartbeats later, he sat up and gained control of his senses. His encampment was plainly visible. His men were sequestered on a nearby hillside beside a deserted tenant's wattle and daub hut. His stallion Lucifer was staked beside him. Nothing was amiss.

Calmed by a deep breath, Robert puzzled over his experience. A seasoned warrior, he never panicked, even in combat, but his fierce need to reach his future wife shocked him as her face floated into his waking memory. She was blonde. She was blue-eyed. She was beautiful. She was not, however, his betrothed.

A shudder fell over him as he reached for his saddle blanket and wrapped it around his shoulders. Her face haunted his dreams nightly. Indeed, the woman was lovely, but he did not know her.

Olde Gylda of Hampshire had warned of this woman's power over him, but when his father banned the soothsayer from the castle, the warning had vanished from his thoughts. Until now. Who might this mysterious woman be?

His betrothed, she was not. Charissa Fitz-Maurice, the only child of the Earl of Mowbry, had been his intended since her birth, nearly fifteen years ago. Their union ensured a peaceful alliance would hold between the two earls for generations to come.

In the intervening years Robert had visited Charissa only a few times. He recalled a pretty little thing with sparkling green eyes and shiny dark hair. Unsettled by the thought, he squirmed uncomfortably. Sensing unease, Lucifer whickered softly and nudged his master's head, his velvety muzzle nuzzling Robert's ear.

"I know, Luce. I woke you, did I not?" Robert hooked an arm under the big black's head and rubbed his face against the stallion's smooth cheek. "'Twas naught but a dream, me thinks. I have one too many women on my mind." Lucifer bobbed his head as if he agreed, making Robert smile.

"You, my friend, did not witness my shame the last time I called on my betrothed. You were out relaxing in the mews beside a dainty filly." Lucifer snickered.

That had been shortly before Charissa's thirteenth birthday. When the two were left alone, conversation had been sparse.

"Aye, 'twas embarrassing. We sat there with nothing to say to each other. Busy bumbling for words, I was not aware of her hound puppy sneaking up behind me. I should have been forewarned because Lady Charissa's eyes were bright and her smile wide. I thought her good-humored because I was visiting. No. Her pup poked his head under my arm and stole the biscuits off my plate, skidding out of the room on his fat belly before I could stop him. My lady shrieked with laughter and called in a cheery voice for the reprobate to behave."

Lucifer stomped and blew air out his nose. Robert laughed.

"*Whoa*, boy. Thanks for the sympathy. 'Tis true I was caught unawares and unsure of myself. Was she laughing at me or at her pet? 'Twas silly for me to be red-faced and flummoxed over a pup's antics, but I could think of nothing else to say. I threw back my cup of ale and excused myself. That was one, no, two years ago."

'Twas an experience he would gladly forget.

What had happened to his sense of humor? He should have laughed about the little dog's sneak attack. Instead, he had sat there ill at ease with Lady Charissa. Being with her had felt ... *wrong.* Perhaps their awkwardness would be relieved when they learned more about each other. He hoped so.

Ever the opportunist, Lucifer lipped Robert's pockets searching for an apple. "No, boy, nothing there." He scratched the soft ears for a moment and admired the long-lashed, dark eyes that tracked his every move. Then he pushed the beast's head aside with a gentle pat. "Time to settle down and sleep." Attuned to his master's changing mood, Lucifer moved away to tug at the tasty long grass next to his stake. His beast may not have much advice to give, but he listened well.

Feeling less on edge, Lord Robert stretched out on the grassy knoll. A ceiling of stars twinkled above his head, so he searched for a sign. A sign of what, he knew not. Something exciting needed to happen in his life ... and soon.

At three-and-twenty, he was known across his father's lands as a stalwart soldier, having seen his share of battle. As heir to the earldom, Robert valued his father's opinion above all others and sought to please him in all things. Now of an age to take a wife, he must follow through with the union arranged by his father and Mowbry.

Hitherto, the idea of marriage never occupied his mind for long. But that was before this blonde woman inhabited his dreams. What should he make of her? Might this be a trick of some soothsayer to dishonor him as the heir?

Alone with his thoughts under the night sky, Robert got his sign. As if on command, a star fell and glistened as it streaked along a path to the horizon before him. Should he make a wish?

He shut his eyes and freed his mind. What did he want most of all? *Ah,* yes, there 'tis. *I wish to love a woman who loves me in return.* Springing to his feet, he ran forward hoping nearness would help him see where the shooting star coursed as it faded from view.

Happy with his wish and pleased with his luck, Robert shushed Lucifer's questioning *nicker* and sprawled again on the hillside to contemplate his marital future. His party would arrive at Castle Hertford in two day's time. Robert vowed to the heavens to straightaway send a rider with a message to the Earl of Mowbry inquiring about Charissa's readiness to marry.

If reluctant, she might need a nudge to remind her the time had come to do her duty. *Yes, 'tis a solid plan.* He would forget all about the blue-eyed beauty of his dreams.

Satisfied with his course of action, Robert settled back with his hands under his head to await daylight. "Aye, Lucifer, all will be well. I am sure of it." Still listening, the stallion snorted his response.

Staring at the canopy of stars above, Robert drifted-off, vaguely aware his vision of a green-eyed miss had morphed into a blue-eyed lady.

Chapter 3

Ashley felt the presence of someone close to her face before she opened her eyes. Was it Abasi? *Please, no.* Every ounce of her body hurt at the moment, and she wasn't prepared to put up a tough front. He was sure to smell her vulnerability. Where was he now? He had been there watching her when the winds came. She remembered the horrible sensation of being whirled into the black and shuddered. What did he want from her anyway? Did he know about the stone?

Her skin tingled with the knowledge she was being watched. Ignoring it, she rubbed her aching brow with both hands, hoping it was anyone but Abasi waiting quietly for her to recover. Lying flat on her back, she stretched, testing each leg, ankle, and foot for damage. Relief flooded her when her joints flexed as they should.

Thankful the damage was minimal, she gathered her courage and opened her eyes expecting to see the face of someone she knew. Instead, she met the eyes of a very old man whose face was inches from her own. She jerked away, but the hard ground kept her pinned beneath him.

"Do not fret, my good woman. Are ye hurt?"

Did he say *my good woman?* Where *was* she? The ancient man had long, white hair that hung down around her face like a curtain as he bent over her. An odd-shaped hat that was not quite a tam or a nightcap, tilted to one side on his head. His eyebrows poked out in front of his face in tufts that shadowed his eyes. Shifting to get a better look, she discovered one eye was a walleye, which lent him a frightening demeanor since it stared at her with an unrelenting glare. His good eye peered into her face with dismay, as if he feared for her life. Maybe she wasn't okay.

Before she could even think about moving to get up, the old man's mouth stirred again, making his scraggly beard twitch as he spoke. "Have ye suffered a fall p'rhaps?" He patted her cheek with spindly fingers.

She needed space to think. Placing one open palm in the center of the old man's chest, she pushed him away. He obliged her by fastening those long fingers, surprisingly strong, around her wrists and pulling her into a sitting position. Shocked, she discovered the man wore nothing but a dark brown robe, banded at the waist with a piece of rope. It was short enough to reveal a pair of rickety ankles, the bones of which glowed with a pearlescent color above his sandals. Giggles erupted behind him telling her he was not alone.

As if on cue, two heads popped out from behind the old man's body, one on either side of him. He stepped back in between them and made the introductions. "I am Edmund, of Ashdown and these are my daughters, Meggie and Alice."

Meggie, wearing a small cap that fit like a baby bonnet over her long, dark hair, stared at her with wide eyes as if she had dropped from the heavens like a toad. *Hmph,* maybe she had at that. Opposite her, Alice rested her chin on her father's stooped shoulder as she, too, watched with great interest, her springy red hair frothing like a halo around her face. Their loose-fitting, cream-colored, woven dresses were banded at the waist with a simple rope belt. Well-worn half boots made of a soft, leather-like material were on their feet. Together the three might have stepped out of the painting of peasants that hung above her mother's couch at home. It was disorienting.

"Might ye be hurt or ill?" the old man asked again.

Scrambling to her feet, Ashley struggled to regain her composure. *"Uh,* no, I'm not ill," she squeaked. At least she thought she wasn't. The old man nodded in relief, his good eye following her every move.

She searched around her feet expecting to see the glowing stone, but it was nowhere in sight. Dread surged through her. Had these people taken it while she was out? A quick look around told her that was unlikely. All they had with them was an empty three-wheel wooden cart.

She couldn't lose that blasted rock before Uncle Zeek got to see it, so where was it? How could it disappear from underneath her without a trace? And now that she thought of it, where had this narrow, dirt lane come from anyway? There were no tire tracks so it couldn't be the same one she and Zeek had driven in on. Besides, it lacked that chalky quality. With a growing sense of alarm, she realized a more immediate problem than a lost stone or a dirt lane.

I am not anywhere near the dig site.

Ashley's eyes tracked over her surroundings in hopes of spying something familiar, only to find nothing she recognized. Just how far had that wind blown her?

The sun was shining, the sky blue, and the pungent smell of lavender hung in the air. Honeybees buzzed around some pink flowering thing in the field beside her when her world went woozy for a moment. *Will munchkins pop out and a good witch float down?* Maybe she should be happy it was a dirt lane and not a yellow brick road. What was happening to her?

"She looks green around the edges," Alice said. "Like midsummer pond moss."

"Hun-uh," Meggie disagreed. "More the shade of my new Sunday shawl."

Sensing an ensuing argument, the old man cried, "Hush, daughters!" He waved his arms to quiet them and they ceased, but not before Alice had reached behind her father and pinched Meggie's arm. She yowled causing her father to turn his wall-eyed stare on each of them in turn.

Ashley ignored the sisters, swallowed hard, and focused all her attention on the old man's good eye, hoping to steady herself.

"I'm so sorry to be a bother. Please let me explain. My name is Ashley Duvall, and I am an American student here on a summer archeology dig with my uncle and twenty-four other students. I think the strong winds a few minutes ago picked me up and deposited me here." She paused long enough to blow out a breath. "I'm a little shaken, I guess."

The old man's face scrunched. As her words registered, he and his daughters stepped behind their rough-hewn cart as if they needed it for protection. The three peered with caution from side to side at the surrounding quiet, above to the cloudless blue sky, and then to each other. Their eyes told her they did not believe what she said. She had to admit no evidence of a storm was visible around her. A knot formed in her gut while she waited, willing them to speak. Not one of them obliged.

"I-I got separated from the rest of my class," she said, her hands pleading her case with palms up. "I'm part of the university archeology dig by Stonehenge? Perhaps you could tell me how to get back there?" She felt stupid saying she was lost, but she really *was* lost.

All three sets of eyes narrowed as if they were confused and did not understand what she said. She tried again. *"Uhm,* unfortunately, I have no idea where *here* is or, *uhm,* how to get back to my group. Could you please help me?" Ashley's smile wavered as black threatened the edges of her sight.

Finally, the old man sucked in a strand of his scraggly white beard and spoke, "What storm ye mean is a myst'ry, and I fear I know not what ye portend by 'Uhm-er-i-cuhn.'" His voice dropped and the last syllable tipped timorously out and rolled downhill, like he would be struck dead for saying it.

Of course it had stormed. That whirlwind came up fast and passed even faster. Could they have missed it? Of more concern was the last part.

"You've never heard of America?"

All three shook their heads with certainty.

"What means she, Father?" Meggie spoke in soft tones above his ear.

"Who might she be? Look at 'er! She be wearin' breeches

36

like a lad," Alice added with a gulp.

Ashley's smile faltered. Do they really not know about America? *Breeches?* The way they examined her clothes made her uncomfortable. Her friend Jazz back in Texas always told her she had no fashion sense, but then she was working at the dig site. What was so unusual about a pink tank top and khaki cargo capris? Her work boots weren't feminine but necessary for fieldwork.

Oh, yeah. Alex's red bandana still wound around her head Indian-style. Was that the offending item? She gave an impatient swipe at the stubborn strand of hair that once again defied the confines of her headband.

A chill found its way down her spine a moment later when all three still followed her with watchful eyes. So now what should she do?

"Uhm, so sorry to be such a bother. Maybe I'd better use my phone and call my uncle, okay?" Ashley unbuttoned the back pocket of her pants, dug out her smartphone, and prayed it would show service bars this time.

"Fuh-own?" The old man formed the word like he was speaking in slow motion. The redhead's eyebrows shot up and the brunette's mouth flopped open. Another time she might have laughed at their shocked faces, but right now befuddlement and anxiety ruled her. *Who are these people?*

"Yeah, if I can catch up with him you won't have to do anything at all." She hoped. Ashley pressed the button and the phone dinged to life, displaying its colorful icons. *Hang it. A full charge, but no coverage bars at all.*

Reception at night seemed to be the only service available the last two weeks, and it didn't look like it would be dark for a while. So here she was--lost and no cell phone. Why would she ever think good luck would come her way?

Ashley gave up and shut down her phone to save the juice, praying nighttime would come soon and her chances of reaching her uncle would improve.

Her companions had the strangest expressions when she

glanced up from her phone. What did they think she was holding? *Sheesh.* If she didn't know better she'd think they were rattled and scared to death of her phone, judging from their expressions. This was modern day England, right? How could they not know about cell phones?

She took a step toward them as she started to speak and they stepped back as if one mind governed three bodies. If the old man could have sprinted, he would have led the retreat to safer ground. They obviously wanted no part of her device.

Then it hit her. What if she weren't in England anymore? Her pulse quickened and she tasted bile. Just where was she? How was she going to return to camp? She wanted nothing more than to be safe and sound back at base camp for the night.

Ashley stuffed the phone back into her pocket and buttoned the flap a heartbeat before her emotions tsunami'd up from her toes, engulfed her brain, and spilled over.

"I'm so sorry. I don't know what to do. I'm in a foreign country. I don't know where I am or how to get back to base camp. I don't know anyone to ask. And I can't even call for help because there's no *freaking* phone service in the area. *Uggghhh.*" Hot tears slithered down her face. The highs and lows of this day were too exhausting.

Fully realizing the severity of the mess she was in, her legs gave out and she sank to the ground. Overwhelmed, she couldn't keep it in. Two years' worth of troubles burbled out of her as if she had tapped into an underground spring.

The old man and his daughters huddled for a moment, deciding amongst themselves what to do with her before they approached.

"There, there now," the old man crooned, patting her gently on the back and then wiping her face with his grimy, long sleeve. "Nothing can be so bad it cannot be fixed by a nice meal and a place to sleep. We will take ye to the Earl of Hertford. He will know what to do with ye." That surprisingly firm hand latched onto her arm and the old man trained his good eye on Ashley. "Come now."

With little breath left to wheeze out her consent, Ashley merely nodded. Too unsteady to walk, the girls helped her sit in their ancient cart before heading on down the dusty road. The old man tottered along beside them.

Relieved for the moment, she felt downright silly sprawled across what was nothing more than a large wheelbarrow, but sobs still racked her chest keeping composure at bay. What was wrong with her? She didn't recognize herself all wimpy, crying and faint prone, yet look at her now. "You are all so ... kind. Th-thank you." Ashley wiped her runny nose on the heel of her hand and tried hard for a winning smile. "Perhaps they'll have ... a landline I can use ... there."

No response again. She noted the worried eyes of her new friends still darted from one to the other as they pushed her a little faster.

Chapter 4

Some time later, Ashley awoke from a satisfying dream to the hum of voices above her, feeling content and flushed. It took a minute or two to remember where she was and tag those voices with their owners--the old man and his daughters. She remembered shutting her eyes, but how had she fallen asleep when jouncing along in the wooden cart meant she felt every bump in the dirt road? Intending to sit up and join in the conversation, she hesitated when one of the daughters said, "She cares not if her legs drape across the handcart. She be no lady."

Really? Hmm, her mother might not approve, but was it wrong to play possum and hear what else they had to say?

"Yer no lady in yer sleep, Alice. Why should she be?" That must have earned a bump from Meggie because there was a *yip* right before the cart lurched to one side.

"Poor little mite," their father said. "She must be in some kind of trouble to be such a watering pot. I wonder from whence she comes." The man rambled on as slowly as he walked, judging from the squeal of the front wheel as it took its time completing each rotation. "Even as she sleeps, the tear right there," he paused, and she imagined a finger near her eye, "says all is not well with her. Worry was written in her big, blue eyes."

One of the daughters--maybe Alice--added her own concern, "Are ye sure we should 'ave taken 'er up, Father?" Ashley felt the tickle of hair touch her body as the girl leaned over her. "What strange bits and baubles she hath. I've ne'er seen the like." She hesitated. "Might she be a witch?"

A witch? That comment shocked Ashley who almost gave away her game. Then the wheelbarrow knocked the thought out of her brain as it glanced off something hard and careened sharply to the left, nearly dumping her out onto the road. "Watch yer side, Meggie. Ye make me do all the pushin'."

"Sor-ry." Meggie overcorrected and almost dumped Ashley out the other side. Still pretending to be asleep, Ashley moaned and shifted herself to the center of the cart, this time flopping a hand over her eyes so she might not be seen peeking out. "How kin I 'elp it if ye push us into a stone."

"Quit yer fussing, daughters." One sister yowled at the injustice, but the old man continued, "Shush now, Alice. I swear ye hath scrapped with Meggie since the day she was born and ye tried to bean 'er with a milk jug."

Alice made a growl deep in her throat but obliged by going back to her initial accusation. "Might she be a wicked woman, Father? Mayhap she be mad like Olde Gylda of Hampshire. If we take 'er to the earl, what will he do with 'er?"

That got Ashley's attention. What *would* this earl do with her?

"Now, daughter, ye know Gylda is not mad. 'Tis a powerful witch she be and knows it. But remember the earl listens only to his wizard on questions such as these."

Did she hear them right? They spoke of a witch *and* a wizard? They believed this? Where *was* she, anyhow?

"If the earl be not in residence, we will hope to find Cedric in his stead, and we may rid ourselves of this burden. Then Cedric can deal with Hertford, and we shall not be 'eld to account if things go astray."

"What noises that gimcrack in 'er drawers made," noted Alice. Ashley almost jumped when a finger poked softly above her pocket. Did the girl think her phone might make a noise if provoked or had she seen Ashley tapping it with her finger and was trying to do the same? A long pause with just the sound of the squeak in the wheel made her contemplate sneaking a peek to see what was going on. Before she had a chance to do that, the old man sighed and said, "What other wonders she must 'ave in all those pockets of 'er breeches."

She decided then and there she would not pretend to sleep through a search of her pockets. A moment later, the jig was up when Ashley's shoulder slammed into the ground and her limbs flew in different directions.

"Now ye done it."

"Tis yer fault, Meggie. Ye hit that tree root like I knowed ye would."

"'Twas *ye* not payin' attention. Not aye."

Discombobulated for real, Ashley fought to find her feet as well as her voice.

"Did-did I do something wrong? Is it my turn now to push?" Pretending sleep-fluster was easy as she staggered about for a step or two. "Are you still taking me to the earl?"

The old man glared at his squabbling daughters and spoke in a soft voice to Ashley. "So sorry, my good woman. I would push the cart myself, but, alas, I can no longer manage a heavy load."

Ashley winced. She shouldn't have made these nice folks push her while she eavesdropped on them. Worse, memory of that pleasant dream involving her medieval horseman rolled across her brain and left her cheeks as hot as they had been when she awoke. She started to offer an apology when the old man *ahem'd* and said, "We shall see Castle Hertford once 'round the next bend. We should arrive before dark."

"The earl lives in a castle? A real castle? They should have some kind of phone there, right?" Wide-awake now and everything else forgotten, her eyes followed where the old man pointed.

Yuck. Why was her mouth so dry? Had it been open while she slept? Had she drooled? She wiped her hand across her mouth just in case before she reached into her cargo pocket mid-thigh to pull out her water bottle. Popping the top, she shot a stream of water into her mouth. Shocked faces greeted her a moment later.

"Oh, forgive my manners. I only have this bottled water, but I can share if you'd like. See, it has a sports top, too, so you can just squeeze water out, and it's sanitary and everything."

Hang it. That blank expression appeared again. This time they all stared at the water container like she had committed a crime by having it. Maybe that was it.

"Okay, I know it isn't green to carry a plastic bottle, but with no water source at the campsite, there isn't a place to fill the stainless steel kind."

No reply from the white-faced three. She shook it off.

"So, let's get going. The sooner we start walking the sooner we get there."

Geez, that's exactly what my mother would say.

A shadow crossed Ashley's mind as she thought longingly of her mother and the safety of her life back in the States. She forced herself to take a deep breath, pulled off her bandana, and swung it in the air as if to hurry her peculiar little parade onward.

Chapter 5

"What is it, Cedric?" Lady Elena bobbed up and down at the wizard's side as he surveyed the ashes of his offering. The wizened old man said nothing, but his eyes glowed with a peculiar spark Elena recognized.

"You see something, do you not?" Her eyes roved over his craggy face, searching for the answer.

Moments before, Elena had observed Cedric use his skill with a mortar and pestle to pound and mix his special herbs and other sundries. After wiping his hands on the front of his robe, he had set the dubious-looking mixture on fire, burning it to ash right before her eyes. Now he busied himself examining the ashen results of this labor as she hounded him with her questions.

In the habit of visiting Cedric several times a week when he was in residence, Elena was certain the old man adored her. However, judging from the sighs now escaping him, she was also certain if she were not the Earl of Hertford's daughter, he might not be so accommodating.

Over her fifteen years Elena had pestered Cedric until she was familiar with all the soothsayer's tricks to foretell the future. She loved the odd quarters the wizard inhabited next to the gatehouse. Her eyes traveled fondly over shelves of dusty jars with strange-looking, unidentifiable contents. Dried plants hung upside down from the rafters, and racks of animal bones gleamed in the morning sunlight from the one small window above the worktable.

Is dust always visible in the light or only here?

A smile broke out across Cedric's face when she caught his eye, as if he now understood his discovery. Whether he was aware of it or not, his eyebrows revealed the thoughts passing through his active mind. Independent of each other, those brows bounced, twitched and quirked up until he nodded in satisfaction.

Still, her old friend bit his lip and divulged nothing. Did he intend to chew the information and digest it first? In frustration, Elena rolled her eyes at this obvious ruse to drive her to distraction.

At last Cedric's liquid old eyes twinkled as they landed on hers, and he boomed out the result of his study. "You are to have a female visitor."

"Yes. Oh yes! 'Tis so lonely here with no other maidens. How many years hath she? Please tell me she is of an age with me. Please?"

Cedric's grin displayed a mouth filled with yellowed teeth. "You need not fear, my child. She is a maiden and will come to you soon."

Delighted, Elena clapped her hands and danced a little jig. A moment later, the soothsayer's smile froze into a vacant look that made her stop and shiver. He spoke as if he had just received a message straight from the air. "There are other things you must know."

"You are scaring me, Cedric. Out with it."

His rheumy eyes focused affectionately on Elena before he took a deep breath and plunged ahead. "This person is from a far off land and her secrets are hers alone to share."

A shadow crossed his wrinkled face. "You must protect her with all you are, Lady Elena, as there are those who will not understand her. Bring her to me as soon as she arrives." He threw up his hands to indicate it would be useless to probe him for more, because he had said all he would say.

What was he holding back, she wondered? What did he know he would not risk saying?

Nevertheless, the outcome was more than satisfactory.

She hugged Cedric with a quick but intense hug and shot out the door, tossing her thanks over her shoulder along with a grin for her favorite fortuneteller.

The old man stood in the doorway with the same peculiar smile on his face as before. When would he reveal everything he knew?

∞∞∞

"*El-ric.* Elric, where are you?"

Eighteen months older than Elena, Elric had been her only confidant and playmate for years. Despite the fact their training now took them in different directions, they were still close. To her mind, however, lessons on fighting with a broadsword were much more exciting than those on stitching a straight seam.

On a run, Elena passed through the bailey sure she would find her sibling in the great hall in the presence of food. She was not wrong. Already in his usual place, Elric delayed his meal for no one and dug into a prime cut of sirloin. Long, lean and growing, her brother spent his days in perpetual hunger, if being the first to a meal and the last to leave were any indicator.

Elena slid into her seat next to him with a simple, "Of course," muttered under her breath. Elric did not pause as he speared another mouthful with his dining knife. A smile tucked in place, Elena purposely kept her secret her own until he glanced up from his food and gathered something was afoot.

"What is it, Elena? I heard you screeching my name from the gate house."

"So you sat here like a pig at the trough and never once bothered to reply? Why should I tell you anything?"

Elric snorted, "Because you would find me here in a moment." Grinning, he waggled his knife at her, a bit of beef precariously balanced on its tip. "And, you have no one else to tell."

True, but that fact made her want to pull his hair out. Her eyes narrowed when she gave in to the impulse to grab a handful of his shoulder-length, golden hair. A tad quicker than she, he snatched her wrist midair. It was a game they never tired of.

"No, no, let me be, sister." Tossing his hair to one side with a snap of his head, he laughed through a mouthful of food. "What have you to tell? Did you find a new litter of kittens? Did you get out of embroidery for the day because Drusilla is sick again? What is it you are about?" Elric slurped a sip from his cup as he questioned her, his golden eyes mirroring her own over the rim.

Brothers. Why was she not blessed with a sister? If their guest turned out to be a friend, she would never have to put up with his nonsense again.

"This morning I visited Cedric ... " Elena would love to have dragged out this incredible news making him work for each tidbit, but she was too excited. " ... who told me the most wonderful thing. We are to have a visitor, a *female.* A *young* one."

Now Elric was all ears, all sparring aside. Meat on his knife was poised for inhaling, yet he wheeled in his chair and stared wide-eyed at Elena, who responded by plastering a smirk across her face. As an eligible man, Elric welcomed a young lady as much as she did.

"What? When? Who?"

His knife dropped with a clank to the pewter plate sending his meat skidding off the table. The errant bite flew onto the rush-covered floor where one of the many castle hounds waited for just such a moment and gulped it down whole.

Elena burst out laughing at her brother's excitement. Would he jump up and head to his room to wash and don festival finery?

"Cedric would not say, but I can tell she will be someone of great interest," Elena crowed, her next words spilling out. "She hath come from a 'far away land' and hath secrets to share, and I must protect her. *Mysterious*, is it not, Elric?"

She took a breath and sighed happily, absently scratching the ears of the still-hungry hound that nosed her lap hoping for another treat. "He would not say when to expect her."

"'Tis Cedric's way. He loves when we hang on his every word." Elric paused and his eyes glazed over. "What possibilities this presents."

"Indeed. Cedric is eager for her arrival, too. He could not hide it from me."

"*Humph.* Do not tarry, sister. We should go to the parapet to see if we can spot anyone coming before Master John finds me for shield and buckler practice."

A serving girl dished potatoes and a slice of quail onto Elena's plate. "I shan't be long. I am too nervous to eat."

As Elena popped a potato neatly into her mouth, the earl's spinster sister appeared unexpectedly at her elbow.

"Slow down, child. Nothing disturbs the digestion like forcing food down in a hurry."

Elena groaned as silently as possible at this intrusion. Every interaction with Lady Margaret pained her. The woman, now the chatelaine, had come to live with them upon the death of their mother when Elena was a baby.

According to Elric, their aunt had all the warmth of a marble statue in the dead of winter. Somehow she had never been able to bring herself to show any love for her niece or nephews.

Their brother Robert, the earl's heir, was untouchable, but not so the younger two. It was there her true power lie. Both were ruled by the iron discipline Lady Margaret prided herself with dispensing.

"Now tell me, children, why are we so agitated?"

Elena pleaded with her eyes for Elric to step in and answer. Her distaste for her aunt could never be entirely contained. He winked at his sister and turned back to face Lady Margaret. "Cedric believes we will soon have company at Hertford."

"Oh my, is that all? I shall believe it when I see it."

Their aunt never saw eye-to-eye with Cedric and resented the earl's reliance on his seer. She may not have been able to control her brother, but she could dampen the enthusiasm his children had for the old man's tales whenever the opportunity presented itself.

"No need to make haste for *that*." A sneer settled across Lady Margaret's features as she took her place at the table. She gave the beast at her feet a boot to the nose before signaling to the servant girl to bring food. Then, once again, Elena watched in agitation as her aunt proceeded to do what she did best: *make life miserable for her dear brother's children.*

Chapter 6

The sun was low in the sky as Ashley and her companions halted in front of the portcullis of Castle Hertford. Awed by the sight of the castle when it first came into view, Ashley was dumbstruck now as she gazed up at the magnificent stone structure surrounded by an honest-to-goodness moat.

Furthermore, as she took in the scene around her she began to be aware there was nothing of her modern world in the surroundings. No parking lot, no ticket booth, no gift shop signs anywhere.

"Well, Dorothy, you're not in Kansas anymore," she muttered, fighting the feeling of dread taking up residence in her stomach.

Edmund of Ashdown, having trudged along steadily beside Ashley, was startled by her words. He picked up his pace as if he were suddenly panicky to get across the drawbridge and inside the portcullis to divest himself of her.

"Hurry now, my good woman. The gate comes down at sunset and we must be within the castle walls."

This had to be a dream, or maybe she had hit her head falling out of the cart. She paused a moment as she inspected the castle exterior and murmured to no one in particular, "Do you suppose the Wicked Witch of the West lives here?" Her situation was getting more surreal by the moment.

As she scanned the area, she spotted Meggie and Alice peeking at each other from the corner of their eyes. A big-eyed Meggie mouthed the word "witch" at her sister with a head jerk in Ashley's direction.

They do think I'm a witch!

Another time she might have laughed, but they were not joking.

∞∞∞

Entering the castle grounds the travelers were besieged by Elena and Elric who swooped in with a warm, if inelegant, welcome to Castle Hertford.

Since the earl and Lord Robert were out on separate missions, Elena made sure Lady Margaret was occupied with harassing the cooks in the kitchen so the responsibility would rightfully fall to her and Elric to greet any visitors. This particular one she was most anxious to meet, and with any luck, she and her brother would have the maiden all to themselves.

Master John had released Elric from his lesson when he was unable to focus, so he had wasted no time in rejoining Elena on the parapet. After a long afternoon of watching and waiting, they spotted their guest. It was the unusual dress that harkened her arrival. Elric had been the first to identify the lad leading the rather unlikely foursome with the cart as female.

Once Elena detailed the oddity of this young woman's clothing, they were certain this must be their long-awaited caller from a land far away. Now, as the girl stood before them, Elena bounced on her heels in pure excitement. She executed her best curtsy as Elric introduced them.

"Welcome to Castle Hertford. I am Elric, second son of Cryspyn Spycer, the Earl of Hertford, and this is my sister, the Lady Elena." He bowed so dramatically with his hand scraping the ground before him that Elena giggled.

Their young guest did not behave as expected.

She swayed precariously from side to side as though she might swoon, staring first at Elric, then at Elena. Her eyes roamed over each with nary a blink. Next, she shifted her blank gaze to the castle and around the bailey at their many servants hard at work. Her mouth flapped like a hooked fish gasping for air but no sound came out. A moment later, her eyes rolled back in her head and her legs buckled.

"Oh, my," Elena gasped. Her hands flew out in an awkward attempt to save the girl from falling.

Thankfully, the man called Edmund, of Ashdown pushed his cart forward and caught her as she landed in the cart bed with a gentle thump. His daughters gave each other a knowing nod before training their eyes on her and Elric to see what their responses would be.

Disconcerted by their guest's swoon, Elric appeared to have no idea what to do next, so Elena gathered her senses and decided for him. "Cedric told me to bring her to him, so ... " She waved her hands in the direction of the wizard's quarters.

When Elric had no better solution to offer, there was no choice to be made. He *humphed* and appeared all too happy to motion for Edmund and his entourage to follow them to Cedric's quarters.

As they started that way, Elena noticed her brother's eyes trailing over the visitor's long, slender body, her luxurious wheat-colored hair, and lovely face. He's smitten, she thought, which made her think for a moment she should have wished for a handsome, young man for herself. *Ah, well.*

The young lady's odd behavior and appearance was confusing, but what an interesting friend she would be.

Friend.

Elena had never had a female friend before. She could not keep from grinning as she skipped to keep up with Elric's longer stride on the way to Cedric's chamber.

∞∞∞

The cart with its infernal squeak announced them, allowing Cedric to meet his guests at his door.

"Well, well, our caller hath arrived." He smiled at the faces looking earnestly at him as they gathered outside his lair.

That is, all the faces except that of the maiden, whose body sprawled across the cart. Not expecting this, Cedric patted the girl's head before looking up to see five sets of expectant eyes searching him for the next move. He was not sure what that next move should be either. He did know he wanted time to examine this person and get to know her without all their questions peppering him at every turn.

"Please leave our guest with me, and I shall escort her in to sup with you when she awakes."

Upon hearing those words, Edmund, of Ashdown could not leave fast enough. Relief flooded his good eye, and in his rapid retreat he told Cedric he would claim his cart on the morrow. His offspring scurried after him without pausing for so much as a goodbye.

Elric and Elena eyed each other and nodded their agreement to Cedric's request. They had no other option but to trust him, so they hastened to the great hall to await the pair.

Content to be alone with the young woman, Cedric wheeled her through the door and closed it firmly to keep any prying eyes or ears at bay. He examined the girl with deep interest and considered checking into her pockets while she slept, but thought better of it. He gently shook her shoulders.

The girl stirred, then jerked to life a moment later, clearly astonished by her environs. Her head all but swiveled as she took in the jugs and shelves of wizard goods, her eyes widening in panic.

Like a turtle on its back trying to right itself, she tried to get out of the cart. Her long legs and arms flew in awkward circles about her body as she spilled herself onto the floor and scrambled to find her feet.

"Holy m-mother, where am I? What's in those p-pots? Who *are* you?" She backed into a small, rustic table and sent several jars flying to the floor. Sticky liquids oozed out of them with a nasty smell she could not identify, prompting horror to etch her face. Cedric grabbed her arm and steadied her with his calming touch before she did more damage.

"'Tis all right, my child. You broke nothing I cannot replace with ease. Sit you down over here and tell me your story." He eased her onto a tall stool and gave her a serene smile. "My name is Cedric and this is my chamber."

∞∞∞

Ashley responded to the man's smooth voice and sat still as directed, cognizant her own will had fled from her body and gone into hiding. Thus, she sat and absorbed the details of the old man standing in front of her.

Gray-bearded and old, he was definitely more vital than Edmund, of Ashdown. A palpable awareness ringed him like an aura. His eyes, bleary with age, held a sharpness that was taking her in as quickly as she was him. The dreary, brown robe he wore was so voluminous it could have housed much of the contents of the room within its folds.

"Are you a wizard or m-medicine man or s-something?" Her eyes popped wide as she stared intently at a jar right beside his head holding an item that looked distinctly like a bat wing.

"Yes, indeed. My duty is to advise the earl on many things. Please, child, tell me your name and how you come to be here." Cedric peered into her eyes as he spoke, and she was comforted in an instant by his pleasant, rumbling voice.

How did he do that?

Ashley summoned her faculties to return to her. "That's just the problem. My name is Ashley Duvall, but I don't know much else right now. I do know where I'm supposed to be, but obviously I'm not there, and I have no idea where I am or how I got here."

Her wavering voice rose with each comment, and she feared she was growing more agitated as she gathered steam. "At the risk of sounding like I've lost my mind, I think I may have somehow gotten *really* lost, like jumped out of my own ... time period?"

Her voice ascended into the stratosphere on her last words, but finding no noticeable change in Cedric, she plowed on. "Or, I'm dreaming and this will be a funny story tomorrow, or I *am* crazy, or ... "

Cedric threw up his palms to halt her rant and smiled to re-assure her. "I can help you with some of that, so calm yourself, my lady, and let me sort this out for you. Now please, tell me how you got to Castle Hertford."

Taking a deep breath, Ashley told him about her trip to England, her job on the archeology dig, and the stone with the weird writing. She told him about waking up after being swept up in a storm and seeing nothing familiar.

She retraced the journey to the castle with Edmund, of Ashdown and his daughters, and finished with meeting Elric and Elena. Throughout her tale Cedric nodded as he listened, but never revealed his thoughts aloud.

She folded her hands in her lap and gaped pleadingly at Cedric. "Have I truly gone back in time? Can *you* help me go home? I am so scared. Everyone will be searching for me, and my mom will have been called, and I can't let her think I'm gone for good." Tears streamed down her face so she mopped them away with the backs of both hands.

Cedric's face held the very essence of sympathy when she looked up. He tapped his lips for a moment in thought, and then patted her shoulder to comfort her. "Yes, you have gone back in time, child. I knew by my own methods this morning you would be coming here."

What?

He gifted her with a look that wrapped around her as effectively as a tentacle, rendering her helpless to answer. They stared at one another while Ashley's brain did flip-flops and her breathing all but stopped. Cedric reached out and put his hand on her shoulder so she could catch her breath. Still it hitched in the back of her throat.

"I believe we can help you go back home again, but not right away."

"Oh..."

A bone-deep chill gripped her, but when Cedric put both hands on her shoulders, the worry disappeared.

Freaky.

"From what you tell me, you sent yourself here where the stone originated by chance. Perchance through a portal? Though I cannot be sure what spell you used."

He twirled an eyebrow tuft in thought. "Do you remember any of the 'weird writing' on the stone?"

Cedric dropped his hands to his sides and waited, silence prevailing in the room until Ashley's thoughts caught up with the question.

She hauled in a deep breath, rubbed her hands up and down her arms, and wished Cedric's hands were still on her shoulders. For some reason that made her think better.

Marshaling her self-control by sheer willpower, she backtracked through her actions to find an answer to his question. Had she simply attempted to read the inscription on the stone? Had she done that aloud?

Yes, that's it. It all came back to her.

"Ced-Cedric, I don't remember how it was spelled, but I thought it read something like *tuh-will-in-ahm-sir.* Is that right?"

"Very likely. What else do you remember?"

"I-I think I said it at least three times being goofy. You know, in different voices since no one else was around to hear me."

"Goo-fee? Ah, I think I understand." He paused in thought as if working out the details. "You cast a spell on the rock by chanting its inscription."

"It was kind of a chant, I guess. I said it kinda high and then low and then high again." She mimicked what she remembered doing. Her flighty thoughts settled for a moment on something he had said. "There *is* such a thing as a portal?" Her heart pounded in anticipation of what he would say.

"Yes, child, there is. I am acquainted with those who have traveled in time so I have some knowledge of what you speak."

Ashley put her hand over her heart to keep it from beating out of her chest at the confirmation.

"I know of one who is said to be a time walker, but she hath never shared her experiences with me in detail." He sought Ashley's eyes, admitting, "I must question her more closely next time."

Ashley struggled to keep her emotions in check as the reality of what he told her sank in. "Just what is the year, Cedric?" She braced for his response, her mouth going dry.

"The year is thirteen hundred and sixty-three."

Her entire world rocked. Her shock was like a live thing in the room reverberating off the walls.

"You can't be right," Ashley moaned, even though she knew he was. She dropped her head into her hands and sat motionless for a time. It must be true. It made sense of all she had seen and heard since regaining consciousness on the side of the road.

When she had recovered herself, Cedric gifted her with a fatherly nod and asked her the same question in a soft voice. Could he be trusted? She saw no danger in his sympathetic expression, so she wiped her eyes and dug into her back pocket for her passport. Cedric did not hesitate as he took it from her outstretched hand.

She and her classmates were told to always have their passports on their person when at a dig site in case a Stonehenge officer stopped by. It was against the law to dig in the area without papers and proper ID. For once, she was glad she had followed the rules.

"Open the cover and look at the first page."

He studied the small, blue book Ashley handed him. She

watched in fascination as he smoothed his hand in wonder over the plastic lamination on the front before opening it. Inside he saw the picture of Ashley in full color, and looked up in pure awe.

"This likeness is not drawn or painted. The letters are perfectly formed. How can that be?" Ashley's smile grew as his fingers stroked the ridges of the embossed stamp over her face.

"Look at the 'Date of Issue' beside the picture, Cedric." His eyes jumped to the date printed to the right of her face and he stilled.

"Unbelievable! So far in the future? That is over ... six hundred and fifty years from now."

"Yeah, it is. Now look at the 'Country of Origin' and tell me what you see."

"It says 'United States of Am-er-ee-kuh. Where would that be?"

"I'll draw you a map when I find something to write on, Cedric." Now Ashley was beginning to enjoy the upper hand of knowing more than a wizard.

"You'll be astonished by the shape of the world." She didn't know how she could even begin to tell him all that would transpire between his time and hers. It gave her a sense of power to be so knowledgeable, and her confidence returned with each moment it took the old gentleman to respond.

∞∞∞

Cedric's mind hummed with the possibilities she presented. He would do his best to send her back to her world one day, but she could tell him so much he decided he should keep her for a while. At present, he needed to address the more practical things.

"Ashley, did you bring anything else with you?"

"Uh, yeah, I have a few things. My passport ... " She held out her hand for Cedric to hand it back to her. "A water bottle, a book of matches, a hair clip, my cell phone, half a chocolate bar, and a flashlight."

She searched each of the pockets of her cargo pants for the items and placed them on the little table before her. "Oh, and my bandana." She dropped it with a flourish on top of the pile.

Cedric's eyes shined with delight as he cataloged this treasure trove of goods from another world. He could spend all night merely looking at them, but he remembered his promise to Elena.

"Please put these away now, and show them to no one else." He hesitated. "There are those who will be quick to call you a witch if they see these things and may wish to do you harm if they grow too afraid. We will peruse each of your possessions on the morrow here in the privacy of my chamber. Now, we must dine with the others in the great hall. They are awaiting your presence. You, my child, must be starved."

Ashley grinned, "Right you are, Cedric. I believe it has been, *hmm,* hours and hours and several hundred years since breakfast."

Cedric bobbed his head in agreement and smiled at her joke. She was proving to be a resilient young woman. That would bode well for what was sure to come, he thought.

"You didn't tell me what *tuh-will-in-ahm-sir* means, Cedric."

"Ah, that I did not." His lips twitched up on one side. "'Tis Welsh for *a hole in time."*

"Well, that explains a lot." He watched her mull over that tidbit of information as she loaded up her things and strode out the door he held open for her.

In the time it took to close his door and turn back to her, the sunny smile once gracing her face had become something more circumspect. In fact, upon closer observation, he could see her eyes filling with tears.

"Do you think I'll ever get back home?" Her question hung as heavily as the moisture in the night air.

Cedric gave her a shrug, but could find no words to comfort her. He knew not if Olde Gylda of Hampshire could help the girl, nor did he want her hopes to rise only to be dashed.

Ashley bit her bottom lip, dried her eyes and grumbled, "Hey, where's a pair of ruby-red slippers when ya' need 'em?"

Cedric opened his mouth to reply before realizing he had nothing to say to this. Yes, he had much to learn about this young woman.

Chapter 7

Night settled over the courtyard as Ashley made her way with Cedric to the great hall. Her eyes darted around the open area exploring everything in the dim light. Huge torch sconces placed well above their heads lighted the way along the thick walls of stone leading them to the great tower.

To reassure her, Cedric explained the tallest part where she would sleep was called the donjon. It hovered over the courtyard he referred to as a bailey. Those terms were new to her so she repeated them under her breath in hopes she might remember them.

A breeze shifted and the smell of roasted meat whooshed up her nose sending her hunger escalating. Her step quickened as she followed the scent, forcing Cedric to *harrumph* in his effort to keep pace.

A warm, merry scene greeted them as they stepped into the great hall. Despite the late summer day, a chill had taken hold of the evening. A fire roared in the massive stone hearth at the far end of the hall, eating the dampness with every flick of its flames.

The girl she remembered as Lady Elena called to them as they climbed some steps to the high table to find a seat. Her brother, sitting next to her in the largest chair at the center of the long table, jumped to his feet to greet his guest.

Getting a solid look at him this time, Ashley almost fainted again. A younger, smaller version of the medieval man she had seen in her vision at the worksite stood before her. The look in his eyes as he greeted her wasn't the same either. Meeting his gaze, she felt nothing like she had before. Still, the resemblance was strong. Was that a coincidence or just her vivid imagination?

Cedric moved to the center of their little group to make the introductions. He started, hesitated for a moment, and then began again more sure of himself. "Please meet Elric, the second son of Cryspyn Spycer, Earl of Hertford, and his sister, the Lady Elena. May I present Lady Ashley Duvall, of the United States of America."

Ashley shot a raised eyebrow at Cedric, but seeing his bland expression played along. Why had he promoted her to nobility? *Lady Ashley?* She had to admit she rather liked the sound of that.

If the earl's children received her as a noblewoman, she would be afforded more respect from servants as well as lords and ladies. Was the old wizard trying to ease suspicions regarding how she came to be at Hertford Castle? *Maybe so.* If she relaxed and paid attention, she might not embarrass him.

Elric and Elena bowed and curtsied so Ashley did her best to follow suit. She went down with sheer grace, but came up more unsteady and awkward than she had hoped. With introductions out of the way, Cedric took his seat next to Elena, and Elric motioned for Ashley to sit to his right as their honored guest. She couldn't help sneaking peeks at him every few seconds. The resemblance to her mystical man was incredible.

As soon as they were seated a stone-faced, older woman descended upon them, a deep frown embedded in her sour face. Introduced as Lady Margaret, Elric and Elena's aunt, the woman had not one thing to say to Ashley or anyone else. The opposite of her warm and welcoming niece and nephew, she nodded to acknowledge Ashley as if it pained her. The woman then seated herself with such distaste evident on her face it was amazing no one else noticed. The lady eyed the chair Ashley sat in and glared at her with narrowed eyes.

How odd. What had she done to deserve that?

Then she figured it out. She must be seated in this woman's

usual place at the table.

How embarrassing. Was a place at the table so important? Should she sit in another chair and let the woman have hers? Surreptitiously, she checked the others to see what she should do. Judging from their expressions, no one else paid any attention to the woman or cared if she was unhappy. They ignored her.

With Lady Margaret's intrusion conversation had all but stopped, and the once congenial atmosphere melted away. The silence prompted Elric to call for servitors and wenches, who eased the discomfort by appearing moments later with delicious smelling food and drink.

Someone had even thought of Ashley's needs and presented her with a wet, warm towel with which to wash her hands and face before she ate. She had never been served like this before. Not bothering to hide her pleasure over the attention paid to her, she decided she could get used to it.

Ashley feasted her eyes on platters of mouthwatering roast meats, some dripping in fragrant sauces, potatoes and garden vegetables heaped in big bowls, and a dense-looking crusty bread that made her mouth water. Something in a basket smelled sweet. Elena caught her looking and told her it was boiled raisins. *Hmph, interesting.*

Trying to copy table manners, she watched Elena and Elric intently. Not having a dining dagger attached to her person as others did, Elric speared the juiciest looking morsels with his and deftly placed them on her pewter plate. Meanwhile, Elena ordered a proper knife to be fetched for her use from the kitchen. She almost snorted in delight at that. Eating with a dining dagger. Imagine!

As tired as she was, Ashley worked hard to enjoy the feast sitting as upright in her chair as Elena. Her back wanted to slouch against the chair like at home, but she suffered in hopes of fitting in. It was difficult, too, to converse as expected when all she wanted to do was shove as much of the savory food into her mouth as possible. She hadn't realized how hungry she was.

Elena and Elric had many questions for her, and some were hard to answer given Cedric's advice. Without consulting the old seer, she knew to be vague about the location of the United States of America. She copied Cedric and referred to it as a "far away land across the western sea."

This news made Lady Margaret's mouth form an even harder line and turned her eyes into mere slits. Not being world travelers themselves, or so they said, the explanation seemed to satisfy the brother and sister and chatter skewed in many directions.

Ashley found if she answered any uncomfortable question with one of her own, the siblings were so anxious to impress and please, their account left their previous question unanswered. They never noticed. Cedric did the same, so Ashley felt sure she would make it through dinner satiated and unscathed.

Wine with dinner flowed freely, and as soon as Ashley's goblet drifted toward empty, someone filled it again. Her head began to swim, and she realized she had better slow down or she'd be in trouble. To her surprise, she was not alone.

"Oh, look at our falconer, Master Obelyn," Elena giggled as she pointed to a small, bald man in a brick-colored robe at the lower end of the table. Plainly tipsy, the man's face drowsed over his plate, his hawk-like nose threatening to imbed itself in his food. "I do fear he is deep in his cups tonight."

Deep in his cups?

Ashley almost squirted wine out her mouth on that one, picturing the man immersed in a big cup of wine, his head bobbing gently on the surface. Okay, she was giddy. Now it was time to quit sipping her drink or she would make a fool of herself.

"What does a falconer do?" Ashley ran the back of her hand over her chin with a casual swipe in hopes of catching any wine that may have dribbled down it.

"He trains and cares for the falcons we use for hunting."

Wide-eyed, Elena turned to Ashley. "We must go falconing, Lady Ashley. You will love it. My merlin is most beautiful and a joy to fly."

Ashley thought the only merlin she had ever heard of was a wizard like Cedric. Growing up she thought wizards were a myth; now she wasn't so sure. Snapping out of her wine trance, she nodded, her head bouncing up and down. "Shounds fun, Elena."

She didn't just say "shounds," did she? Over-articulating to compensate, she tried to sound normal. "I'm game for anything you want to show me." Should she have said "Lady Elena?"

A runner interrupted that thought, arriving with a parchment for Elric. Surprised, he opened it and announced with some trepidation the arrival of the earl and two guests expected around midday on the morrow: Aaron Fitz-Maurice, the Earl of Mowbray, and his daughter, Lady Charissa.

Elena explained to Ashley that Lady Charissa had been pledged to wed her oldest brother Robert, the Earl of Hertford's heir, for many years. The earl and Robert visited Lord Mowbray and his daughter periodically to maintain the bargain. Theirs would be a political merger to cement the alliance between the two noble families and their lands.

During this last visit the two fathers had decided Charissa was now ready to be married to Robert in a ceremony to take place by the end of the week. She was told Robert was away tending to tenant business on the far side of Hertfordshire, and would not be home for two days. He would arrive a day later than his intended.

Elric wondered aloud if Robert had been informed Lady Charissa and Lord Mowbray were coming. Ashley was thunderstruck by that statement. Was marriage undertaken in such a cavalier fashion? Turning to Elena for some reassurance, she saw the girl was practically palpitating with excitement over having more than one visitor and would be of no help.

What is the rush?

"Elric, have you met Charissa?"

"Only my father and Robert visited Charissa, but when I was about ten she and her father came here. Lady Charissa was eight, I believe, so there is much about her I do not remember."

Ashley gaped. *No way.*

"You told me you're seventeen, didn't you? So *Lady* Charissa is only *fifteen.* Didn't you say your brother was twenty-three? She can't be ready to marry, can she?" The horror must have shown on her face because Elena tried her best to calm the waters.

"She is only a little younger than I, and I was ready two years ago. Father granted me permission to choose my husband, so although offers have been made, I have accepted none."

"What do you mean by *ready*? According to whom? How can anyone so young be ready for marriage?" Ashley had difficulty keeping her voice below screech level.

Unabashed, Lady Margaret glowered into Ashley's eyes and answered, "A maid is ready, Lady Ashley, when she can bear a man's child."

Oh. My. God.

Ashley was about to proclaim the system barbaric and a wretched business for women, when she caught Cedric's eye and backed down.

"I see," she began in earnest, "it's just different from the way things are in America." She paused feeling the need to continue, but then thought better of it. To her dismay, Cedric nodded his approval and changed the subject before Ashley could find out if Elric was promised to anyone.

Geez, at eighteen, they must think I'm an old maid.

She had thoroughly enjoyed sitting next to Elric. While he didn't fill the impossible standards of her vision, he was a tall, good-looking young man. His muscular build was easy to detect through his rich robes. Elric had stolen glances at her throughout the evening and she was certain he was interested in her because he flushed a deep rose color whenever their eyes met.

As she spent the evening looking back and forth between beautiful Elena and handsome Elric, she was struck by the similarity of their looks. They could have been mistaken for fraternal twins. They each had the same dark golden hair and soft golden brown eyes, tweaked a bit as needed to be masculine or feminine. Attentive to everything she told them, they seemed to like her as much as she liked them.

By the end of dinner, Ashley had learned a great deal from her hosts regarding the castle and its occupants. Happily, a heart-felt rapport had sprouted among the three young people. Even Lady Margaret had not dampened their enjoyment. Ashley might have landed in far worse circumstances, she realized. She would thank Edmund, of Ashdown and his daughters for delivering her here if she ever ran into them again.

When Cedric moved to retire for the night, Elena popped up before Lady Margaret could budge. She curtsied goodnight to her brother and Cedric, and led Ashley up the spiral stairs at the end of the hall toward the sleeping chambers. Lady Margaret's hard, squinty eyes followed Ashley's attempt at a curtsy and drilled into her back as she and Elena walked away. Did Elena feel those dark eyes on her back, too?

The stairs to the family floor of the donjon were steep and uneven as they wound upward, leaving Ashley struggling to keep up with Elena.

"Oops." Ashley stumbled on a step. "Have I had too much wine or are these stair steps different heights?"

"Ah, 'tis not your imagination, Lady Ashley. They were built like this to slow down an invader if the castle should be under siege. I guess it works," Elena tittered, as Ashley tripped again. "The steps will be easier for you in a few days."

"Good to know I'm not just 'deep in my cups,'" Ashley snickered, jumping over the last two short steps to reach the top.

They stood at the center of a circular hallway with rooms opening all around. "With Lady Charissa arriving soon, I know not where to place you, Lady Ashley. If you do not mind, there is a small chamber next to mine where you should be quite cozy. I shall be close by if you need anything."

"Sounds perfect," Ashley articulated, this time with precision. She was relieved to know she wouldn't be by herself. "Is the bathroom close by?"

Taken aback by the question, Elena faltered. "We will order washing water for you now, if you would like, and my maid will deliver the hot water to your room. 'Tis what you mean?"

"Maybe later, but I, uh," Ashley balked, wondering how graphic she should be and pantomimed to the best of her ability what she meant. "I need to relieve myself. Pee? Use a potty? Toilet?" How to explain?

"Oh, I am sorry, Lady Ashley. Of course you need to use the garderobe. A lidded bucket can also be found in your room for use in the night, if needed. Servants will dispose of any soil in the morning. But please, let me show you to the garderobe now."

Ashley followed Elena away from the sleeping quarters and through some double doors at the far end of the hall. A blast of putrid air greeted them as they entered what smelled like an outhouse. A long bench with several holes cut into it served as a row of toilets.

Not much privacy here. Surely people did not use the room at the same time, did they? Ashley calculated this room was at least on the third floor from the ground and couldn't help but wonder where the refuse went.

As if reading Ashley's mind, Elena offered an explanation. "There is a shoot that carries soil to the moat."

Ashley peered down a hole to see what she meant and was overcome by the fumes. This was smellier than any privy she had ever used anywhere. Unfortunately, everything just dropped straight into the water below.

Ugh. So this is why people got sick in medieval times. No sanitation.

She searched around for water and saw a small pitcher and some clean towels neatly stacked on the side and an empty basket beside them, but nothing resembling toilet paper. Was that to be used in place of tissue? *Hmm,* time to check out the contraption in her room.

Ashley tried not to hold her nose and said through a weak smile, "Well, I think I'll wait until I'm in my room, okay?"

Elena nodded her agreement, looking worried over the obvious rejection of the garderobe, but pointed out in a cheerful voice her own chamber situated next door to Ashley's room.

"You will sleep in here then. Before I leave you, it seems you will need some clothing, as well. If you do not mind my asking, what happened to your companions and your trunks?"

"Good question. I wondered when someone would ask that. The truth is, I have no idea. One moment I was sitting in the hot sun in the middle of a field, and the next thing I knew, I was swept up in a sudden storm. I was transported to the side of an unfamiliar road where Edmund, of Ashdown and his daughters found me. My uncle and the other members of our group don't know where I am, and all my things are with them."

"Oh my, you have had troubles, have you not? Concern yourself no longer, dear Lady Ashley. My wardrobe is filled with gowns, and since you are close to my size, you may dress in one of them. If 'tis in need of altering, Mistress Black, our head seamstress, will make the adjustments. We shall set about all of it on the morrow so you are ready to greet Father and our visitors.

"I hope I'm not too much of an imposition. You're so kind to let me stay here, Elena." Ashley scrunched her brow. "Hey, should I be saying *Lady* Elena?"

"I have waited forever for a friend my age, Ashley, so my wish is for you to stay here an eon. Besides, I think Elric fancies you."

Ashley's blush spoke for her.

"In answer to your question, when 'tis only the two of us or Elric or Cedric, Elena will serve. However, with others here for the betrothal, 'twould be best to call me Lady Elena." She paused with a sideways grin on her face, "Oh, and always be formal with Lady Margaret or she will probably lecture you as she does Elric and me."

"Got it. Formally, you are Lady Elena and privately you can be just Elena, but always use Lady when addressing the ... *Dragon* Lady." Ashley narrowed her eyes and did a fair impersonation of Lady Margaret's slitty-eyed, disapproving stare.

"Yes." Elena giggled at the silliness, but a moment later her expression turned wistful. "I am very happy you are here, Ashley. Cedric foretold your arrival, and 'tis rare he is wrong, but he did not say how long you would be here." She sighed and met Ashley's eyes. "Please, stay for a long time."

"Perhaps I will." Ashley's heart thudded with anxiety over whether she would have any choice in the matter.

Her worries relieved for the moment, Elena finished her instructions. "I shall send for your washing water now. Oh, and I will ask my maidservant Anna to locate a night shift for you as well. Do ask her to assist you with anything else you might require."

"Thank you, Elena. You think of everything."

Goodnights were exchanged and Elena left Ashley alone to survey her quarters and search for that lidded bucket-thing.

$\infty\infty\infty$

Would she ever sleep tonight? So much had happened since breaking camp it seemed like weeks had passed rather than a single day. In the silence of her room, Ashley thought about Uncle Zeek and the others on the trip. Would they be looking for her? Would they have notified her mother of her absence? *Dear God, please don't call my mom and scare her.* What would they think of her disappearance?

It had felt great to clean up. Her mom would have called it a spit bath, and Ashley smiled at the memory as she put on the nightgown Anna had given her. It was somewhat scratchy with too many nubs to be called comfortable, but she'd manage.

She didn't know what to do with her own clothes. They were dirty and not something she would wear here again, even washed. Would there be pockets in the clothes Elena loaned her? If not, she would figure out something to do to hide her stuff.

Ashley's eyes roamed around the room examining its contents. A narrow bed curtained with white muslin took up most of the space. An empty, open-faced wardrobe next to it reminded her she had no other clothes. A straight-backed chair stood rigidly against the wall like a forgotten soldier. Beside it a fat candle glowed on a sturdy table beneath a super skinny window cut into the wall near the ceiling.

Warmth spread through the room from the small fire behind a low hearth. Something burned in the grate that was not coal or wood. Its musty smell hung thickly in the air. The room decor was limited to a fluffy animal skin on the floor and a thin tapestry depicting some long ago hunt draped over the wall behind the chair.

Few places existed to hide anything in here. Though she had no need to keep her things on her person, she didn't want anyone to take them either. They were her link to her own world and proof she was who she said she was.

A shudder passed over her. It was one thing to be an alien from another country, yet quite another to be an alien from hundreds of years in the future. The first would be treated here with respect and interest. The second might get her hanged for being a witch.

She must be careful and listen to Cedric. With all she owned tied up in her bandana, she folded her clothes in a neat little pile and deposited them at the foot of the bed. Satisfied she had done all she could at the moment, Ashley snuffed the candle and climbed under the covers.

Exhaustion seeped through her and burrowed deep in her bones. Ashley exhaled a fluttery sigh one last time before drifting off to sleep, wondering if her dream man would make an appearance. She certainly hoped so.

Chapter 8

Her blue eyes sparkled and flickered in the firelight as though a dozen fireflies had taken up residence in them. Filled with longing, her eyes slid over his body, making him reach for her to wrap his arms around her curves and pull her to him. Then her warmth thinned and she melted into smoke, her eyes glowing like the last coals of a dying fire.

Shaken by his reverie, Robert dismounted his stallion and turned the great beast over to his groom to rub down, feed, and stake for the night. Normally he would care for his animal himself because he was quite attached to Lucifer, but thoughts of his dream woman addled his mind and body. Elusive and intangible, the wench left him restless and unsatisfied.

Fortunately, he had performed his assigned mission many times before so work garnered little space in his head. As was the custom, Robert had led a unit of twenty men on their trek around the perimeter of their vast grounds for a full moon cycle.

During that time his task was to oversee the collection of tenant rent and approve a new roof here or a new well there, or some other kind of repair. His father prided himself in maintaining happy tenants and wealthy holdings.

It was not a bad job. His men liked him and deferred to him, allowing for a smooth journey. Still, if this were all he could expect for years to come, he would die of boredom. Perhaps that was the reason his mind insisted on replaying the image of the fascinating blonde woman? He sighed in exasperation.

Lord Robert had grown up ready to do anything to prove himself to his father, and wore the scars he had accumulated in the process as badges of honor. He excelled in sporting events. He was a superb swordsman and an accomplished archer, with anything of a physical nature easy for him to master.

Marked by the same golden hair and eyes as his siblings and mother, it was obvious he belonged in the Spycer family. Robert believed his broad shoulders and lean frame, along with his squared jaw and high cheekbones, gave him a commanding appearance not unlike his father's. While not exactly vain, he knew he cut a handsome figure in his armor, since females of all ages had a hard time not gaping at him. The last few years he had not hesitated to take advantage of their notice.

With only the ride home on the morrow, his men were off celebrating the end of their sojourn in the settlement a short distance away. Excited about the drinking and whoring ahead of them, they had taken off with haste, but Robert was too unsettled to join in as he once had.

As dusk dwindled into darkness, he hung back, sitting upon a rock on the very top of a hill at the edge of their encampment. He watched the lights flicker on in the hamlet below, one cottage at a time. If he were to go there with his men, women would fight for his attention as they had since he was a lad of fourteen, but he did not want that tonight. With so much on his mind, he was anxious to return to Hertford Castle and pursue his plan to claim Lady Charissa.

Then again, perhaps not.

Doubt filled his head. What if his betrothed did not respond to him physically? What if he did not respond to her? Why did he dream of the mysterious woman and not his intended? Were the gods sending him some kind of message? Reflections rolled around and around in his head with no clear result presenting itself.

What did he want from marriage? That was a hard question for him. Did he want his marriage to be like that of his parents? Memories of his mother had dimmed over the years. Now, the way she made him feel stood out more than her physical appearance or the sound of her voice. Affectionate and caring, she had hugged him so much his father had admonished her for it, saying she was coddling him. The earl would not stand for that with his heir. He still missed his mother's reassuring touch. He would want his own children to have the security and love of a mother's arms.

And what of his father? The Earl of Hertford was an intelligent, powerful man. All of their people respected the earl, who was judicious and fair in his dealings with them, but he was not a beloved person. Kindness was not one of the earl's attributes. Since his wife's death, he had become a hard man for all except Elena, who could soften their father to get what she wanted with ease. Perhaps she reminded him of their mother.

The earl would never admit to being soft, in any event, but particularly not with his sons. Robert and Elric fought hard for each concession. Robert lived in fear of disappointing his father, having been taught that honor is chief among a man's strengths. He was proud to have never dishonored or lied to his father in any way.

Yet, he wanted more from his own marriage and the children he would bring into the world than his parents had. Theirs was an arranged joining of two important families. The dowry his mother brought to the union nearly doubled their family lands.

Had they been happy together? His mother had done her duty in birthing three healthy children, but had she and his father loved each other? He did not know.

While he had never witnessed them argue with each other, he had never heard them laugh with each other, either. He wanted love and laughter in his marriage. Would he find a love match with Charissa?

That helped articulate the question bothering him at the moment. "What do I know of Lady Charissa? What kind of person is she?" The sound of his voice echoed over the empty space around him.

In the few times they had encountered one another, she had been prim and proper, smiling and laughing only at her silly hound pup. Was she spoiled as the only child of Mowbray? Did she mistreat servants, make snide comments about others in their absence, or enjoy making life miserable for everyone around her?

God's blood, he had described his aunt! Was Lady Charissa simply a younger Lady Margaret? The thought of being trapped in a marriage for life with a termagant like her chilled him.

On the other hand, the blonde woman who inhabited his dreams seemed to be the exact opposite. She was velvety warm and enticing to hold with a smile that lit up her face and made her blue eyes twinkle. No hint of evil surrounded her. She felt right in his arms, and he was at home with her. She would be a loving mother for his children.

He shuddered again, this time with disgust for his mental wandering. Lady Charissa was real and he would wed her. The mystery woman was no one he knew, nor was he bound to ever meet her. With few women of his station available, she would have crossed paths with him by now if she were real. Thus, 'twould be far better to do what was expected of him.

Frustrated in mind and body, Robert took off on foot for the village. Maybe downing a cup of ale or three with his men might settle him enough to sleep without dreaming of *her*. Tomorrow, if weather permitted, they would arrive at Hertford Castle, and he would know the answers to his questions, for better or for worse.

Chapter 9

Ashley's morning was not off to a good start. Shouts and movement from the courtyard below made her think she was back in Uncle Zeek's camp. When she tried to jump up for a day at the dig site, her body refused to budge. Worse, she could hear her mother knock on her door and tell her to open it, but she couldn't answer her or move a muscle. Horrified, she screamed, but no sound came out her mouth. Just when she feared she might be dead, her brain kicked into gear, and she slipped out of her half-awake frenzy into the real world. Or, at least as real as it could be for a modern girl waking up for her first morning in 1363 England.

She shook off the eerie dream and reacquainted herself with the room. Sunshine streamed in through the narrow window and she realized it must be well into the morning. Had she slept later than anyone else on the premises? Nothing like making a good impression.

A knock at the door snapped her to attention, and she now suspected whoever was out there knocking had probably been there throughout her dream. She threw the covers off and raced to the door, reaching it just before she blacked out for a moment. Not so fast, she chided herself.

"Well, good morning, sleepyhead!" Elena all but sang as she sauntered into the room with an armful of clothes. Wearing a deep red gown with little white and pink flowers nestled in her flowing, golden hair she was the picture of medieval perfection.

"Hey, Elena, sorry I slept so late. What time is it?" Embarrassed, Ashley attempted to finger comb her tangled hair, but soon gave up the battle as a lost cause.

"'Tis mid-morning, but worry not. You needed the sleep, I am sure. Here is a selection of suitable garments for you to wear. Anna will be in soon with a tray of food so you may break your fast while we dress you."

The next few minutes were an experience for Ashley in more ways than one. While she struggled to make sense of the clothes Elena gave her, she had not expected to turn around to find her modern clothes on Elena. The girl had Ashley's bra on backwards over her own clothes and was examining the material with interest.

Now that's just cute.

"This cloth stretches and bounces back. What makes it do that?"

"It's called elastic, Elena. It's in lots of underthings for comfort because it moves with your body."

"I see. What is the purpose of this garment?"

"Well, bras are supposed to enhance a woman's breasts and keep them from bouncing around. You need to turn it around."

"Oh." She followed directions and put it on again, still over her dress. "I see how that makes more sense. Does it make you look bigger than you are? Men like that, do they not?"

"Yeah, we suffer a lot for their attention even in my country." Smiling, Ashley held out her hand and Elena reluctantly gave up the bra. "Here, let me show you how it works. This is a push-up bra so it has a little cushion for your breasts to sit on which makes them appear bigger and fuller." Ashley fastened it behind her back and modeled for Elena.

"*Oh, my.* It doth as ye say! I should like one of those."

"Perhaps you can wear it one day, Elena. After all, you are loaning me all your clothes. I can share, too."

Elena's smile bloomed as she lifted her own breasts to see what the effect would be.

"I would love to try it, dear friend." She caught sight of Ashley a moment later, a question falling out of her mouth with little thought.

"Why are you wearing a belt between your legs?"

Ashley's eyes dropped to her thong underwear before rolling them to the heavens. How to explain? Why *did* women wear such skimpy panties? *Hmm.*

Just as she opened her mouth to form an answer, a popping noise sounded. Bored with waiting for an explanation of a thong panty, Elena had moved on to the snaps on Ashley's capri pants. Ashley chuckled as Elena gleefully snapped and pulled them apart dozens of times, enjoying the sound they made and the way they held the cloth together.

"Whatever you call this, 'tis ingenious."

"They're called *snaps*. I guess because they make that sound. I have to admit I never thought about it before."

"*Amazing.* Where might I find clothing like yours, Lady Ashley?"

"Yeah, well, that's a bit of a problem right now. Those are my work pants and since I don't have my other clothes, those arc all I havc."

Elena held them up in front of her body to check for size. "Do you think I might don these one day?"

Ashley grinned. "What do you think your family would say if you showed up to greet them wearing my clothes?"

"*Ah,* you are right," Elena sighed. "They would not understand, would they?" Ashley shook her head in agreement, a smile still twitching about her lips.

"Perhaps I may clothe myself in them one evening when we retire for the night?" Hope spilled from Elena's entire person as she clutched the item to her chest. How could Ashley refuse that?

"Of course. That is the perfect solution."

Anticipation of the treat to come glowed on Elena's face as she tossed the coveted possession back to Ashley.

"I'm going to need some help with your clothes, Elena. I don't know where to start."

"Mine are not as exciting as yours, but we had better have

you dressed before my father arrives. Females who cannot do as instructed earn his wrath. 'Twould not be the way to begin with him, Lady Ashley."

Her stomach flipped in response to Elena's description of her dad, prompting her to dive into the pile of clothing with renewed zeal.

In its abundance, it all seemed so cumbersome for a balmy summer day. Ashley insisted on wearing her own underwear, but Elena was equally as insistent the thin linen chemise had to be worn too. Though she wanted to omit the slip, Ashley wound up with it over her bra and panties. She thought of it as a giant skinny t-shirt since it covered her from her neck to the floor and was cut in a T-shape with sleeves to the wrist.

A crisp blue linen kirtle, Elena called it, went over the chemise and copied the same shape. It was fitted through the torso, flaring from the hips to the hem at her feet. The sleeves flared the same way at the wrist. The neckline was a wide scoop neck, both modest and flattering.

Not designed for a marathon, the material pooled around Ashley's ankles. That extra fabric helped because it meant there was no need to lengthen the gown to compensate for her extra inches. Elena assured her she would get used to lifting her skirt as needed. Ashley doubted that.

Even though she was convinced she looked ridiculous, Elena was not yet finished with her. She presented a gorgeous, sleeveless thing she called a surcoat, which was a long vest Ashley was to add for the arrival of the earl and company.

It was *gorgeous*.

Elena called the dark blue, densely woven fabric damask and pointed out the beautiful silver embroidery around the edges. The result was truly lovely, but Ashley was worried she would melt under all the layers.

Next, hose and garters and a pair of extremely pointy shoes were handed over for Ashley's consideration. Oh, my, these were too much. She nearly offended her new friend when she sat down on the bed and cackled like the Wicked

Witch of the West. With a shoe popped over each hand as a puppet, she exclaimed, "I'll get you, my pretty, and your little dog, too."

Her new friend tried not to stare at Ashley as though she had lost her mind. Obviously, Elena missed the reference, having no idea what Ashley was doing.

It turned out to be a moot point since she couldn't shove so much as her big toe into Elena's shoes. Since the skirts were so long and would cover her feet anyway, they agreed Ashley could put on her own socks and boots. She would have to wash out the socks tonight since they were mud-crusted from the dig site, but they would do for now.

Bread, cheese and ale arrived with Anna while all this was going on, and the servant did her best to help as needed. Ashley couldn't believe they served ale for breakfast but chose not to say anything. Her mom would have a cow over that.

Dressing Ashley's long hair with an intricate, tiny braid circling the crown, Anna tucked fresh lavender into it as a finishing touch. The blonde curls streaming down her back to her shoulder blades were quite fetching, Ashley thought.

Elena scampered to her chamber next door for one last accessory and returned with a narrow, embroidered belt to fasten around Ashley's hips. She and Anna stepped back to admire their handiwork.

According to them, Ashley had gone from a lad to an enchanting noble maiden. She *was* a Lady Ashley now. She had to agree the overall effect was nice, even though she looked like a character from some medieval festival back in Texas.

Anna was cleaning up the breakfast mess when the trumpets blared, heralding the arrival of the earl. He was right on schedule.

Elena snatched the surcoat Ashley had shed in the stuffy room and threw it on her new friend. Grabbing Ashley's hand and pulling her out the door, Elena hustled them down the castle stairs.

Ashley cursed each treacherous step all the way down,

stumbling only a dozen times or so along the way.

"Slow down, Elena. I'm gonna break my neck if I step on this dress."

"I beg your pardon. I must be in the bailey to present my father with a stirrup cup or he will not be happy."

"*Ah, geez,* what's a stirrup cup?" Ashley swallowed her apprehension even though she was certain the earl was not going to like her as much as his children did.

"Watch closely, my friend, and you will see how it goes. 'Tis nothing to warrant concern. Find Lady Margaret and stand on the steps with her, and I will introduce you to my father as soon as he dismounts."

Elena sped off to the kitchen for the earl's stirrup cup, leaving Ashley to fend for herself. Her confidence fled with Elena. As she stood there flustered, she saw what she thought was the back of Lady Margaret heading out the door to the courtyard, so she followed.

As expected, Ashley wound up standing beside Elena's aunt on the steps in front of the entrance to the great hall. To her amazement a thrilling scene fit for a movie unfolded before her. She ignored being examined from head to toe by Lady Margaret and made a point of returning the same drippy smile the woman had given her.

The sound in the bailey was intimidating and fierce. Dust swirled as two distinct troops rode into the courtyard, side by side, each flying the standard of their respective family.

The red and gold of the Hertford crest flew beside the earl who was riding the biggest black stallion Ashley had ever seen. The earl was followed by a detail of at least a dozen men wearing what she now knew to be red and gold surcoats over their armor. Sparkling swords flashed at their sides.

A short distance behind Hertford, the Earl of Mowbray sat astride a gleaming white charger, looking most imposing. The forest green and gold of the Mowbray standard flew above a small, white mare positioned directly behind the earl, carrying a petite, dark-haired maiden. They, too, had guards behind them wearing the green and gold over their armor. The bright colors against a startlingly blue sky were breathtaking in their splendor.

As the impressive unit came to a halt, Elena led a line of servants bearing cups to the side of the horses and handed them up to the soldiers. The men drank the contents greedily, and wiped their chins in unison with the backs of their hands. Their synchronized movement caused Ashley to stifle a giggle.

The earl reached down from his horse, plucked Elena off her feet, and balanced her in front of him on the saddle. He placed a grand smacking kiss on her cheek much to Ashley's surprise. She sensed this was more of a family tradition than a formal one, and it made her smile to see the earl greet his daughter so warmly. Maybe he wouldn't be so bad. Blushing prettily, Elena kissed her father's cheek in return before he placed her once more on the ground. Thus the stirrup cup saga ended, much to Ashley's relief.

With the greeting ceremony over, more trumpet calls had the Mowbray squad sent back through the portcullis to make camp outside the gates. The Hertford soldiers moved in the opposite direction to their quarters on the backside of the grounds, all as Anna had explained they would do.

The earl, Lord Mowbray, and Lady Charissa dismounted. Their squires and castle grooms were left to tend their mounts as the three walked toward their small audience.

Ashley sucked in a deep breath to ease her nerves and only then became aware of Elric standing next to her. She had been so enthralled by the scene playing out in front of her she had not seen him arrive. Heartbreakingly handsome, he stood tall next to her in his own red and gold finery.

She waited for him to say something regarding her changed appearance when it became apparent he wasn't looking at her at all. His eyes were pinned on Lady Charissa. One glance told her why. Lady Charissa was approaching him with a huge smile, and her sparkling green eyes were locked on Elric's.

This should be interesting.

With Elena bobbing excitedly at his side, the earl and his companions stopped in front of them. Lady Margaret preceded Elric and Ashley down to the foot of the stairs where introductions were to take place. The earl had been eyeing Ashley with real interest since he spotted her upon dismounting. Ashley could feel her knees tremble under her skirts and prayed it wasn't obvious to the others.

The earl was a formidable man who appeared to be in his late forties. Resplendent in the Hertford red, he sported a neatly groomed, grey beard, and silver-streaked, dark hair that glistened brightly in the sunshine.

"Good day, Lady Margaret, Elric," the earl boomed as he nodded to each in turn, towering over all of them. "Pray tell, who is this charming young lady with you?" An innocent question, perhaps, but all could feel the sharpness of his tone.

Ashley cringed.

As Elena and Elric jabbered a defense, Cedric's rumbling voice interrupted them from behind, causing Ashley's heart to fly out through her chest. At least that's how it felt.

"My lord, may I present Lady Ashley Duvall of the United States of America. She arrived yesterday from her travels around our land. We would invite her to visit with us to share her experiences before she goes home to America, if it pleases your lordship."

The earl raised one eyebrow impossibly high as he cast a long, calculating look at Ashley. His gaze snaked down her body and back up to meet her eyes. He clearly did not accept Cedric's words at face value, and Ashley was sure she would be explaining herself to him all too soon. Unexpectedly, the earl plastered a smile on his face and proceeded to welcome her, as a good host should.

"It pleases me greatly to have guests from afar. Welcome, my lady. You shall have to tell us more of your journey, Lady Ashley. I have ne'er heard of a place called America, so you must be well-traveled."

What an understatement, she thought, but summoned the courage to curtsy and reply, "Yes, indeed, my lord." She sucked in a nervous breath, wondering if she had addressed him correctly. She'd have to go over all this again with Elena.

Having established Ashley's identity, the earl finished the introductions. Ashley mumbled and curtsied her way through them, following Elena's lead as much as possible. Lord Mowbray examined her with a wan, but agreeable smile. Older than the earl, he had dull gray hair and a bushy beard to match.

She was quick to note how Lady Charissa's face instantly fell when she heard Elric's name. *Whoops, he's not Robert, is he?* Had no one warned her Robert would be missing? From what she observed, no one else noticed Charissa's reaction.

When the earl motioned Mowbray to move inside, Lady Margaret snagged the man's arm and led the way with the earl right behind.

Elric never took his eyes off Charissa and stepped up to escort her into the hall, leaving Ashley and Elena to follow behind them with Cedric in tow.

$$\infty\infty\infty$$

The banquet hall was bustling with excitement. Candles on wagon wheels hanging from the rafters lighted the dark room along with torch sconces mounted on the stone walls. Workers were everywhere, buzzing among themselves while waiting to serve the new arrivals.

The earl settled himself comfortably in the lord of the manor's chair, motioning Lord Mowbray to sit to his right, with Lady Charissa next to him.

Lady Margaret and Cedric sat to the earl's left. Elric piled in next to Charissa, with Ashley and Elena seating themselves next to Elric despite the ugly look Lady Margaret gave them for doing so.

Ashley and Elena might as well have been seated next to Cedric, since Elric completely hogged the conversation with Charissa. At ease with Elric, the girl laughed in a pleasant way whenever he tried to amuse her.

"You must sample the beef, Lady Charissa. It is aged to perfection and as delicious as you," he declared, waggling his eyebrows in her direction.

Appalled, Elena rolled her eyes at her brother's pathetic attempt at flirting, mouthing his words in an exaggerated fashion toward Ashley to mock him. Delighted that Elena taunted Elric as easily as Ashley would her own brother, she bit her lip to keep from giggling. She had to admit, though, she was a tad put out at having been so soundly dumped by Elric.

Wine and food flowed freely, but Ashley was uncomfortable under the earl's blatant stare, a perplexed look upon his face. She noted it was Elric, however, who had the earl openly fuming a short time later. Undaunted, Elric continued to flirt, ignoring the fact this sweet girl was his brother's betrothed.

Ashley observed the earl, who was still glaring at Elric, beckon a servant and whisper in furious tones into the man's ear. Unless she was mistaken, the earl would find some way to occupy Elric until Robert arrived home.

∞∞∞

The moment the earl rose from his chair to indicate the end of the meal, Lady Margaret had his ear.

"Brother, if I might have a word with you."

Mowbray, well satiated, was bid to go to the earl's map room and wait for him there. Now cornered, the earl turned to Lady Margaret who hissed her warning to him.

"Your children and that disgusting wizard have invited a *witch* into your home." Her sneer said there was more. "The *lady* wore garments the like no one hath seen before, and something is disturbingly wrong in her manner of speech and behavior. You must send her away before she harms us all."

The earl hated his sister telling him anything and was used to brushing off her urgent warnings of one thing or another. This time he could sense she was actually in earnest.

He bit back a snappish response. "I will talk with Cedric this afternoon, sister, and get to the bottom of it. Meanwhile you are not to take matters into your own hands. We have enough to do to get our Robert married to Lady Charissa this week without adding to the difficulties. Leave Lady Ashley to me."

Knowing she would not argue with her keeper, the earl observed Lady Margaret purse her lips and *harrumph* her consent to his edict. As was her custom, she would take her obvious anger to the kitchens where she would harass the servants, unfettered by his authority.

He turned his attention to Elena who was enthusiastically escorting Charissa toward the keep to settle the girl in her chamber for the rest her father had ordered. The two were chattering nonstop. His daughter was thrilled with her new sister-to-be, her radiant face filled with happiness.

Elric had watched them go with a long face, much to the earl's disgust. Did his second son not understand Lady Charissa belonged to Robert?

As he contemplated collaring Elric for a heated discussion, Master John arrived as ordered to spirit the disgruntled young man off for an afternoon's work on his weaponry skills. *Ha.* That should keep the lad out of trouble. He would postpone that firm talk with his errant son to before the evening meal.

But now, where had this Lady Ashley gone? He wanted to question her privately while the others were occupied, and now would be the perfect time.

Unfortunately, she was nowhere to be found in the great hall or the bailey. He was not pleased to put off the meeting. Trudging the stairs to the map room and Mowbray, he questioned why a bad feeling about this girl had settled in his gut, but it had. Experience told him not to ignore it.

Chapter 10

Cedric watched Ashley comfortably enter his chambers as if she had inhabited them for years. Gone was the stuttering, stumbling girl of yesterday. *What a strange miss.*

She plunked down on the same stool she had sat upon before and made herself at home examining the nearest jar with unfeigned interest. He chortled a moment later when her eyes doubled in size as she came to realize the jug in her hand held eyeballs. She hastily put those watery ones down and looked up to meet his smiling eyes instead.

"You are managing quite well today, Lady Ashley, for someone as far from home as you. However, surely you have many questions for me."

He removed several dusty jars from a high stool in the corner and searched for a place to put them. Finding nothing suitable, he jammed them into the midst of the others on a nearby shelf. Finally, he dusted off the seat top with his spindly fingers and placed the chair across from Ashley, hitching up his robe as he sat down.

"*Yup.* Only about a thousand questions, Cedric, but what I really wanna know is if there's any way you can help me go home."

Ashley squirmed in her gown and pulled uncomfortably at the neckline. A moment later she figured out she had to pull up the back of the gown to give herself more sitting room in the front. If she did not know how to sit in feminine attire, Cedric surmised, then she clearly had no previous training as a lady.

"*Hmm,* yes, I'm sure you do want to know about that."

Cedric eyed her surreptitiously and smiled to himself. She certainly had spirit, and while he would help her, he himself had about a thousand queries to be answered.

"I shall think on what we can do, Lady Ashley, but meanwhile I should like to examine the items you displayed for me yesterday. Are they with you?" Cedric peered at her person, searching for the possessions he hoped she had brought with her.

"Yeah, I've got 'em, but I sure miss my pockets."

Ashley dug under her skirt to release the bandana holding her goods that were suspended from a cloth belt tied at her waist. Cedric dutifully looked away and marveled at how this girl was so unaware of exposing her legs in such an unladylike fashion. Perhaps these Americans had no modesty.

Ashley plopped back down on the stool, untied the scarf and opened it on her lap. Cedric leaned forward and studied the contents intently. What did he want to look at first? The small book she had called a passport he had held already, so waiting to hold that again was no hardship.

The flagon of water arrested his attention, perhaps because the container was the biggest article she held. Of what was the vessel made?

"May I?" Cedric lifted the bottle off Ashley's lap to examine it. "*Oh,*" he cried in horror when it squished and crumpled under his touch. He dropped it onto her scarf afraid he had broken it.

Ashley laughed. "No worries, Cedric. It's made of plastic. You can drop the stuff and it won't break. Where I'm from, water is bottled to insure purity so it can be taken anywhere with ease. We recycle bottles like this most of the time, but sometimes we just throw 'em away."

Cedric tentatively picked up the bottle again and squeezed it. To his surprise the strange jar reclaimed its former shape when he loosened his grip. He found Lady Ashley's eyes watching him delightedly.

"What amazing matter to reclaim its shape by itself," he

commented, somewhat embarrassed by his actions. Even that was not all. Lady Ashley showed him the mouth of the jug called a "pop-up sports top." He told himself he had to test its pop over and over again to be sure it was doing what she said it would do. *Mesmerizing.*

"Puh-las-tik, you say. *Hmph."* Cedric looked up from this marvel of the twenty-first century to recognize the humor in Ashley's eyes.

"Yeah, well, it isn't all that great, Cedric. People aren't always good at recycling, and these bottles cause problems as waste. That's not to mention people tire of buying water."

"Water is not *free?"*

Cedric felt his jaw fall open, so he clamped it shut to hide his shock. Were people so callous as to deny others the life-giving substance? The thought was barbaric.

"What if they have no water?"

"Well, water is available in lots of places if it's not bottled. But even then we've already paid for it since we all pay our cities to clean the drinking water that comes out of our faucets at home and everywhere else."

Cedric did not understand what she was talking about and scrunched his face in protest, despite his best effort to keep calm. "Please explain, Lady Ashley."

"Don't worry, Cedric, bottling is not much different than those wine flasks everyone uses here. Same concept, just water. No one goes without water to drink." Her brow furrowed over his concern.

Relieved, Cedric accepted her response with a nod. His fingers hesitated for a moment before giving the sports top he still held one last pop. Then he handed the bottle over with a sideways grin, recognizing he did not want to give it up quite yet.

"Hey, I was wondering, Cedric, is your water safe? I have only seen people drink wine or ale."

"Ah." Finally, something he could speak about with confidence. "You are observant. To be sure, 'tis safer to drink the

spirits if you do not know the right spots for fresh water." That settled, he wished to move on to the other articles she still held.

He directed his gaze rather pointedly to the objects in Ashley's possession and hoped she would go on with explaining her valuables. Happily, she got the message. *Intelligent child.*

She next chose a small item and held it up for his inspection. "This is just a hair clip. Watch, hair is held if I twist it up because there is a little spring built in." She demonstrated. "Chip clips like this are made out of plastic, too. Just the kind you can't see through. If I remember correctly, plastic is a product made from oil, but don't ask me how, 'cuz I can't tell you the process."

Cedric took the object and examined it before squeezing it as she had shown him. Sure enough, it held the front of his robe closed when he placed the two sides together and attached the clip to the material.

"What a curious and helpful device." His mind promptly started detailing many uses for this small thing called a clip. Would that he could experiment with it or create a design for one. He would gladly wait to view whatever else she presented him, if only this were his for a time. Should he ask?

"And these two things you're gonna like a lot, although they won't last long. Do you have a candle I can light for you?"

What would she show him now? Cedric grabbed an aged candle from beneath a table and held it while Ashley presented something she called a "book of matches." The small paper she held in her hand had an image on it with the words "LaCasita Mexican Restaurant." She explained it was a place to eat where she lived, not unlike an inn but with no guest rooms. Flipping open the folded parchment, she twisted out a small stick she swiped against a rough spot at the base of the square. To his amazement, a fire sparked to life.

"Now *that* is useful."

What wonders this young lady had in her possession. She did not disappoint. However did this match thing work?

"Where do they hide the flint in something so small? Is the tiny twig the tinder? Are there more?"

"'Fraid not. But look at this, Cedric. A flashlight has much better light than a match. The bad part is the batteries will eventually die and there is no way to buy new ones here." She held the small object in her hands and flicked a switch on its side.

Cedric stared around him in awe as the little light lit up most of his chamber. *It hath no flame.* 'Twas not hot since she touched it without hurt. What made a light such as this? A twinge of uneasiness shot through him. Was she truly a witch? What would Olde Gylda think of Lady Ashley?

"This is a high intensity flashlight that throws a lot of light."

She unscrewed the top and pointed out the essentials under the clear cover. He had never seen such things before as "bulbs and batteries." Unlit, it was only a small object, but when lighted it filled the room with brightness. The power of the sun was captured in the room. A frown consumed him as he wondered how anyone accomplished this without witchery?

"The electricity in our houses is kind of like this," Ashley answered as if reading his mind. "It's permanently wired into our walls and lamps, so we only change out the bulbs when they burn out. Candles aren't used except for romantic dinners or if the lights go out due to a power outage."

Cedric nodded sagely, but feared Ashley understood he was only following her words and not their meanings. His mind raced to make sense of what she was saying, but still he did not understand her explanations.

What was a "power outage?" He rubbed his fingers in circles at his temples, wondering if his eyes were bugging out of his head.

Ashley reached out and snared one of Cedric's hands, placing the flashlight in his open palm. He flinched, expecting what he was not sure. To his amazement, the small tube was feather-light in his hand. A smattering of braveness surfaced when he cautiously pointed the light into the darkest corner of his quarters.

"My, my," he muttered aloud, as the light uncovered a pot of saffron he had thought long gone. *How wonderful.* He warmed up to the new light, forgetting Ashley's warnings regarding the things she called batteries, and flashed the light into all the dark recesses of his cell.

That is, until he stumbled over a small barrel in his attempt to look into a grimy cupboard on the back wall. Fumbling the little flashlight, he caught it a moment before it smashed onto the stone floor.

Sheepishly, he apologized for his lapse and reluctantly returned the fascinating instrument to Ashley, wishing with all his heart the little tool were his to keep. That was an impressive invention he wanted to use again. But with other treasures to examine, he barely contained his excitement at what she might show him next.

"Now this is the coolest thing I have." Ashley carefully handled the object she held named a "smartphone."

"Unfortunately, it won't do nearly what it is capable of doing because it operates off a satellite for most of its applications. Still, I can show you a few things it does."

Not even bothering to decipher the majority of her strange words, Cedric hovered over the small rectangular thing in Ashley's hand. "It doesn't seem cold."

Ashley snorted. "'Cool' is just an expression, Cedric. This is primarily used as a phone to talk to people who are a long way away. I won't be able to show you that because there is no satellite."

"And a satellite is ... ?" Cedric was hesitant once again. Might she show him what she held without all the explanations? He was pretty sure by now he would not understand what she said anyway, but he needed to at least sound as if he did. A wizard had his pride, after all.

"Satellites are units sent up into the sky that send signals

time walking experiences with him. Cedric replaced the pestle in the mortar and turned to face Ashley to tell her thus, only to shake his head in consternation and turn away. Once again, she had ungracefully hoisted her skirt up to her waist to tie the bandana to her undergarments. *How will she ever pass for a lady?* Cedric massaged the deep wrinkle between his eyes.

"I shall go to Olde Gylda for help, but do not repeat to anyone where I have gone. She is not in favor here and 'twould not be looked kindly upon. Tonight I will tell the earl I hath need of travel to find herbs for my work and plan to leave at dawn. 'Tis best he knows not for what we search."

"Agreed." Ashley shook out her skirts and used the palms of her hands to smooth the material down in the front and back.

"I shall tell the earl you are a very important and powerful person in your land and he must treat you with great respect." If only he were sure she would not commit similar indiscretions in front of the earl. "That way you should be safe here until I return. Olde Gylda will undoubtedly be able to help you, and I shall not be more than a few weeks."

"*Weeks?* Wow, I was hoping to be back home in a couple of *days.*"

She took a deep breath and groaned her distress, looking deflated. He could not help but pity her as tears filled her eyes, threatening to spill over their brims. "I don't mean to sound ungrateful, Cedric. Things are different here and everything seems to take much longer. I just know my mother is probably frantic by now and I hate to think of the pain I'm causing her."

Cedric smiled warmly, reassured by her words. The lass was worried about her mother. How dangerous could she be?

"I understand, child. I shall do my best to find out how to return you to her."

He stood and moved toward the door. "Now, you had better run back and find Lady Elena before she worries you are missing."

Apparently, he had said the magic words. Lady Ashley immediately perked up and dried her eyes as she hopped down from her stool. "Cedric, you're the *best.* I promise I'll draw a map of the world for you the first chance I get. You've been awesome."

Ashley threw her arms around him, hugged him tightly, and then sped out the door. Cedric was left to stumble and catch his breath wondering what had hit him. *She was, indeed, resilient.*

Chapter 11

The slant of the sun was sharper when Ashley headed out of Cedric's chamber and wandered aimlessly down the long, narrow corridor heading back to the castle. *What time is it?* Cedric had told her she shouldn't pull out her phone to check the time like she used to. Besides, her battery would die. While nice to not worry about the time, without a schedule she was even more lost.

A moment later, she knew she had taken a wrong turn somewhere because she found herself approaching a small garden. Soft-colored, fragrant flowers created a palpable serenity in the place. Lavender and rosemary and even a climbing rosebush she could identify, but the rest were unfamiliar.

As she bent down to smell the lavender, the sound of voices drifted toward her on the warm summer air. She listened intently and to her surprise recognized them. Elric and Charissa were here.

Oh, my.

As she rose from her crouched position to search the area for them, she spotted a shady arbor as a likely source of the sound. Ashley couldn't quite understand what they were saying, but judging from the tone and the soft laughter, they wouldn't want to be interrupted.

Turning to leave unnoticed, Ashley came within a breath of running smack into Lady Margaret who carried a wicked looking pair of garden shears and a wicker basket.

Oops.

"Oh! Lady Margaret, you startled me," Ashley said in an

unnaturally loud voice. Lady Margaret glared at her like she was truly a madwoman. She forged on undaunted. "Lady Elena suggested Lady Charissa and I visit the garden since the day is so beautiful. Is there anything we can help you with?" Ashley blinked wide-eyed at Lady Margaret whose head jerked in different directions as she searched the grounds.

"I do not see Lady Charissa about."

Having picked up on Ashley's less-than-subtle warning, Charissa sang out in a cheerful voice, "Here I am, Lady Margaret." She skipped out of her hiding place as innocent as could be and sailed over to where the older lady held her ground.

"'Tis a lovely day, is it not? If you are here to cut some lavender or rosemary, may we do it for you?" She hooked her arm through Ashley's and adopted the same bland smile. Ashley bit her cheeks and managed to maintain her composure over how silly the two of them must look. She dared not make eye contact with Charissa.

Lady Margaret's eyes narrowed to slits and her nose twitched as if she smelled something vile. Yet, with nothing obvious to complain about, she was forced to hand the basket and shears to the two girls.

"You may cut enough lavender to fill this bin. Add a few sprigs of rosemary too. When finished, bring it to the kitchen and I will see the cuttings get put to good use added to the rushes in the guest chambers."

Suspicion lay in Lady Margaret's eyes as surely as pollen lay in the many blossoms of the garden. Yet, having nothing else to remark upon, she pursed her lips and stalked away. It was such a Wicked Witch of the West moment Ashley almost hummed the tune, but Elric chose that moment to burst forth from the arbor.

Both girls wheeled on him and shushed him with their hands and frantic faces. Elric bobbed his understanding and slid wraithlike back into the protected area where the girls joined him.

"That was a close call," Ashley informed them in a soft

voice.

"Thank you so much for saving us, Lady Ashley," Charissa whispered.

Elric nodded in solemn agreement. "'Twould be more than awkward to explain our presence to Lady Margaret."

"Hey, you don't have to tell me anything. I couldn't care less if you two are together, but from what I understand about this betrothal business, awkward might not begin to describe it."

Elric's jaw jutted out. "'Tis not fair Robert is betrothed to Charissa only because he is the eldest." He paused to lower his voice again. "She hath said not a handful of words to him in as many years, yet today the two of us have talked nonstop." Shrugging off his resentment, he smiled at Charissa with regret apparent in his eyes.

"'Tis true, Lady Ashley. Lord Robert and I have not seen each other in nearly three years, and we had little to say to each other when we last were together. I must admit I did think Elric was Robert when I arrived, but the comparison ends there."

She smiled with soft eyes up at Elric who hungrily held her gaze. The heat all but radiated between the two of them.

This is not going to end well.

Ashley snapped the shears open and shut a couple of times and broke the spell holding the two lovebirds. "Well, unless you wanna be surprised again, I suggest we cut these flowers and disappear inside ASAP."

Two sets of eyes swung questioningly at her and Ashley automatically explained, "ASAP ... *as soon as possible.*"

Elric and Charissa nodded, only slightly confused. Then the two girls set about cutting the requested sprigs, while Elric disappeared out the back of the arbor.

∞∞∞

"So, Elena, you said you turned down marriage proposals, but you haven't told us who asked you."

Ashley was sprawled across Elena's bed with her arms behind her head and one leg hanging off the side, her foot tapping the floor. Elena could not stop smiling as the three young ladies chatted while getting to know one another. After saying their goodnights below, they were enjoying a little girl-talk in Elena's chamber. Ashley continued to fidget while she watched Elena brush out Charissa's long hair.

"Oh goodness, they are not anyone you would want to hear about." Elena's disrespectful tone regarding her suitors made Charissa giggle.

"Try me. Come on, Elena, spill. Dish!" Ashley teased.

"*Spill? Dish?* Dearest Ashley, you do say the strangest things." Elena's snicker turned into a grimace. "Oh, my. I hate to think about them."

"Did your dad find 'em or did they find you?" Ashley had trouble imagining how these match-ups worked.

Charissa turned to face Elena, most interested in what she had to say. Lost in thought, Elena tapped the brush on her temple while she pondered the question. *"Hmm,* Father would not let me say no if he were the one proposing the union." She resumed brushing, this time on her own hair. "Fortunately, 'twas they who sought my hand, so Father let me refuse them."

"Okay, time to name some names, Elena."

"Yes, Elena, tell us please. Might I know them?"

"Good question, Charissa. Only two have offered." She breathed a quick, half-hearted sigh. "Have you, by chance, encountered the Baron of Bedford?"

"Of course I have." Charissa gave an involuntary shudder. "*Oh, my.* He frightens me." She paused for a moment to let the shiver pass and then scrunched her nose. "And, he is ... *old,* is he not?"

"Yes, I believe he hath seen well over forty seasons. That, however, is not the worst of it. He simply made my skin feel like spiders were crawling over it whenever he took my hand, so I could not fathom being married to him." Elena's face puckered like she had sipped the bitterest ale imaginable at the thought of Bedford.

"Eewwww," Ashley grimaced, thinking how awful it would be to be coerced to marry someone who made her stomach churn. "Who's the other guy?"

"Ah, the other one was not so very bad. 'Twas Pierce Wilkins, the son of Sir Charles Wilkins, who lives nearby. He is a sweet lad, but unexciting. He fawned and pawed over me with sticky fingers until I could take it no longer. He is pudgy, forever hath a drippy nose and is anything but a scholar. I begged Father to let me say no. He was not much impressed with Mr. Wilkins either, and my brothers laughed at him behind his back, so 'twas not a match that had any hope."

"Not much of a choice, Elena." Ashley wiped her nose with the back of her fingers as she thought of the drippy-nosed suitor. "Seriously, if your dad had insisted would you have had to marry one of them?"

Elena had enjoyed telling the tale of her ill-matched admirers, and Charissa had easily laughed along, but now they had serious faces. Charissa was the first to state the situation matter-of-factly. "Of course, Lady Ashley. Once an arrangement hath been made there is no choice.

Ashley heard the wistfulness in Charissa's voice, and judging from the look on her face, Elena hadn't missed the underlying complication either. Like Ashley, Elena had probably recognized the furtive looks Elric kept sending Charissa's way throughout the evening meal. Charissa had flushed every time their eyes found one another. Now, looking from Charissa's face back to Elena's, Ashley didn't know what to say to break the tension building there.

She opted for humor, pinched her face into a sneer, and let classic valley girl fly, *"Get. Out."*

Charissa and Elena looked appropriately shocked. "I could never marry someone like tha-at. *As if*." Ashley threw her hair over one shoulder and tossed her head for effect. *"Gah,* I would like totally run away. Or what*ever*."

Looking at their stricken expressions, Ashley couldn't control the urge to giggle any longer and unleashed a very un-lady-like snort. That gave her away. Relief flooded their faces, allowing Charissa and Elena to erupt into laughter.

"Oh, my. We thought you had lost your senses." Elena wiped tears from her eyes as she and Charissa grinned at each other.

"Sometime I'll teach you that language. It's teen-speak in my country. Or at least it used to be." Ashley wondered how she'd ever describe a valley girl and upspeak to them.

The cloud that had hovered moved on, leaving the mood brighter, but she hoped the message was clear: Lady Ashley Duvall would never be part of an arranged marriage.

Chapter 12

"Do I *have* to wear this hat-thingie? It makes me feel like a nun."

"'Tis called a coif and its job is to cover your hair neatly so the veil and coronet sit properly. 'Tis very lovely on you, think you not so, Charissa?" Elena turned to her soon-to-be sister for confirmation. "The little pink flowers on her coronet match the pink of her cheeks."

"Yes, indeed, Elena. We are all beautiful ladies, are we not?" Charissa paused long enough to perform a pert curtsy for Ashley's benefit. "'Tis a special occasion, Lady Ashley, and we should dress our best."

Charissa pushed into place her golden crown that held the sheer fabric with gold leaves embroidered around the edges. Her green velvet gown was exquisite. The girl's sparkling green eyes shone even greener, and the gold surcoat with the ermine trim was richly elegant, making her skin glow.

Elena's headdress featured lavender blossoms woven into a tight circlet to match the color of her dress. The two were enchanting medieval misses from the pages of a childhood storybook.

When she looked at herself, however, Ashley saw an actor waiting to go on stage in some costume drama. Comfort would never be hers with this *thing* on her head. Maybe if it didn't go under her chin it might not be so claustrophobic.

"Well 'tis certain you must look your best, Charissa." Elena adjusted her skirts and donned a surcoat with silver embroidery that matched the silver stitching on her veil. "The feast tonight will be the first time you and Robert have been under this roof as a betrothed couple."

"'Tis so, but I would be more cheerful if my stomach would quit somersaulting. If only it were Elric." Neither Elena nor Ashley knew what to say about that.

"Hey, I'm gonna be glad to meet this brother Robert I've heard so much about." Ashley slipped into the dark blue and silver surcoat on loan again from Elena. She grimaced as she tugged on the ties of the suffocating coif in hopes of more breathing room. *Nope, still none.* Disappointed, her attention shifted to her shoes. "I don't think I can walk in these pointy, clown shoes." For emphasis, she took two steps and stumbled over the long narrow ends of the slippers, falling hard into the side of Elena's chest of drawers. The impact sent the brush and hairpins atop the dresser scattering to the floor.

"I should give these back to Lady Margaret and put my boots on."

"No!" Elena and Charissa cried in unison. Ashley cringed and raced to pick up the hairbrush and pins, like somehow speed would make everything better.

Elena took a deep breath and patiently explained, "Use Lady Margaret's slippers today, but you may wear your boots tomorrow and until the shoemaker finishes the pair ordered for you."

She smoothed Ashley's headdress like a mother hen tending her chick, tightening it again at the neck. That made Ashley roll her eyes in frustration and wonder if she might faint. "We are expected in the great hall now so my father and Lord Mowbray can inspect us before Robert arrives. According to Anna, the runner appeared an hour ago, so Robert is not far behind."

"Okay, now *my* stomach's queasy. You know I don't pass inspection with your father, Elena. He never says anything. The dislike simply shows in his eyes. Mark my words, I will screw up this arrival in some way and he'll order me off the property and then heaven only knows where I'll go. You just watch."

Charissa and Elena did just that. As Ashley's arms flailed as she railed, their lips quivered in their attempt to keep from laughing at her dramatically acute distress. Finally, Charissa could hold it in no longer and blurted, "You are beautiful, Ashley, and all you must do is stand there."

Ashley's breath caught and she was aghast at her own behavior. Here she was going on and on about nothing but a little discomfort. Meanwhile, Charissa was trying to quell her nerves at meeting the man she had not seen in three years who would be in her bed by the end of the week.

In her mind's eye, Ashley pictured her mother's face with a raised eyebrow and disappointment pursing her lips. *Ashley Marie Duvall, you are acting like a spoiled brat.*

"I'm so sorry, you guys. I'm usually not this self-centered. You two are so perfect and I'm so out of my element it makes me crazy." She took Charissa's hands in hers. "This is your show, Charissa. Elena and I have got your back."

Charissa's eyes twinkled. "Thank you, Lady Ashley. I am truly happy to make a friend of you. 'Twill all be fine even though I know not what you will do with my back."

Ashley grinned, but before she could answer, Elena grabbed both her new friends and herded them out the door. "My brother must be served the ceremonial stirrup cup so I need to be in the bailey before he is. Let us go there at once and join my father and Lord Mowbray."

Ashley bumbled along behind her friends, her pointy footwear slapping the floor with every step. Not stopping to ask her questions, Elena blurted, "Why do you call us *guys*, Ashley? What means this word?"

Man, how to explain that one.

∞∞∞

"I don't know what Cedric told your father this morning,

but he looked at me like I might set him on fire with the flick of my wrist." Ashley tromped up the kitchen stairs behind Elena. "Did you see how he actually took a step back when we stopped to talk to him?"

"That I saw," Elena snickered. "I swear he hath never acted like that before. He would not even approach me since I was beside you. Mayhap 'tis not a bad thing. We passed inspection with nary a word from him."

"Too bad Charissa has to stick with her dad. Somehow Lord Mowbray doesn't seem too impressed with me one way or the other." She paused as she surveyed the kitchen scene. Cooks and servitors were hustling about with preparations for the upcoming feast. "What are we doing here, Elena?"

"I am here to fill Robert's stirrup cup with his favorite wine."

That made Ashley flush in embarrassment at having followed Elena into the kitchens like a puppy tailing its mother. "*Geez,* I should be standing on the steps in the bailey right now, huh? I'm sorry my head isn't in the game at all this morn--."

Watch trumpets blared, causing Ashley to all but jump out of her borrowed shoes. Startled, Elena juggled the cup she had just filled before gaining control and clasping it tightly to her chest. The entire kitchen clicked into a higher gear like someone had flipped a switch. The effect was electric. The hairs on the nape of Ashley's neck stood up and waved as the current of excitement took hold of her.

In her rush to get to the ceremony, Elena wheeled on her heels and scooted past Ashley on the narrow kitchen stairs. As Ashley turned around to follow her friend, one dastardly shoe didn't make the full turn. The pointy tip caught on the top step. That made her lurch forward and step on the back of Elena's gown. She flailed for balance and teetered for a moment before toppling into an unsuspecting Elena. With nothing to grab for safety but air and each other, the two tumbled down the steep staircase, landing at the foot in a heap of velvet, satin and spilled wine.

Ashley bounced off the top of the pile, fearing the worst. "I'm so sorry, Elena. I'm such a klutz. You aren't hurt, are you?" Finding Elena's hand, she tried to pull her to her feet, but halfway up as Elena got her legs under her, she groaned in pain.

"*Oooh*, my ankle," Elena sat back down and rubbed it fiercely, trying to make the hurt go away.

"*Ah,* man, it's starting to swell already." Ashley bent over her broken friend, totally responsible for her injury. "I'm so very sorry, Elena."

"I know 'twas an accident, Ashley, but now I should be outside with the others at the head of the line with my stirrup cup in hand." Tears of frustration threatened to spill down her face as she poked at her rapidly swelling appendage. "I cannot walk on this. You must play my part, Lady Ashley."

"Oh no, Elena. I can't do that." Ashley shook her head with every ounce of finality she could muster.

"You must, Ashley. My father will not forgive me if no one is there to serve Robert the ceremonial cup. *Please*?" Pain and anxiety pinched Elena's pretty face. "*Please, Ashley?* You saw me do it for my father. 'Tis not hard. Take the cup and *go*."

Put like that, refusing her friend was not an option. She grabbed the cup, hiked her skirts, and ran for the courtyard. A dozen steps later she stumbled again over those wretched shoes. This time she kicked them off not caring where they landed. Naturally, one smacked into a kitchen helper headed for the bailey, and the other tripped an old cook who wasn't agile enough to get out of the way. "Sorry!" she yelled to them, relieved they both appeared more affronted than damaged by the unwarranted assault. Reaching the side door to the bailey, Ashley heard Elena shout to her to refill the cup from the fountain outside the door. "Got it," she hollered back, now with one less mystery to solve. *Apparently they do drink water sometimes.*

The line of servants with cups formed at the base of the imposing front steps leading up to the great hall. Ashley kept her head down and filled the cup with water. Thankfully, the wine had spilled down the stairs in the fall rather than on them. *Too bad Robert won't get the wine he likes.* She jumped into position at the head of the line and caught her breath.

The servant girl behind her tipped her head sideways and cocked a brow at Ashley. A moment passed before she realized her coronet had twisted to the side in the tumble, making her more fallen angel than lady. Feeling the circlet with her fingertips, she placed it back in the center of her head and checked with the girl to see if she had it right. The lass smiled at her and helped set her dress to rights, grinning widely when she discovered Ashley wore nothing on her feet. Ashley opened her mouth to attempt an explanation, when the trumpets blared again. At the last moment, Ashley thought to exchange cups with the girl, so Robert would be presented with wine rather than water. *Whew.* Now she was ready.

The fearsome beasts erupted into the bailey, snorting and stomping and way bigger from this angle than any horses in her memory. Ashley sucked up her courage and led her line of cupbearers to meet the riders as she had seen Elena do only yesterday. Her eyes were fixed on the stirrup cup she held. What if she fell over her train despite the fact she was shoeless, and once again spilled the liquid, this time in front of everyone? Silently, she cursed herself for getting into these untenable situations.

∞∞∞

Entering the castle grounds, Lord Robert was somewhat surprised at the formality of the greeting prepared for him. Yes, they had been gone for a full moon cycle, and yes, he expected to be greeted by his family, but something was different here. His eyes tracked over all the familiar faces of those who dwelled within the castle walls and were now lined up and dressed in their best to meet him. Only one explanation fit.

Visitors must be afoot.

Halting the procession in the middle of the courtyard, his eyes searched and landed upon the Hertford standard flying on a pole next to the great hall doors. Directly beneath it flew the standard belonging to the Earl of Mowbray. He could not believe his good fortune.   *Charissa must be here.*

Robert wanted to fly from his horse and find her at once. Instead, he had a ceremony to endure.

The approach of the stirrup cup bearers on his right, with his sister at the lead in her usual blue gown, only partly held Robert's attention. He was mostly focused on the steps to his left where the Earl of Mowbray stood next to his father.

Where is Charissa? Why can I not see her?

With his attention diverted, Robert was late in realizing Lucifer was nuzzling under his sister's arm, bumping her hard enough to knock her down. Robert reined him in, patting the high-spirited animal to calm him while he continued to search for Lady Charissa among the throng on the steps. This was a ceremony he could complete in his sleep. Thus, when his sister thrust her hands above her head to serve the cup to him, he mechanically pulled her up and sat her before him on his giant steed. He wanted nothing more than to be finished with this business so he could move on to find Charissa. But the moment Robert leaned down to place the ceremonial kiss on her cheek, she turned her head to him and started to speak. Robert's mouth found lips, not cheek.

A jolt of electricity shot through him upon impact and he reared back with alarm. He had accidentally kissed his sister on the lips, had he not?

Why does my spine tingle with pleasure?

Dismayed by his own reaction, he forced himself to look down at the girl. His eyes widened in surprise as they fell upon a lovely face clearly not his sister's.

The maiden kept her eyes glued on the cup she held almost prayerfully in her lap, and seemed as shocked by their contact as he. A modest blush crept across her cheeks that he found delightful.

Robert was in awe. He had not found Charissa in his search for her on the steps. That meant this demurely coifed beauty who shyly would not look at him must be the lady he would marry. Robert put his hands on either side of her face, kissed both closed eyelids and breathed a gentle, *Charissa.* Then he set his mouth firmly over hers.

His lovely lady stiffened, but then her hands loosened and deserted the stirrup cup. It miraculously stayed balanced on the saddle between them as her fingers slid up to his shoulders. If she intended to end his kiss, that message shriveled in the fire that sparked between them. Her lips moved along with his and her hands clutched him with a tight grip.

Pleased with her response, Robert was in heaven as he slipped a hand behind her head to cup it gently, deepening his kiss. His chosen fit him as perfectly as the stars had foretold. This beauty melted to butter in his arms and clung to him to keep from dripping off the saddle.

A need for air forced Robert to break his lock on Ashley's lips. He pulled her into an embrace as he smiled over her head at their families on the steps. Robert hoped to see them smile back, happy the two would be so well matched. To his bewilderment, he was met by a carnival of ghastly expressions, their faces contorted in horror. His father's flesh was an unhealthy purple. Lord Mowbray held his hand over his sword like he wished to use it. Lady Margaret appeared to have fainted with a disgruntled Elric holding her up, and a smaller coifed lady with a stricken face stood between the two men. Aghast, he pulled back and lifted the chin of the lovely lady beneath him, wishing for answers to be found in the emerald green eyes he so vividly remembered.

A pair of crystal *blue* eyes reluctantly rolled up to lock onto his. Robert's breath abandoned him. He knew those eyes. In haste he ripped the coif from the girl's head, spilling golden curls about her where Charissa's dark tresses should have been.

'Tis she!

Straight from his dreams, the lovely blonde woman lay nestled in his arms ... and in front of his betrothed for all to see. Too shocked to move his body, only his brain scrambled.

"What have I done?" he muttered. A joyous refrain of *'Tis she* took up residence in his brain over a furious *No* and blocked out any other thoughts.

As if to break the spell, the forgotten stirrup cup chose that moment to take flight from its precarious place on the saddle. It spewed wine as it spiraled to the ground before pinging along the cobbles of the bailey, the only sound to be heard in the otherwise deafening silence.

Chapter 13

Those tawny eyes looking at her with a mixture of dismay, confusion and wonder sent Ashley's body into stun mode. She couldn't speak or move, but her mind raced as she stared into the eyes of her medieval man.

He was perfect and he was real. His big hands were still holding her firmly in place, just as they had when he kissed her. The taste of him now burned like a brand into her soul. *Robert?* The man haunting her dreams, both waking and sleeping, was the brother of Elena and Elric? How was this even possible? Was she meant to be here? Is that why she had seen him at her worksite before she was swept away?

Her mind kept spinning the same questions over and over again like the color wheel on her computer when it got stuck. She was unable to make it force quit so she was rendered speechless.

∞∞∞

Elena had limped with the aid of a servant to the top of the stairs outside the great hall in time to witness the infamous kiss. She was positive Robert had mistaken Ashley for Charissa.

What else would he have thought?

The time for this revelation lasted only a moment, however, before all hell broke loose. Ashley was dumped from

Robert's saddle like a discarded lap dog. Robert flew in a fury off his mount, flung the reins at his groom, and then sent Ashley a withering look before striding across the bailey toward his father. None of this had been Ashley's fault, but Elena worried Robert and her father would blame her friend anyway.

Dear Lady Ashley was standing where she had been dropped, completely flummoxed. From Elena's perspective, Robert's kiss had devastated the girl's senses as she made no move to join them or explain herself. Her new friend kept looking from Elric to Robert and back again.

Elena wished she had better prepared Ashley for Robert's appearance, but she had never dreamed of the need for it. Elric was a younger, smaller version of Robert, but she had never noted until now how they differed. They were but her brothers. Robert was a powerful, fierce-looking *man*, and at the moment, not a very happy man.

A glance at her father made her even more concerned. His face was so red she feared he might explode with rage. Or was it embarrassment? He had to recognize Robert's mistake, right? Was it the possible failure of the alliance with Mowbray that had him apoplectic?

Elena's eyes bounced from the confused face of Charissa to Elric and back. Oddly, Charissa did not appear to be overly concerned with what had just happened. Elric stood directly behind the girl and reached out a hand to covertly hold her waist in a show of support. Had he lost his mind?

Elena's eyes snapped back to her father. Did he see Elric? Thankfully, he was busy glaring holes through Robert and unaware of his younger son's actions.

Hope shone in Charissa's eyes as the girl judged her father's reaction to the kiss. Did she want Mowbray to reject Robert and leave her free to marry his brother? Was that an option? Elena braved a peek at Elric and found the same tangle of worry and hope residing in his eyes.

Lady Margaret, who had careened into Elric's arms in a faux faint during the kiss, now stood on her own two feet.

Goodness, the woman had no shame. Elric had reluctantly snagged their aunt before she hit the ground, when Elena was sure he would rather have let her fall. Lady Margaret's face did not show its usual look of scorn. 'Twas obvious her aunt was enjoying the discomfort of others too much.

"I did not ... I do not ... I never ... " Whole thoughts eluded Robert's tongue as he stood before them attempting to describe what had happened. Elena was sure he did not know himself. 'Twas not surprising words failed him before their angry father.

She had some rescuing to do, she thought grimly, as she took up a place at the foot of the steps between Ashley and her father.

"Dearest brother, Father, Lord Mowbray, and Lady Charissa, 'tis all a terrible mistake." Elena's heart pounded as all eyes fell upon her. "In my hurry to get to the stirrup cup ceremony, I tripped over Lady Ashley and we fell down the kitchen stairs."

Elena dismissed her attendant with a wave of her hand. "I hurt my ankle, as you can see, so I made Lady Ashley fill in for me in the presentation of the stirrup cup."

All eyes had shifted from Elena's swollen, damaged appendage to Ashley, still standing where she had been dropped. Not waiting for any comment, Elena focused her attention on her oldest brother. "Dear Robert, I know you have not been introduced to Lady Ashley, and it hath been years since you were with Lady Charissa. Thus, I believe you mistook her first for me and then for your betrothed." Elena let this sink in before adding in a heartfelt rush, "Especially with all three of us done up in coifs that hide our hair. And, Lady Ashley *is* wearing one of my gowns."

Robert appeared to have heard only part of her explanation. Elena watched him find Charissa and absorb the expression on her face, gauging where things stood between them. Robert's eyes landed on Elric's hand resting on Charissa's waist, and his eyebrows shot sky high. A moment later, when

Charissa turned her face toward Elric and heat flared between the two, Robert's mouth opened in amazement.

Robert had seen *something* lay between his betrothed and Elric. What would he do? Her brothers had always been the best of friends. Would Robert view this as a betrayal? The color slowly drained from Robert's face as his eyes roved over everyone present before settling on Charissa. "Please forgive me, Lady Charissa."

The earl needed no further explanations, because he sunk into Elena's with the fervor of a starving man given meat. He turned to Lord Mowbray, who had remained eerily quiet. "What a mess, Mowbray, but an honest misunderstanding, what say you? I know my son would never have dishonored our lovely Lady Charissa." At this, he patted Charissa on the back to display his affection for her as a father-in-law-to-be.

"So it would seem, Hertford." Mowbray examined his daughter's face, but seeing no signs of distress, turned to Robert to greet him. "So sorry to confound your homecoming, Lord Robert. Our arrival here at Hertford was unexpected, was it not?"

Robert tore his eyes from his examination of Charissa long enough to accept Lord Mowbray's kind words with a bow. "Unexpected, but not unwanted, Your Lordship. I thank you. Your forgiveness is much desired." He turned back to Charissa, took her hand and bowed to her, adding, "As is yours, Lady Charissa."

Charissa blushed and curtsied her acceptance of his apology and the tension eased. Looking anxious to move the center of attention elsewhere, Charissa spotted Ashley, bewildered and standing apart from everyone, and called to her, "My dear Lady Ashley, please come and let me introduce you to Lord Robert." The girl giggled as she said it.

Bless her. Elena was astonished Charissa had not only recovered nicely but had the presence of mind to now find the whole business amusing. Or was she repaying Ashley for her save in the garden yesterday from the dreaded Lady Margaret? Her new friends had regaled her with that story.

As she hobbled forward to take Ashley's hands, Elena added her own affirmation. "Lady Ashley is a dear friend, Lord Robert, though she hath been here but a short time." With the blessings of her two friends, Ashley had no choice but to step toward Robert and give him her hand as she curtsied.

The response of the pair as their hands touched made Elena imagine a lightning bolt had zapped the joining. Ashley recoiled and grasped her hands to her chest, her eyes wide with shock. Robert's face had gone from penitent to disturbed, his eyes narrowing to slits. What was wrong with them now, Elena thought. Worried, her eyes darted from the two to her father, but fortunately his attention was on Mowbray. She searched for something to say to ease everyone's discomfort, but her mind was overtaxed. Robert mumbled something unintelligible to Ashley, and Ashley answered with something equally unintelligible, leaving Elena overjoyed to have the difficult moment pass at last.

The earl hastened everyone inside and to the feasting tables. Charissa took Robert's arm and followed her father and Lady Margaret through the door. At well over six feet, Robert towered over the tiny Charissa who had to crane her neck to meet his eyes. Elena was pleased when Elric came to their rescue and offered to escort her and Ashley. Elric rolled his eyes first at one and then the other, and all three burst out laughing. Despite snorts and snickers, they managed to contain their nervous laughter before the others noticed them.

"What else can go wrong?" Elena squeaked.

"Oh, *never* ask that," Ashley groaned. "The universe will prove to you it can find *something*."

"I think the universe may have already had its say, Lady Ashley." Elric spoke in a low voice, his smile dying.

"What mean you, brother?" Elena's brows pulled together in concern.

As they entered the great hall Elric lowered his voice to a whisper to keep it from echoing off the walls. "Anyone who had eyes and was attentive did not miss the connection you and Robert made with your kiss."

Ashley's eyes flashed to Elena for confirmation. "Tis true, my friend. I saw it, too." Tears welled in Ashley's eyes as she acknowledged what Elena and Elric believed to be true.

"I never intended that to happen, you know? It just *did*." Ashley caught and held Elric's eyes for a moment. "I think I now understand what has happened with you and Charissa." She paused, her earnest gaze fixed first on Elric and then on Elena. "What are we going to do?"

The question hung in the air like a storm cloud over the rest of the night. Would the betrothal of Lady Charissa and Lord Robert be ill-fated?

∞∞∞

Robert escaped to his room as early as possible without offending their guests. Undressing in the comforting confines of his chamber, he tried to clear his befuddled mind. His behavior in the courtyard still made him cringe. He had been so sure the beautiful woman in his arms was Charissa, that he was yet dumbfounded at how the events had unfolded. He had shared with no one that the lovely blonde inhabiting his dreams was in reality Lady Ashley. Who would believe him?

The mere thought of the woman had his body remembering flaming sensations while his mind fought for good sense. Lady Ashley had felt so right in his arms it was as if he had found home. He still felt the warmth of her lips and the way her body fit perfectly against his. He had known the moment she had surrendered to his touch, giving back what he gave to her. But she was *not* his betrothed. *What now?*

Robert threw his tunic on the chair by his bed and shrugged out of his shirt and undergarments before flopping naked on the featherbed. The evening had been something close to a disaster, although everyone had tried hard to make it a success.

Sweet Elena. She had worked to make up for the inauspicious beginning at the stirrup cup fiasco, but her efforts seemed to have been in vain. Lady Charissa had chosen to put a brave face on it all, but her cold, clammy hand said she was anything but comfortable with him. She had said all the right things and laughed charmingly, but joy never reached her eyes.

Ah, those shining green eyes. They did not sparkle for him.

They did, though, come alive whenever Elric was near. What was he to think of that? Elric had always hero-worshipped him as the big brother who showed him the way forward in all things. Yet Elric had been hard-pressed all evening to look him squarely in the eye.

Why?

Elric would never contest his betrothal to Lady Charissa. At least, he did not think he would. It had been set for years and Elric had uttered no complaint. What had changed in his absence to create this strange awkwardness?

The answer to that question zinged into his brain as the image of Lady Ashley Duvall arrested his attention once again. Who was she? Why had she taken up residence in his dreams? From whence had she come? This story about a far off land did not ring true to him. Was she some kind of witch?

That would account for his dreams. Had she bewitched him? Every single time he touched her during the evening's dancing, he had thought his body would come away with black soot where their appendages joined. Even now, hot tingling spread to his core, arousing him. Who could have imagined his dream woman would come to life in his own home.

This is blasphemy.

His traitorous mind gave him no relief. He had tried not to stare at Lady Ashley all evening, but his eyes would seek her person on their own when he was not otherwise engaged. More than once his eyes had found Ashley's, and he was sure he detected a longing in them that matched his own. *God's blood.*

What was he to do?

Charissa was indeed lovely, yet Ashley's charms were far more pleasing to him than that of his betrothed. His body heated as he thought of Ashley dancing throughout the evening, her tall, elegant body calling to his with its silky sultriness. She was alluring even when she was not sure of the dance moves.

He smiled as he remembered how untroubled she was to dance like a peasant without shoes. *Ah,* his barefoot beauty with the golden mane. Again, his body flamed to life.

Awck.

She was *not* his. Why did his mind wish to betray him as surely as his body? He turned on his side and tried to sleep, even as his thoughts reached out to Ashley, wondering where she was and if sleep had found her.

∞∞∞

Ashley rubbed her teeth vigorously with a towel. Elena had taught her to use white wine to rinse her mouth, followed by a thorough chewing of parsley as the only tooth brushing available to her. Forget rinsing. She wanted to gulp the wine down and wash away the day.

No, she didn't. Not really.

She would always remember the day she'd met the man of her dreams ... literally. It was just her luck he was taken. The man would be married in a matter of days to her friend. Groaning, she tossed aside the much-abused rag and chomped viciously on a mouthful of parsley as she brushed her hair.

What a tangled web things were in now. She wanted Robert with every fiber of her being, but he was promised to Charissa. Charissa wanted Elric, and Elric wanted Charissa. Where did Robert stand in all this?

When she had said goodnight to Elena, the girl was still

troubled about the events of the day. She must not know what to do either.

There had been no talk of a sleepover tonight. All three girls had gone to bed, promising to meet up in the morning to go falconing with Robert and Elric. That was bound to be uncomfortable.

Ugh.

She needed to go home before she made matters worse. Her mother would be beyond frantic by now. Maybe, just maybe, Cedric would make it back faster than planned.

Ashley spit out the remnants of parsley into a small bowl and decided to rinse out her mouth with the rest of the white wine. Then she wound her hair up on the crown of her head and clipped it with her chip clip before sliding into bed. No one would realize what was holding up her hair before morning. She was too tired and too dispirited to braid it like a good little medieval girl. She grimaced.

Would she dream of Robert again? She was in danger of losing a part of herself if she stayed here much longer. Already the routine, the dress, the people ... Robert ... all were getting too familiar.

Cedric? Where are you?

Chapter 14

Falconing. Never in a million years did Ashley think she would experience falconing. *Humph.* Make that a mere 650 years. Yet, here she was, standing beside what Elena called a cadge of falcons. The padded wooden frame was built to carry hooded hawks to the field. These sleekly beautiful birds sensed what was in store for them and sat alertly in their cages, their heads twisting to take in all the movement around them. She couldn't wait to see them in action on the hunt.

The young people had gathered at dawn in the courtyard after breaking their fast with bread and ale. Ashley and her stomach still couldn't get used to drinking ale for breakfast, but the bread was just-baked warm and delicious. It settled her insides considerably with its yeasty goodness.

Robert greeted her with a nod of his head. Elric grinned at her from behind Robert. Charissa gave her a shy smile and Elena hugged her, whispering encouragement in her ear. At least no one seemed putout or too unhappy with her. Hopefully, the day would smooth over the problems of yesterday.

Ashley had wanted to wear her own clothes thinking pants would be perfect, but Elena had nixed that since the ladies would be riding sidesaddle. The thought of a sidesaddle sent a wave of bile up her throat. She rode astride with no problem, having learned at camp years ago. Just the thought of a sidesaddle made her completely uneasy despite Elena's assurances she would be fine.

Elena had outfitted her in a lilac cotton kirtle with a heavier grey surcoat drawn over it for warmth in the cool morning.

Ashley got to wear her own boots because she had no proper shoes to fit her for this adventure. Anna had helped Ashley pull her hair back in front and secured it with a little, silver-laced cap at her crown. The sides and back flowed down her shoulders. Best of all, she had cinched her worldly possessions into a leather pouch which now hung from the girdle at her hips.

Elena and Charissa were similarly dressed. Elena in blue and silver; Charissa in green and brown. Each wore a kind of half boot made of soft leather. Their hair was loose and flowing too, shining in the lights of the early morning.

Ashley couldn't contain her delight as she surveyed the guys. Deliciously male, Elric and Robert were both clad in leather. Elric's slightly fitted, brown-leather tunic was worn over a billowy, long-sleeved, white shirt with matching breeches. Beside him, Robert was the man in black, wearing a black-leather tunic and breeches. Yes, *man* described him best, Ashley thought. Nothing was soft about Robert so his choice of black suited him. Both trod about in supple suede boots, reaching knee high and tied with leather laces. Each sported a cap boasting a puffy feather.

Elena called her name for the second time, and Ashley worked to pull her attention back to her friend. She fought brain fog and guilt for not wanting to listen to Elena as she explained to her how to mount a horse onto a sidesaddle. Upon closer examination, however, Ashley noted this saddle was structured differently from those she had seen at riding competitions. She was not exactly sure what the difference was never having ridden on one before. That prompted her to sit up and pay attention or risk humiliation.

"Ashley, 'tis simple when there is a mounting block like this one. You step here with your left foot and throw your right leg over the pommel. Keep both feet on this side of the horse." She demonstrated the move. "Then you adjust your weight evenly so you can keep your balance."

"Thanks, Elena. It's easy for you. At least you could fumble or be awkward to make me feel better, ya' know." Elena grinned at Ashley's good-humored whine. She gracefully dismounted and motioned for Ashley to try.

"Ye shall do it with ease." Charissa did her best to encourage Ashley, prodding her with smiling eyes to give it a try.

The young groom held the pretty, gray mare still while Ashley attempted to follow Elena's instructions. To her surprise, she dropped into the sidesaddle with a plunk, feeling not nearly as graceless as she thought she would. The girls clapped and cheered their approval, and any tension in the morning among them dissipated along with the mist.

Ashley was so heartened by her unexpected success she stroked the mare's neck and whispered sweet words to her until the fuzzy ears of the beast twitched.

To Ashley, they made a dizzying procession when they left the castle, crossing under the portcullis and across the bridge in single file. She and Elena rode shapely mares of varying shades of grey with neat little black hooves, while Charissa was at home upon her graceful, white mare. Elric sat tall upon a big-boned, red roan, while Robert rode his black stallion.

Master Obelyn, in dark leather, had the falcons in two cadges mounted between a solid pair of workhorses. He traveled behind them to keep a careful watch on the birds. As Lord Falconer he would serve as chaperone since Lady Margaret did not believe falconing was a "lady's province" and refused to accompany them. Ashley wondered if anything *fun* was a *lady's province* in that old dragon's view.

Behind Master Obelyn, two servants carried food hampers on the backs of their saddles as well as the items necessary for the hunt. On leashes strapped to the servants' arms were four hunting dogs, jumping and slavering on each other. They were overjoyed at being out of their kennel and ready to work. Their unadulterated doggie-grins made Ashley happy.

The morning was crisp and clear with sunshine trying to break through the thick summer foliage of the trees. Ashley had not been outside the bailey since her arrival, and she exalted in the newfound freedom. Once away from the castle, they left the road and headed into a stand of dense-look-ing trees. By now Ashley's right leg was beginning to numb in its ungainly placement. Shifting her position, she wondered if she would ever last in this torture device until they reached their staging area.

They all were silent as they kept a slow pace for the better part of an hour through the dense trees. Every now and then they scared up a bird or startled a small animal that took off in the underbrush, heard but not seen. Gentle whinnies and an occasional snort from the horses echoed in the morning air, punctuated by a yap or two from one of the dogs.

The underbrush melted away and they found themselves in a clearing. The grasses here held a pungent, earthy smell that reminded her of home, sending a pang of homesickness through her. She did her best to shake it off and focus on her surroundings.

From the chatter around her, she understood this was the perfect spot for falconing. *Excellent news!* Relief flooded Ashley as her cramped limbs ached for release from the confines of the sidesaddle.

"Over here, Lady Ashley!" Charissa dismounted, using a fallen tree trunk in place of a mounting block and handed her reins to a still-mounted Elena who led the animal away. She grabbed the bridle of Ashley's mare and positioned the animal beside the trunk.

"Why does getting off look so much worse than getting on?" Fear scrunched Ashley's face. Charissa's eyes twinkled once again at Ashley's dramatics as she stilled the mare with a hand on its cheek. Then Ashley surprised her by all but fall-ing out of the saddle. Charissa caught and steadied her landing with her free hand until Ashley had both feet firmly on the ground, amused relief flooding through both of them. Elena neatly slipped down without a block a short distance away. Thankfully, Robert and Elric were huddled with Master Ob-elyn around the falcons and missed her bungled dismount.

"Now what, Elena?" Ashley wiggled the toes of her right

foot trying to reestablish circulation.

"Now we prepare to fly the falcons. They are hooded at present in their cadges and tied with jesses to their perches." She pointed to a nearby cadge where tiny leather straps tethered a falcon's feet to its perch.

Elena pulled out a pair of long, leather gloves from her saddlebag. "We must put on gauntlets before handling them. Their claws can tear into a hand or an arm in an instant."

"Sounds delightful," Ashley muttered, taking the gauntlets Elena handed her as if they might bite.

"'Tis in truth not frightening at all, is it Elena? The dogs will be set loose in the brush to scare up the game birds for us. Then the falcons are unhooded and fly off to catch them."

"Charissa hath the right of it." Elena held up a shiny, feathered object on a long string. "See these lures? They are used to persuade our falcons to circle back with their prey and drop it in favor of the swinging lure. Of course the lure has a piece of meat on it. Then the hounds retrieve the game bird."

"Simple enough in theory, ladies. S-o-o, is it time to meet the falcons? If I wait much longer I'm afraid I'll chicken out."

"Chicken out?" Elena looked in confusion to Charissa who shook her head.

"Sorry. I mean lose my nerve." Her two friends nodded but still looked puzzled about the chicken reference. She'd have to be more careful about how she phrased things.

They hurried over to where Master Obelyn had five birds of different sizes and colors perched on a rack open to the field. All were hooded and still strapped to the perch. Ashley noticed a tiny bell attached to the leg of each bird.

"Why the bells?"

Robert answered her this time. "Our falcons are still wild, but they have been trained to let us hunt with them. The bell is attached so we might find them if they do not come back right away."

"Oh, I thought they were tame." Ashley mulled this information. "Why do they come back at all?"

"They know I keeps 'em fed, and they likes that, m'lady." Master Obelyn presented his birds with a wave of his hand.

"*Ah,* so they're little opportunists. Smart birds." Robert smiled in agreement and her heart skipped a beat.

"Ashley, this is my new merlin. She is beautiful, is she not?" Elena had donned the heavy gloves and was proudly lifting a beautiful small bird that had stepped easily onto her hand. The merlin, now unhooded, was a compact bird with golden-rimmed eyes and legs, and a body of mottled browns. Elena stroked the white and brown spotted chest of the little lady. The merlin's button-black eyes darted intelligently around her, taking in every slight movement.

Charissa walked up beside Elena and stroked the bird, too. "She is exquisite."

Ashley was not convinced she wanted to hazzard the sharp little beak if it decided to take a bite out of her hand and held her ground. Maybe if she asked questions they wouldn't notice her reluctance to touch Elena's merlin.

"If these small birds are merlins, what are the other two bigger ones?"

Elric was quick to present his beautiful blue-gray peregrine. This falcon was finely detailed with markings that made it look most exotic. Not to be outdone, Robert reached for the largest bird on the perch and unmasked a gorgeous creature he called a gyrfalcon. It had a splotch of gold over the beak but otherwise was a stunning black and white. The predatory nature of this bird was immediately obvious to Ashley and she instinctively backed away.

Robert frowned.

Had he taken offense at her reaction or did he simply want her to like his falcon? She was relieved to discover it was the latter when he told her in a hushed voice to put on her gloves and walk slowly to him. Fear slashed through her. She had to force her feet to move until she stood beside him.

"Hold out your arm with your hand palm down and he will sit on your glove."

Ashley would rather have put her hand out to a rattle-snake at the moment, but it was Robert asking this of her, and somehow she couldn't refuse him. Besides, her mouth was so dry she couldn't have said no anyway. With her heart in her throat, she held out her arm next to Robert's as instructed, and sure enough, the gyrfalcon stepped calmly over to her hand.

She was shocked at how light this falcon was. Around two feet tall, he weighed next to nothing. Seeing Ashley had frozen in place, Robert reached over and let the falcon step back onto his hand.

"That was a little scary, Lord Robert. Thanks for taking him back. But ... please. Show me how you fly him." Robert gifted her with a heart-stopping grin and was off with his gyr-falcon to demonstrate before she had regained her equanimity.

The rest of the morning was spent setting the falcons free to hunt for game. Beating the brush came next as they walked behind, rescuing the game birds from the hungry falcons with tasty treats offered on the lures. There would be plenty of food for dinner tonight, Ashley thought, as her friends worked their magic with the falcons. Finally, she gave it a try with one of the merlins and was amazed the little bird flew right back to her hand without a lure. Master Obelyn told her she was a natural at falconing, and Robert smiled at her. Life was good.

Shortly before noon, Elena's merlin tried to catch prey twice its size and fought the larger bird to the ground. The dogs got involved, and before the scrap had ceased it was apparent the little merlin was wounded. In her scramble to get to her downed bird, Elena managed to trip over an oak root and fall headlong into the brush. She got up with only a minor scrape or two on her face and hands, but her previously injured ankle had not fared so well.

Master Obelyn rushed to the merlin's aid and took it back to the cadge. Worry evident on their faces, Elric and Charissa carried Elena to a nearby log to sit while they examined her injury. Ashley plopped down next to Elena and squeezed her hand in what she hoped was a comforting gesture, not knowing what else to do. She could see Elena tried to hold back the tears as everyone gathered around, but it was clear to all the girl was in pain. The little bird hadn't fared much better.

"She looks to 'ave broken a wing, m'lord." Master Obelyn finished his examination of the falcon and wiped his hands on his breeches. "If we 'ead back to 'ertford soon, it kin be mended, m'thinks."

Everyone's eyes sought Robert's. The decision to stay or go would be his to make. It was also apparent Master Obelyn would not rest until his bird had been doctored. Elena surely needed to go back, so Ashley was not surprised when Robert dutifully proposed to return to the castle post haste.

"No, no, no!" Elena cried amidst her own pain. "Please do not spoil the rest of the day for everyone because I am such a klutz and fell down. Is not that what you call it, Ashley? Klutz?"

Ashley grinned and gave her friend's hand another reassuring squeeze. "That's exactly right. You clearly have been hanging around me too much." Her smile fell when her gaze landed on her friend's face. "If you are as uncomfortable as you look, you'd better go back, and we should just go with you."

The others murmured their assent to this plan, but Elena would not budge. "No, I insist you stay and enjoy your luncheon. Cook will be most put out if we go home and her delicious food is not eaten."

Master Obelyn took advantage of an opening to not only be of assistance but also take his leave. "M'lady might ride back wit' me and m'lads, if ye wants to stay 'ere."

Hesitant, Robert nodded to himself before announcing his decision. "Go home, Master Obelyn. We shall follow."

"Oh, no, Robert. 'Tis broad daylight so you need not have a chaperone. You must stay. Eat. Enjoy the day. I shall be fine."

After a bit of fussing and discussion, this seemed agreeable to all. The old falconer expertly packed up the equipment and secured the birds in their cadges. With Master Obelyn's help,

Robert bundled his wounded sister onto her horse, and moments later, she and the falconer were headed home with their two servants and the dogs in tow.

Charissa and Ashley waved goodbye to Elena and watched as the lumbering little cavalcade disappeared into the woods. Then they spread the luncheon out on a blanket thrown over a nearby grassy knoll shaded in part by a giant oak. As they worked they chattered nonstop about the merlin's scrap with the hounds, Elena's damaged ankle, and other events of the day.

Cook had arranged a mouth-watering lunch. Ashley was starving from the morning's exercise and couldn't wait to sink her teeth into the cold chicken and venison. Thick slices of crusty bread and golden wheels of cheese added to the feast. An almond cake and a jar of sweetmeats waited in the second basket along with several bottles of wine and a jug of mead.

Charissa was unpacking the cups along with the pewter plates, when a blinding flash of lightning, followed by an ear-shattering crack of thunder, blasted the sky.

∞∞∞∞

The tethered horses shied and whinnied their alarm at the thunderclouds breaking above. Elric sprinted over to calm them, speaking to each in turn. Running to the center of the field, Robert assessed the danger. From which direction had this storm come? It had been lovely only moments ago, but they had been so deep in the forest they could only see the sky directly above them. Now what had been blue sky and sunshine had become a furious swirl of black clouds overhead. He turned back to their encampment at a run as a loud crack of thunder reverberated through the nearby woods.

Elena and the falconer had been gone but a little while and would likely get drenched, but he could do nothing for them. If he took his party to his father's hunting camp a short distance from where they stood, they had a chance of finding suitable shelter. Without it the heavy rain would soak them.

Elric met his eyes and yelled over the horses, "To the lodge?"

"Aye," Robert shouted back. "'Tis close." He turned to help Charissa and Ashley who had begun throwing things back into the baskets in a frenzy of haste and terror.

Elric held the reins of all four horses and struggled to keep the spooked animals under control as he led them to the girls. Robert met him and snatched the reins of his stallion and the two mares, so Elric could fasten the baskets on the back of his roan.

The wind whiplashed the clearing, and a driving ice-cold rain pelted into Robert's skin. He held the bridle of Charissa's mare while providing a knee for her to mount the beast. She slid into the saddle and took the reins, controlling the scared little mare with remarkable ease.

When he turned to assist Ashley, he saw her face was whiter than his shirt, and her arms were wrapped protectively around her body. Her formerly pleasant mount danced in front of her, whinnying in fear with the whites of its eyes on full display. She impressed him with her bravery as she took a deep breath and stepped in to mount her horse.

Crash!

Lightning arrowed through the sky with thunder on its heels. The little mare reared back on two legs and charged at Ashley, who tumbled to the side just in time to escape the sharp hooves. Before Robert could release his hold on the reins, he was jerked around. The terrified animal took off, forcing him to roll over Ashley.

Both were on their feet before two beats of Robert's frantic heart had pounded. Already mounted, Elric turned to pursue, but Robert bellowed, "Let her go!" The mare bolted through the underbrush and streaked out of sight.

Elric turned back as Robert scooped up Ashley and settled

her astride his stallion. He jumped on behind her and wheeled his panicked steed around. With everyone mounted, he led Charissa and Elric at a gallop through the trees toward the lodge.

Once out of the clearing and in the shelter of the trees, the pelting rain lessened to a steady patter. When Ashley snuggled into his arms, Robert was captivated by her touch. It felt right for him to hold her. Using his free arm he could not stop himself from pulling her flush to his chest. Despite the storm he had a fleeting hope it could perhaps take a bit longer to get to the camp.

Boom!

Another streak of bright light slashed through the woods and a tree beside them cracked into two pieces. Charissa screamed as the huge branch teetered overhead before crashing to the forest floor, inches from them. All three were forced to tightly rein in their fear-stricken animals. Ashley shuddered and latched onto Robert, burying her head in his chest. He muttered reassurances in her ear as he urged his horse to move ahead.

All thoughts of taking his time vanished as the patter of rain turned into a downpour.

Chapter 15

The hunting lodge showed itself as a dark blob in the distance that took shape as they approached. A rugged-looking building, it nestled into a small clearing that appeared to Ashley to be divided into two parts. A shelter for humans huddled on one side, and a mews for beasts squatted on the other. The thatched roof over both stayed solidly in place, defying the sharp winds that plastered the wet to her bones.

Robert slid to the ground, taking Ashley with him, and handed the reins of his still skittish stallion to Elric, who already held the bridle of Charissa's mount. Robert reached up for Charissa and whisked her from her saddle.

"Get inside!"

Ashley needed no further encouragement from Robert as she and Charissa raced to the wooden door. It took both of them throwing all their weight against it to make the thing give way and open. They staggered inside and pushed the slab of heavy wood shut to keep the driving rain from coming in behind them. The two were drenched from head to toe. Puddles formed around their feet as they stared into the dark room. The smell of damp earth, mildew, and closed quarters greeted them.

Another crack of thunder exploded directly above their heads. Ashley dashed to a window fearing Robert and Elric had been hit. Charissa was at her elbow, the girl's face crumpled in concern. The yellowed oilcloth and the eerily dark sky prevented them from seeing much of anything, but then Robert yelled to Elric, who answered, and she knew they were unhurt.

"Do you think Elena and everyone else got home okay?" Ashley's worry was palpable in the darkened room. "They were ahead of this, right?"

"I am sure they did, Lady Ashley. She hath Master Obelyn to care for her, and he will be sure she is safely returned." Charissa spoke calmly as she turned from the window and peered through the gloom. "Flint, tinder and a candle must be here somewhere."

"Yeah, a little light would make me feel better for sure." Ashley started across the room and banged into what seemed to be the side of a table. "This is ridiculous," she grumbled, rubbing her injury to make the pain ease.

Fishing inside the surprisingly dry leather pouch at her waist, she plucked out the tiny flashlight she knew was there. Without another word she flicked it on and shined the high intensity light around the room. "*Ah,* there it is." The tinderbox sat next to a candle on the mantle of a fireplace across from the window.

Striding to the hearth she heard Charissa gasp behind her. "Ashley, that light!" Her voice wavered. "'Tis coming from your hand!"

Ashley couldn't help but chuckle. "Oh, this? It's called a flashlight. You like it?"

She directed the light at her friend and promptly quit smiling. Charissa swayed as though she might swoon, the color having fled from her face. "It's not dangerous. It's just a flashlight, not magic. These are made and sold in my country for just this kind of thing."

Before Charissa could respond, the door flew open behind them. Ashley spun around to find Robert and Elric standing in front of the open doorway, silhouetted by the rainwater streaming into the room. The light from her flashlight glowed in their faces, giving them an otherworldly vibe.

They did not move, their nearly identical scowls making her shiver. Ashley made an effort to sound calm. "Guys, get in here before we all drown. Can one of you get a candle going so I don't have to use up the battery in this thing?"

Elric was the first to recover. *"God's blood,* Ashley, what is that thing?"

Robert shut the door with a thump and glared at the flashlight in Ashley's hand.

"You are a witch."

"No, Robert, I'm just from a different place, that's all."

She held out her arm holding the flashlight loosely in her palm. "If you light the taper, I'll show you what this is, and you'll not be so amazed."

Ashley aimed the light to shine on the mantle. Robert strode to the tinderbox and opened the lid. A flint lay inside, but material to light was absent. In the firebox below, dry logs were stacked with enough kindling to light. Another stack sat to the right of the grate, so once a fire got going she was sure they would soon be warm and dry.

"Give me your tinder box, Elric. Mine is wet."

Elric grimaced. "'Tis in my saddlebag." Groaning, he turned to go.

Another strike of simultaneous lightning and thunder slashed across the room just above their heads. Panic flared in Charissa's eyes. Elric shouldn't have to go outside in this weather when she could light that fire in an instant. Ashley made up her mind to risk it.

Robert was working hard to get a spark off the flint in hopes of lighting the dry kindling when Ashley stopped the nonsense. "Oh, *please.* Charissa, hold this and let me use a match."

She shoved the flashlight into Charissa's hand and focused the light on the fireplace. Charissa's eyes were huge, but she held the little flashlight without faltering. Ashley rummaged through the rest of her possessions in her pouch and pulled out the book of matches and her bandana. Drying her hands thoroughly with the bandana, she flipped open the matchbook cover, selected a match, closed the top securely, and struck it. A flame snapped and crackled to life on the stick she held. Bending to the fireside, she lighted the twigs and moss in the firebox using her free hand to block any drafts.

As luck would have it, the dry moss took hold and a fire flared to life in seconds. "There! That's much better, don't you think?"

Satisfied with her success, she blew out the tiny matchstick, threw it into the blaze, and stuffed her belongings back into her bag. Wheeling to face her companions, she expected them to thank her. Instead, they stared at her, their faces white and their thoughts unreadable.

Ashley took a deep breath, lifted the flashlight from Charissa's hand, shut it off and held it up for all to see. "Don't worry, Charissa held the flashlight and nothing bad happened to her, did it?"

The light from the fire was now bright enough for them to see what she held. "It's only a flashlight. Here is the on/off switch, this is the light bulb, and inside are batteries that power the light. All anyone has to do to make the light work is flick the toggle button." She demonstrated by snapping it on and off a couple of times.

"Robert, take it and give it a try."

Brow furrowed he accepted her challenge and picked up the object from her open palm. He pushed the switch as instructed. The light turned on exactly as Ashley said it would. He waved it around the room, amazement shining in his eyes. He turned it up to his face and stared into the light, casting his face in eerie shadows.

Elric wanted his turn and wrestled it from Robert, flashing the light into the corners of their dreary room. Both were now excited about the new toy. Moments later Elric held the light under his own chin, as Robert had earlier, and began entertaining them all with goofy, scary expressions. How odd, Ashley thought, boys with toys in any time period played the same games.

Ashley smiled at their enjoyment, but was once again

ready to end the impromptu party to keep the batteries from dying. "So time's up. Sorry to disturb your fun, gentlemen, but the energy in these doesn't last forever. I want to keep what juice I can for any further adventures."

Robert snatched the flashlight from Elric's hand and held it out for Ashley to take. Thankful for his help, she reached for it, but Robert clenched his fingers around it at the last moment and held it up to his chest. "Indeed, Lady Ashley, where is this far away land from whence you come?" He quirked an eyebrow at her and waited for her reply.

Startled by this sleight of hand, Ashley searched Robert's face to determine his intent. His tawny eyes glittered and the fierceness of his expression made her heart skip a beat. Appealing to Charissa and Elric for support, she found the same raised eyebrows and questions reflected in their eyes. Her body compulsively shuddered, making her shake until her teeth rattled.

Charissa broke the moment with a shiver of her own and moved to stand before the fire. "We all are drenched to the bone, and the fire is not yet hot enough to dry us. Are there any drying blankets here?" Charissa asked through blue lips, rubbing her hands together vigorously over the struggling embers.

"I shall fetch them." Elric disappeared into a side room.

Robert had not taken his eyes off Ashley, but finally yielded when Elric returned a moment later to pass out towels for everyone.

Robert looked down at the homespun cloth he held and back up at her. His expression was blank. How pathetic and bedraggled she must look to him.

Without warning, he captured her with his towel, pulled her to him, and energetically began drying off her shoulders and arms. Trembling, she submitted to the treatment without a fight, not sure if he was angry with her or what.

"Here, let us dry you. We can talk later." Good, she thought, he might not burn her at the stake today. That relieved some of her anxiety.

Robert helped her remove her sodden surcoat and carefully laid it over a wine barrel to dry. He rubbed the sleeves of her thin bodice robustly with his towel. Ashley stood still, like a small child being tended to by a parent, and gazed up into Robert's face.

Some of the intensity was still there, but she read a different emotion in his eyes now. What was it? She noted the little pucker between his brows as he concentrated on his task, the firelight sparkling in his eyes, and the determined thrust of his squared jaw. It was a beautiful face. How astonishing it was to find him real flesh and blood and not some kind of mystical mirage.

See-sawing the towel across her backside, his face sprouted a smile. "You seem to be enjoying this, Lady Ashley." His rumbling voice sparked an unfamiliar warmth deep within her person. "I do not think I have ever seen you stand still this long."

Ashley picked up on his teasing tone. "I don't recall asking for any help, Lord Robert." She cocked an eyebrow at him and sent a seductive smile his way. At least she hoped it was seductive as heat rushed to her face. This guy did something to her insides without even trying.

Before she could blink, Robert spun her around so her back was against his chest and drew the towel back and forth across her breasts. "You do not want my help?" His whisper crackled in her ear making that bit of warmth flash into fire.

Ashley's stomach capsized. "N-n-no! P-please c-continue." Her breathing was erratic and her heart galloped. She gloried at his touch in spite of being somewhat intimidated by him. Ashley's eyes wandered hazily over the front of her dress as the towel worked its way down her body and froze. She had let Anna dress her, and she had not worn her bra. There for all to see, her nipples stood erect and clearly visible through the wet fabric of her clothes.

Ashley snatched the towel out of Robert's hand and tossed

him the dry one she still held. "Don't forget to dry yourself, Robert." Could she sound more idiotic? The man scrambled her brain just by standing there.

She wrapped the wet towel around her middle and covered her perky nipples to the best of her ability. She had better tamp down the fire in her core before she did something foolish.

Robert straightened slowly and frowned in response to the sudden change in her. She cringed at the hard set of his face. She couldn't just tell him what the problem was. Nervously, she turned to Elric and Charissa in hopes of rescue only to find Elric deeply engaged in drying off an entranced Charissa. The two were murmuring to one another and obviously enjoying themselves.

Ashley moved back toward the hearth and hovered above the flames, patting the towel over her hair to dry it. Was it the towel, the fire, or her hair that smelled like wet animal? Would he notice? She couldn't think of anything to say to Robert, so she kept her face to the fire, hoping the heat would mask her flushed cheeks.

Feeling his eyes on her, she smiled wistfully over her shoulder. She could only pray the top of her gown was drying sufficiently to hide her nipples. "The fire feels so good," she babbled, and immediately cursed herself for sounding vapid.

Robert took the cue and nodded his agreement. He gifted her with a lopsided smile that made her pulse race, and began to dry his face with the same drying blanket he had used on her. He shed his tunic and tossed it aside on the battered trestle table in the center of the room. Empty wine barrels stood in for chairs around it. Sitting on the nearest one he pulled off his soggy boots. With a glint in his eye, he stood and stripped off the wet shirt that clung to his body.

Ashley could not look away. Did he know what he did to her? Wearing only his breeches, Robert planted himself in front of her. His body glistened in the firelight that highlighted the ripples on his lean, well-muscled frame. He could have been a mythological warrior god, his body glorious in its beauty.

Her hands fell to her sides as she gaped, no longer able to hold up the towel now hanging limply in one hand. Robert's grin widened as his eyes rested on her chest. She followed his gaze to find the sheer fabric on the front of her still transparent and clinging to her very erect nipples.

She stilled for a moment before the blood rushed to her face. Her breasts had betrayed her again. *Gah.* She countered his bold stare with her wadded towel launched at his head. "*Robert!*" She sounded like a parent scolding a naughty child. Spinning back to the fire she hid her face. "How embarrassing," she moaned.

Robert sneaked up behind her and offered a sincere apology. His breath tingled on her neck and made her squirm in a new, delicious way. A nervous giggle bubbled up through Ashley that erupted in an unladylike snort. Robert laughed at the sound, which prompted Ashley to accidentally snort again.

From that point it was game on. Robert tickled her and snorted back until the two were laughing and playfully snorting at each other, flopped in front of the fire. Peals of laughter came from Ashley as she stretched across Robert's lap, twisting and gyrating in her efforts to keep him from tickling her. Really, it was all too silly, but so much fun.

Elric and Charissa joined them in front of the fire to ask what was so funny. Ashley and Robert halted at the question, read each other's eyes and cracked up again. Sucking in breath, Ashley found her voice, covered her chest demurely, and tried to explain to them how the wetness of her clothing was a bit too revealing. Silently questioning each other, Charissa and Elric wondered what they were missing, before shrugging it off as giddy fun.

∞∞∞

Robert glanced at the faces across from him as talk quieted. Charissa was sitting with Elric wrapped around her like a second skin. He and Ashley mirrored that, the back of her head resting against his chest, his legs on either side of hers. It all felt completely comfortable and right. The only trouble was Charissa was *his* betrothed. He was shocked to think he had hardly noticed her all day. Had he talked to the girl at all? He could not remember doing so.

On the other hand, Robert could recall Ashley's movements throughout the day with ease. He had been physically aware of her at all times. From the moment they had first touched astride his destrier at the stirrup cup ceremony, Ashley had stolen his attention, and he feared, his heart. Looking down at her cuddled in his arms, he was convinced she felt the same. She was beautiful, intelligent, modest, and charming. In short, she delighted him. Everything about the day had been new to her and perhaps terrifying at times, yet she had gamely given her all to each activity. He liked her spirit.

Elric murmured something to Charissa, and she smiled radiantly up into his face. Yes, Robert could see their connection. The couples gazed serenely into the fire that now crackled and sizzled, the sounds of the storm outside having settled into the patter of a steady rain.

"How long hath ye been in love?"

The question slipped out of Robert's mouth before he had time to check it. His voice was smooth and unthreatening, yet Charissa's breath hitched and Elric swallowed visibly. *There it was.* The situation no one wanted to address was now out in the open. The gauntlet had been dropped.

Charissa flushed, her face flaring scarlet as she sought Elric's help. He opened his mouth, but words deserted him. Ashley's body tensed in Robert's arms, so he squeezed her hand to reassure her. "I am not angry, brother. Look at us. How can we be unhappy when it appears we have found our other half?"

This time it was Ashley who gasped. Elric drew a deep breath and adjusted his death grip on Charissa's hand as he waited for Robert to explain. "Perhaps we are all awestruck, or maybe this is how 'tis meant to be." Robert smiled down at Ashley who was looking up at him in wonder. "Charissa is yours, Elric, as you are hers. I know not what our father or Charissa's will say, but I will not hold her to our betrothal bonds."

Everyone was speechless for a moment. Then everyone started talking at the same time. Elric and Charissa laughed and cried, ending up in each other's arms locked in a fierce kiss.

Ashley's face brightened with delight as she watched Elric and Charissa rejoice, but her face flickered her uncertainty as she met Robert's eyes. He gathered her to him, smoothed the damp hair from her face and answered her unspoken question with tenderness. "Yes, Ashley, I do think you are meant for me. We knew it the moment we touched, did we not?" He paused for a moment and Ashley could not resist adding, "If not in our dreams?"

Robert was stunned. Did that mean she had dreamed of him as he had dreamed of her?

Commotion on the other side of the room interrupted his thoughts.

"I am going to search for a few more drying blankets." Elric jumped up and marched to the side room. "I'll be back shortly."

What was he up to? He'd like to have his brother's head for interrupting his moment with Ashley.

"I shall ... help him." Charissa followed in Elric's path and disappeared into the side room. She shut the door firmly behind them.

Ashley sat up and stared at the closed door. "Did someone say 'Don't follow us,' or did I imagine that?"

Robert laughed, his eyes twinkling now in understanding. "Do you think they tire of our company, my lady?"

"I think they want to be alone." Ashley's eyes held a naughty glint he had not seen before.

"What should we do while they are g--"

Ashley's mouth found his in answer and they melted into

one another. Yes, this is what he longed for. Her lips were soft on his but they set him on fire. What was it about this woman he could not get enough of? Like her dream self, she filled more than his arms. She filled his soul.

Time passed in a sweet haze. The fire died along with the deluge. The sun popped out as if it had never been gone. The door to the side room scraped as it opened, alerting Robert of the interruption to come. He nudged Ashley to stand and struggled to find his own feet.

Elric peered around the edge of the door and smirked when he saw their unkempt state. With a roll of his eyes Robert indicated it was safe to come out. Elric pulled a sheepish Charissa along behind him. It was no secret how each couple had spent the intervening time.

Still, the four had difficulty making eye contact with each other, so Robert took charge to ease the tension. "The time has come to leave if we are to reach the castle before nightfall." Everyone nodded agreement, scanning the room for what needed tending before they could leave.

"I will fetch water to douse the fire." Elric headed outside for the rain barrel while Ashley and Charissa began setting the room to rights. Robert's mind was already on the trip home as he set out to saddle the horses.

"Robert!" Elric caught his brother's attention as he left the lodge. "We must talk."

Robert strode to the barrel where Elric busied himself filling a bucket with rainwater. He waited for his brother to begin, wondering if Elric had the same concerns he had.

Elric's words spilled out in a rush. "Much as we wish it, Charissa and I do not believe our fathers will agree to release you from your betrothal. Too much is at stake in the alliance of the two estates."

Yes, that was his concern, too. "You may be right, little brother." Grimly, he looked Elric in the eye. "What do you suggest we do?"

Elric hesitated, his eyes straying to Charissa and Ashley as they walked toward them. Placing the full pail at his feet, he reached out a hand for Charissa who ran to him. He tucked her protectively under his arm. "We think we should be discovered coming in tonight after hours by Lady Margaret. She will automatically think the worst and raise a furor in the family."

The plan was a bold one and Robert was unable to hide his surprise. Elric pressed on. "Then you will play the wronged partner and refuse to marry the less-than-virtuous Charissa." Here Charissa grinned up at Elric who winked at her. "Our fathers will have no choice but to let us wed. You will then be free to form a union with whomever you choose." At this, his eyes darted from Robert to a wide-eyed Ashley.

Robert let out a low whistle. "I see. T'would do it." He reached out and lifted Charissa's chin so she had to meet his eyes. "Is this what you want, Charissa? You will be ruined."

"'Tis the only way, Robert. No one will remember the disgrace once we are married awhile."

Robert desired to do just as she and Elric wished, but what of his own honor? "I cannot let Charissa be disgraced knowing I am equally to blame." Robert stepped away in disgust with himself for thinking otherwise. "T'would be dishonorable."

Charissa grabbed his arm and made him look at her. "Would your honor prefer you wed a woman in love with another man? Would your honor prefer *you* loved another woman?" She paused to let her words sink in. "I see no honor in either, sir."

Robert peered for a long time into Charissa's eyes, reading the resolve he found there. Finally, he nodded and cocked his head to the side. "You are sure?" he questioned, his eyes moving from Charissa to Elric.

"Yes!"

Their unison answer broke the somberness of the moment. Robert smiled when he heard Ashley breathe a sigh of relief next to him. "Then 'tis decided." Robert opened his arms and Ashley dived into them.

After a rather lengthy celebration of the decision, the lovers reluctantly broke apart. "Let us be quick to finish here and go home." Robert's eyes still glowed from the fervor of Ashley's kiss. "We have much to plan en route to see this happens tonight."

They soon found themselves back in the saddle and happy despite their still damp clothing. They rode toward Hertford Castle with hope in their hearts all would go as planned.

Astride his stallion, Robert pressed Ashley to his chest, frequently nuzzling her neck. The fates had ordained he choose this woman and his heart rejoiced. In the span of two days, she had become so much more than a dream. She would be his life from this point until death parted them.

The journey home took almost no time at all as they plotted their evening's strategy. Awkwardness had abandoned them somewhere along the way in favor of high spirits. If it went well, all would be right with Robert's world.

What a difference an afternoon can make. Robert's heart smiled.

Chapter 16

Damien Lundene, Baron of Bedford, stood on the parapet of Hertford Castle and sucked in a lungful of the freshened, rain-cleaned air. He needed to calm himself or he would regret his decision to come here.

Yesterday, a rider had delivered the invitation to him to attend the nuptials of Lord Robert and Lady Charissa. No surprise there. What was a surprise was the snubbing he had just received from the chit he intended to marry.

Having arrived several days early hoping to renew his pursuit of marriage to the Lady Elena, he had found her alone in the passage leading to the great hall. Upon their meeting face to face, she had tried to hurriedly brush by with her nose in the air like she knew him not.

Her actions had angered him so thoroughly he had grabbed her and handled her far too roughly. Lady Elena's unexpected rebuke had sent him fuming to the parapet like smoke to the sky. No one looked upon him with disdain and got away with it.

Yet, he could not shake the shame that dogged him. Never before had he treated a woman so harshly. The resulting terror and revulsion on Lady Elena's face made him ill. She was Hertford's darling. He had gone too far in treating her badly, and he knew it. All she had to do was complain to her father, and he would no longer be welcomed here.

God's blood! What was wrong with these young women? Why did they not do the duty they were born to do?

He was a wealthy, titled land owner and he needed an

heir. Hertford had no objections. It was that blasted little hussy who refused his hand.

As Bedford glowered from his lookout above the road leading to the portcullis, he became aware of movement below. It was nearing sunset and the gates to the castle would soon be closed. He counted three horses and four riders, with a female riding in the lap of a man on the first big animal. Something about this sight drew his attention beside the fact they were moving at a rapid pace to get inside before the portcullis dropped.

Wait.

He recognized them. It was Lord Robert and his brother Elric. *Ah,* then that must be the Lady Charissa, Mowbray's spawn, in front of Robert. *No.* He spotted her small frame and dark hair on the mare between the brothers.

Who is that blonde woman, perched in front of Robert?

The baron watched as the young woman turned her face up to meet Robert's and received his kiss on her lips. *Who is this?*

As the riders approached the gates, his fascination grew as the girl sat upright, careful not to lean against Robert as she had been. What an interesting development. Lord Robert, to be wed in a few days time to the Lady Charissa, was clearly enamored with another woman--and in front of Lady Charissa, no less.

The earl would not be pleased with this news. He would hold on to the information and use it to his advantage if Elena ventured to tell her father of the encounter in the hallway. His little indiscretion would be nothing compared to the collapse of the impending nuptials of Lord Robert and Lady Charissa.

Smirking in satisfaction, he noted his hands had unclenched and his palms were pressed against each other as if in silent prayer for his newfound scheme to work. His sly smile became a full-fledged grin. Bedford spun on his heels and went to join his host in the great hall for the evening festivities with a lighter heart.

∞∞∞

Ashley and Charissa were chattering and still in high spirits as they slipped through a side door into the keep from the courtyard. The two had left Robert and Elric equally excited, having finalized the details of their plan on the ride back.

Wishing to avoid the earl and Charissa's father until they were clean and changed, the girls scurried toward their rooms. No one was sure how the two fathers would react to an account of their chaperone-free afternoon. If they appeared as usual in their places at dinner, perhaps there would be few questions.

As they rounded the corner to the bedchambers, Ashley ran smack into Elena who was obviously in a hurry.

"There you are!" Elena hugged each girl with a fierceness Ashley immediately found suspicious.

"Okay, your ankle appears to be better, but has something else happened?" She examined Elena closely. Stress radiated off the girl in waves.

"Oh, nothing, except your horse, Ashley, came in riderless not long ago." Elena's fists were clenched at her sides. "In a panic, Father sent men out to search for you. I am surprised you did not see them."

"*Ah*, well, so much for acting nonchalant."

"What mean you, Charissa? Nonchalant about what?"

"Come on, Elena, there is so much to tell you. We'll fill you in while we get cleaned up." Ashley grabbed Elena's arm and half-dragged, half-carried her into Charissa's chamber.

Finishing each other's sentences, Ashley and Charissa described their eventful afternoon with Robert and Elric. Elena sat motionless on the bed with her hands folded in her lap throughout the tale, her face moving from amazed, to astonished, to dumbfounded. When the tale was told and the course of action revealed, Elena was truly speechless as she tried to absorb and make sense of the new world order.

"Hey, are you all right, Elena?" Ashley hated the sadness on the girl's face. Her effusive friend was never this quiet. Was something else wrong or was she offended by their plan? Unease shot through her. Elena would not report their ruse to her father, would she?

"Lady Elena, 'tis what we all wish." Charissa watched closely for a response slow in coming.

Elena closed her eyes for a moment and shivered. Her eyelids fluttered when she opened them, but her eyes stayed unfocused. "I am happy for all of you. If your strategy works all will be well, and I should like nothing more than you two as my sisters."

"Why do I believe there is more?"

"There is ... I ... Something happened to me this afternoon." Elena's voice trailed off.

Charissa and Ashley eyed one another. What could that be? They had been apart only a few hours.

"What troubles you, friend?" Worry now edged Charissa's voice.

Tears slid down Elena's cheeks and she brushed them away with her fingertips. "The Baron of Bedford arrived this afternoon, unbeknownst to me. I encountered him in the passageway this afternoon."

"*No way!*" The older suitor who scared her was here? Ashley promptly sat down beside Elena and signaled for Charissa to sit on their friend's other side.

"Tell us all," Charissa urged.

Ashley knew whatever had happened had been traumatic enough to make Elena extremely upset. The usually sunny girl sat between them slumped and ashen, like the life had been sucked out of her. Ashley reached for Elena's hand and squeezed it in a show of sisterly support. She willed the girl to continue.

"I thought if I pretended I did not see him, he would let me pass." Elena sighed and struggled to find the words. "It-it must have been the wrong thing to do." Her strangled cry rent the room.

"He hurt you, didn't he?" Ashley felt the heat of anger wash over her.

"He frightened me more than he hurt me," Elena sniffed, thrusting her chin up. "I thought I was past him safely, but then he gripped my arm just before he jerked me around to face him."

Charissa gasped, her eyes wide.

"His face was an inch from my nose as he demanded I say his name, but I was panic-stricken and could only stare at him. My silence made him so angry his face purpled. His vile breath on me turned my stomach until I feared I might cast up my accounts."

Ashley could not contain her dismay. "Oh, Elena, he would not have dared do that if we were with you. I'm so sorry."

"As am I," Elena whispered. "He glared at me hatefully until I cringed and cried out. I could not help it. The sound echoed down the empty hall. I prayed someone would hear and come to my rescue." Elena dropped her head as if ashamed. "He grabbed me by the shoulders and dug his fingers into my skin to keep me from calling out again. Then he forced his mouth on mine."

Elena put her face in her hands and said nothing for a moment as Charissa rubbed her back to comfort her. Dragging in a clean breath, Elena sat up, her spine rigid. "It did not last long. I struggled against him until he pulled away, but not before he bit my lip and made it bleed. When he stepped away, his eyes never left my lips. For a moment I thought he understood he had gone too far and would apologize, but a blackness settled over his face. It was as if he were satisfied to have placed his mark on my body." Her hand wiped over the red spot on her lower lip as if the motion might make it go away along with the memory. "Then he turned his back on me and stomped away."

It was now Charissa and Ashley's turn to be speechless. Who could imagine anyone treating the perfectly pliant and sweet Lady Elena in this fashion? Ashley was the first to speak. "He physically threatened you! We can't let him get away with this. You have to tell your father."

"You must, Elena. No gentleman would ever treat you that way."

"Indeed, but Father will not be happy to hear it. The baron is his friend. I believe he *wants* me to marry him because it is a good match. The baron's lands adjoin ours and I would never be far away which would please my father. He was disappointed I turned down Lord Bedford when he offered."

Ashley arched a brow in disdain for the man in question. "Would your father still want the union knowing the baron *bit* you? Besides, if your father accepted your decision earlier, why is Bedford even here?"

"He is here for Charissa and Robert's wedding." A faint smile played around her lips. "Our guests will be confounded by an unexpected couple, won't they?"

"Do you fear the baron hath not given up his suit?" Charissa got back to the root of the problem, ignoring the reference to her first betrothal.

"*Yes.*"

Tears sprang into Elena's eyes, but then her expression hardened as her fingers rubbed them away. "He may not be a man to take no for an answer, but I will not change my mind. Nonetheless, I think he is here to sweeten his offer in hopes my father will accept it in spite of my wishes."

"*Ouch.*" Ashley chewed her lip until a new battle plan emerged. "We can't let that happen. We're really gonna have to have your back tonight. But no worries, my friend. Charissa and I will divert Bedford at every opportunity so you won't even have to talk to him."

"Yes, 'twill be a thorny night, but we shall see it through." Charissa's chin came up. She was ready to take on Bedford at his worst.

A grim smile played about Ashley's lips as she did her best to reassure the two all would end well before morning. If only someone could do the same for her and Robert. This baron sounded like a nasty piece of work.

A knock at the door startled them. It was Anna with hot water. She helped Ashley and her new friends scurry about the business of washing away the day's woes and donning their feminine armor for the coming battle.

∞∞∞

To a casual observer, Ashley thought, the assembled guests behaved in an ordinary way that night. They laughed, talked, ate and drank as expected. To the plot's participants, however, the underlying tension was as real as the unwanted guest.

The earl himself introduced Ashley to the Baron of Bedford, whose eyes seemed to peer right through her clothes. *Yuck.* She took an instant dislike to him. Of course Elena wanted nothing to do with the man.

His face held an insufferable smugness, like he knew something no one else did. He was not tall, but a solidly built man, with sharp features and bushy, black brows over dark eyes. The silver hair at his temples gleamed in the candlelight. The guy never doubted he was a handsome, powerful man and wanted everyone else to acknowledge it too, especially Ashley.

A chill passed through her as she puzzled over why he cared what she thought of him. The baron may have been a strikingly handsome man, but the energy pulsating from him was not positive. Something about him was unsettling, as if he were not quite comfortable in his own skin.

As the diners were being seated, Elena's face lost all color when she was directed by her father to sit next to Bedford.

When attention shifted to the other side of the earl, Ashley smoothly stepped in and moved the trembling Elena over one seat. She would sit next to Bedford herself, rather than make her friend suffer the attentions of this man. Ashley would manage to put up with him for one night. To her relief, Bedford only quirked an eyebrow at her when he realized Elena was not beside him, but he said nothing.

Charissa and Robert were settled on the far side of the earl, with Elric on the other side of Elena. Robert tried to keep his eyes off Ashley, as much as Elric tried to keep his eyes off Charissa, but Ashley wondered if they were fooling anyone. Twice she caught the baron watching her when she sneaked a glance Robert's way. He would have no reason to suspect her of an attachment to Robert, would he? It made her shudder just to think of it. The man was like the creepy uncle in a horror movie--nice looking on the outside but scary rotten underneath.

The earl was in a good mood, as was Mowbray. To them, the young ones were uninjured from their afternoon adventure, and Elena's damaged ankle was not as bad as first suspected. The two men enjoyed making good-natured sport of Ashley, teasing her for having her mount arrive riderless. She laughed and took it well, happy she was not being scolded and promised to improve her riding skills.

Lady Margaret chided that falconing was not a lady's pursuit and declared they would have done far better to have remained within the fortress walls. This received groans from most, but an acknowledging laugh from Bedford, who was then rewarded with the regard of an overly flirtatious Lady Margaret. The rest of the evening she batted her eyes at him if he so much as looked in her direction.

Serves him right, Ashley thought. Let the old bat seek him out. Surely, she did not think he would be drawn to her, did she? He needed an heir. But then, maybe nasty was drawn to nasty. Lady Margaret was about the same age as Bedford, Ashley speculated. On the other hand, the man needed to save his flirtation for a lady who welcomed it, and who more deserving of Bedford than Lady Margaret?

"You found something amusing, Lady Ashley." Bedford watched her face intently. *Gah.* Ashley was aghast. The man *had* been watching her since her introduction to him. And, judging from the leer he bestowed on her, she was the one now in his sights.

"It's nothing you would find humorous, my lord." She swiveled toward Elena to shut him up. It didn't work.

"My dear Lady Ashley, you are quite lovely." His lips nearly touched the shell of her ear, making her cringe and wish he would leave her alone. The smell of his heavy, cloying scent filled the air around her. To her chagrin, when he sat back he eyed her from head to toe. "You are finely formed and elegant in body with a beautiful face." He paused and shook a finger at her. "Yet, there is something different about you I cannot place."

Ashley held her breath. Could the man know something about where she had come from? Did he know her secret?

The baron hovered over her, tickling her ear with his hot breath. "You glow with self-assurance, unlike that little Hertford wench beside you." Ashley's head whipped around in disgust and scowled at the man. "That *wench* you speak of is my friend."

"*Ha!* You have spirit, Lady Ashley. I do like a woman who can challenge me."

Ashley was repelled by the heavy-lidded look he gave her. She could not grumble to anyone because she had all but asked for his interest when she moved Elena and sat next to him. He continued to openly assess her attributes which totally creeped her out. *Ugh.* She felt dirty, yet he had laid not one finger on her. No wonder Elena found him repugnant.

"In fact, my lady, the idea pleases me greatly." He reached out to place his hand on top of hers. Ice filled her veins at his touch and she wanted to throw that hand back in his face. She braced herself and tried to smile sweetly.

"Perhaps, Lord Bedford, you should hatch *another* idea." She wanted to scream for him to remove his hand, but instead he seemed to take her statement as an encouragement for his advances. Finally, she jerked her hand from under his, pretended to catch a sneeze, and hid her hand in her skirts.

"Bless you," he and Elena chimed.

Thank you for noticing, Elena.

Ashley dutifully thanked Bedford before turning to Elena to babble about the rainy weather and perhaps catching cold and so on. Elena took her cue well and did her best to hold Ashley's attention until the baron shrugged and began conversing with Mowbray on his other side.

As the end of the evening neared, Ashley was as exhausted as if she had played a game of keep away all night. With occasional assistance from Charissa, she had skillfully kept Lord Bedford from Elena's side throughout the evening. As a result, Bedford had become increasingly amorous, and she had been forced to fend off his wooing more than once.

A confused Robert caught her eye and questioned her association with Bedford by sneering at the man. She rolled her eyes and shrugged. Well, what else was she to do? Robert couldn't spend the evening next to her, and at least she was sparing Elena more distress. She would have to get the word to him soon that Bedford had bullied a terrified Elena, and then he would understand. What he would do with that information she didn't know. Would he confront Bedford? Complications were developing with every minute spent in Bedford's company.

At last the interminable evening's entertainment ended. The earl rose and invited the men to his map room for a new drink imported from France called *eau-de-vie*. The girls welcomed this news and said their goodnights trying not to look like schoolroom children released from a scolding.

Taking Ashley's hand to bid her goodnight, Bedford purposefully flipped it over and kissed her palm. She almost lost her cool when his cold tongue lightly touched her skin.

Why did that palm kiss make her feel violated? Her stomach churned. Hadn't she thought Bedford a stomach churner when Elena first told them about the baron? She'd called that one right.

Thankfully, Charissa's father was next in line. She gave him such a warm goodnight he fumbled his response and turned red in the face.

The three girls raced up the steps to Elena's room, with Ashley only tripping twice on the stairs, where they would ready for stage two of the evening. Ashley's heart pounded.

Out of the frying pan into the fire?

∞∞∞

Lord Bedford nursed his drink in the map room until Mowbray deemed it time to call it an evening. Robert and Elric had left early with other activities in mind they were not sharing. Their father had retained his good humor and let them go, choosing to talk hunting with his old friends.

Bedford had done some serious thinking during this time, letting Mowbray carry the conversation with the earl. Upon Mowbray's departure, he decided he would pre-empt any designs young Robert might have on Lady Ashley by letting his feelings be known.

"Hertford, I admit I came here with the intention of renewing my petition for the hand of your daughter, but her mind hath not changed."

"So 'twould seem. I am sorry, Damien, but she hath a mind of her own, and I vowed to let her use it in finding a suitable husband."

"Yes, well, it seems I must look elsewhere." Bedford cleared his throat, signaling an end to that topic. "What of Lady Ashley? She is an attractive possibility and your children are enchanted with her."

"Aye, that they are." The earl's tone indicated this pleased him not. "She hath proved to be a favorite." A hint of anxiety could readily be heard in his voice and Bedford was quick to pick up on it.

"I take it you agree not?"

"An incident occurred, a mix up, you understand, causing some confusion when first she arrived, but since then she hath been an unassuming guest. I cannot object."

"Yet, you have reservations about her?"

"I know not where this United States of America is found of which she speaks. That makes me uncomfortable, as doth the unusual language she uses. Before Cedric departed for regions unknown, as he is wont to do, he did instruct me to protect her in his absence."

"Why would she need *your* protection?"

"I know not, but he said she is an important person in her country and warned I should afford her my deepest respect."

"How fascinating." Bedford was all-ears now. "How comes she to be here?"

"She was separated in a storm from her party, or so the story goes, but the others she describes have not been found."

"So, you are unsure of the length of her stay, or if she will be a permanent visitor?"

"Hmm, yes. She hath not been here long, yet I sense she somehow will be the cause of trouble for me. I would be relieved if she left here." The earl's face showed surprise with his statement as if the truth of it was new to him.

"Ah, so you would not be opposed if I pursued her for my own?"

"No, sir, I would not. With that said, I must add I know not of her parentage, nor whom you would ask for her hand or the status of her dowry."

"The lack of a dowry is not a concern of mine, as well you know. If there are no family members to ask for her hand, then I see no reason why you, sir, cannot fill that role since she resides here."

"I follow your reasoning and I cannot help but concur. Still, I am hesitant to make decisions for Lady Ashley until Cedric returns. He did leave her under my protection."

"Such nonsense, Hertford. Think you not she would be safe under my care? Would you not wish to keep her from upsetting your life? You and your children would be free of her." He had the right of it regarding the earl's feelings toward Lady Ashley, and he could sense the earl shift to this logic. He pushed for consent. "Let me pursue her and we shall see what happens."

"'Tis no harm in that. It might be the best solution for her if her own people do not claim her."

Lord Bedford smiled to himself, drained the last drop from his cup, and said his good night. That had gone better than expected. He could forget that troublesome lass of Hertford's now his road with Lady Ashley was clear.

Chapter 17

The plan to break the betrothal of Robert and Charissa was a simple one in Elena's mind. Elric and Charissa were to meet in the courtyard after midnight. There they would wait for her to wake Lady Margaret to tell her Charissa was not in her bed and could not be found.

Lady Margaret would roust a servant out of bed to carry a torch for her as she searched the premises. Elena was to stay with Lady Margaret, persuading her to check the courtyard, where low and behold, Elric and Charissa would be found in each other's arms. Lady Margaret would raise the alarm whereby Hertford and Mowbray would realize the betrothal must be broken and a new one needed. Charissa would be disgraced by their dishonorable rendezvous, but forgiven once she married Elric.

The plot was complicated almost immediately when Elena tried to awaken Lady Margaret with the news of Charissa's disappearance. Lady Margaret, in her attempts to flirt with Bedford at dinner, had consumed way more wine than was her usual.

Elena first called softly to Lady Margaret upon entering her chamber but got no response. Then she yelled in her aunt's ear. Still nothing. The snoring older woman did not surface when roughly shaken, so Elena decided the lady was out cold and their plans would have to be altered.

She was on her way back to tell Ashley about Lady Margaret's failure to awaken when she rounded a corner and bumped into Charissa's father.

"My lord, you startled me!"

"My lady, what are you doing roaming the halls alone at this hour?"

Elena thought she might as well alter their scheme since the opportunity presented itself. "I need your help, my lord. I come from Lady Margaret's room where I went to wake her to let her know Lady Charissa is not in her bed. Unfortunately, she would not come round, so you find me here."

This captured the earl's attention and the teasing demeanor of a moment ago transformed to concern.

"I was preparing for bed and remembered Lady Charissa had asked to borrow a belt for the morrow, having forgotten the appropriate one at home. I took one of mine to her room to save her the trouble of borrowing it in the morning, but Lady Charissa was not there. I have searched everywhere inside, but she cannot be found. Now I am worried about her."

"There, there, my child, Lady Charissa is a most responsible young woman. Go back to your quarters. I am sure she is fine."

This confused Elena. Why would Charissa's father not wish to find her? "But, sir, she--"

"Enough, Lady Elena. I am sure you missed her and she is asleep while you roam the corridors. Go now without another word." Lord Mowbray shooed her back toward the keep so she had no choice but to go. As she hurried off to see Ashley to determine their next move, she glanced over her shoulder only to find no sign of Charissa's father. It was as if he had simply disappeared. *How odd.*

Elena charged through Ashley's door and threw herself on the bed. "'Tis all a mess. Lady Margaret would not wake up no matter how hard I shook her. On my way back here to tell you, I encountered Charissa's father. I thought he might discover Charissa and Elric as well as Lady Margaret, so I told him of his daughter's disappearance."

"Quick thinking, Elena."

"Yes, but he calmly told me Charissa was a responsible girl

whose whereabouts I had probably missed in my search and sent me back here."

"*What?*"

"Yes. Whatever shall we do now?"

Ashley began to pace the small space in her room over this unexpected turn of events. "Perhaps we need to call it off for tonight. Who would've thought getting someone to look for Charissa would be difficult? We'll have to try again tomorrow night."

"Yes, but ... " Elena pounded the bed with her fist. "I wanted this over tonight."

"I know. Same here, but it'll be okay. This will serve as our dry run."

∞∞∞

Ashley wasn't sure she could stand another night of tension, but there was no other alternative. "Hey, wait here. I'll go down and explain to Elric and Charissa that it's over for now. Elric can tell Robert. We'll talk to Charissa in here and see if we need to revise anything from her end before we try it again."

"Somehow I think she hath not minded waiting with Elric." She grinned at Ashley with a knowing look on her face.

"*Uh-huh!* I think you're right. I'm sure Elric's made good use of the time. Perhaps all is not lost." The thought of the two lovebirds together in the dark made her smile, too. She banged open the door and called over her shoulder, "Be back in a flash."

Ashley scampered down the stairs in record time, handling the uneven steps with precision. Elena had been right about that as well. She unbarred the side door to the keep and slipped out into the night, listening for her friends.

Nighttime sounds abounded. Owls hooted nearby, and in the distance, dogs yapped out a melody that prompted a refrain from their counterparts within the bailey. Charissa and

Elric were not the only two beings appreciating the night. Her thoughts turned to Robert. Where was he now? What would he think of the postponement? She would love to have time alone under the stars with him right now. *Ah,* well. Tomorrow night might be better.

She was about to call out to the pair when an arm reached out and encircled her middle. Her backside smashed against the hard body of a man. "Going somewhere, Lady Ashley?" The cold, calculating voice of Lord Bedford blared in her ear. He reeked of alcohol and his grip on her body was too tight.

"Let me go!" Ashley gasped for breath, rattled by the sudden appearance of the man who had harassed her friend. He pressed her tighter instead.

"I was enjoying the night air and thinking about you, my lady." His mouth nuzzled her neck as he held her fast. "I am happy to see you, but what brings you outside? Are you meeting someone?"

He sounded jealous, she thought, as his hand slid from her hip slowly down to her bottom, where his fingers possessively cupped her flesh and squeezed.

"No!" Ashley yelped, squirming to avoid his touch. He chuckled at her discomfort but refused to let her go. How could she get away from him without making him more suspicious than he already was?

She resolved to stick with what little plan they still had. "Charissa isn't in her bed, and we haven't been able to find her inside, so I thought I'd look for her out here." She pushed hard against his arms, hoping he would release her. He didn't budge.

"She is with Elric, is she not?"

"Why would you say that?" *How could Bedford know?* The man scared her. She tried again to free herself from his hold, but he would not let her go.

"Now, now, my Lady Ashley, where do you think you are going?" His laugh had taken on a dark edge.

"*Let go of me.* You have no right to hold me this way."

"*Ah*, there you are wrong, my lovely. This very evening, the earl approved my suit for your hand in marriage."

Bedford whirled her around to face him. Holding both her wrists firmly behind her back, he pressed her to him. "With no male authority governing you, Lady Ashley, you are now under Hertford's protection. He is obliged to act on your behalf and hath granted our union. You, dear one, are to be my baroness."

Bedford moved in to kiss her, but Ashley erupted in anger at the audacity of the two men deciding her future. She was not Elena. She was not Charissa. She was Ashley Duvall, and no one was going to force her to marry. She abruptly kneed Bedford in the groin. That made him keel over in agony, but he did not break his hold on her wrists.

Ashley kicked and screamed with all her might at the baron and was only slightly aware of movement on either side of her. Elric and Charissa had heard the commotion and were hurriedly approaching from the bailey on the left. Frustrated with the hellion, Bedford secured both of Ashley's wrists in one hand before he grabbed her gown with the other and ripped it to the waist.

Fighting with all her strength, Ashley was overpowered by Bedford who quickly reclaimed and held both her hands in his. Charissa shrieked in horror at this proof of the baron's violence. Elric stepped behind Bedford and trapped the baron's arms behind his back. With one fierce jerk, Elric pulled him away, instantly freeing Ashley.

The voice of the Earl of Mowbray boomed from Ashley's right. "Cease this now! *Hell and damnation!* What is going on here?"

So the earl wasn't as calm as Elena had thought about his daughter's disappearance. Thankfully, he had been worried enough to check outside in the bailey for her. Bedford was now outranked.

The furor stopped and quiet fell like a blanket over fire, snuffing out the flames. Lord Mowbray surveyed the scene, looking from one to another, taking it all in. Holding her torn bodice together, Ashley struggled to catch her breath. A trembling Charissa stood beside her.

Bedford looked bored with it all, but he could not shake off grim-faced Elric, who hung like a bulldog locked on the baron's arms. Lord Mowbray shook his head in disgust and zeroed in on his daughter with cold fury. "Charissa, why are you not in your bed?"

"I ... I ... We ... " Charissa cringed at the rage disfiguring her father's usually placid face.

Elric released Lord Bedford with a flourish and stepped in front of Mowbray. "My lord, Lady Charissa and I wish to be wed." His chin tipped up in defiance.

The world stopped spinning for a moment.

Stunned, Lord Mowbray's eyes burned orange like dragon eyes in the dark. "Impossible! You are betrothed to Lord Robert, *daughter*, not this pup."

Elric ignored the slur. "My lord, she loves me and I love her. We wish to be married." Charissa could only nod vigorously, unable to speak.

A sharp voice from behind Lord Mowbray cut through the night. "Lady Charissa and Elric have been caught unchaperoned, Mowbray. She is compromised in her troth to Robert." Lord Mowbray wheeled to face Hertford, but was speechless. The earl was right.

Bedford winced at the sound of Hertford's irate voice. The furious earl's gaze skated over Ashley's ripped bodice before he squared to face Bedford, shaking his head sadly. "Damien, what have you done?"

"It seems I have taken myself a wife, Hertford. Lady Ashley is compromised, too."

Ashley's brain imploded. Her knees weakened and her vision blurred like rainwater running down a windowpane. Strong arms grasped her hips from behind to keep her from falling. *Robert.* She sighed with relief knowing he had arrived and was standing behind her next to Charissa.

"No, no, no, he cannot marry that wretched girl!"

A drunken Lady Margaret wove her way across the bailey with a servant holding a torch above her head. Elena trailed her aunt but was unable to stop her. All heads turned to stare at the woman. Her aging face sagged in misery upon learning that the man she had flirted with so successfully at dinner was now set to marry someone else.

The instant Lady Margaret reached her brother's side, her eyes rolled back in her head and she fainted. This time no one thought to catch her, and she sank in a heap of white skirts on the cold ground.

Chapter 18

Lady Margaret's dramatic entrance had paused the scene long enough for everyone to take a breath and wait expectantly for Hertford to speak. He was still seething. He jerked his sister up by one arm and almost threw her at Elena and the servant. When Elena quaked at this, Ashley knew they were all destined for trouble. The earl's fiery gaze burned them as he surveyed those gathered. After a long, impassioned moment, he fumed in a dangerously quiet voice, "Go to your chambers. *Everyone.* We will deal with this in the morning. Do not come to me. I will summon you." The earl spun on his heel and stalked off.

Robert's hands left her hips, and her security vanished with their departure. She whirled to face him, but Robert only flashed his hurt in her direction before he turned and strode purposefully away.

Stricken, Ashley could not breathe and thought she might die. Memories of panic attacks after her father's disappearance swamped her senses. Squatting, she put her head between her knees and fought for breath.

She remembered all too well the feeling of abandonment then and recognized it now, watching Robert walk away. Surely he did not believe her compromised? She would never marry Bedford. He had to know this was a setup, didn't he?

Why can't I get my breath?

Her strength dissolved and she crumpled to the ground, a sob finally leaking out from deep inside the walled-off part of her heart where her tenderest feelings dwelled.

Charissa and Elena appeared at her sides to pull her to her feet. Elric whispered in her ear, "I shall speak to him, Lady Ashley. He knows not what transpired here." He left quickly under the watchful eye of Mowbray. Her friends walked her toward the castle, reassuring her that things would work out. If only it were true.

As the girls toppled into Elena's room, Ashley became aware of Elena and Charissa sobbing, too. It had been an emotionally exhausting evening for all of them. How selfish she was to be thinking only of herself. That made her flagging energy return, enough to help her propel them onto Elena's big bed. There had to be a solution for the mess she was in.

"I cannot believe our plan fell apart so incredibly." Elena pulled up a corner of her bedding and dried her tears with it. "'Tis my fault for not waking Lady Margaret. If she and I had gone out into the courtyard instead of you, Ashley, none of this would have happened."

"Do not forget, Elena, Elric and I were discovered as planned," Charissa reminded her friend.

"True, but why did I not hit the old bat in the head with a brick, if needed? Anything to have awakened her."

Picturing that, Ashley snorted through her tears. "Why, Lady Elena, such violence. I do believe I *have* been a bad influence on you."

A wail burst from Elena. "No, you have taught me to think for myself. The violence is all me."

"*Whoa.* Slow down, Elena." Ashley was horrified the girl had taken her words the wrong way. "I was teasing you. What happened tonight with Bedford is in no way your fault. What neither of you know is your father, Elena, granted Bedford's bid for my hand in marriage when they met after dinner. That's why when I would not cooperate with him, he ripped my gown to compromise me. It's how he secured his claim."

Still grieving over her fallen status with her father, Charissa gasped and gripped Ashley's wrist. "The earl agreed to let that horrid man marry you?" A deep scowl marred her pretty face. "How can that be? The earl is not your father."

"You are mistaken, Ashley. My father would not make you marry someone you do not choose."

"*Ah,* but there you have it, Elena. I am not you. He fears me for some reason, I think. Perhaps he believes I *am* a bad influence on you."

Ashley smiled ruefully at her friend and shrugged. "He would like me to be gone from here, and foisting me off on the baron suits him just fine." She puzzled for a moment trying to fit all the pieces of the evening together. "What I don't understand is why Bedford has decided to turn his attentions from Elena to me. I come with no money or land. Why me?"

"He needs an heir more than either of the other," Charissa replied. "You or Elena would fill his requirement, and Elena hath turned down his offer once already and will do so again."

"That still does not explain why my father granted his bid for you, Lady Ashley."

"Well, Bedford had an answer for that one, too. He said the earl had a right to act for me since I had no apparent male authority to do so, and I was living here."

Her friends' faces fell. "If 'tis so, Ashley, you shall not break this union easily." Elena's bottom lip jutted out in commiseration.

"'Tis true. Our fathers are powerful men, and they will do what they please with us whether we wish it or not."

"Is that why Robert walked away?" Ashley's quavering voice betrayed her emotions.

"Yes. If Father insists on the bond, Robert will be able to do nothing about it, especially if Bedford compromised you."

"What if we say Robert compromised me first?"

"Then Father would realize tonight's discovery was a plot, and Robert's honor would be in question. Father would never forgive him for breaking his bond with Charissa."

"Yes, Robert would be ruined in the eyes of the earl. Believe me, the only thing destroying my bond with Robert tonight was my being unchaperoned with Elric. Lord Hertford broke our betrothal for Robert's sake, not mine. I am not sure Father will ever forgive me for humiliating him." She stifled a whimper by covering her face with her hands.

"Then there is only one thing to do."

"What is that, dear Ashley?" Elena's face brightened.

"I am, like, totally running away." Ashley half-joked in her valley girl drawl. Her fake smile dropped like a shade leaving her face darkly serious. "I won't stay here if I have to marry the baron."

"Oh, no, Ashley. You cannot go." Elena was visibly crushed at the suggestion her friend might leave permanently.

"You cannot leave by yourself. Where would you go?"

"Good question, Charissa. You'll have to help me figure that out. If we can find Cedric, I bet he'll have some answers." Ashley hoped her face showed more bravery than she felt.

"Yes, that is the logical step." Elena wrung out a cloth from the evening's now cold wash water and passed it to Ashley. "Cedric holds much sway, 'tis true. He will surely be of help, but do try to discuss this with my father. Mayhap you can convince him to drop Bedford's suit. Cedric did leave you under his protection, did he not? That should not include marrying you off to anyone."

"I'll give it a shot, but if he can't be persuaded to change his mind, I'm outta here." Ashley finished washing her tear-streaked face and tossed the washcloth back to Elena for emphasis.

They talked long into the night with Elena and Charissa eventually dropping off to sleep. Ashley was left alone to fret over the events of the last twenty-four hours. What had begun with such promise had ended in pain for all of them. Certainly, this would be an evening none of them would soon forget. Charissa had been brave to thwart her father, but standing up to him had been devastating. Even if she and Elric married, she had displeased her father in ways unimaginable to her only a few days ago.

The same could be said of Elena. She had always had her

father under her thumb. Now she was appalled by his treatment of Ashley, and uncertain if her father's anger applied to her too. Would Elena now be forced to marry? Ashley wondered if she had dragged her new friends into difficulties they never would have experienced if she hadn't encouraged an independent streak in them. Then there was her situation to consider. Wandering the countryside by herself in search of Cedric was a scary proposition. What would she do for food or shelter if she didn't find him right away?

Once outside the castle walls she would be alone in an unfamiliar land. Still, being forced to marry Bedford was far worse. That simply could not happen. Yet, how could she stop it if what Elena and Charissa said was true?

The last thing she remembered, a rosy light was seeping into Elena's room, but when Anna knocked on the door to rouse them it was full daylight. Rubbing the crick in her neck, she grinned at Elena and Charissa who were still asleep. The three had been curled around each other like a pile of kittens. Kittens, who had survived one storm but knew the next was coming.

Chapter 19

Dawn was fighting to break through the black shell of night when the confines of Robert's chamber closed in on him. His frustration and confusion over the night's events had intensified over the hours, leaving him feeling like he might explode. At the moment, hitting something greatly appealed to him, so he decided to go to the armory and practice with his mace.

All was quiet as he passed the sleeping quarters of the keep on his way out. By contrast the clatter of pans and the voices of the kitchen workers echoed off the stone courtyard. The smell of baking bread greeted him from across the bailey. Two yellow dogs skittered around him vying for his attention, one playfully nipping his backside before being shooed away. Robert was in no mood for fun.

Minutes later he was hard at work, beating bound hay into submission with a nasty looking mace.

Thwack.

He did not know what to make of last night's debacle. After their time together at the lodge, he thought Ashley belonged to him, yet at dinner he had watched her give her attention to Bedford. When he had silently called her on it, her response was to shake her head and smile at him. What did that mean?

Thwack.

He did not want to think about the courtyard nightmare. Having heard the expected commotion, he had walked into a completely different scene from the one they had all planned.

With her gown ripped to the waist for all to see, Ashley was horrified, but Bedford's face was calm. He acted as though nothing had happened he was even moderately sorry about.

Thwack.

Elric had explained to him Ashley was a victim who had fought the baron after he grabbed her in the courtyard. While that was likely true, Robert had to admit all those things combined had shaken his confidence regarding Ashley's feelings for him.

Robert wanted to go to his father and explain everything. He had been able to talk to the earl about anything bothering him ... until this. Their open relationship was a source of pride for both men. His own dishonesty had crippled that connection.

Thwack.

Robert wanted nothing more than to stake his claim on Ashley and thwart Bedford's unscrupulous suit. If he did so, however, he would reveal he was part of the plot for Elric and Charissa to be found together. That would destroy his honor and Elric's too. Charissa and Ashley would be ruined. What a sticky spider's web he had stepped into by agreeing to Elric's plan. He and Ashley had been trussed-up like flies by Bedford's web and no one seemed capable of saving them.

Thwack.

∞∞∞∞

The Earl of Hertford dragged himself wearily from his bed having thrashed around the remainder of the night. Cast off bedclothes lay wadded in a heap on the floor.

What was he to do? He loved his children and was a fair man and a good father most of the time, so why were all three of them miserable at the moment?

Marriage was marriage and had a purpose to fulfill, did it

not? A good match meant an heir would be likely, the bloodlines were solid, and alliances would be beneficial. Why did his children not respect this? Did they not understand love would come later, if it were truly important to them? That is what had happened years ago when he had married their mother. Her death had left him alone to manage their children's futures all by himself. He missed his Beatrice and her warm and wise counsel every day. Elena was the very image of her. Perhaps that was the reason he indulged his daughter as he did. Was that his mistake?

He feared he had erred in allowing Elena the right to turn down offers she did not want. Women were to serve their fathers and husbands, not the other way around. She would be securely wed to Bedford at this point and mothering children of her own if he had had his way.

Hell and damnation.

Why did she not see Bedford was a perfectly decent man? *God's bones,* he was a *baron*, not some peasant who had wandered in.

Leniency had won him nothing but trouble. Elena's distraught face last night had chilled him to the bone. She was his baby and the sweetest child a father could hope to have. Nonetheless, she had glared at him like he was the very devil for not shooting an arrow through Bedford's heart.

It must be this Lady Ashley. She was the variable in his puzzle, and since her arrival, his orderly world had been turned upside down. He would not be held responsible for what he might do with the girl if Cedric did not hurry back.

He sighed and struggled to get his head cleared. By rights he must hear Bedford first, he supposed, to gain an insight into the baron's situation. What was in that man's mind when he settled his attentions on Lady Ashley? By God, he would find out or there would be hell to pay.

∞∞∞

Bedford examined his reflection in the glass as he washed his face. He had not known what to expect upon arriving at Hertford Castle, but he never would have imagined what had transpired. Had he succeeded beyond his wildest expectations or was it all an unqualified disaster?

If Hertford insisted on his subsequent marriage to Lady Ashley, Bedford would not care if he were sullied in the process. He would leave with the lovely lady as his wife and be well on his way to having an heir to his riches and lands by nightfall.

Besides, he liked this fiery female. She possessed intelligence, pluck, and courage that would provide robust sons for him. Her body glowed with health. Her straight, white teeth gleamed when she smiled. Much to his chagrin, he had not managed to win the lady in the manner he would have preferred. There would be time for wooing once he had her safely ensconced in his home.

He would keep Robert's secret tryst with Lady Ashley to himself unless pressured. Nothing would be gained with his friend if he implicated the man's eldest son in a dishonorable scheme.

His conscience niggled when he thought of his clash with Lady Elena. Hertford would wage war against him if he learned of it. What had bedeviled him to treat his friend's daughter like a strumpet?

God's blood.

He was tired of living without a wife. He was lonely. He wanted female companionship *and* an heir. Was that so bad? Why was finding a wife so much harder this time than it had been with Anabel?

Her father had arranged their marriage yet she had come to his bed happy to be with him. They had enjoyed a fine life together. If only she had been able to bear him children. She had been slight in build, dark-haired and dark-eyed, lively and fun. Sadly, with each babe she lost, her step slowed a little more, until ... His chest felt like unseen forces were squeezing him. He had best not think about Anabel now.

Bedford wasted no time dressing, straightened the fur collar of his surcoat, pulled on his best leather boots and went off to see Hertford.

The moment he walked into the earl's map room, Bedford knew this meeting would not be easy. The tension in the air was thick. He flashed on the way he felt standing on the battlefield before the call to fight. Hertford was stalking to and fro in the room like a caged beast. When he turned to face the baron, his eyes were wild.

"There you are, Bedford. I am anxious to hear a full accounting of last night's fiasco from you before I give audience to anyone else. We have been friends and allies for many years, and I do not wish that to change because of a mere slip of a girl."

"I agree with you, my friend. I am sure we can come to a suitable agreement regarding the lady in question."

"*Hmph.* Please define what you deem that agreement to be, sir."

"Simply put, I would marry the Lady Ashley at once and return home with her as my wife."

"I do not understand your method of pursuing her, Damien, especially your actions in the bailey last eve. How came you to be there and why was the lady in such a state of dishabille when you were found?"

"*Ah,* I understand your confusion. The encounter was not planned. The Lady Ashley interrupted my reverie in the bailey after my visit with you. Although she sought *me* out, she was unprepared to complete the seduction she initiated. Of course, I did not mean to rip the bodice of her gown." Bedford's voice was properly apologetic. "I do not know her reasons for bewitching me, but suffice it to say I am not unhappy with the result. I want her for my wife."

Hertford nodded his understanding of Bedford's account. Needing time to think, the earl urged him to go break his fast in the great hall while the others were interviewed. After his friend left the room, the earl thought about Bedford's explanation of his regrettable behavior. He was surprised the man showed no sign of remorse, but rather smugness, as if he had gotten exactly what he wanted.

Bedford should have apologized and begged to be released from any obligation to marry. Instead, the baron wanted Lady Ashley.

How confounding.

Well, what more was left to say to the man? Normally, the two would decide the woman's fate, and she would live with their decree. This female complicated that because she was not his daughter. How was he to deal with her?

He pondered the issue, pulling his hair to relieve the headache throbbing in his temples. He would summon her. If Lady Ashley accepted Bedford, this part of last night's unfortunate events would be resolved. Then he and Mowbray need only focus on the Elric-Charissa-Robert wreckage.

A vague unease troubled Hertford that all these parts made up a whole, yet how they fit together eluded him.

∞∞∞

Ashley dreaded the showdown with Elena's father. It was apparent to her that the man had gone from indifference to disgust in his attitude toward her. There would be no sympathetic ear to bend. Elena and Charissa sent her off with advice on handling the earl, and she would do her best to plead her case. Still, nausea soured her stomach. She would not accept a life with Bedford.

She was a Texan, a citizen of the United States of America.

What would her mother say if she knew her daughter might be forced into an arranged marriage--and in the fourteenth century, no less? Would this be her *Wizard of Oz* moment? Would she wake to find she had been hit on the head and arrive back in her own time?

Much of this experience she didn't want to be a dream. Robert might be a personification of her dreams, but his kisses were real flesh-and-blood kisses. Her friendships with Elric, Elena and Charissa were the best of her life. She would never want to give up any of them.

All, she thought, with the exception of the mighty Baron of Bedford. In trying to save Elena from the advances of Bedford, she had unwittingly invited them upon herself. Could she convince Elena's father to wait for Cedric and delay the impending marriage to Bedford?

Ashley threw open the door to the map room with a vengeance and stalked in. She vowed she would not appear to be a docile female who bent to anyone's will. The earl would be forced to bend to her. She hoped.

The earl wheeled to face her when he heard the door slam open. He was not a happy man as his dishevelment revealed. Atop his head his hair stood in peaks like sheaves of wheat where he still pulled at it in annoyance. His eyes burned with a feral glaze to them, making him an altogether fierce and unyielding presence. Not at all what she wanted to find.

"Good morrow, Lady Ashley." The earl gave a nod to her and stood tall, surveying her with narrowed eyes like a lion its next kill.

"Good morrow, my lord." Ashley stood as tall as she was able in defiance of the power she felt emanating from the earl. "You wanted to see me?"

Something changed in Hertford's face as he observed her rigid stance and his eyes softened. "Yes, child, please sit down and let us discuss the mishaps of last evening." He motioned for her to sit at the map table and took up a chair opposite her. He smiled in her direction, but his eyes were now narrowed and penetrating. "Please help me understand how you came to be in the courtyard with Lord Bedford."

A reasonable question, she thought. "It's all a big misunderstanding, my lord. Just before bedtime, Elena popped into Charissa's chamber to give her a belt Charissa wanted to borrow and couldn't find her. She and I hunted everywhere but had no luck. We thought we'd better tell Lady Margaret because we were afraid something might've happened to Charissa. When Elena couldn't get Lady Margaret to wake up, she came back to tell me. I suggested we look out in the bailey, even though Elena said we should stay inside. I figured a quick look around couldn't hurt, so I poked my head out the side door and took a peek. That's when Bedford grabbed me."

"You were not going outside to meet him?"

"Of course not."

"He said you were trying to seduce him to trick him into marrying you."

Ashley was so indignant she barely caught her breath enough to answer the charge. "Lord Bedford must be a coward who doesn't want to tell you what actually happened."

"And what would that be?"

"He doesn't want to tell you he took advantage of my surprise appearance at the door by assaulting me. He doesn't want to tell you I kicked and screamed to get him off me. If you examine his legs today you'll find bruises to prove it. He doesn't want to tell you he intentionally ripped the top of my dress because I wouldn't do what he wanted." Ashley paused dramatically. "That's what *really* happened."

The earl's eyes arrowed into her and pierced her confidence. "You are asking me to believe you? You, an unknown, unaccompanied woman from a place no one knows should be believed over a friend and ally of mine since childhood? A friend who can give you a title, a fortune, and a family, if you could but persuade him to marry you? Surely you see my reluctance to accept what you say, Lady Ashley."

Thrown back in her face in this fashion, Ashley saw how

ridiculous her story sounded in light of what Bedford proclaimed as the truth. She sputtered, "But it is true, my lord. I do
not want to be married to Lord Bedford. I do *not* care to have
his name or his money, and I definitely do *not* want to mother
his kids. I pretended to be interested in him at dinner only because Elena was terrified of what you and Bedford would do.
She worried you would override her decision to turn down his
offer and she'd be forced to marry him. I put myself between
them as a favor to Elena, and it just backfired for me. The baron
interpreted that interference as interest. I can assure you I am
not interested in Lord Bedford." Ashley shuddered as her tirade
blew itself out.

"So, whom *do* you wish to marry, Lady Ashley?" The earl's
sharp tone sliced into her anger.

Ashley was momentarily stunned and her mouth fell
open. How should she respond to that question? Did he know
about her relationship with Robert? Her mouth opened and
shut two more times before she finally mouthed, "I wish to
marry a man I love who also loves me."

The earl never had a chance to respond. The door thumped
open again, and Bedford burst into the room. "I could not help
but overhear my Lady Ashley, Hertford. I would ask you to
grant me a few moments of privacy with her to address her
love for me."

Shocked by the interruption, Ashley groped for words to
deny the request, but Hertford found his voice first. "Certainly,
Bedford. I need to consider all this, so take your time and call
me when you are finished." He hustled out of the room a little
faster than his dignity would allow.

Ashley hopped out of her chair and turned on Bedford,
having no difficulty expressing her feelings to him. "I have
nothing to say to you, sir. I want nothing to do with you. Let's
be clear about what happened yesterday. You attacked Elena
in the hallway and scared her to death. I put myself in your
way last night only to protect her."

Ashley warmed up to her task and unleashed her pent up

temper on Bedford. "You need to stop this ridiculousness and go home. Look for some other female somewhere else who wants what you offer. No. One. Here. Wants. You."

Stung by the slap of her words Bedford was mum for a moment and stared blankly at her. He sank into a chair beside the map table and put his face in his hands, looking to Ashley like a deflated tire. Still, he said nothing.

Ashley was not prepared for this reaction. She had expected him to be a windbag and blow back all kinds of expletives in outrage. She replayed what she had said to him and instantly was sorry her refusal was so cutting.

From his perspective, all he wanted was a wife and a family, not something really awful. Both men made decisions for the women in their lives until she arrived on the scene and upset the balance. Would Elena have defied him if Ashley had not influenced her otherwise? Maybe her twenty-first century notions were to blame for this mess. What should she do? Apologize?

Still, Bedford said nothing. Filled with shame for her cruel words, Ashley plopped back into her chair. "I'm sorry I spoke to you in such a demeaning way, my lord. My mother always says my mouth moves too fast for my brain."

The baron looked up sorrowfully, resting his chin on his hands. "Thank you, Lady Ashley. I must confess I do not understand why it hath been so hard to marry again. I find myself behaving in ways I know are wrong." He shrugged and shook his head. "I should never have forced my regard on Lady Elena, but she angered me by treating me as if I did not exist. Then you gave me the idea at dinner that you might welcome my suit, and I must admit, I like that idea." Bedford slid out of his chair and crossed to Ashley. "I think we two suit one another rather nicely. I like your fire. Your heart. Your wit."

He took her hands in his and pulled her up to stand before him. "How can I make you understand? I want a wife who loves me as much as I love her. I know from experience love can come from an arranged marriage because I loved my first wife with all my heart. Anabel died in childbirth and the babe, my son, shortly after."

How unbearably sad, Ashley thought, as she watched the baron's dark eyes fill with pain. Having missed her father the last two years, she knew something of the heartache the baron described. Tears began to flow down her cheeks.

The baron took her face in both hands and used his thumbs to wipe away her tears. He stared into her eyes with such a depth of emotion Ashley was spellbound. As if his kiss could heal her pain, Bedford sealed his lips over hers. It was not the arousing kiss of a lover, but a sweet kiss from one who understood sorrow.

When the door banged open a moment later, Ashley started and pulled back to end the kiss, but the baron's lips clung to hers a bit longer. The tiny hairs on the back of Ashley's neck stood to attention and announced who had entered the room. In horror, she put her hands on Bedford's chest and pushed, but the baron's arm slipped around her waist and pulled her back to him.

No. This is not happening. Not again.

Her eyes flew to Robert's in silent apology as he stood a step inside the doorway. The hurt in his eyes said it all. He had seen that kiss. How could she ever explain? Not knowing what else to say, Ashley spoke softly and distinctly as one would to a frightened child. "*Robert*. It is not what you think."

Robert did not wait for an explanation. He spun on his heel and fled from the room. Ashley gave chase, but Bedford seized her arm and whirled her around to face him. She began to protest, but he silenced her with a finger to her lips.

Bedford's words spilled forth in a quiet rush. "Make no mistake, Lady Ashley, I know of your tryst with Lord Robert. I saw the two of you on horseback returning yesterday and the kisses you shared. It was obvious Lord Robert and Lady Charissa were no longer paired, as it was you who sat in Lord Robert's lap enjoying his attention."

"No. You're wrong!" Panic engulfed her.

"No, I am not. You know Lord Robert cannot have you without exposing others, but I have no such reservations in claiming you for myself. You do not want me to tell the earl what I know. I want *you*, Lady Ashley, and I am willing to do whatever it takes to make you my wife." He released her gently, but firmly.

Aghast, Ashley stumbled from the room in despair. Why had she ever thought the man had a heart? Bedford all but declared it was game-on in some bizarre war for her hand. He was determined to win at all cost, yet Ashley had only one thought ... *Robert.* Whatever was *he* thinking?

Blindly, she ran down the passageway toward the great hall and smacked into the Earl of Hertford. He captured both her arms and held her fast.

"Lady Ashley, what on earth are you about?"

"My lord, I ... I must--." Ashley's mind would not function.

"Lady Ashley, you are clearly distressed. Go at once to your bedchamber until you regain control of yourself." Irritation made the earl testy. "I take it your talk with Bedford did not go well."

Ashley shook her head. The man was in no mood to listen to her, and he would check with Bedford, anyway, to find out what had happened to send her off in tears. She needn't tell him. Much to her dismay, he turned Ashley around and summoned a guard to see her to the keep. She had no choice but to do as he bid.

By the time they reached her door, Ashley was wallowing in misery. Elena and Charissa were watching for her and quickly dismissed her escort, hustling Ashley into Elena's room.

Ashley tried to recount what had happened with Elena's father and Bedford, urgently explaining she must go find Robert before it was too late. Charissa and Elena cringed over the tale of Bedford's kiss and agreed Robert's assumptions must be checked immediately.

Charissa washed Ashley's face with a cool cloth dipped in

lavender water to calm her. Elena produced an old, hooded cloak for Ashley to wear to hide her identity as she searched for Robert around the castle grounds. When the three girls stepped out of Elena's room on their way to let Ashley out the side door, they came face-to-face with one of Hertford's guards.

"Ye must go back to yer chambers, m'ladies. I have orders from the earl to confine all three of ye to yer quarters until further notice. If ye be needin' anythin', 'twill be sent fer and brought to yer rooms."

"*What!*" Elena's indignation threatened to overwhelm her.

"I must speak with my father," Charissa demanded.

"T'will do no good, m'lady. He was with the earl when the order t'was given."

"Let me guess," Ashley added with cold certainty, "Lord Bedford was with them too."

"Right ye are, m'lady."

"*Damnation.*"

Ashley and Charissa stared in amazement at the usually placid Elena who shook her head in abject frustration at them. Grabbing their arms, she dragged them back into her chamber before either girl could speak.

Chapter 20

Steam rolled off his feverish body when Robert stepped out into the bailey and his heat crashed into the cooler air. His face still flamed and he hoped no one stopped him before he got back to the deserted armory. He needed time to recover without having to act like all was right in his world.

At the moment, nothing was right. He had been so sure of his course. Hours of swinging his mace had helped him determine to take matters into his own hands. He would go to his father and demand Ashley not be forced to wed Bedford. He would tell his father everything and risk his own honor as well as the fates of Elric and Charissa--*anything* for Ashley.

He had marched up to his father's map room to fight for the woman he loved, only to find her being tenderly kissed in the arms of Lord Bedford. His heart had stopped.

Robert had been confused before, but now he was completely dumbfounded. Had their afternoon together at the lodge been naught but a dream? Did she love him at all? He still tasted her on his lips whenever he thought of kissing her. The indescribable sensation of her in his arms haunted him.

Was it not the same for her? He had been so certain at the time, but now ...

What had she said? *It's not what you think.*

God's bones. What else should he think when another man kissed his woman? Especially when that other man had already compromised her, supposedly against her will?

Robert flung himself on top of the battered hay and threw an arm over his eyes. Exhausted from a sleepless night and hours of bashing things, perhaps sleep would claim him for a while. Was not everything supposed to be better after rest? He more than wanted it to be true because right now he was too devastated to move.

∞∞∞

The earl found Lord Mowbray hunched in his chair in the map room wearing a forlorn expression and twisting his hands every which way, deep in thought. Likely, he was still scandalized over his daughter's behavior last eve because no one had expected the well-mannered, malleable Charissa to behave so outrageously. The man had his sympathy. Hertford still struggled with how his own child was capable of such dishonor.

Analyzing the situation as objectively as a father could, he knew Robert was the better choice in a husband for Charissa. It was Robert who would inherit the title, the land, and the fortune. Elric was a reputable lad, but his second son. All would be Elric's only if some misfortune took Robert, God forbid.

Furthermore, Lord Mowbray had to be aware Elena's marriage to Elric would still secure the alliance with Hertford, for that was important to both men, but it would not be as comfortable for his daughter. Mowbray would have thought of all that, but had Charissa? Was she still so young and naive she only had eyes for the boy in front of her? And Elric was a *boy*. A soft boy who should grow to be a man not unlike Robert, he hoped, but certainly not the soldier-hardened man Robert was today.

The earl's reflections drifted to Charissa's face as he remembered it the night before, and there he had to pause. She had goggled at young Elric as he stood tall and demanded her hand like he was truly her lord and master. He smiled as he thought of his younger son jutting out his chin and stating his case. Perhaps the boy did hold some promise.

His fatherly intuition told him Charissa and Elric would be heartbroken if not allowed to marry. Should the prior marriage bond be reinstated with Robert or should he allow Elric to make a match above his station, despite his actions?

Bedford, who had been sitting nearby, offered to leave, believing the two fathers might require privacy, but Mowbray signaled him to stay and that pleased the earl. The mess to be settled was not news to Bedford and his opinion was valued.

"So, Mowbray, what do you propose we do with marriage plans for Lady Charissa?"

"That is all I have been thinking about, Cryspyn. I do not believe I shall be able to persuade her to go forth with marriage to Lord Robert. After the events of last evening, 'tis doubtful he will wish it."

"Aye, I have not spoken with Robert today, but it would seem you are correct. What of Elric's press for her hand? Will you honor his bid?"

"*Hmph.* Seems honor hath little to do with it." Mowbray offered his friend a wry smile.

"True enough," Hertford winced. "I am not accustomed to discussing my sons and their honor in a negative light, yet I understand your feelings. Elric hath never caused a day's trouble in his young life. I know not how any of this happened."

"Yes, I agree, yet I think all need not be lost. Lady Mowbray and I set up the marriage contract to Robert primarily so Charissa would always remain close to us. With the death of my wife, this is even more of a concern to me." He shifted forward in his chair ready to make his pronouncement. "Thus, since I wish to keep a strong alliance with you, my friend, it matters not whether she marries Elric or Robert. I would have wished for her all that will be Robert's as the next Earl of Hertford. She hath chosen otherwise. I believe if those concerns are not enough to hold Charissa to the contract she hath with Robert, then it should not matter to me."

"Are you saying you will give your blessing for Charissa to break with Robert and wed Elric instead? She hath been betrothed to Robert for many years." The earl was not sure he wanted this outcome. Rewarding Elric for his duplicity bothered him, yet his friend was right about the bond between families not being damaged by the change.

"'Tis so. Charissa disgraced herself and by rights should be returning home a ruined woman. Since she and Elric want nothing more than to marry, I believe we should consent."

"But you know Elric, as my second son, hath a limited inheritance."

"Aye, I do. I will help close the contract by giving Charissa a generous dowry and a sizable cut of land adjoining yours to help out the young ones. With no male heir to whom I may leave my lands as 'tis, 'twill go to my brother's son upon my death. I would rather it be left to Elric and Charissa than to my nephew."

"'Tis a solid offer, Hertford. I should accept if I were you," Bedford said. The baron had been watching this exchange with intense interest, which made the earl curious about his friend's support. Still, the encouragement was just what he needed.

"Very generous of you, Mowbray. This is a fine settlement for Elric. He is in his chamber anxiously awaiting word of his fate and expecting the worst."

Mowbray's eyes twinkled as he heartily shook his old friend's hand and agreed to work out the details of the marriage bond later in the day. They immediately sent word to Charissa and Elric of their now impending nuptials, keeping the wedding in three days as announced, with a new groom in Robert's place.

"Mowbray, would you object to a double ceremony? If Hertford hath no objection, I should like to say my vows to Lady Ashley the same day."

"*Hmph.* So you are going to wed again, Bedford? I see no reason to host two feasts when one will do, eh, Hertford? I cannot but be in good humor now Charissa's future hath been settled."

"If you will vow to protect her as Cedric required of me, I see no reason to delay. I perhaps feel a twinge of guilt in handing over my responsibility to you, Bedford, but-"

"-you want to be rid of her, yes?" Bedford finished for him.

"Yes, indeed, my friend. Indeed." The earl felt a ripple of unease pass through his body. He did not trust Lady Ashley, yet his own daughter enjoyed the girl's company. Did he or Elena have it right?

Quiet ruled the room for a moment, each man with his own rumination, until the earl broke the spell by adding a caveat. "We three agreed earlier today on a guard to watch over these young ladies, did we not? I believe it wise to continue to keep them confined to their wing of the keep until Lady Charissa and Lady Ashley are married. What say you?"

Both Mowbray and Bedford nodded their heads with vigor.

"They have created enough difficulty as 'tis, running about at all hours, and I think we shall rest easier if they are kept in their chambers," Mowbray said. "My child is always complaining she hath never enough time with ladies her own age. She should welcome these hours with her friends before she marries."

"An excellent suggestion, Hertford." The baron was so quick to concur Hertford wondered what else worried the man. "A most excellent plan, indeed."

"Well, 'twill rankle Charissa, I can assure you. Still, her disgraceful conduct yesternight deserves some punishment. She shall endure it. Keep the cats caged, so to speak. After all, she is to marry the man she desires, so we shall call it her penance, aye, gentlemen?"

"Aye!" The baron and earl nodded their agreement enthusiastically.

Hertford served his *eau-de-vie* with pleasure and both Mowbray and Bedford could not help but smile. They all had reason to be pleased. Had they not used their power success-fully today to broker solutions for the difficulties they had faced? Surely, a celebration was deserved. Satisfied with him-self and all he had accomplished, Hertford leaned back in his chair and sipped his drink. *Ah, 'twas good to be a lord.*

Chapter 21

Three snarling felines streaked back into Elena's room with claws extended, hissing at the very walls. Or so Anna described them once they were inside and the door was shut. She had arrived moments before the three realized they were not only confined to chambers but also a summons had been issued for Charissa to report to the earl.

That news pitched them all into an even higher furor as speculation abounded as to why the earl summoned her. Was Charissa to be dishonored and sent home? Would she be forced to marry Robert, despite her wishes? Or, would she be allowed to wed Elric? Anxiety was etched into Charissa's face as she solemnly hugged Elena and Ashley before heading down to meet her fate.

Ashley threw herself face down on Elena's bed and let her emotions steamroll over her. How could things be in such a mess? She could not bear the thought of Robert believing she had betrayed him. How could he possibly think she would choose Lord Bedford over him? Yet that must be what he believed. Seared into her mind was Robert's stricken face as he stood at the earl's door.

She had to reach him in person to hold his face between her hands, look him in the eye and tell him exactly what had happened and why. She had to make Robert understand she loved him, she was forever his, and would never be unfaithful to him.

Wow! Where had that come from? She *loved* him?

She searched her heart to find she *did* love Robert. She had never felt that about a guy before. She had *liked* a number of guys, a few a lot, but love? That was a new thing for her. It made her ache to think of Robert hurting over anything she did, but to be hurt over the baron? *Ugh.*

Ashley heard a moan and raised her head to find Elena eyeing her with a sad face. *Did I moan? Gah.* It was time to find her self-control. Ashley sat up, wiped away her tears with the heels of both hands, and turned to face Elena's watchful, golden eyes. "We need a new plan. I will *not* marry Lord Bedford. *Ever.* I will not let them do this to me."

Elena sighed and slipped onto the other end of the bed opposite Ashley. "I wish it were that simple. As women we have no way to prevent marriage if our fathers and the baron are in agreement. Why, here we are all but locked in our rooms. We can be starved into submission if they so desire. Who would stop them?"

"But it's so unfair, Elena. They're *your* fathers, not mine. I shouldn't have to answer to either of them. I have to get out of here and find Robert."

"Yes, dear friend. We shall think of something. We will find a way."

A knock at the door interrupted them. Anna presented herself to tell Ashley *she* was summoned to the earl's map room. Incredulous, Ashley cocked her head in Elena's direction. "What now? I suppose I'm to be married to the baron today before I can plot my escape?"

"Perhaps." Elena's sorrowful eyes told all.

"Are you *serious*?" Ashley jumped to her feet and paced the room. "I was being facetious. They wouldn't make me marry him today, would they?" A shudder ripped through her at the thought.

"Nothing prevents them from having the ceremony today if they choose."

"Then I'll act like I'm sick. Maybe I can throw up on Bedford and he'll be so disgusted he'll call it off." Alarmed by the whole business, Ashley was becoming more distraught by the minute. "Elena, what am I gonna do?"

Sliding off the bed, Elena grasped Ashley by the shoulders and held her still. "Right now, Ashley, you must go hear my father's words. Once we know what he hath decided we can plan what to do next. Go before he is angered you have not answered his summons."

Elena was right. Ashley had no choice but to find out what they had in store for her so she nodded her agreement. The wild fear in her heart hardened into determination. She would go with her head held high. No submissive miss was she. Ashley turned without so much as a glance in Elena's direction and marched from the room.

∞∞∞

As before, Ashley purposely did not knock as she threw open the door to the map room and charged in. She expected both earls and the baron to be thrown off balance by her forceful interruption, but to her surprise the room was empty. She was instantly deflated.

Now what?

Had she taken so long they had stomped out in fury? Would she be taken to a dungeon? Placed in the stocks like a thief? Her agitated mind spit out a stream of wretched punishments, each one more extreme than the last.

Trying to calm her racing pulse, Ashley breathed deeply and let her eyes wander about the room, this time taking in the solidly male surroundings. Her heart fluttered in dismay as her eyes landed on the huge metal armor hanging on the wall. These men were warriors. Actual warriors. How was she to fight back against them?

A tall mirror flanked the armor and Ashley caught sight of herself. Her eyes had black shadows streaked under them like a football player at game time. That's what happens when you don't sleep and are stressed out of your mind, she thought. Some warrior she was. What a mismatch.

Her hair still sported her plastic chip clip, a remnant of her attempted escape. Without the big cloak to cover her head it would be noticed. She pulled it out not wanting to have to account for the strange clip to the earls or the baron. She ran her fingers through her hair to straighten out the tangled strands and only partly succeeded. In the process she fumbled the clip and it went skating across the hard floor, landing somewhere behind a decorative screen in the corner.

She pulled out the pouch always attached to her person containing her treasured possessions and prepared to pop the clip back into the bag. Yet when she walked to the screen and searched behind it, the clip was nowhere to be seen. *How odd.* She had watched the thing skid all the way under the screen. Muttering an expletive to herself, she got down on her hands and knees to hunt for the clip.

Unexpectedly, the door slammed open and the earl and the baron entered, joshing and jawing in high spirits. Ashley froze where she was. How would she explain why she was behind the screen on all fours? This was not the way to win a war.

"I believe that was a success, Hertford. Mowbray was beaming, Lady Charissa glowing, and Elric over the moon."

"Aye, I believe we made the right call. There is no better match for Elric, and he is truly besotted with the girl." The earl poured a drink into two cups and handed one to his friend for a toast. Their goblets clinked making Ashley jump at the sound. So, she thought, Elric and Charissa will be wed. Robert would be free. At least something was working out right.

"Your guests may be a bit confused when they come for the wedding and find a different groom." Bedford smirked at the thought. "However, the two families will be joined as before, so all will be well."

"Are you still of a mind to marry Lady Ashley the same day?"

Ashley held her breath, clenching tightly the pouch she

held in her hands. Her fingers recognized the shape of her cell phone in the squished bag and an idea popped into her brain. She soundlessly reached in and pulled out her phone. Pressing the button to turn it on, she prayed she had silenced its sounds the last time she had used it. The phone powered up and to her relief made no noise. In seconds she was looking at the picture of her dad winking at her on the home screen as if he were lending his silent support.

"Aye. Why not? We cannot keep the girl under guard in her room forever, ye know." The two men laughed, their voices booming off the stone walls. Ashley set the camera to video and tapped record, holding the phone up between the slats of the decorative screen. The two men were framed squarely on the face of her phone.

"Alas," the earl sighed, his grin fading. "I am having second thoughts about forcing Lady Ashley to wed, Damien." The earl put his cup down on the table with a thud and dropped heavily into his chair. "I am not the girl's father and I am surely overstepping my bounds by insisting she marry you. Her people might claim her on the morrow. And, I have to admit, I am uneasy about Cedric's response to the marriage. My gut tells me when he returns he will not be pleased at how I have chosen to protect her."

"You think too much of that old wizard, my friend." The baron took a seat opposite the earl to plead his case. "No man is here to give permission, save you. If the girl is married to me, what can Cedric or her people do?"

"True. Yet, her guards tell me my daughter is most unhappy with my decision to force Lady Ashley to wed and furious because I confined them all to chambers. I am in for unhappy times in dealing with her."

"Aye, I am sure Lady Elena will come 'round. Do not worry, Cryspyn, you can be sure I do not intend to beat Lady Ashley into submission." The baron grinned broadly at the earl. "I want the girl, and I think it shall not be long before she bends to me. We will have a happy union."

Grudgingly, Ashley had to acknowledge the sincerity in Bedford's voice, so she was not surprised by the earl's reply. "Aye. 'Tis done then, Damien." He paused for a moment deep in thought and then his brow furrowed as if puzzled. "Did we not send for the lass?"

Ashley stopped the camera and sat very still.

"We did. I shall fetch a servant to find her."

"While you are gone I shall inform Lady Margaret she needs to prepare for two weddings in three days. You will meet me here shortly to deal with Lady Ashley?"

"Indeed!" Damien was already out the door and gone.

The heavy steps of the two men echoed down the corridor before Ashley poked her nose out from behind the screen. She held down the button on her phone to shut it down. As she opened her bag to put it away, her eyes happened to fall upon the chip clip in *front* of the screen. The stupid thing must have bounced off the wall and skidded back out. She snatched it up and shoved it into her bag along with her phone.

What to do now?

She decided she would wait for the men to return and pretend she had just walked into an empty room and was waiting for them. She would play dumb while they informed her of their plans. Then, she would high tail it back to Elena's room to decide how to get out while the gettin' was good.

Three days. She had three days to make herself disappear from the castle. She had proof on her phone the earl knew he had no power over her to force her to marry, but who would care? No one but Cedric knew her real identity. She would be stupid to flash her phone around and show everyone her video. She'd be hung as a witch. He was her best hope to stop this nonsense. Where was he anyway?

Charissa and Elena were chattering and giggling when Ashley opened the door to Elena's room. They abruptly stopped and looked guilty when she stepped into the room.

Noticing Charissa's reluctance to greet her face to face, Ashley tried her best to reassure the girl. "It's okay, Charissa. I don't hate you or Elric for your good fortune. It's what we all want. It just sucks I'm stuck with the baron unless we can figure out how to get me out of here."

Flopping on the bed between her two friends, Ashley encouraged them to continue planning her flight from Hertford Castle. They told her they could still get messages out to Elric through Anna. Perhaps he could devise a diversion that would take the guards away from their door long enough for Ashley to slide out the side door to the bailey. Of course, from there they had no way to see her through the portcullis, and no one had any good ideas about where she would go from there.

A particular worry was that last part. What *would* she do if she did vanish from the castle? She felt the chill of panic take her as she fought to imagine a future on the other side of the castle walls. Her dream of going home to her family was further away than ever.

She contemplated the two friends before her, so generous with their help for her. How could she tell them who she really was? Would they still want to be her friend when they knew her secret, or would they feel betrayed by her silence? What would her mother tell her to do if she were here? If only she could call her up and ask her.

And, where was Cedric? He had said it would take him two weeks, but she believed deep down he wouldn't be able to help her when he came back anyway. A grim smile twisted on her face as she thought Cedric was probably like the wizard in the *Oz* movie--more bluster and noise than actual wizard. Cedric might be able to influence the earl to keep her from marrying the baron. As for getting her back home to the good old U.S. of A., she didn't think it would happen. He knew little more than she did about how she got here.

Bottom line? If she couldn't make it home, then she had to make a life here that involved Robert and her friends. She couldn't be running away to places unknown, now could she?

"Ashley, would you be able to find the hunting lodge again without one of us with you?" Elena asked.

Charissa brightened at the suggestion. "Yes, Ashley, that is the perfect place for you to go until we can contrive something better."

"There is no reason for my father to search there, since we never told him 'tis where you sought shelter yesterday."

"True, Elena. I might be able to find it in the daytime, but not at night. I'd be lost and scared silly."

"Daytime is good." Elena squinted as she plotted the next step. "Now we have to determine what the distraction will be to cover your escape tomorrow morning."

Before either of her friends replied, a fist banged on the door, and a new voice was heard calling Elena's name from the hallway. Her brow puckered in puzzlement at the disturbance, Elena slid off the bed to answer the door.

Ashley peeked around the doorframe and recognized the head cook from the kitchens standing in the hall holding an oversized tray of steaming, delicious smelling food. This was the cook Elena had said was her father's favorite when he was a child. The woman squinted with the authority of one who had stirred a few steaming pots in her time.

Elena frowned. "My goodness, Tilly, you never leave the kitchens. What are you doing here?"

Her face still flushed from the kitchen fires, the woman shushed Elena with a tiny shake of her head so the sentry would not see. Loudly, she teased, "Well, m'lady, are ye goin' to stand there and stare at me, or are ye goin' to let me in?" Her eyes glittered in the torch light of the hallway. "The day is no' gettin' shorter and I 'ave to get back to me post."

Truly, amidst all their plotting the day had moved on, and darkness was closing in. Ashley's stomach flipped over once and complained about its empty status.

Standing beside Elena, Charissa giggled at the girl's obvious fluster at finding the cook at their door and gave her friend a hip bump. "Move over, Elena, and let the woman in!"

Elena warily stepped aside, shutting the door behind the old lady right in the face of the posted soldier who had sniffed and gaped his interest in the food. Charissa and Ashley were licking their lips and admiring the delicacies as they cleared the small table for the over-sized tray.

Elena waited until Tilly put her load down, then grabbed her arm and made the woman face her. "What is going on? You must tell me why you are here."

Ashley was about to tell Elena to give her suspicions a rest and appreciate the great food, but the servant nodded in agreement before she had the chance. "Aye, miss, ye've got the right o' it. Ye always were a quick one, m'lady." She wiped her hands on her apron, shoved a flyaway handful of frizzy hair behind an ear and spit out her concern. "I come to help Lady Ashley out o' the trouble she's in."

Ashley dropped the cover she had lifted from the shepherd's pie, letting it bounce and flip off the table without a flinch. The cook now had her undivided attention.

"Aye!" Tilly smiled at Ashley and picked up the lid, wiping it on her already soiled apron before placing it gently on the edge of the tray. "Anna and the rest o' the servants 'ave been angry 'bout 'ow that Bedford fellow treated Lady Ashley last night." The old gal caught Ashley's eye and winked at her. "They thinks highly o' ye, m'lady. Now, after the man behaved so ugly to 'er, the master insists she *marry* 'im? 'Tain't right."

She paused for a moment and then shook her head, her mouth puckering like she had sucked a bitter lemon. "Everyone been buzzin' 'bout it all day. I got to thinkin' and remembered what me ma showed me when I was but a wee one. There is a way out o' this very room even if 'tis locked and guards are standin' outside the door."

Elena's face was a mixture of suspicion, wariness, and intrigue. "Whatever can you mean, Tilly?"

"This be an old, old castle and me mum was 'ead o' the kitchens 'afore me, ye know. In them days, the folks 'ere might be attacked at any time. They was ruthless years, me lovelies. The last thin' anyone wanted was fer the women and children to be trapped in the keep with no way out o' a castle o'er run by the enemy."

Clearly enjoying her momentary status, the wizened old woman halted briefly for dramatic effect and to confirm she held each girl's full attention. "This 'ere room was built with a 'idden door what opens onto a stairway what then delivers a body into the outer bailey right next to the portcullis."

"You're kidding!" Ashley groaned in disbelief. This was right out of an old movie.

Tilly drew herself up to her full height and gave Ashley a haughty look that made her choke on her laughter. "'Twas not a laughin' matter, m'lady. If the women were captured they were raped, killed, or both. The children were oft killed, too, as no one wanted to be bothered by 'em or risk 'avin' 'em seek revenge when growed up."

Ashley swallowed hard. "I'm sorry, Tilly. I meant no disrespect, I can assure you. I-I didn't know that happened."

"I had not thought of a hidden stairway," Charissa said, easing the tension in the room. "I have heard of them, but never thought I'd see one myself. 'Tis exciting."

Elena was more indignant than amazed. "It must be hidden well! I have slept in this room my entire life."

"'Tis true, m'lady." Tilly's black eyes twinkled at Elena's bewilderment. "If I 'ad longer I would make ye look fer it to see 'ow long it takes ye to find it. As 'tis, I 'ave to get back to work 'afore Lady Margaret knows I be gone."

The girls didn't wait for their visitor to finish speaking before they were busy searching the walls and looking behind the bed and the wardrobe. For a moment, the old cook smiled and shook her head at them, enjoying her superior knowledge. Then she calmly walked over to the large tapestry on the inside wall next to Ashley's room and began to roll it up.

The girls stopped and stared at the wall hanging. At the bottom a fine lady and her child looked longingly up at an angel perched at the top of a winding staircase. "It's behind this tapestry?" Elena cried. "Now I understand. I worried for years there was something seriously wrong with those two if they wished to go to heaven before their time." She sighed. "Why did no one tell me it was designed to hide escape stairs?"

Carefully rolling up the tapestry to just above her head, Tilly motioned to Ashley and Charissa to hold up the roll so there was room to work under it. She then began to feel each stone in the wall from below one side of the tapestry to the other. To their delight, moments later she pushed and a rock moved in with a groan.

"*Ah,* there 'tis." Tilly's crinkled face betrayed her satisfaction. "Ye see, this one pushes in givin' ye a grasp of the stone underneath. It pulls out like this." She demonstrated, revealing the handle of a lever behind the stonework. The girls gasped as one at this discovery. Ashley blinked twice to be sure of what she was seeing.

The cook used all her considerable weight to push down and the handle budged slowly, grumbling its reluctance to move after so many years frozen in place. As it gave way, the outline of a jagged door began to appear before them.

Elena was so shocked she sputtered, standing rooted before the opened door. Tilly laughed and patted Elena's cheeks. "'Tis good we found it, m'lady." She turned to Ashley who was peering through the opening to the dark passage behind it. "Be careful goin' down there, m'lady. Those steps 'ave not been used for many a year and there is no tellin' what lurks down there."

Her caution having been delivered with all the authority she could muster, the old cook declared her job finished. She told the girls to enjoy their dinner and slipped out before they could question her further.

Flummoxed, Elena marveled over this revelation. *Amazing.* Still holding the rolled tapestry above their heads, Charissa and Ashley were so excited they couldn't quit chirping about the discovery. Finally, Elena thought to push a tall dresser from across the room to a spot next to her friends so they could place the roll atop it.

Charissa moved to a branch of candles and began to light them to use in exploring the dark stairs. Ashley's stomach made them all freeze when it released a disgraceful, unladylike gurgle. Charissa burst out laughing. "Well, if the stairs have been here for a century or more, they are not going anywhere anytime soon. I think we can savor Tilly's excellent dinner while 'tis hot and then explore."

"Excellent plan!" Ashley felt her face flame, but she had to laugh along with her friends. The smell of the shepherd's pie and something with cinnamon in it wafted through the room, making them all forget any notion of starting down the stairs for now.

Ever the taskmaster, Elena insisted they at least drop the floor length tapestry and place it behind the dresser and in front of the hidden door. They could roll it up again when they were ready to explore, but it would be out of sight should anyone pop in unexpectedly. Once tucked away, the girls fell upon Tilly's gift with great relish.

No need for a diversion now, thought Ashley. She dipped a finger into the warm cinnamon-rum sauce smothering the bread pudding and sampled it with a satisfied smack.

Perhaps she really could escape successfully.

Chapter 22

The Earl of Hertford sat alone in his map room thinking about the events of the day and feeling tired to his bones. It would seem all had worked out well. His friends were still his friends, Elric would have the wife he desired, and Lady Ashley would no longer be his problem. All the day's needs were met. And yet, something deep inside him warned all was not right. But what? He truly did not know, but found his feet headed into the women's wing of the donjon before he had time to reconsider.

Noting the guards outside his daughter's door, he wondered if he had gone too far in confining the girls to their chambers. Yet, as he got closer, unmistakable giggling and high spirits sounded from within. He smiled to himself and his chest unclenched. Elena was enjoying her friends. He knocked on the door in the next instant, needing to see with his own eyes all was well with his child.

A moment before the door opened movement in the room ceased.

"Our tray is ready to go back to the kitch--*Oh!*"

He was the last person they expected to appear at their door. Lady Charissa stood before him as frozen as a statue, holding the remains of their evening meal on a serving tray. His carefully affixed smile wilted a mite, but not waiting for an invitation, he strode past the girl into his daughter's chamber. Suddenly, the room was airless and too warm.

Elena was the first to gather her wits and run to him, giving him a hug and a kiss on his cheek. Yet, somehow she was stiff and awkward in his arms. That frightened him because it had never happened before. Did part of her hate him for his actions with the two young ladies? Granted, he did not visit Elena in her quarters often, but she and her friends were acting oddly. Was he mistaken or had he spied Lady Charissa and Lady Ashley sneaking looks about the room like they were guilty of something? Was that only his imagination run amok?

God's blood.

Facing these three girls was like being a gawky twelve again. Struggle as he did, nothing entered his mind to say past the usual hello. All three young women stood grinning before him, and somehow every aging bone in his body knew they were hiding something from him. For the life of him, he knew not what it could be.

This day had dawned to a daunting mess yet had resolved itself satisfactorily all around. Might they be happy about that? Yes, that must be it, he thought, as he said goodnight and made his way back to his own chamber.

Deep down he knew he was wrong.

$\infty\infty\infty$

"Wait, what was that sound?"

"What sound? I heard nothing." Charissa's breathing was louder than her whisper.

"Hold the light higher, Ashley." Elena peeked over their shoulders into the depths below.

Holding a branch of candles, Ashley bravely leaned out over the stairwell that loomed like an abyss below them. The stairs had not been used in many, many years, but Ashley had not given thought to what that would mean until now.

"Listen!"

Silence prevailed for a long moment to prevent their voices from echoing down the stone walls around them. New noises were heard. Rustling and scratching sounds bounced off the walls from below and up steps structured more like a ladder than a stairway due to their steep drop.

"I think it sounds like rats."

"*Ugh!* Just what I need to make my escape memorable, Elena--rats in a dark stairwell."

"'Twill help you make it through the passage quickly. I should not want to be down there any longer than necessary. It smells."

"And thank you for your support, too, Charissa." Ashley pinched her nose and rolled her eyes at her snickering friend. "You are welcome to go with me to the door on the other side, you know."

"Ooh, I had not thought of that, Ashley. Of course Charissa and I shall accompany you. I want to know exactly where it exits anyway."

"Must we?" The grin froze on Charissa's face at this bold idea.

"If we are extra loud and shine the light before us, won't the rats find a place to hide until we pass? I don't know too much about them, but aren't they more afraid of us than we are of them?"

"Thou must not have seen the rats in the stable, dear Ashley. Those vermin are this big." Elena's hands split to show a foot wide. Ashley moaned.

"And they can gnaw through your slipper in a heartbeat." Charissa snapped her fingers for effect.

Much to Ashley's horror, Elena and Charissa appeared deadly serious. A moment later they erupted in a peal of laughter when they simply could not contain themselves any longer. Ashley smacked each of them a good swat on the backside for their tease.

"Just for that, there is no way I am going down these stairs and to the exit on my own. You *will* be coming with me." Ashley paused to inspect the thick cobwebs over the filthy stairway. She noted it was now as quiet as a graveyard beneath them. All the scratching had stopped. "What say we wait to do this until morning when the critters are more likely to be asleep? I'll be ready to make a run for it, especially with you two making lots of noise right behind me."

"Wonderful idea, Ashley." Charissa was already inching back up the steps to Elena's room.

"No need to stress yourself tonight since you are not going anywhere until morning." Elena wasted no time in following Charissa.

"You two are absolute chickens, aren't you?" Elena and Charissa snorted their agreement, nodding effusively as they stepped back into the chamber.

"I'm really gonna miss you two."

Elena and Charissa's smiles fell as the reality of their parting with Ashley in the morning hit them. Their eyes grew large and their cheeks puckered as it occurred to them she was, in fact, leaving.

"Oh, don't look so sad. You know I couldn't bear to stay away forever. I have to disappear until Bedford is gone and Cedric is back." She needed to change the subject before she got too choked up. "Besides, y-you have to tell me how to get to the hunting lodge. I'm not sure I remember the way."

It hurt to think of *never* seeing her friends again, yet that might be the case. If Cedric helped her go home to Texas, how would she get back? Could she really leave Robert and her friends behind if she was not certain she could return? Right now the answer to that question was a big, fat *no*.

∞∞∞∞

The first rays of morning light sneaked across Ashley's face and woke her. Had she slept? Wriggling her weary bones only confirmed her doubts. Sitting up, she fondly studied the sleeping faces of Charissa and Elena. How had she ever found such perfect friends? They were honorable, loving, guileless females whose beauty ran bone deep. She could never replace them.

With a jolt of adrenaline straight to the heart, Ashley remembered what lay ahead of her for the day. Would she be able to find her way to the lodge by herself and then wait for help to arrive to take her someplace safe? Anxiety clenched her chest until she struggled to breathe. What other choice did she have? If she stayed in the warmth and security of the castle, she would soon find herself married to the baron and on her way to a new home.

That thought made her decide to shake her friends and wake them, keeping as quiet as possible. With an urgency they all felt, they dressed Ashley in her own clothes and then covered her from head to toe with Elena's oldest, dreariest cloak. She would blend in enough with everyone else to pass through the portcullis.

Needing an early start since she would have to walk to the hunting lodge, Ashley hugged her friends one last time. Tears blurred her vision as she scurried down the steps of the escape stairs. Elena held the torch high over Ashley's shoulder, with Charissa right behind stomping on each tread to scare away any remaining four-legged fiends. The door to the outer bailey opened just as Tilly predicted in a small alcove next to the portcullis. Ashley reluctantly shooed Elena and Charissa back through the door. Then she closed it firmly, took a deep breath, and prepared to step out into the open.

"Alice, if ye canno' get out of me way, how am I ta see where ahm goin'?"

"Aw, shut yer trap, Meggie! Yer always tryin' ta make things difficult."

She was saved.

Those familiar bickering voices were music to her ears. Meggie and Alice could be trusted to take her to the hunting lodge and help her. Ashley's heart beat a fearsome tattoo as she waited until they were next to her before casually stepping out to stand before them. To their credit, neither woman gave her away to the soldiers because their mouths dropped open to somewhere around their knees. Ashley motioned for them to step into the alcove, and then explained in a rush her need to escape the castle and go to the Hertford hunting lodge.

The sisters told Ashley they had heard all the latest gossip the castle servants had to share having arrived the night before. That meant the baron's decision to marry Ashley was old news. What they did not understand was her desire to flee the castle. Why would she not wish to stay and wed a handsome lord?

Did she not understand that she was a lady and not a peasant? As a lady she did not need to run away. They told Ashley all about their night at the castle while punching each other at intervals and treading all over each other's telling of the tale. Ashley pieced together that having slept inside the great hall, as was the custom for young women traveling without protectors, they were fair game for any lecherous lord. The two had watched in fear as the earl and his guests drank themselves into a happy stupor at dinner.

What happened next was the scary part. The Earl of Mowbray had caught Meggie's eye, grinned lewdly, and crooked a come-hither finger at her. Meggie had hidden behind her sister and then faded into a dark corner to stay out of sight until the lords left the hall. Sadly, the story they told was all too true for peasant women. If a lord wanted to use their bodies for a night, they had no choice but to let them.

Different rules applied for ladies, however, so Ashley realized she had some explaining to do to make them understand. To their minds, Bedford was a gloriously handsome man who was rich and the master of a lovely manor nearby. He was not young, but he was not so old, either. They did not understand why Lady Ashley would refuse to be a baroness.

Looking into their puzzled faces, Ashley told them she would explain everything once they passed through to safety on the other side of the portcullis. Too curious to say no, the sisters shared a speaking glance. Meggie tapped her toe impatiently, while Alice shot an assessing look at Ashley. Finally, they nodded in rare unison and motioned for Ashley to pile in between the sacks of flour they carried in their cart. Once settled, they used Ashley's cloak to cover both her and the cart. They tucked in the sides to make it look like a blanket holding goods in place.

To Ashley's surprise, the two displayed some acting talent. Meggie and Alice started an argument about which sister held the eye of a stable lad named Jamie. They started through the watch at the portcullis, gaining only a knowing smile and a hoot or two from the men stationed there.

Checking to see if they were out of danger, Ashley peeped through a small hole in the cloak. For a terrifying moment she spied a guard eyeing her covered cart with narrowed eyes. Meggie must have noticed it, too, because she let out a shriek at her sister that made the man's head swivel to her. Once all eyes were focused on her, she sprouted a sloe-eyed smile. That sparked the guards to shout a few more lewd remarks in her direction and shake their heads at her. Meggie sashayed on through the portcullis beside her sister and the cart as if she had nothing to hide.

Ashley was cramped and ready to erupt by the time Meggie and Alice deemed themselves far enough away to let Ashley out of her misery. Once uncovered, she rolled out of the cart and fell hard onto the ground. Her numb legs refused to hold her up. The sisters each grabbed an arm and stood her on her feet--just like old times. She required support until her legs regained enough feeling to allow her to walk on her own. Ashley hugged both girls and warmly thanked them for coming to her aid.

"'Tis nothin', m'lady. Glad to be of service we are, but ... " Meggie shrugged her shoulders at her sister, who finished the thought. "We do no' understand why ye are leavin'."

"It's simple. I don't want the baron for a husband. I want Lord Robert. He wants to marry me."

Ashley didn't think she would ever see the sisters speechless. But there they were, mouths open and tongues hanging out. Well, maybe not out, but she did enjoy their shock. Robert was like a god to them. Their eyes swept her up and down in that way females have of assessing each other's assets.

Their faces betrayed their thoughts. Clearly, they were impressed that in the short time Ashley had lived in the castle, she had managed to capture the hearts of two such desirable men. They eyed *this* Lady Ashley with new respect. She struggled to hide her smile. If her friends back home could see her now.

∞∞∞

Finally, the roof of the hunting lodge poked through the tree line. It had taken hours to trudge the distance from the castle to the lodge, and Ashley's feet hurt. She shed her cloak as the sun warmed the day, shocking Meggie and Alice once again that she would walk about wearing so few clothes.

Meggie whispered loud enough to Alice for Ashley to overhear. "The lady hath no sense of propri'ty, doth she?"

Alice answered in an equally loud voice, "Mayhap 'tis why the menfolk like 'er." Ashley caught the meaningful nod of agreement between the two usually squabbling sisters and turned away to squelch her giggle.

"Lady Ashley, when we get to the lodge, we shall leave ye there and hie 'ome. On the morrow we will bring ye some proper clothes that will cover all of ye and no' give ye away as a lady." Alice offered up her most charitable smile as she elbowed her sister. Meggie punched her back without hesitation. "We shall bring food with us as well, m'lady, so no need to worry yerself 'bout starvin'."

"I can't thank the two of you enough. Without your coming along when you did, I don't think I would've escaped so easily." The sisters preened over this and held their heads higher. "You're very kind to help me. Lord Robert will thank you, too, I'm sure. Meanwhile, I have some bread and cheese with me so I'll be fine until then."

Considering all the gossip the sisters had shared along the way, Ashley decided to ask one more question. "Listen, before you go, can you tell me where Cedric might have gone? He mentioned visiting a friend who might help us locate my countrymen."

"Cedric, ye say?" Meggie thought a moment. "Aye, he would likely be talkin' 'bout Olde Gylda of Hampshire. She lives in the hills a ways from 'ere. We kin ask round 'ome fer ye to see if anyone knows fer sure."

Alice chimed in before Meggie had quite finished. "We kin tell ye on the morrow."

"That would be great! Thanks a bu-."

Before Ashley could finish her sentence, Meggie and Alice had already darted through the door to the lodge, excited to see what it held within. Ashley shook her head at the temerity of the two as she followed them inside.

For the first time Ashley thought things might work out for her. Apparently, the friendship between Cedric and Olde Gylda was no secret. Why, she mused, had Cedric wanted her to keep his destination quiet? Did the earl dislike the old woman that much?

Meggie and Alice busily examined every inch of the lodge. Ashley plopped down on one of the barrel stools to wait for them to finish, her thoughts turning to the castle. When had her disappearance been discovered, she wondered? By now the jig must be up. Elena and Charissa planned to pretend she was ill and confined to her room, but that ruse would not hold up for long under the earl's scrutiny. She shuddered. What would she do if the baron came after her?

Pronouncing the lodge rather ordinary, Meggie and Alice ran a nonstop commentary on every detail, but they did help her start a fire. They saw no problem with that since no one would be close by to see the smoke and give her away. After all, the place was deep in the forest with no one around it for miles. Ashley's concern was for nothing. Or, so they said.

The sisters cheerily waved goodbye and set off for their home, hoping to reach it by sundown so as not to worry their father. Ashley sent her regards to the old man, and that pleased them. Ashley was confident they would keep her secrets and come back with the proper goods to help her. Lord Robert would be grateful to them for helping his lady and that was as good as insurance for their assistance.

Looking around the dingy main room of the lodge, Ashley remembered the last time she had been here. Robert had claimed her as his, and she had claimed him right back. Much had happened in the meantime. Now Charissa and Elric would wed, but she was stuck with an amorous baron she did not want, and a confused Robert. She vowed to find him in person to clear up the misunderstanding keeping them apart. Thinking of that mess, her heart thudded in misery and her stomach clamped into a knot from the sheer anxiety of it all.

Ashley removed the knapsack attached to her waist along with the leather pouch carrying her valuables and dropped them on the floor. She hunted through the larger bag and pulled out a hunk of bread. Nibbling on it made her stomach settle. Breathing easier, she spread her cloak on the floor in a warm sunspot and curled up, intending to nap. With nothing left to do, sleeping would pass the time as well as anything else. Her mind, however, would not quiet, racing from one thing to the next.

Thoughts of her mother and brother flowed through her. Would she ever see them again? How long had she been gone? It seemed like only a few days here, but maybe it was much longer on the other end. What if they had already given up on her and no one was still looking for her?

Then there was her life here to think about. Yes, she actually had a life here. In fact, she had friends who loved her and a beautiful man who wanted to marry her. The mere thought of

Robert sent deep shivers to her toes. She wouldn't think about the baron since he provoked shivers of a different kind.

She had much to be thankful for, yet here she was, alone and lonely, in a lodge deep in the woods. Would she ever find her rightful place in the world? And in which world might that be? Having started the day early and with little sleep the night before, she succumbed to a fitful slumber despite her over-worked mind.

"Ashley, what are you doing here?"

From a distance she spotted her father as he looked down on her sleeping form and nudged her awake. He was standing above her prone body when joy zapped through her, waking her instantly. She was back in her body now as he scooped her up in his arms.

He smelled of wood chips and sweat, the same as he had so many times in her life when he had come in from working in the yard. The scruff of his beard was prickly and it rubbed her cheek as she hugged him hard. Putting her down solidly on her feet, her dad stepped back and surveyed her. "You look like you could use a little sleep, Ashley. Maybe I should leave you to rest."

"No!" she shrieked. "No, you can't go away. I've just found you!"

Her dad threw back his head and laughed at her. "I'm not lost, Ashley. I have just not been able to get back to you until now. It's complicated to explain ... just don't worry." As he spoke the words, his form became hazy and his image dissolved. Joy and desolation swamped her at the same time. She had seen her father. He didn't look sick or unhappy at all. He was glowing with good health and he had laughed his rumbly laugh. She had to tell her mother Dad was okay. They didn't need to be sad anymore. He was happy and must be in a good place.

Ashley awoke with a start, gulping air as if she had been drowning. The hair on the back of her neck prickled announcing she was not alone.

∞∞∞

Robert approached his family's hunting lodge with real trepidation. Would he be too late and find Ashley no longer there? What if she had not found the place at all? Fear gripped his insides as he thought of all that might have transpired since he last saw his beloved. Thanks to Elric, who had found him asleep in the armory, he now knew of Ashley's plans for escape and the whole story regarding Bedford's unwanted attention. A chill ran down his spine as he recalled the moment it hit him Ashley did, indeed, love him. He had not been wrong. She had no feelings for the baron at all. Perhaps it would work out for him and Ashley as it had for Elric and Charissa. *It has to. I love her.*

Sliding off his destrier, he tethered his stallion to an oak well out of sight inside the tree line. He crept up to the nearest window and peered through its oily surface. His heart skipped a beat before speeding up in excitement. There she was in her golden beauty, curled up on her cloak like a cat in a sunspot, waiting for him. Robert smiled and something deep inside him clicked into place like a key in a lock.

He slipped inside and closed the door. Not wanting to wake her quite yet, he padded softly across the room and knelt beside her. In her sleep she twitched and smiled adorably. Did she dream of him?

Without warning, her eyes flew open and she launched herself into his arms, holding him as if he might disappear at any moment. Thrilled, he rocked her back and forth, with fingers tenderly shaping her body.

Robert pulled back and gazed intently into her eyes. Finding the answer he sought, his mouth possessed hers. It was some time before they separated enough to gaze into each other's eyes once more. Still, they did not speak. Choked with raw emotion, Robert bent down and covered her face with his. Butterfly kisses touched her eyes, her nose, and her forehead. He leaned back long enough to smile at her.

∞∞∞

When next he claimed her mouth, whole new feelings sprouted having nothing to do with butterflies. Lying back, Robert pulled Ashley down on top of him. All thought vanished as she stretched out and plastered herself against him. She could not get close enough. Robert understood and rolled her under him as he answered her passion with passion of his own. His every move told her she was his.

Ashley had never felt such belonging in her life. Robert possessed her and she him. It was a feeling that made her shudder with pleasure as she kissed him and pressed him to her heart. Her legs wrapped around him in an effort to pull him even closer as she felt all of him against her. She would be his forever.

Wait!

Forever?

Would she be here the rest of her life? Would she *never* go home to her family? Somewhere in the recesses of her brain, her mind demanded she halt this lovely, insane joining before it went too far. She had to be honest with Robert. He didn't know her secret, and she had to come clean.

Robert was showing her with his very being how much he loved her, touching, holding, stroking her. When she stiffened and lay still beneath him, he drew back with the certain knowledge something was wrong.

Gazing into his worried, hazel eyes, she wondered if it were possible to ever adequately explain to him what troubled her. It had been heaven to find each other, and they both knew it. She met and held his gaze, filling it with all the love in her heart. At last, those eyes softened, and she saw him visibly begin to relax. Still, questions lurked there demanding an answer. How to begin?

"I love you, Robert."

She meant what she said, but Robert heard in the tone of her voice there was more she had not spoken. Rather than replying, he cocked his head in question and smiled his crooked smile as he pulled her to a sitting position. Squeezing her hands against his chest, he held them as if he feared she might jump up and run away.

"I have not been honest with you," Ashley blurted. The suddenness of the declaration caused Robert to draw back and drop her hands as if he had been burned. All his former insecurity over the baron snapped back into his eyes.

"No, there is no one else, Robert. That's not what I mean."

"Good, because I love you, Ashley."

He let out a pent-up sigh of relief and gratefully clasped her hands in his own once again. With his heated gaze never leaving her face, he proceeded to kiss each finger, making Ashley all but melt into a puddle. Couldn't she just forget this honorable stuff and pick up where they'd left off? She sucked in a ragged breath and tried to focus.

"You don't know who I really am or where I come from, and it's time you did." Her voice was so tight in her throat her vocal cords ached.

Robert read her distress and took her face between his big hands, rubbing her cheeks gently with his mace-calloused thumbs. "Let me make myself clear, Ashley. I care not who you were or where you came from. You are here now, and that is all that matters to me." He moved to take her mouth with his, but she placed a hand over his lips to stop him. She would never get another word out if she gave in to him now.

"It isn't that easy, Robert." Ashley shook her head slowly, but never broke contact with his beautiful eyes. "The only one I have shared my secret with is Cedric, who has gone on a mission to help me get back home. That's why he left soon after I arrived. He told me to tell no one my story for fear I might come to harm, and I have honored his request. I have felt like a liar and a cheat at times, since I have grown to love you and Elena, and Elric and Charissa like my own family. I understood his reasoning and so will you when you hear what I have to say."

Chapter 23

Robert looked longingly at her mouth as she spoke. If she didn't get his full attention now he would never truly hear her confession.

Rising unsteadily from the floor, she held out her hand to him. "Come," Ashley said, smiling down at him. "Let's sit at the table here so I can show you what I am talking about."

She pulled a reluctant Robert to his feet and sat him on a wine barrel at the trestle table in the center of the room. His eyes still roved hungrily over her body.

Ashley moved around the table to pick up the leather pouch from the floor where it sat beside her cloak and took her seat across from him. Of course he would rather be making love than listening to any story she told. She sighed heavily. Perhaps she should forget all this and just love him.

Sucking in a noisy breath she dropped the pouch without ceremony on the tabletop. No one, including Robert, had ever asked her why she wore the pouch. The bag had been on her person every day for safekeeping because the items inside were too precious to lose.

Perhaps they thought the pouch held only feminine fripperies, or perhaps they were too polite to ask her outright. Even Elena had never broached the subject. Now the ashen look on Robert's face told her he knew this small bag contained something important.

"Robert, do you remember the flashlight and match I showed you and Charissa and Elric when we were here last?"

Hesitantly, Robert nodded.

"Well, that is only part of what is here in my bag."

"Are you trying to tell me you are a witch?" His voice was soft and non-accusatory.

Ashley smiled. "That's it exactly!"

Robert flinched.

"Wait! Let me rephrase that. Cedric was afraid if I told anyone else, I would be proclaimed a witch and perhaps hung or burned at the stake or something equally grim."

"So you are not a witch?" Robert cocked his head to the side, tensely waiting for her to answer.

"No, I am not a witch. I told all of you then, I am simply from another country."

"So why would that get you killed?"

"Because I didn't tell you everything." Ashley took a deep breath, reached across the table and put her hands out in a silent plea for Robert to take them. He obliged, holding them with a tight grip and waited. His head turned slowly back and forth as if bracing himself to hear some awful thing

"Robert, I come from a time period and a country in the future."

A guffaw burst from Robert, but seeing Ashley's serious face, he stopped, shook his head and smiled warily.

"You think I'm joking or crazy, but I'm neither. The United States of America is a country across the Atlantic Ocean that doesn't exist in this year of 1363. Explorers won't land there until 1492."

Robert dropped her hands, drew back, and folded his arms against his chest. "You believe this?" His frown deepened into a scowl. "You want me to believe you come from a time over a hundred years from now?"

"Actually, more like 650 years from now. My country is a powerful and successful nation."

∞∞∞

Robert's jaw dropped open in disbelief at what he heard.

"I know, Robert, I know," she crooned. "This sounds completely bizarre, but I can prove all this to you with some of my possessions." Robert opened his mouth twice to speak and found nothing to say. Finally he shrugged and motioned her to continue.

Ashley reached into her bag and pulled out the flashlight and the book of matches. "You remember these, right?"

Robert picked up the matchbook and stared blankly at the picture on the cover. A flame had sprung from the little stick when rubbed. He put that item down as if it might combust on its own and grabbed the flashlight. This was the real fascination.

"Look closer at the flashlight. Now in the light of day, tell me what it's made of."

Robert examined the flashlight he and Elric had played with. He had not even considered that. A bright yellow, the material was something he did not recognize. He remembered marveling at the little bulb that lit up and the batteries that powered the light when Ashley turned it on for them. Yet he had never thought about the possibility of any of these things coming from a time in the future.

"I see," Robert said in a low voice. "I do not know of what it is made."

"We call the substance plastic, Robert. It's quite common in my time period, having been invented somewhere in the 1900s. At least I think so. I should have paid more attention in Mr. Gillette's history class in high school."

Reaching back into her bag she pulled out a bottle and a smaller, clam-shaped object she said was for her hair. She placed them on the table next to the flashlight and the matchbook.

"These things are also made of plastic. Just different kinds."

As the afternoon wore on and Ashley explained her treasures, Robert's eyes were glued to her face as she answered his questions. He did his best to respond as he thought she wanted him to. In truth he was not happy about the world Ashley inhabited before coming to Hertford because it was too different from his own. Why would she want to stay with him when her dazzling world awaited her return?

Dutifully handling the objects she presented, he listened intently to her explanations of each. His fingers glided over her picture on the passport with care, and he stared incredulously at the date beside it. He worked to keep the glower off his face as he became more and more sure she would not wish to stay with him at Hertford.

He did break into a smile when she shared the remains of her chocolate bar with him. Chocolate was a new experience, and it tasted delicious.

Robert was in awe of Ashley. Her description of coming from the future made sense to him. In his mind she was one of a kind since he had never met anyone remotely like her, but then, his world was not a large one.

His eyes scanned over her odd dress. Elric had described what she was wearing when she arrived and it appeared to be what she was wearing now. No respectable lady of his time would ever wear what she had on, yet she was not of low birth. Or was she?

He thought of his wish upon the falling star that seemed so long ago and guessed he had been granted his wish. How was he to know the girl of his dreams would be from the future? It was difficult to comprehend.

Last, Ashley placed what she called her smartphone on the table. "This is the last and most important item I have to show you, Robert. I confess I have shown only portions of this to Cedric. There is a battery inside I will not be able to recharge once it dies, so I must even now use it sparingly. Before I show it to you, let me explain what my life was like before I wound up here and found you."

Robert interrupted, "I am sorry, Ashley, but I must first take care of my destrier. Lucifer hath been tied to a tree for too long and needs to be groomed and fed before dark. I will return shortly."

Robert escaped the lodge, sucking in the fresh, forest air with the need of a drowning man pulled from the water.

∞∞∞

Through the hazy window, Ashley saw Robert run his hands through his hair with unmistakable desperation. Poor guy. He feared what she would tell him next. How hard it was for him to assimilate a future world that was beyond imagination in his. If she could spare him the details she would, but the truth of her situation was inescapable.

Robert strode with purpose toward his stallion and she wondered if he would return. She wouldn't blame him if he left her. Was a future even possible for them? While he seemed to be taking in what she told him with intelligence and sympathy, she knew he was guarding his real feelings. A talkative Robert had become a concerned Robert.

Lucifer? That was the black stallion's name? Somehow it fit. Was this all a trick of the devil? Give her a man she would want for a lifetime, but do so in a time period she should not be in. She laughed at herself. What the devil was she to do?

Ashley got up from the table, put everything back in her pouch except for the phone and dug in her other bag for food. Finding what was left of the bread and cheese she decided to make a picnic in front of the fire. Maybe it would rekindle memories of their last fireside visit.

She shivered remembering how she felt when Robert kissed her. Why had she ever brought this up? *Hmph.* Oh yeah, he would find out sometime, wouldn't he? It might as well be now when he was all hers and there would be no interruptions.

She thought of Elena and Charissa. What would they think

when they heard her story? Would Elric believe her? She massaged her temples in hopes of warding off a headache.

Ashley rekindled the fire that had died while she slept, precisely as Elena had taught her. It was a skill she never imagined she would need only a short time ago. She sat back on her heels and surveyed the meager food spread out on her cloak. It would have to do.

Now where was Robert? When she opened the door she found him standing on the other side, staring up into the darkening sky. Her man certainly did need some space, didn't he? Feeling her presence, Robert turned and smiled at her. That was a good sign.

"Hey," Ashley called. "There is bread and cheese if you're hungry."

"I am. I brought some food with me, too. 'Tis only saddle rations, but 'twill fill the belly." Robert held up a saddlebag and stepped to her, grabbing her around the waist with his free arm as he swept inside.

"*Ah,* you built a fire, I see. Not bad for a creature from the future. Or did you cheat and use one of your fire sticks?" He tickled Ashley's ribs and a giggle of pure relief exploded from her lips. At least he found some humor in all of this.

That giggle provided Robert his opening, and he threw down his saddlebag in order to tickle Ashley with both hands. Moments later they were lying in each other's arms before the fire, giddy and grinning at each other.

Robert had succeeded in kissing her nearly senseless, and Ashley was so happy she thought she might pop. Maybe, somehow, they would make all this work.

As they supped on dried venison, berries and nuts, in addition to Ashley's bread and cheese, Ashley explained her world. She told Robert all about her home in Texas, about her dad disappearing, her mother's sadness, her little brother's worries, as well as her Uncle Zeek's graduation gift.

She described her high school, her friends, her car, her cat named Toby, television and movies, music and anything else that popped into her head. Robert asked an occasional question. His expression told her she might as well have been a bard telling a tall tale. It all sounded wondrous to him.

As Ashley wound down, Robert asked to see the thing she called a phone. She grinned. "You're gonna like this, Robert. Phones are so awesome. We live and die by them in my world 'cuz they do everything. Mostly we talk to each other voice-to-voice or face-to-face, but we can write instantly to each other, too. We send mail, take pictures and send them to each other, watch those movies I told you about, and on and on." She giggled. "I sound like some kind of advertisement, don't I?"

Robert raised an eyebrow. *"Oops!* Sorry. An advertisement or ad is a message of some kind aimed at getting you to buy a product. I mean I sound like I'm trying to sell you something and I don't mean to."

Robert nodded and got up to retrieve the phone from where it still lay on the table. He sat down and pulled Ashley onto his lap, so he would be looking over her shoulder while she showed him the phone. Ashley pressed the button and waited for the thing to come to life. She described to Robert how only part of the phone's capability worked in his world.

First, she took a picture of Robert and then one of the two of them together. She held her arm out as far as possible to get the best shot, calling it a selfie. Robert was impressed with picture taking and took two of her before she could stop him.

Next, she went to her photos and scrolled through them, showing Robert all the people and places in her life. She hated not taking more time with each, but she was always aware of the battery going down. When she got to the video of Bedford and his father, she paused.

"We haven't talked about the baron and your dad. Have you thought about how we're going to explain our relationship to them?"

"Aye, I have thought of little else. I do not have the power to make them do as I wish, nor do you, Ashley. They can decide who and when you marry since you are but a female."

"Robert, do you think I am 'but a female' to be treated like that?" Ashley held her breath while she waited for his answer.

The corners of Robert's mouth tipped up into a grin at the absurdity of her question. "No, Ashley, to treat you that way would be to steal from you your very soul. I cannot imagine you in a subservient role."

"Thank you, Robert. I hoped you would say that." She took a deep breath and thought for a moment, forming her next question. "Would you believe both your father and the baron know they don't have power over me?"

Robert's brow cocked dubiously at her.

"Yup! In this video they both admit they are doing whatever they want to do. They wonder if they will be challenged by my people if they show up to claim me." Noting the look of incredulity still on his face, Ashley smiled. "Let me show you."

She played the video twice. The first time Robert only marveled at the fact he was looking at his father and the baron on the face of the little phone. Ashley told him how that had happened before she replayed the tape. It was clear his father and the baron were making up the rules as they went along.

Robert agreed they must challenge the earl and his agreement to wed Ashley to Bedford. What did Robert want to have happen then? That was the question she wanted answered.

∞∞∞

Lovingly, Robert beheld the animated face of the woman in front of him as she told him her tale. The question he did not want to ask bubbled up to the surface in spite of his efforts to banish it.

Why would this strong, intelligent, beautiful woman, who belonged to another time with all the wonderful things he had seen with his own eyes, want to stay with him? What did he have to offer her but his undying love? He believed she loved him, but would their love be enough to compensate?

His mind would not allow him to picture life without Ashley. Yet like a wild bird, if he caged her by keeping her at Hertford, he would only make her wish to return to the freedom of her former life.

Before Ashley could pursue her line of reasoning any further, Robert twirled her around on his lap, so she was facing him. He picked up her hands in his and looked deep into her eyes. "My dearest Ashley, I love you. I love you with all my heart and always will. But now, you must answer the real question. Will you continue to search for a way back to your world or will you stay with me and be my wife in this one."

Chapter 24

Ashley's eyes nearly crossed with the power of his question.

He loves me? His wife? He wants me for his wife!

Her heart stuttered and she choked on her next breath. How was she to honestly answer Robert? She wanted him in her life more than anyone else, yet she felt a strong pull to her own world she couldn't deny. Should she give up everything in her world to stay with him?

She thought about the wild ride her adventure in his world had been thus far. It had been exciting and filled with emotional highs and lows the likes of which she had never experienced before. Robert was a once in a lifetime love. There would never be a Robert in her world, but could she happily leave her family and her world forever without looking back? Could a time-crossed love survive?

And what about that time continuum stuff always in time travel movies and books? If she had children with Robert, would she upset that balance and screw up the future for generations to come? All this confused her. Tears rolled down her cheeks.

Robert pulled her close. Her face nudged into his shoulder while he stroked her hair and her back. Finally, Ashley pulled far enough away within the circle of his arms to look him squarely in the eye. "I love you, Robert. With all that I am, but I don't know what to do."

Gently, Robert smoothed the hair wet with tears away from her face, "I know, sweeting. We must find Cedric and ask his advice. If there is no way to return you to your world, there will not be a question, will there?"

Ashley nodded, wiping her nose on the back of her hand. "If he hath found a way, then we shall decide what is to be done," Robert said. Emotionally exhausted, Ashley only bobbed her head in reply.

They stretched out in front of the fire where Robert held her snuggled against his chest. Thoughts danced in her head as randomly as the licks of flame in the hearth. Perhaps they would find a way to make it all work. Her eyes fluttered shut on that hopeful note and sleep soon eased her tired brain.

∞∞∞

As planned, Robert was awake and ready to go at first light. Ashley had told him about her escape from the castle with Meggie and Alice, the daughters of Edmund the Olde. He had never spoken to either of them, but he knew who they were. The sisters were supposed to come back at dawn to bring Ashley suitable clothing and food. To avoid gossip over finding them together, Robert was to go hunting and stay away until the sisters had made their appearance and gone home.

When Ashley playfully whined over being left alone even for a short time, he wickedly gave her a kiss goodbye she would never forget. Drugged by those kisses and unable to move, Ashley lay sprawled on her cloak. Before he left Robert whispered in her ear, "Sweet dreams."

Some time later, Ashley rolled over and pushed to her feet, smiling dreamily to herself and stoked the embers of last night's fire, building it to a roar again. The crackling logs took the damp and chill out of the morning and made her feel less lonely.

She picked up her leather pouch from the table, stuffed once again with her precious possessions, and tied it on her belt. The heel of last night's bread sat wrapped up in a piece of linen next to Robert's saddlebag. It was still edible so she nibbled on the crust as she settled down to wait before the fire.

Lost in thoughts of her home and family, voices outside arrested her attention. Fear zapped through her. Was it Abasi? Should she run and hide? Then reality surfaced and she remembered where she was. Feeling silly for letting her overactive mind wander, she shook it off wondering if she would always be fearful of that man and reminded herself that Meggie and Alice were due to arrive.

Hoping to confirm the presence of the sisters, she glided to the window on soundless feet to peek out. No one was there. Intending to peek out the door for a better look, she tiptoed over and grabbed the handle, but it whooshed open on its own. A hard body slammed into hers.

Huge hands roughly grasped her shoulders. Shocked, she looked up into the dark, grim face of a man she didn't recognize and unleashed a shrill scream.

"Gotcha' my fine little miss!" The man's fish and onion breath threatened to knock her out. "I 'ave her!" he shouted over his shoulder to the other men, now gathering behind him. "The baron will be pleased ta see ye, m'lady."

Horror shot through Ashley with a force momentarily stunning her. *The baron? No!* She and Robert planned to face all this together. She couldn't do it alone. Not now.

Before she thought about moving a muscle, the men surrounded her and she was swept off her feet and placed on the saddle. Another of Bedford's men pressed her so tightly against his armored chest she thought she might not be able to breathe. She gasped for air and he loosened his hold only slightly. In another moment they galloped full out, six men, two abreast, heading back to Hertford Castle. Ashley felt her eyes roll back into her head and all went blank.

∞∞∞

Robert tossed his head back and breathed in the fresh smelling morning air. The mist had mostly dried, leaving the forest teeming with animals scurrying about in search of their own breakfasts. Birds called out their morning songs; otherwise, the quiet was so deep one could practically hear the vines grow. *What a glorious day to be alive.*

Ashley would be waiting for him and they would figure everything else out together. Robert had bagged two pheasants and a quail. His thoughts were on bragging to Ashley of his hunting prowess when women's voices drifted to him from the direction of the lodge. He determined easily that it was Meggie and Alice chattering in loud, unhappy tones. It was another moment, however, before he recognized his worst fear: *Ashley was gone.*

Ye gods, this was his dream come to life!

He had been warned yet he still had left Ashley unprotected. How had he not seen this coming? What was he to do now? How could he make this right? He cared no longer if the sisters found out he had been with Ashley all night. He strode into the lodge, scaring the two speechless. That was not an easy thing to do. Meggie and Alice were renowned talkers.

Once they identified Lord Robert and realized he did not intend to slit their throats, they relaxed enough to tell him Ashley was nowhere to be found. They said she must have left in a hurry as the fire was still blazing and a bit of bread had been dropped by the door. He shuddered when he saw her cloak still spread on the floor in front of the fire. How sweetly she had lain there sleeping when he had left her.

Robert's heart ached even more when he examined the ground outside, finding evidence of multiple horses and men's footprints all around the entrance to the lodge. Remnants of that forgotten nightmare skittered through his mind of soldiers on horseback carrying his love away. He should have known. Why had he so thoughtlessly left her alone? He did not have to think twice about who had taken Ashley and where he would find her.

He threw the game birds on the ground in front of Meggie and Alice. Without another word, he saddled Lucifer, who mercifully had not been found by the baron's men in the mews, and took off for the castle.

With due caution, Meggie lifted the birds to avoid getting blood on her tidy, white apron and inspected them. Alice ran after Robert. "Will m'lady be needin' the clothes we brung her?" When she got no response, she turned back and snatched the birds from Meggie, splattering blood down the front of both of them. "M'lord give 'em to *me!*"

"Bosh, I picked 'em up first. Now look what ye've done to me nice clean clothes, Alice." Meggie grabbed the necks of the dead birds, pulling hard. "Give 'em 'ere or ye'll be pushin' that cart all by yerself."

Robert had not heard a word screamed at him by the battling sisters behind him. It was the battle ahead that drew him like a flame to the air.

∞∞∞∞

Lord Bedford paced the length of the parapet as he had for the last three hours. The castle had been in an uproar since early yesterday evening when it had been discovered Lady Ashley was not chambered with Lady Elena and Lady Charissa.

Those meddling females had made sure Lady Ashley had had all the time she needed to make her escape. They claimed to have no knowledge of where she had gone, but he did not believe it for a moment. Though they had cried and gnashed their teeth, the two young women held firm and had not given up any information regarding their friend.

The soldiers had not started out looking for Ashley until dawn, so Bedford had spent the night sleepless and filled with worry. He cringed thinking about Ashley on her own with no protection. She might be lying by the side of the road, having fallen victim to a wild animal or worse, been raped or killed by thieves.

Was the thought of marrying him so awful she would take such a risk with her life? Surely, not. He offered her a life of relative ease with her friends nearby. Who would run from that?

His mind refused to contemplate the fact no one knew the whereabouts of Lord Robert. They were likely together and a night had passed, but he chose not to say anything to Hertford. After all, he wanted help reclaiming Ashley.

Hertford had not connected Robert with the disappearance of Ashley. He had told his friends with a rueful chuckle that Robert was probably licking his wounds with the help of some willing wench in Hertford village. Bedford winced as he thought about another wench who might have been all too willing.

The three lords had decided they must go after Lady Ashley. Bedford's men were to search through the forest, Hertford's the village, and Mowbray's along the river. They would find her, hopefully, before too much trouble followed her. Still, he paced.

A cry went up from the watch a short time later, and the baron ran to the end of the parapet to see what caused it. He made out his own men, under his standard, riding back to the castle. Lady Ashley appeared to be held in the lap of one of his men in the center of the small brigade. At least, he did not see Lord Robert. Anger flooded his veins, only moderately tempered by relief.

What should he do now? The answer popped into his head before he had finished forming the question. He wanted Lady Ashley. They would be wed tomorrow along with Elric and

Lady Charissa. He stalked to the stairs, gaining determination with each step. He would meet her in front of the great hall and she would soon agree she had no choice but to accept him.

Chapter 25

Ashley surfaced with the pounding of the horse's hooves echoing the pounding of her brain. For a moment she was utterly disoriented, but reality slammed into her and stuck like mud thrown at her face.

"So yer awake, m'lady, are ye?" Her captor grinned and more nasty air blew in her face. Did all these soldiers have breath fit to kill? "We'll deliver ye back to the baron in no time. 'Tis the parapet ye can spy behind that big oak tree."

Ashley could only grimace. She had lost. What would the earl do with her now? Would the baron have gone home in disappointment? *Ah,* but these were his men she reminded herself. No, he would be there waiting for her. And, he knew about Robert as well as Charissa and Elric. Had he told the earl what he knew? If only she had not been caught so soon.

She braced for the coming conflict. She did not want to tell everyone who she was as she had told Robert last night. How then would she protect her secret and herself? Her head pounded double time as they approached the castle.

She could see Elena, Charissa and Elric standing behind their fathers who flanked Lord Bedford on the steps of the great hall. Elena and Charissa were apparently out of room arrest. *Ah,* yes, the need for that vanished when she disappeared.

She would love to have been a rat in the wall when the earl remembered the escape stairway in Elena's room. He deserved to be tricked when he was the one who held them prisoners. Her eyes shifted grudgingly to the baron who was glaring fiercely at her. She sighed. However would she get out of marrying him now?

All in all, no one looked happy or smiled a welcome as she and Bedford's men rode into the bailey. Ashley's body was shaking as she was helped down from the saddle. Her legs buckled under her when her feet hit the ground, but she stiffened her resolve to be strong. Miraculously, her legs stiffened too.

Ashley's eyes sought Elena's and found much sympathy there, but no solution for the current situation. Elric held Charissa's hand, both looking uncomfortable they could do nothing to help her.

The earl would not look directly at her, she noted. What was that about? Had they told him the whole story or were they still in cover-up mode? She should tread lightly until she found out if any of their secrets had been exposed.

Lord Bedford seemed to be smiling, but the smile on his lips bore no relation to the glittering look in his eyes. He vibrated with anger. Every muscle he moved said he was not a man to tangle with, yet that was exactly what she had done.

Bedford stepped forward and took Ashley's hand, lifting it smoothly to his lips for a kiss. He turned it over and kissed her palm, looking squarely into her eyes and daring her to flinch. *So that's how it's to be. He'll be nice to me as long as I don't oppose him.*

Fat. Chance.

"You are returned unharmed to us, Lady Ashley. I trust your little outing was not too trying," Bedford said, glibly through gritted teeth.

"On the contrary, my Lord, it was the best night of my life," Ashley gloated, her chin rising at least two inches.

Bedford's eyebrows shot up at her open insolence, then his eyes blackened and narrowed. Ashley wondered if he would hurt her. She should know better than to always take the bait.

"You would be wise, Lady Ashley, to keep your tongue behind your teeth until you learn to bend to me." Bedford's voice, quiet and silky in her ear, was meant only for her to hear. "And bend to me you will."

Ashley opened her mouth to tell him to go to hell, to leave her alone, that Robert would save her, and about a million other things. Wisely, she shut it before she pushed him too far. She would bide her time and wait for the right moment to strike back and end this mess.

Bedford took her hand and tucked it securely under his arm and strolled imperiously with her toward the others. All her friends stood there with such stricken faces, Ashley needed to ease their worry. She gave them a huge grin and winked like a fellow conspirator at them.

Mowbray's forehead furrowed and she glanced at the earl in time to see Hertford's face freeze into a dark scowl. Her friends tried hard to contain their grins in response. At least she had managed to lighten the moment for them.

Ashley knew Bedford had not seen her smirk, but he knew intuitively she was undermining him. He turned to her and inspected her odd, unladylike appearance with disdain.

"You will wish to change clothes from your journey and refresh yourself, Lady Ashley. Then I will expect you to meet me without delay in the garden arbor." He bowed, turned on his heel, and strode in the direction of the garden before she could respond.

Hertford and Mowbray did not wait for any further greeting, but turned and went back inside the great hall, deep in a private discussion of their own. The moment they were gone, Elena flew off the steps and into Ashley's arms.

"I never thought I would see you again!" She hugged Ashley, squeezing every ounce of air from her lungs.

"We have all been so worried about you. There was no way to know if you had made it safely to the lodge--"

"--or if Robert had found you," Elric finished for his sister. "He was greatly relieved you still wanted him, but furious I had let you go on your own."

"Tell us, Ashley, what happened after you left us," Charissa demanded.

Ashley smiled at all the questions and the concern on their faces. "I'll fill you in completely but you better tell me everything that happened here, too, so I don't say too much when I talk to the baron." Her smile faded. "He seems more obsessed than ever to go through with this wedding, so let's talk while I change and wash up. I stink of fish and onions like Bedford's men."

"I will tell you later what she says, Elric. Go now and please keep an eye on the baron while we help Lady Ashley dress." Elric lifted an eyebrow at being dismissed by Charissa, but then smiled and nodded indulgently at his lovely betrothed's orders before he headed after the man in question.

∞∞∞

Ashley smoothed down the sleeve of her blue gown and stopped to collect her thoughts before striding into the garden. She was determined not to be the cowed little miss Bedford wanted her to be.

To thwart him she had taken her time dressing. The baron's expression and stance told her he was displeased so much time had passed.

Ah, poor baby.

Bedford met her at the gate and pulled her, jerking along, to the back of the garden to the spot where Charissa and Elric had first found each other. The arbor was the perfect place for a lover's assignation because it was quite secluded. Too bad it was Bedford beside her instead of Robert.

As if reading her mind, the baron all but shoved her onto a bench and glared down at her. *He has quite a snit going, doesn't he?* No one would be around to help her should he get too aggressive. She'd better be careful not to antagonize him too much.

"We must reach an understanding regarding our relationship, Lady Ashley, and I think now 'tis time to do so."

"I agree." The baron didn't know half of what she wanted him to understand.

"First, my lady, we are to be married tomorrow as planned along with Lord Elric and Lady Charissa." Ashley huffed air out her nose in disgust. Bedford's mouth formed a cruel line. "Do not be a petulant child with me, Lady Ashley. I demand respect and you shall give me such."

"But I cannot figure out, my lord, why you insist upon marrying *me!*" Ashley tamped down her frustration several notches, but she wanted to scream. "You don't love me and I'm sure I don't love you, so what is this all about?"

"Heirs, Lady Ashley, heirs. 'Tis about having an heir so my line goes on and my lands and people are not left leaderless." The baron rubbed his forehead, nearly as frustrated as she. "Do you doubt what I say?"

"No, I know about your need for heirs, but why do you want to force me into providing a son for you. Why not find a lady who would be honored and proud to be your wife? Clearly, I'm not that lady."

"Your face and your body please me. You are young and healthy and will provide me with strong sons and daughters."

Ashley cocked a brow at him and shook her head. He ignored her, plucking a budding rose from the arbor and spinning it between his fingertips. "I am your lord and I will decide whom I shall marry. No male authority governs you other than the Earl of Hertford who hath given you to me. This is not your decision. You, as a female, are to be compliant and do as you are told. You shall wed with me and you shall be my wife and mistress of all I possess."

Ashley's hopes were as decimated as the rosebud Bedford now crushed between his fingers. There would be no changing this man's mind with logic. He had rutted these ideas in his brain and no amount of pushing, pulling or digging would free his thought for anything else.

Surely Robert would realize she had been kidnapped and

come for her. He wouldn't let the baron wed her without a fight. She would go with the flow until the right opportunity presented itself. It would. *It has to.*

Slowly, Ashley raised her eyes to the baron and smiled. He appeared taken aback by her change of heart and for a moment she felt guile flash through her smile. She quickly covered it, so when Bedford examined her face more closely, he thought her sincere. He cautiously straightened and waited for her to speak.

"Then, it's as you require, my lord." Ashley folded her hands in her lap in her best imitation of a biddable medieval girl.

The baron smiled at her and held out his hand to her in invitation. "Since we are to be wed, you must call me Damien."

"As you wish, *Damien.*" Ashley gave him a smile showing all her teeth. *More like damned Damien or Damien the damned, but Damien it is.* She purposely did not take his hand and he slowly withdrew it. "There is a feast this evening for Charissa and Elric so I should go now, *Damien*, and help them prepare for it."

"*Ah,* 'tis for *us* as well, Lady Ashley.

"Uh, right. Well, I have to go now."

Ashley rose and turned to leave the arbor. Damien seized her arm and pulled her to him, covering her mouth with his. Ashley opened her lips to protest only to find his hot tongue thrust into her mouth. She all but gagged at the invasion. One hand groped and grabbed her breast while the other pressed her so hard against him she was defenseless. She was at the point of panic, not being able to breathe, when Elric's voice cut through the peacefulness of the outer garden.

"Lady Ashley? Lady Ashley, are you back there? Lady Margaret is looking for you in the great hall. Lady Ashley?"

The baron's hands slid down to cup her bottom. He squeezed her soft flesh to his satisfaction before reluctantly releasing her. Lust still filled his eyes as he placed Ashley away from him. He set to rights the front of her bodice where he had savagely pawed her breast and called to Elric in a loud, firm voice.

"She is here, Elric. Tell Lady Margaret I will send her on her way."

Ashley stood motionless, momentarily shocked by the baron's actions. Finally, she caught her breath and understood Elric had saved her. She spun around and raced out of the garden, never slowing when she heard the baron laugh and call after her, "Until later, *my love*."

Chapter 26

Ashley sat morosely next to Lord Bedford during the evening's feast. She didn't want to be the wet blanket for Charissa and Elric, who glowed with excitement on the eve of their nuptials, but where was Robert? Had his search for her taken him to the wrong place?

To add to her misery, Damien the Damned pawed her every few minutes, unable to keep his hands to himself. If he was not feeding her sweetmeats, he was kissing her hand, her lips, her cleavage, or any other part of her body he desired. She knew he was sending a message for all to see that she belonged to him to do with as he pleased. If the meal didn't end soon she was ready to stab him with her dining dagger.

Seated on Ashley's other side, Elena did her best to engage her friend's attention so she would not be forced to give it to Damien. It didn't help much. He openly ignored Elena, and grabbed Ashley's shoulders to turn her to him whenever he wished.

At one point the hairs on the nape of her neck stood up, and she was sure Robert had entered the great hall. Hope surged through her for a moment, but scanning the crowd methodically, she could find no sign of him. Dejected, she sat with her elbow on the table and her cheek in the palm of her hand.

Ashley felt Lady Margaret's wrath without looking at her, even though the woman was seated at the far end of the table. The old girl couldn't contain her jealousy or her anger because she probably believed evil should be heaped upon Ashley's head for her wicked ways with men. Somehow she knew Lady

Margaret would not hold the baron responsible for his roving hands and leering looks at her. No, in that lady's mind it was always Ashley's fault, never his.

Ashley sighed and fondled the tip of her dining dagger with her thumb. A moment later, Damien stiffened next to her, and she sensed something was wrong. She directed her attention first to the door hoping maybe Robert had walked into the great hall, but she couldn't see him anywhere. Disappointed, she sneaked a glance in Bedford's direction.

Instantly, she knew something was *really* wrong. Damien's expression was blank. His dark eyes popped and his face was rapidly losing its color despite his deep tan. His hands clenched spasmodically at his throat. Then it hit her.

"Lord Bedford is choking!" Ashley shrieked. *"He can't breathe!"*

The earl, who had been engaged in a discussion with Mowbray, spun around in his chair and began shouting and banging on Bedford's back. The rest of the great hall held a frozen tableau, with all faces turned to them in alarm.

Hitting his back would not dislodge the substance stuck in his throat. Ashley was sure of that. Why did no one perform the Heimlich maneuver on him? Then it dawned on her she was the only one in the room who knew what that was, let alone how to do it. Selfishly, she thought about just letting him die. She wouldn't have to marry him. Problem solved! But when blue tinged the baron's face, she panicked. She couldn't sit here and let the man *die!*

Ashley jumped up so fast her heavy chair crashed to the floor and she stumbled over it in her haste to get into position. She shoved the earl aside with strength she didn't know she had. Grabbing Bedford from behind, she jerked him out of his chair and to his feet. As if through a tin can, she heard people yelling and telling her to stay away, but she ignored them. Bedford was terrifyingly unresponsive, and if not for the adrenaline surging through her body, she would have had difficulty holding him up.

She thrust her arms around his waist and followed the

instructions exactly as she had been taught. She made a fist with one hand and placed her thumb above his belly button. Then she grasped that fist with her other hand and delivered four upward squeeze-thrusts as hard as she could into his abdomen. On the fifth try a piece of beef shot from his mouth. It smacked Lady Margaret squarely in the chest as she bounced up and down on the opposite side of the table screaming for Ashley to "Desist at once."

Leaning heavily on the table with both hands, Bedford gasped again and again as he struggled to regain his breath.

Pandemonium broke loose in the hall. No one had ever seen anything like *that* before and everyone was talking and laughing and reenacting what they had just witnessed. Lady Margaret's wits apparently cracked into ice shards and fell to the ground at her feet because she had no words. Elena, Charissa and Elric hugged Ashley all at once as if she were a hero who had vanquished a foe.

Still fighting to compose herself after the effects of her adrenaline surge, Ashley caught sight of the earl. Like the calm in the midst of the storm, he stared at her like she was not of this world. Why would he do that? His eyes narrowed as he frowned at her. *Ah,* now she understood it. He thought she was a *witch.*

Mowbray cheerfully patted Bedford on the back. "I thought you would die, friend, truly I did. 'Twas certain you could not gain your breath no matter how hard Hertford thumped you trying to dislodge that bit of beef. If I had not seen it with mine own eyes, Damien, I would ne'er believe a mere slip of a girl could save you as she did." He shook his head in sheer awe. "And the look on Lady Margaret's face when that meat struck her breast is one I shan't soon forget!" He threw back his head and laughed at the memory. Lady Margaret, who had been seated once again by a servant, glared reproachfully at Mowbray before directing her ire once again at Ashley.

The earl had had enough of the cheering and hugging. He pounded his fist on the table and demanded all take their seats. Glowering at Ashley, his voice boomed out over the room full of people. "We are fortunate our good friend, Lord Bedford, is still well and among us thanks to the quick actions of Lady Ashley." The room erupted in cheers, hoots and fists on the table until the earl quieted them. "We would, however, ask her to share with us what ... *magic* she performed to save him so effectively."

He raised a brow and stared at Ashley in a direct challenge to prove she was not a witch. Cheers burst forth once again, this time cheering for the magic to be shared. The earl scowled at his people who were not viewing Ashley as a witch at all, at least not a bad one. They were thoroughly impressed she had saved Bedford.

Ashley wasn't sure how to proceed with a description of the Heimlich maneuver. Bedford was recovering quickly, which made her smile in spite of herself. How could she not be happy about actually saving a life? She turned to the earl. "My lord, there is no magic here. In my country, this maneuver is taught because it works. Lord Bedford needed to cough and he couldn't, so I coughed for him by doing what you saw me do. I used no magic. Any of you could have done the same thing." She nodded as much to herself as to the earl and the crowd. "No magic, just knowledge of what to do."

All around the room, people nodded and accepted what she said, since they had seen for themselves how it worked. The earl seemed vaguely troubled, yet he said nothing. His breathing miraculously restored, Damien's face was filled with wonder. Ashley plunked down beside him. "How are you feeling?"

He must have thought her an angel the way he croaked, "You *saved* me." Before she could respond, the baron bounded to his feet and rasped emphatically to all, "Hear ye, hear ye!" All eyes were on the baron, now fully recovered. The room buzzed with expectation. "I wish to reward Lady Ashley for saving my life. I shall grant her *anything* she wishes, be it jewels or finery or whatever pleases her. Tomorrow I shall formally pledge to give myself to her as her husband in marriage. But tonight I give my pledge freely, for she hath spared me an untimely death." Everyone whooped and cheered. All talked nonstop to anyone who would listen about which specific riches Lady Ashley should choose. The baron sat down pleased with himself and his generosity to his betrothed.

Ashley didn't think she liked where this was going. She wanted Lord Bedford, Baron of Bedford, Damien the Damned, Unwanted Betrothed to go home, not say he wanted to give her the moon. She spoke quietly to him, "I would have saved *anyone* who was choking. It happened to be you, so don't think it means anything special."

"You could have let me die, my dear, but you did not. Surely that means something."

"Granted, I couldn't let your life end over a bite of meat, my lord, but it doesn't mean I want to marry you. I don't. I don't hate you, and I don't wish evil upon you. I only want you to go home and leave me alone."

Damien didn't seem to hear her. "I told you, my *love,* I would grant you anything you wish and I mean that. Would you like jewels or new gowns? A lovely mare, perhaps? What will it be, dear heart?" His eyes sparkled almost as much as the light off the silver sides of his hair.

Ashley rose to her feet, her blood pumping, and tapped a pewter cup with her dining knife to quiet the room. "I have decided what I wish Lord Bedford to grant me for saving his life. You all heard him say he would grant me anything I asked." She paused dramatically, ensuring everyone heard her words. Damien all but grinned in anticipation of what riches she would demand of him. "Thus, I wish, my lord, for you to grant me freedom from my betrothal to you. I. Do. Not. Wish. To. Marry. You."

Voices rocketed around the room with everyone yelling and talking at once. Ashley sat down, cocked an eyebrow at Damien and looked directly into his eyes.

"You know I will not grant you that, so why do you ask it

of me?" Damien spit out. His face had lost its wondrous glow in but an instant and was now dark and forbidding.

Ashley leaned forward and put it to him straight. *"Ah,* but your exact words were 'I will grant you anything you wish.' You did not say 'anything but your betrothal to me', did you? You said whatever pleased me and this pleases me."

The baron lurched to his feet and calmed the rowdy crowd. He plastered a smile upon his face and laughed a brittle laugh. "Such a jest, Lady Ashley. Of course you do not wish to break your betrothal to me." He chuckled again, but no one believed it a jest. Lady Ashley's grim face belied any joking about something as serious as marriage. "She tells me she would choose a ruby necklace as her reward, so rubies 'twill be!" He raised his cup in a toast to the room and half-hearted cheers punctuated the uncomfortable silence.

Not to be outdone, Ashley rose to stand beside the baron and the crowd hushed to hear her speak, unsure of what would happen next.

"He lies!" Ashley declared, vehemently.

The crowd caught its collective throat and silence choked the room. "I asked for no such necklace and Lord Bedford knows I did not. I ask for only one thing and that is freedom from my betrothal to him. If Lord Bedford cannot grant it, he has no honor, for everyone heard him set the terms of his offer."

Once again, pandemonium exploded in the room as all had something to say about this stand off between Lady Ashley and Lord Bedford. Lord Mowbray shook his head and closely examined the potato on his plate, moving it from side to side with a finger. Elena, Charissa and Elric shouted their support to Ashley. Lady Margaret shrilly told anyone who would listen that Lady Ashley was nothing but a strumpet trying to extort money from the baron.

The Earl of Hertford slowly rose and stood magnificently above the crowd, demanding all recognize his authority over the room. The sound of screeching voices cut off with but a stroke of his hand. He sneered with each word he spoke. "If Lord Bedford wishes to grant Lady Ashley anything at all, it is solely his choice. She is but a woman, and therefore, it is not for her to argue anything. This disagreeable disagreement is over."

His people dropped their eyes and stared in silence at their hands as though they had been beaten with a stick. Yet one man, dressed in a friar's robe with his face hidden beneath its deep hood, rose and addressed the earl. "Then you have no honor, Sire, since you will not acknowledge what all heard Lord Bedford say."

For a moment Ashley expected lightning bolts to rain down from the heavens since the electricity in the room was unmistakable. All eyes flew from one man to the other, waiting breathlessly for a crack of thunder or someone to be struck down or ... *something*.

The color drained from the Earl of Hertford's face, leaving him with no words to respond. The man drew back his friar's hood, revealing his person to the crowd.

It was none other than Lord Robert who stood before them.

Chapter 27

"Robert," the earl breathed. Everyone else was too stunned for speech, staring open-mouthed.

Two beats fell before Ashley's face registered what had just happened. Then without hesitation, she flew out of her chair and bounded down the stairs to the common tables by the door where Robert held his ground. He opened his arms to her and folded her into him, squeezing her tightly. He kissed her forehead and tucked her under his arm before turning to stare defiantly at his father.

Stricken at this unlikely union, the earl's brain was spinning furiously trying to make sense of what he was seeing. *How has this come to pass?* Robert had been betrothed to Lady Charissa until a few days ago, yet his commitment to *this* woman was obvious.

The earl glanced at Elric and Charissa only to find them seated at the table with mouths shut and eyes locked on their joined hands. What was going on here? The chit must have performed her magic on his son, for Robert was obviously smitten with her, but Elric and Charissa were somehow part of it. Of that he was sure. But he had more to consider.

The challenge Robert so carelessly tossed out in front of the entire world was directed at him as well as at Lord Bedford. How was this to be resolved without bloodshed? He could not ignore the insult directed at him in front of his people. Yet he did not want to see his son, *his heir,* destroyed because of this wretched female.

He would pretend as though it were some kind of strange

jest played upon him. That's what he would do. He could not let either Robert or Damien lose his life over this worthless wench no one knew anything about, yet everyone wanted. It was one thing to lose your head over a woman you might want; it was well another to lose your life fighting needlessly over one.

The earl cleared his throat and instantly all eyes were on him. He took a moment to calm himself and spoke in a pleasant voice to all. "This hath been an evening to remember, I would say." He aimed for a chuckle, but it sounded more like a growl to his ears. "I believe 'tis time for all of you to go to your beds, for more celebrations are ahead of us on the morrow." He nodded with a smile to Elric and Charissa as well as the baron standing gravely beside him.

"We have had quite enough excitement for one evening." He raised an eyebrow at Robert and Ashley. "Lord Robert and Lord Bedford will join me in the map room where we will sort out the ... *confusion* of this evening in a civilized manner."

He paused again for effect and then spoke to Ashley as though he had sucked on a bitter lemon. "Lady Ashley, we will *inform* you of the decisions we make." His attention turned to Robert and his gaze softened, a wicked smile playing around the corners of his mouth. "Judging from Lord Robert's curious disguise and his bold words, I believe there is an amusing tale here that must be told. Perhaps I shall share it with all of you on the morrow." He smiled beneficently upon his people for a moment, then spun on his heel and strode out of the great hall, head held high and back ramrod straight.

It was a superb performance, and all were aware he was, indeed, the master of the castle. Furious, Lord Bedford gave Ashley a scorching glance and followed in Hertford's wake.

The room exploded with everyone talking at once trying to understand the scene they had inescapably witnessed. Ashley heard snatches of conversations around her indicating amazement over Lord Robert's appearance as a monk and astonishment that he was now attached to Lady Ashley.

Many were concerned he had irreparably crossed his father, yet the delicious drama surprised and excited them. Folks speculated and bets were taken on whether she would marry Lord Damien tomorrow, or stay with Lord Robert. Many curious eyes assessed her person. Had she made an even bigger mess of things? She wasn't sure.

Ignoring the crowd, Robert turned to face Ashley, gathered her in his arms and delivered a passionate kiss. When lack of air forced him to end it, he breathed hard while he scanned the room for a moment, taking in all the commotion. "Well, that was unexpected, was it not?"

Kissed breathless, Ashley found only enough air to answer, *"Umph?"*

Robert slipped out of the heavy robe and presented it to the friar seated next to him with a simple thank you.

"Wh-what made you come in disguise?" she asked, her breath still heaving. "I couldn't believe it was you and you had come for me."

"Unsure of what to expect from Bedford, I did not want to give him the advantage of knowing I was here to take you from him. Thus, when I passed the chapel as I came in, I slipped in to find a robe to disguise myself."

"It certainly worked well. I thought you were here because the little hairs on the back of my neck tingled like they always do when I'm with you." Ashley rubbed her neck with one hand to demonstrate. Robert gloried at her words and the effect he had on her, pulling her closer. "But I watched for you all night long and couldn't find you. I've never been so glad to see anyone in my life!"

Ashley scrunched her face in distaste over a new thought. "Once again, however, the *men* in the room will decide my fate and I will be 'informed' of the outcome." She took both his hands in hers and reminded him of the facts of her situation. "I will not be forced into marrying the baron under any circumstances, Robert. And I don't want to tell him my real identity just to get out of this marriage. You understand why I can't marry him. So there is no way I can do as I'm told like a compliant little lady should."

"I agree," he teased with a wink. "'Tis why, Lady Ashley, you will accompany me to the map room."

Astonished, Ashley opened her mouth to speak but no words came out. Robert laughed aloud at her speechless response. He pulled her hand to his lips for a kiss, then tucked it under his arm and led her away before she could find her words.

∞∞∞

Lord Bedford steamed into the map room, seething in his own juices. Or so it seemed to the earl.

"How *dare* she, Hertford. How dare she question my honor after I so graciously offered a gift of her choosing for saving my life? Why would the woman do that?"

The earl wondered the same thing, but calmly poured two cups of *eau-de-vie* and handed one to his friend. Both drank deeply, the earl wiping the back of his hand over his mouth as if to clear the way for his next words. "Tell me, Damien, why do you continue this pursuit of Lady Ashley? She must not be invested in you since she had no trouble up and running to Robert's side after impugning your honor. Why not let her go?"

Damien sank into a chair by the hearth and put his face in his hands. He kneaded his brow in frustration. "You are right. It makes no sense. Yet I no longer want only a willing wench in my bed, Hertford. I want a *wife.*"

Damien looked up at the earl, his eyes pleading his case. "Your daughter rejected my suit a month ago, and tonight Lady Ashley hath done the same. I want someone to give me an heir and who else is there? What am I to do now?"

"I would suggest you go to London and look for a wife there, perhaps at court," Ashley answered, entering the room with Robert holding her hand securely in his.

"Still your tongue, Lady Ashley. You were not invited to this meeting, hence you need to absent yourself from my presence now." The earl was shocked she would defy him so openly.

"She was invited by me." Robert kept his voice low and even as he faced his father. "This concerns her as much as it does me, so if she leaves, I leave with her."

The earl glared his displeasure at being spoken to in such a rude manner by his heir. Glancing at Bedford in hopes of a little support, he noted the man sat there pale and cowed, all the fight having been sapped from him. Turning back to Robert, he could see by the set of his son's jaw he would do as he said. His annoyance complete, the earl decided if it were a standoff they wanted, it was a standoff they would get. He would not budge for this little girl even though he had encouraged Bedford to let her go only moments before. She had crossed the line with him too many times. She needed to leave Hertford Castle.

"I'm sorry, my lord, that you don't think much of me." The wench did not back down in the face of his anger. He narrowed his eyes at her in warning, but she continued without pause, "I am not used to people deciding for me what happens in my life without any input from me ... and particularly when something like marriage is involved."

"Lady Ashley," the earl snarled, "no one here has ever heard of this United States of America you say you come from. In this land men determine the futures of the women under their protection. Surely you cannot believe women can judge for themselves what is best for them?" He scowled at Ashley before spitting out his decision on her future in staccato fashion. "You, child, seem to be firmly in my care, so I will decide what is best for you, and that is marriage to Lord Bedford."

As his words registered, the earl watched the girl's expression go from sincere to indignant. *Ha!* He held the power and she did not. She might defy him, but she would not win.

Robert started to speak in her defense, but Ashley shushed him with a hand on his arm. "You see, that's just the problem. You, my lord, cannot possibly understand what is best for me, because you don't know anything about me other than my name and where I come from."

Before the earl could answer, Damien interrupted, "I do not understand how I am such a problem to marry, Lady Ashley. I offer to give you a life as my wife any woman should desire yet you spurn me. I do not understand you."

"I know you don't, Damien." Ashley gave the baron a wistful smile. "What you don't understand is I gave my heart to Robert before I'd even met you."

The earl's eyebrows shot up with that bit of information and then settled into a firm scowl as he scrutinized Robert. *What is this? What has gone on under my very nose with Robert and this woman?* Regret swamped him. If he had only followed his instincts and sent her on her way when he had first met her, all would now be well. His eyes drilled into Robert's. "I believe you owe me an explanation, *son*."

As Robert steeled himself to face his father's wrath, the earl glanced at Bedford and was startled to find the baron had perked up at Lady Ashley's news. He was now sitting on the edge of his chair with a smirk on his face like a cat that had been into the cream. Did *he* know what Robert would say?

"Yes, Sire, I have owed you an explanation far too long." His eyes darted to Ashley, who smiled her encouragement to him. "Remember when I arrived home to all the fanfare and kissed Lady Ashley, thinking she was Lady Charissa? I was embarrassed that I kissed a woman who was not my betrothed. It angered me it was not Lady Charissa's lips I kissed, because the moment my lips touched Lady Ashley's, I knew she belonged to me. I believe she knew it then, too." He gave Ashley a lopsided grin that made her blush a deep red. "When at last I spotted Lady Charissa on the steps, she and Elric were staring into each other's eyes as lovers do. I suspected they had formed the same kind of bond I found with my first taste of Lady Ashley's lips."

"I do not believe any of this, Robert." Disgust dripped from the earl's lips with every word. "Are you saying you and Elric both fell in love at first sight? You are acting like a child, not my heir."

"'Tis true, Father. We all went falconing the next day, and you will recall we had to send Elena home early with an injured ankle. Then we got caught in the rain." Robert and Ashley smiled, their eyes locked on each other. "We sought shelter in the old hunting lodge nearby, and 'tis there our love was sealed."

The earl paled, shooting a glance at Damien to gauge his reaction before asking outright, "Are you saying Lady Ashley is untouched no longer?" Damien looked intently at Ashley, who first giggled her embarrassment, but then stopped when she saw their stunned faces.

"No!" Ashley and Robert yelled, laughing uncomfortably at their unison cry. Ashley paused for a moment, waiting until all eyes were on her. "I'm also not used to everyone talking about my virginity like it's a commodity. Robert means it was there we first spoke of our love for one another."

"Yes, she hath the right of it." Robert leaned in and gave Ashley a kiss on the cheek. "It was clear to all of us that Elric was in love with Lady Charissa, and I was in love with Lady Ashley. It was Elric and his Charissa who came up with the idea of getting caught together after hours. Elric would compromise Lady Charissa and her betrothal to me would be broken. As dishonorable as it sounds now, it seemed the simplest way to break the bond neither of us wanted."

The earl paced back and forth in front of the fire. This was worse than he had thought. Did honor mean nothing to his son--to *either* of his sons? He turned to the baron whose face wore an unreadable expression. What of this did Damien know?

With a grin at Robert, Ashley picked up the telling of the story. "It would all have succeeded as planned except Elena could not get Lady Margaret to wake up and make the discovery. Elena and I decided to call it off for the night since we had no one to catch the lovers in the courtyard. I had gone into the bailey to find Charissa and Elric to tell them, when you, Damien, appeared and assaulted me."

"'Twas not an assault, Lady Ashley!" the baron responded, defensively.

"I'm not sure what you call ripping one's dress to the waist here, but in my country I'm pretty sure we'd call it an assault."

"Enough of this!" the earl snapped, glaring at Ashley to quiet her. He jumped ahead to make his point to Robert. "So, to your mind, Elric and Lady Charissa got what they wanted, but you got thwarted by Damien. Is that correct, Robert?"

"Yes, Father."

"A fine tangle you have woven for yourself. Do you believe Lady Ashley is worth your honor, for that is what she hath taken from you?"

"Lady Ashley hath taken nothing from me, Father. I made the decision because 'tis what I wanted then and still want now. I was uncomfortable having Lady Charissa take the blame for committing the indiscretion because I was equally guilty, but it seemed the best course at the time." Robert turned to Ashley, seeking agreement before shifting his attention to his father. "If I had told you I wanted to end the betrothal would you have agreed to let me do so?"

The earl did not hesitate for a moment. "No, I would not have broken the bond that hath held for nearly fifteen years. I have more honor than that, I can assure you." The earl felt his face heat. His son had never questioned his judgment before. *Why now?*

"Okay, that makes no sense." Ashley could contain herself no longer. "You fathers got together and created a betrothal bond that suited your needs when your kids were babies. So, on the basis of that, you would willingly sacrifice their happiness for the rest of their lives?" Ashley's eyes blazed. "You call that being honorable? How is it fair to them? Especially when

you have allowed Elena to turn down marriage proposals because she didn't want to marry either of the men who offered."

Blanching at her words, Damien sulked, but the earl sputtered as his blood boiled. He glowered at Robert who stepped
in front of Ashley as if he needed to protect her, fearing she
might suffer for her insolence. Insulted and hurt that his son
thought he would strike a woman, the earl forced himself to
calm down. Yet, what upset him most was the wretched girl
was right. Never would he have granted Elric permission to
marry Lady Charissa, and never would he have chosen Lady
Ashley for his heir's mate. He was guilty of catering to his
daughter's whims, as well, but Elena was not his heir; therefore, whomever she married mattered not. He could afford to
be indulgent with her. Glowering menacingly at Ashley, he decided he had had his fill of this child.

"We are finished here. Neither of you hath any authority in
this." He dug in and gave Ashley a withering glare. "I have given
Lady Ashley to Lord Bedford, and I have heard nothing here
that changes my mind."

Ashley rolled her eyes up at Robert in exasperation. Robert pulled her to him, slipping his arm around her shoulders
and turned to his father. "That will not happen, Father. You
have no authority over Lady Ashley. You do not know where
her people are and you promised Cedric you would protect
her. That does not involve marrying her off to Lord Bedford."

"How do you know any of this?" the earl growled.

Robert smiled grimly, meeting Ashley's eyes. "I will not
say. You do not deny it, do you?" The earl remained silent, but
stared at Ashley. What sorcery was this? How could his son
know what he and Damien had discussed?

Damien rose from his chair and turned to confront Ashley.
"You are sure you will not wed with me? I can give you far
more than this pup, who will not be the lord here for many
years. Come, come, what say you?" He tried to take Ashley's
free hand and pull her away from Robert, but she refused to
give it to him.

"Look, Damien, I told you before I can't marry you. I'm not sure why you won't believe me. We are not meant to be together. You need only to find the right wife and that definitely isn't me. Quit looking here to find your lady. She's out there waiting for you ... *somewhere else.*" She slammed her mouth shut fearing she had said too much.

"So you believe Lord Bedford can leave Hertford Castle having been bested by a mere woman and retain his honor?" the earl scoffed. The insufferable chit knew nothing about a man's honor.

"Is that the issue, Damien? You would be too humiliated to grant the wish you said you would give me in front of everyone?" The baron said nothing but shrugged a shoulder sadly and sat down. "Well, if this is what worries you, I believe I can fix it without any further issue."

"And what would you do, Lady Ashley?" the earl jeered, rolling his eyes at her.

Ashley grinned. "I will honestly tell you what happened. I spent the night at the lodge *alone* with Robert, so I am compromised ... again." She chuckled at the absurdity of that, as if it were a great joke. The earl remembered the compromising incident with the baron only a few nights before and winced.

"So, you can tell everyone that when Lord Bedford found out what happened while I was away, he would not marry me and went home."

As she finished speaking, Lady Ashley beamed her satisfaction at her proffered solution. It must have been the truth because Robert smiled at the woman like she was a gift from the heavens. Did he think changing his bride from Lady Charissa to Lady Ashley was of no significance? Perhaps to the Hertford people it would not matter.

Bedford considered what she said and slowly nodded. "Why not?" he shrugged. "'Tis as good a solution as any. I shall leave with my honor intact." He stared longingly at Ashley. "'Tis better than leaving with nothing at all."

The earl slumped upon hearing Bedford's words of acceptance, until it appeared he might fall if he did not sit down first. His world deflated. The wench had won.

No one spoke a word for a full minute as they waited to see what the earl would do. Finally, he turned to his friend. "If this is what you wish, Damien, then I will honor it." Damien nodded.

The earl turned the full force of his power on Ashley. "You, Lady Ashley, and Lord Robert will *not* marry tomorrow. We will wait for Cedric to return before any further talk of marriage will be considered."

Robert started to protest this authoritarian directive, but Ashley grabbed his arm and made him look at her. In soft tones the other two could still hear, she told him, "It's okay, Robert. I think it's the right thing to do, too." Robert took her hands in his, shaking his head unhappily, so she whispered, "Don't worry. My feelings for you haven't changed. We should wait to hear what Cedric has to say, right?" Robert reluctantly agreed, but did not look happy.

Hertford raised an eyebrow at the discordant murmuring between the two and wondered if all was well between them. Perhaps he had a chance to free Robert from her grip after all, if only he had enough time.

Chapter 28

Camped out on Elena's big bed, Elena and Charissa were waiting with wide eyes when Ashley blew in. The storm cloud that had threatened her for days was gone, leaving her happy to enter the sanctuary of Elena's room.

Settling in for a chat, the girls sat cross-legged facing each other, ready to hear Ashley's story. She regaled them with the thrilling tale of her prince charming, and how he had stood up to the evil king to keep her from marrying the wrong man. Or something like that.

Actually, she tried to remember the earl was Elena's dad, and her friend loved him in spite of his distaste for her. She did love telling them again how wonderful Robert was. He had saved her from marriage to Lord Bedford with his appearance in the great hall and during the more recent map room tribunal.

Her friends cheered when Ashley told them the baron had agreed to her suggestion that he accuse Robert of compromising Ashley. They thought it genius. Lord Bedford would refuse to marry her and go home with his honor intact.

"Yes!" Elena cried. "I shall no longer fear running into Lord Bedford in the halls or anywhere else after hours."

"I am so sorry, Ashley, that you must endure the same judgmental looks I suffered when everyone heard about Elric and me," Charissa said, smiling. "It is not a hardship when you realize the alternative is to be wed for life to someone you do not love."

"Here! Here!" Ashley pretended to toast her friends with an

imaginary glass. They all took a deep breath and relaxed while they contemplated the events of the last few days.

Ashley smiled at each of her friends, a wicked gleam in her eyes. "Now, ladies, we'd better settle down and celebrate a certain person's last night as a single lady." She waggled her eyes at Charissa. "Are you nervous about being with Elric tomorrow night?"

Elena giggled, covering her mouth with her hand. "This is Elric we are talking about--my very own brother. The one I have shared my secrets with since I was old enough to have any. How can it be he is marrying my friend?"

Charissa shivered with excitement and wrapped her arms around herself. "I tried not to think about it so much after you left us, but now I know in my heart all will be well. I am nervous, but I know Elric loves me and I love him. I trust him. Whatever our future holds as long as we are together we will be happy."

"I'm jealous, Charissa!" Ashley leaned forward and gave her friend a playful push. "The earl made it quite clear he would not allow Robert and me to even think about getting married until Cedric is back. After my close call with Damien, I'm good with that."

Elena glowed with happiness as she grinned at Charissa. "You will be my sister on the morrow. I shall miss having Elric to myself, but to have a sister hath always been my dream." She reached for Charissa's hand and grabbed Ashley's, too. "To think that I shall have sisters like the two of you is wondrous."

"Well, sisters, it's time to get down to the really important stuff now." Ashley appeared very serious which flustered her friends. "What are we all going to *wear* tomorrow?"

∞∞∞

Preparing Charissa for her wedding was like dressing a

doll. She floated like an angel around Elena's room in her wedding gown. Much to the delight of her "sisters," Charissa had come to Hertford Castle prepared for a wedding. She produced an exquisite gown of ivory silk with a gold and silver brocaded surcoat. Ashley marveled at the beauty of the rich fabrics.

They were delighted to dress her with all the lovely accessories from the golden circlet in her hair to the ivory leather slippers with golden tassels on her feet. She was a true princess standing next to a handsome prince, for Elric looked pretty stunning himself.

Over the last two days, the groom's clothing, originally sewn for Robert, had been reworked to fit Elric. The castle seamstress finished it in time and the result was stellar.

Elric wore ivory leggings under a knee-length, ivory silk tunic with gold braid edging the hem and sleeves. Thick white fur trimmed the sleeveless mantle that topped his tunic, and a necklace of braided gold and silver called a chaplet finished the look.

The two were spellbinding and gorgeous in their splendor.

The ceremony in the little chapel was anything but short, with Elric looking oh-so-very-serious and Charissa mildly terrified. Robert sat with Ashley, squeezing her hand when she got teary. She watched Elena smile the whole time even though happy tears trailed down her friend's cheeks. The earl never cracked a smile, but seemed happy for Elric, nonetheless.

Charissa's father fought back his own tears when he hugged her afterward, and Charissa's eyes glistened then, too. Once the hugging and congratulations ended, Ashley was caught up in the excitement of the crowd and ready to celebrate. A trumpet fanfare announced the end of the ceremony for the benefit of all those not in the chapel and marked the start of the party.

Ashley remembered all the food at the block parties her neighborhood used to enjoy when she was a little kid. She thought that was a lot of food, but this made those events look like dinner with the family.

The tantalizing smell of roasting meats had driven her crazy for the last twenty-four hours. Everything meat from boar and stag to woodcock and snipe had been spitted and roasted over open fires, and now smelled divine drenched in savory sauces. Fish and beef pasties competed with baskets of fresh, thick breads next to platters of sweetmeats, nutmeg custards and a treat Elena loved called marchpane. Ashley recognized it as marzipan.

Most of the residents of Hertford village could be seen preening and strutting around the castle grounds, dressed in their best. Tenants and folks from miles around arrived to enjoy the celebration too. Deep in preparation for the wedding feast for days, the castle kitchens turned out an amazing amount of delicious food and drink for all.

Charissa and Elric could not stop grinning, and they both blushed beautifully over the bawdy teasing coming their way. Ale, mead and spiced wine flowed freely with everyone partaking equally which loosened tongues as the day unfolded.

Ashley was shocked over and over by the ribald ribbing the newlyweds took from villagers and tenants, male and female alike. They left nothing to the imagination regarding what to do in the bedroom on their wedding night. She flushed a deep scarlet when Robert whispered to her what *he* would like to do with *her* on *their* wedding night. *Oh, my!*

Now, waiting for Cedric to return seemed like an impossible task. Robert was immensely pleased with her response and held her next to him the entire evening. She was more than happy to let Robert nuzzle her ear and press her to him for a thorough kissing as often as possible.

Elena did not have a good time. She spent the evening running from a pudgy young man Ashley learned was the infamous snot-nosed Pierce Wilkins. It was obvious to Ashley why Elena had turned down the young man when he wanted to wed her. Deep in his cups, he slobbered his affections in her face whenever he managed to catch up with her. Unfortunately, every time she ducked Mr. Wilkins, she turned around and ran into Lord Bedford.

The baron had been persuaded by Hertford and Mowbray to stay for the festivities, thinking he might spot a willing woman to take his mind off Lady Ashley. When that did not happen, he kept his eye on Elena. Much to her dismay, he would smile, look her up and down like she was wearing no clothes, and then brush past her, making a point of rubbing against her. It made her sweet friend shudder.

With Ashley and Charissa occupied by Robert and Elric, Elena was left alone too often to fend for herself. Ashley found out after the fact that Elena had given up the fight early in disgust. As an excuse to leave the party, she claimed she needed to oversee the preparations for Charissa and Elric's chamber. In truth, she had fled straight to the safety of her own room.

The happy wedded couple got sent off to bed with much pomp and flourish. A short time later Ashley noticed bodies strewn wherever they had fallen all over the great hall. Some snored loudly, while others talked intimately with their lovers in the darkened room.

Clearly, it was time to call it a night even though she hated to part with Robert. He admitted he would waste no time in bedding Ashley on the floor in a corner of the great hall if he were not Lord Robert.

Feeling pleasantly tipsy, Ashley had nothing but thoughts of Robert's goodnight kiss swimming in her head when she started for the stairs to the donjon. The now familiar sound of sisters squabbling interrupted her daydream. She turned to see Meggie and Alice tugging without mercy on either side of a young tenant farmer who was the worse for a cup of mead too many. Her fuzziness gone in an instant, she was alert and ready to question them about Cedric's whereabouts.

The young man's face turned green right before he melted into a heap at their feet and passed out cold. Still screaming insults, the sisters then focused their attention on each other. They paused mid-insult in surprise when Ashley stepped between them.

"Meggie! Alice! Good to see you are enjoying each other's company, as usual." Ashley couldn't help but smile as the two blushed a deep red, completely flustered. "I'm sorry to interrupt, but I wanted to say hello and thank you again for helping me get safely to the lodge." The pair nodded, still dumbstruck. "Lord Robert said you returned with clothing for me as planned. I was kidnapped, you know, and brought back here, so I could not meet you."

"Do ye still want the clothes, m'lady?" Alice's voice betrayed her worry. "Cuz we took 'em back 'ome."

"No, no," Ashley reassured them. "But I do want to know if you have heard anything about where Cedric might be."

"Aye, we 'ave." Officially off the hook for the clothes, Meggie's wariness vanished. "'Tis said Cedric was the victim of a run-in with a highwayman on the road to see Olde Gylda. She found 'im the next day lyin' in the dirt and hath been nursin' him back to 'ealth ever since."

"Aye, 'tis true, m'lady." Alice did not hesitate to put her two cents worth into the conversation. She bumped Meggie out of the way to speak to Ashley. "We 'eard it from the blacksmith who 'eard it from a pedlar who come from Olde Gylda's."

Ashley's heart was racing. Now she knew where to find Cedric. As soon as she could, she would convince Robert to take her to Olde Gylda's. They would make sure Cedric got well so he and Gylda could help her find the stone that would decide her future. Ashley thanked the sisters profusely and left them to continue their argument over the desired young man now snoring softly at their feet.

The night was mostly gone when Ashley crawled into the narrow bed in her own room. Thankfully, it wouldn't be long before she could get to Robert to tell him the news of Cedric. Something told her he might not be as excited as she was. Her stomach twisted into a knot.

How did she want this visit to Cedric and Gylda to play out? Part of her wanted them to never locate the stone so she had no choice about going home again. Yet part of her needed to go home to tell her mother what had happened to her before coming back. It was that part that wondered if the possibility even existed for her to go home and come back unharmed, or whether she might reach home, but never be able to return.

Worse, what if the stone took her somewhere she'd never been, and she would be lost to both Robert *and* her family forever? *Ugh.* She shivered like it was the middle of winter. Too many chilling possibilities presented themselves. Then thoughts of Abasi rolled into her head. Would that wretched man be waiting for her if she returned to the same place? Now that was a dispiriting thought.

Ha! If her new vermilion leather slippers were only ruby red, she wouldn't need that stupid rock. She'd just wind up safe at home in her own bed. Ashley closed her eyes, snuggled down under the covers and let the effects of the mead roll over her.

Chapter 29

The sun beat down on the hills outside Olde Gylda of Hampshire's cottage. Cedric and Gylda, deep in discussion, stood beside Elena, a short distance away from Ashley and Robert. Cedric talked in mellifluous undertones to Gylda and gesticulated with each wave of his hand to punctuate his thoughts. Robert wondered what Cedric was saying since the old wizard was far enough away and quiet enough he could not attend it.

He lifted Ashley's chin and dabbed away the tears streaming down her face with tenderness and his pocket cloth. Without further thought he raggedly mopped the sweat off his own forehead and the back of his neck.

Even though the dreadful hour had arrived, they still delayed her departure as long as possible. In another moment, Robert thought Ashley might become hysterical from crying so hard. He thought perhaps if she did not, he would. Having employed every persuasion imaginable to keep her from using the stone, she was still determined to go back to her home.

In the end, she had made up her mind to see her family once more and tell them where she was. She would not destroy her mother's happiness or her own by disappearing and causing her mother and the rest of her family deep pain. How was she to live happily with him in his world if she did not try to spare them the misery of her loss in theirs? He did not think he could say good-bye, but here he was. The pain of parting was about to send him to his knees.

Robert forced himself to stand tall, stroking Ashley's back and arms as he held her tightly to his chest, telling her again and again how much he loved her. She broke away from his caresses long enough to run to Elena, who was soundlessly sobbing as she stood alone to the side of the others. Wordlessly, she threw her arms around her friend. The two pressed their foreheads together and wept inconsolably until Robert pulled Ashley away.

Cedric moved to stand beside the stone that would send Ashley through time. Robert gave his love one more desperate hug before stepping back and dropping her hands one at a time. Ashley quickly said the words three times as if fearing she would lose her nerve. The winds started blowing and the dust swirling until the angry circle snapped her up, and she was gone.

He was certain he would never see her again.

Robert woke with a start, feeling bereft. It took him a moment to identify the source of the abandonment making him feel so forlorn. Then his dream skittered back into his brain. He dropped his head and tugged at his hair in despair. The dream was but a warning of things to come. Ashley would leave, and he would be alone if he did not find a way to stop her.

∞∞∞

Ashley's eyes popped open when she heard the knock at the door, and she knew it was later than she wanted it to be. She bounced out of bed and paused for a moment to steady herself and gain her footing so she did not faint. Flinging open the door a moment later, she found Elena dressed and ready for the day.

"You must hurry, Ashley. Elric and Charissa are preparing to leave for their wedding trip. Do you wish to tell them good-bye?"

"I do!" A wide-eyed Ashley was now fully awake. "Please help me, Elena. Anna is not here, and I cannot pull the laces tight by myself." Elena was already ahead of her, pitching clothes at Ashley in a steady stream as she found them.

"Have you seen Robert this morning?" Ashley asked as she shed her nightclothes and donned her chemise.

"Aye, he hath long since broken his fast and hath been asking after you."

Ashley hurried to wash her face. The hot water Anna had delivered, probably hours ago, was now frigid. Patting the cold water on her cheeks brought color to the surface and cleared her head. She fumbled with her slippers, trying to put them on as Elena dropped a light blue gown over her head.

"Elena, after I said goodnight to Robert, I ran into Meggie and Alice. Do you remember the sisters who brought me here?" Elena nodded with a smile of remembrance for the odd duo. Ashley fought to find the armholes. "I asked them to assist me in locating Cedric when they helped me escape to the lodge. They found him, Elena!"

"Oh?" Elena mumbled with hairpins stuck in her mouth. She found a free hand and pulled them out in a rush. "Where! Where did he go? Are you going after him? Does this mean you and Robert will wed soon? *Ooh*, Ashley, this is so exciting."

Ashley froze for a moment. She must tell Elena who she was and where she came from. Cedric had seen Ashley through his magic before her arrival, so she was sure Elena was somewhat suspicious about the items Ashley carried. It might not come as a total surprise, yet Ashley hoped Elena wouldn't be angry with her for not telling her all the details sooner.

She admitted to herself she liked fitting in a lot more than explaining her time travel. She had put off telling her tale too long. With no time to explain to Charissa and Elric before they left on their wedding trip this morning, she would hug them hard today. She hoped they would remember her love for them once Elena spilled the beans after Ashley disappeared.

"*Whoa*, slow down. Lots of questions there, Elena. I can't answer all of them yet, so we'll have to talk later." Ashley's transformation from sleepyhead to well-dressed lady had been quick. She ran a hand down the side of her dress and smoothed it across her hips. She didn't look half bad.

∞∞∞

Elric and Charissa were all smiles, attending court like royalty, when Ashley and Elena got to the great hall, both out of breath.

Charissa spotted Ashley and grinned widely. "'Tis time you made it down. I thought mayhap I would leave without seeing you to say farewell."

"Oh no, you wouldn't do that." Ashley cringed, thinking that was exactly what she would do soon to Charissa. She ran to her friend and squeezed her hard, lifting her up off her feet and rocking her back and forth. Tears popped into her eyes as she let Charissa go, turning away to hide her distress. Elric was too perceptive and reminded her gently, "Lady Ashley, 'tis only for a fortnight. We shall be back before you know it." *Ah, if he only knew,* Ashley thought.

According to Charissa, the plan was to spend some time by themselves in one of Mowbray's manor houses, taking time to get to know one another. Then they planned to live at Hertford Castle until Mowbray built them a place of their own. He promised his men would provide protection for the young couple as part of Charissa's dowry. Their life together was off to a grand start. Would she and Robert ever be so lucky?

"I'm sure you're right." Ashley wiped the wet from her face with the back of her hand. "But I'll miss you both." She hugged Elric and whispered in his ear, "Take care of yourselves, okay? I love you both." Stepping back she chewed her lip to keep her composure, but her chin quivered, giving her away.

Robert stood solemnly beside her and witnessed her tender goodbyes to his brother and Charissa. His face told her he digested the real meaning of her words. He reached out and pulled her back to his chest, his arms encircling her as they stood facing the newlyweds. Ashley relaxed into him, re-assured by the strength and security she felt in his touch.

The bailey erupted in activity as Mowbray's men arrived to pack up the trunks and escort the newlyweds to their honeymoon haven. Afterward, the soldiers would come back to Hertford to escort the Earl of Mowbray to his home.

Much laughter, hugging, crying and teasing ensued as the inhabitants of the castle lined up to say their farewells. The procession finally formed and rode out through the portcullis, with Charissa and Elric waving to their friends until they were out of sight.

Lady Margaret dabbed at her eyes, although there were no visible tears, and left on the arm of her brother. Looking now like wilted flowers, Elena and Ashley were left standing with Robert on the steps of the bailey.

"I am rather sad," Elena commented, her brow puckering. "I should be happy for them, and instead I am lonely." She turned to Robert and Ashley. "And then you two will likely desert me. Whatever will I do?"

Robert smiled wanly at his sister before rolling his eyes at Ashley for her response. Ashley said reluctantly, "I have much to tell you both and I don't want to be interrupted. Where can we go to talk?"

"An *intrigue*," Elena smiled. "Precisely what I need to pick up my spirits." Elena's face flushed with pleasure.

"Let us go for a ride, my ladies. I have need to get out in the open myself."

"That's an excellent idea, Robert." Ashley watched his face, unsure of his mood.

"I will tell cook to pack us food left from the wedding, and we can stop for a picnic." Elena's eyes were glowing. "I missed the last one when I hurt my ankle again. Remember?"

"I do," Robert and Ashley replied at the same time. They laughed along with Elena, but in truth, falling in love with each other at the lodge had been unforgettable.

The three agreed to meet a short time later at the stable.

Robert headed in that direction to secure the horses, while Ashley and Elena went to the kitchen to make arrangements for their lunch.

"This will be such *fun*." Elena was delighted and skipped ahead of Ashley in her excitement over the day's plans. Ashley just gave her a lopsided grin, wishing with all her heart it wouldn't crush her friend when she heard what she and Robert had to tell her.

∞∞∞

The day was blue-sky fresh with barely enough breeze to keep the puffy white clouds from gathering and the warm day from being hot. Ashley enjoyed the ride immensely. With no more censuring looks from the earl and Lady Margaret to endure, she relaxed for the first time in what seemed like forever. Well, to be exact, the first time since the Baron of Bedford had entered her world. She breathed easier now he was gone.

Ashley glanced at Robert riding next to her on his big stallion, and her heart flip-flopped. Unbelievably handsome as he sat tall in the saddle, Robert made the guys like Alex from Uncle Zeek's dig look like little boys.

Robert was huge, well over six feet, with more muscles than a body builder. He was tanned, with sun-streaked golden hair that always fell into his hazel eyes. Feeling her gaze upon him, he turned and their eyes locked, his intense expression scorching her to her toes. Grinning back at him like a giddy fool, she knew she was in love.

She could not explain the hold he had over her in any other way. This specimen of all things manly wanted her. How insane was that? Without a doubt she had taken advantage of the lack of female competition here to gain and hold Robert's attention.

But in truth, it was more than that, because she affected

him the same way he affected her. It started the first time he laid a finger on her all those days ago when she gave him the ceremonial stirrup cup, and it was true today. So, if they were meant to be, then a way for them to stay together must exist. Right?

Robert leaned over and held his hand out, palm up, with a silent request for her to put her hand in his. Ashley obliged, smiling ear to ear. Why was it he made soup of her heart every time he touched her? Their horses plodded along in a peaceful rhythm, side by side, held together by the joined hands of their riders. No one was in a hurry today.

"You are beautiful, my love," he crooned. Ashley glanced ahead, not wanting Elena to hear him. *Bless her.* She rode far enough ahead to give them some privacy. Ashley felt her smile widen even more. "Thank you, my handsome lord." Robert liked that.

"What is it you wanted to tell me?"

"After you left last night I ran across Meggie and Alice. Remember them?"

Robert chuckled, "Aye, the sisters who scrap with one another unceasingly."

"Well, I asked them to try to find out Cedric's whereabouts."

Robert tensed. "And did they?"

"They sure did," she replied smugly, certain she was very clever to have confirmed Cedric's location.

"Cedric is not with Olde Gylda of Hampshire, is he?" Trepidation shook his voice.

"Why, yes! How ever did you know that?" Cedric had warned her not to share his destination with anyone else, and she had kept her promise. Had Robert found Cedric and not told her?

∞∞∞

Robert felt a sharp pulsing in his temple. Cedric had been at Olde Gylda's in his dream. How *had* he known that? Wasn't Cedric supposed to be on a mission to gather his herbs and such? Had anyone mentioned Olde Gylda? He knew not. In his dream Cedric had been standing by Gylda when Ashley disappeared.

This was too much of a coincidence. He was well acquainted with Gylda who had worked beside Cedric at the castle until his father dismissed her for practicing the Dark Arts. Robert suspected his father had been terrified of her when she so accurately predicted a farming loss. The earl feared Gylda had arranged that loss, and he had been nervous enough to get rid of her.

Gylda was Cedric's friend and ally, so perhaps it was not such a strange linkage for him to make in a dream, but still ... He realized Ashley was waiting for him to say something. *"Hmm,* 'tis not too surprising as they are old friends." He decided to say nothing about his dream to Ashley.

"Oh," Ashley appeared crestfallen over her news being stolen but recovered. "Well, then you must know where she lives, right?"

Robert *did* know where she lived, but he was loath to take Ashley there so soon. He wanted to put off this search for the stone as long as possible. If he delayed her attempt to go home, they might be able to talk his father into allowing them to marry. Maybe then she would not want to go home. Cedric may not have found the stone yet, or at least it did not sound like it, so perhaps there would be time to change her mind about using it.

"Yes, Ashley, I do," he said, unable to lie to her. "'Tis about a day's ride from here."

"Perfect!" Ashley bounced with excitement on her saddle. "When can we go? I wonder if Cedric and Gylda have found the stone?"

"God's teeth, Ashley. Are you so very excited to go home?" Robert snapped. Ashley trembled, making Robert instantly

sorry for being so sharp with her. He groaned and shook his head. "I am sorry, Ashley. Please forgive me."

"No, Robert, I'm sorry," Ashley countered. "It was rude of me to be so insensitive." She paused a moment. "Remember your dad told us we couldn't marry until Cedric came back, so there is that."

"Aye, 'tis not Cedric that bothers me. I must tell you I have grave reservations about your use of the stone to go home. I do not want you to go anywhere. Having found you I now must fight to keep you." He met her eyes with another searing look of desire. "Why would I want to let you go, even if it is to your own home?" Ashley's eyes were glued to his face when he told her the real problem, "What if you go, and I never see you again?"

Ashley, pale and stricken, found no words to say. Luckily, Elena broke the tension by turning around in her saddle and calling out, "Look over there. 'Tis a splendid place for a picnic. What think you?"

Ashley tore her eyes from Robert's long enough to examine the area around her. "It's a beautiful spot, Elena." Addressing Robert, she added, "We do need to talk, don't we?" He nodded as they turned off the dusty road into a clearing in the woods bursting with wildflowers.

Elena was in shock. For a day starting out with such promise after the departure of Elric and Charissa, it had turned out to be anything but fun. As the threesome settled down to enjoy a tasty luncheon, Ashley had given Robert a meaningful nod before announcing she had something important to tell Elena. Thinking it had something to do with Ashley's relationship with Robert, Elena had answered agreeably. How could that be bad?

Never had she thought Ashley would tell her she was from a time 650 years in the future. She struggled to understand. True, Ashley was different from any other girl of Elena's acquaintance. Yes, she possessed knowledge of things no one else did. Still, who would dream she was from a different point in time?

Elena watched in fascination mixed with awe as Ashley pulled out the items she carried with her in the pouch around her waist. Elena had always wondered what was in there, but never thought it her place to ask.

Her jaw hit her chest when Ashley showed her the moving picture of her own father and the baron. What flummoxed her even more were the pictures of Ashley's family and friends. They were of a life she had trouble imagining.

When Robert explained how Ashley had accidentally fallen into their world, the final puzzle piece fell into place. At last Elena understood all of what Cedric had seen before a "female near her age" arrived at the castle. Ashley told of her search for the stone that would allow her to travel back to her home, and why it was necessary for her to do so.

Tension radiated between Robert and Ashley over this stone and Elena knew she needed to give them a chance to talk without her around. She left them with the remnants of lunch having lost her appetite. Finding a comfortable spot nearby on the shore of a burbling creek, she sat and contemplated what this revelation might mean for her and those she loved.

∞∞∞

Robert sat with his back against an ancient looking sweet chestnut tree, holding Ashley's head in his lap. Examining the size of the tree, he thought they could live in the enormous hollow of its trunk if necessary. Mayhap then they could leave their troubles behind and be together. Ashley held one of his hands and periodically kissed his fingers as she talked to him. He enjoyed her attention, but he was not happy. He may not entirely understand her need to go home to see her family, but he did try.

"Robert, it's something like this. Your mother has been gone for a number of years, hasn't she?" He raised his eyebrows, questioning the direction of her thoughts. "If you had a chance to go back in time to see her, to talk with her, to tell her you love her, would you do it?"

He thought about that for a while and decided her line of reasoning was understandable. She had not said goodbye to her mother. Ashley was all too aware of the pain her mother had suffered by not knowing what had happened to her father.

All that was nice of her and very much in keeping with Ashley's character, he thought. However, it still did not address the question of whether or not it would work as they imagined. What would he do if she did not return?

"I understand what you say in my head, but my heart does not." He pulled Ashley up into a sitting position and placed her in his lap, planting a passionate kiss on her lips. "I cannot let you attempt this if we cannot get assurances from Cedric and Olde Gylda that you can truly go home, and more importantly, return to me. If they are even a little more unsure of the workings of the stone than you or I, I shall not let you go."

Robert was not sure if his possessive words pleased Ashley or not when she bit her tongue and stifled a quick reply. He was upset and she seemed to respect that.

"I hear what you are saying, but I have to try, Robert."

"There is no point in arguing further. We will know not what the real situation brings until we find Cedric and Gylda. Promise me, sweeting, you will listen and not charge ahead with this until you understand all the dangers involved." Silently, he prayed he could thwart the discovery of the stone. As lacking in honor as that might be, there would then be no question of her leaving.

"Sure. Fighting won't help and we can cross those bridges

when we get to them."

"Now," Robert teased, "show me how much you love me."

Only Elena's presence kept Ashley from a complete demonstration of that demand.

∞∞∞

On their ride home, Robert and Elena discussed ways to make their escape from the castle in order to get on the road to find Cedric and Olde Gylda. Ashley made no attempt to hide her smile at their duplicitous talk. Had she really been such a bad influence on the two of them or had they always been like this?

When they met the earl for the evening meal back at Hertford Castle, he dropped a bombshell on them. Because his estate business had suffered neglect too long with all the visitors and festivities, he would be gone a fortnight to London to take care of several matters. With much difficulty, all three of them stifled their responses to his news. Ashley wanted to *whoop-whoop* her delight to the rafters. Instead, she clamped down on the inside of her cheeks and refused to look at either Robert or Elena for a full five minutes.

The earl left Robert in charge and cautioned them Lady Margaret would be watching Elena and Ashley, so they needed to stay close and mind her. *That's not gonna happen.* This would be her best opportunity to sneak away, and once gone, Lady Margaret would be able to do nothing about it for the full two weeks. By then Ashley's dilemma would be solved one way or another. Either she would be gone for good, or she would come back with the stone's help and marry Robert. Lady Margaret would not be able to stop any part of their plan this time. It was perfect.

The earl left before dawn the next morning, having said his goodbyes the night before. It would take his entourage three days to reach London. Even though he expected to encounter no difficulties on the road, he took with him a unit of ten men for protection.

Elena and Ashley awoke bright and early and packed lightly for their trip. They might have to stay with Olde Gylda for a night or two since it would take a full day to get to her place and a full day back.

Ashley was lost in thought as she filled her bag with the few necessities she would need. She made sure her own clothes were in the bag and her other possessions attached at her waist.

Looking around the room, she remembered her first night and what a scared little rabbit she had been. How much she had learned about life here in the time since. She had found true friends and a true love. A tear rolled down her cheek and she brushed it away with the back of her hand. She hated good-byes. What if she were never to see this place and its people again? She shook off her reverie and decided to simply not think about it now. It was too painful to contemplate at the moment.

∞ ∞ ∞

As Ashley, Elena, and Robert sat at a trestle table in the great hall breaking their fast with fresh-baked bread and honeyed mead, Lady Margaret joined them. Robert cocked his verbal arrow and announced to her he would be touring tenant farms on the northeast side of Hertford land. Her eyebrows shot up to within an inch of her widow's peak at this information, but she held her tongue and listened to Robert. Their steward Jeffries would cover for Robert, and Captain Giddings and his men would guard the castle in his absence.

Lady Margaret was quite surprised to hear Robert planned to leave so soon after his father. When Robert recommended she watch over Hertford Castle for him, her eyes narrowed in suspicion.

It was then Robert let fly his arrow.

"Lady Margaret, I must inform you Lady Elena and Lady Ashley will be traveling with me."

"No-o-o!" shrieked Lady Margaret, her eyes flashing from one errant child to the next. "You cannot mean that, my lord. 'Tis not proper for the young ladies."

"Aye, my lady. You are welcome to come with us if you wish to chaperone them to your satisfaction." Robert was quite sure she would reject this notion, and he was not disappointed. As expected, after only a moment's thought, Lady Margaret was all too happy to pluck that arrow from her conscience and toss it to the floor.

"Nay, I cannot shirk my duties here, my lord, especially if all of you are gone. Who would make sure everyone is fed and cared for if I were to go?" Thank you, my lady, for being so predictable, Robert thought, smiling to himself.

"An excellent point, my lady," Robert concurred with as solemn a face as he could muster. "My sister will serve as chaperone for my betrothed, and the two of them wish to do some shopping for our wedding in the villages we will pass through. We shall take men with us, as did my father, to be safe. You need not worry about us." He gave his aunt his most engaging smile. "I am sure you will attend the castle well in our absence, Lady Margaret, and for that I am in your debt." Robert rose and gave her a sweeping bow to seal the deal. The older woman could never withstand his charm when it was turned on her full blast. True to form, she put up less fuss than any of them imagined possible.

Walking back to her chamber to pick up her things for the trip, Ashley was amazed that going home was closer than ever. She couldn't decide if that was good or bad. How would this end?

A shudder ripped through her at that last thought, prompting a quote from *Julius Caesar* to flash through her mind. *"O! that a man might know the end of this day's business, ere it come; but it sufficeth that the day will end, and then the end is known."*

She had been forced to memorize it for a big Shakespeare test in Mrs. Welch's class when she was a sophomore in high school. Funny how it was all but meaningless to her then, but pretty much spelled out her situation now. Well, it might be more than a day before her fate would be decided, but, undoubtedly, she would know it soon.

But which way did she want it to go?

Chapter 30

The morning had been way too long for Ashley. Not an experienced horsewoman like Elena, she was unused to long hours in a saddle, especially a sidesaddle. By the time they stopped at The Bramble Inn in the village of Rickmansworth, she was so sore Robert had to lift her down from her mare. Her limbs had long since given up any hint of sensation.

They walked about the main street to help her legs revive as well as to check out the shops. It was the first time Ashley had been in a village like this, and she was quite taken with what she saw. Always a dedicated shopper, she wanted to go into every shop on the street, much to the delight of Robert who told her to take her time looking.

Elena did the opposite. She admonished Ashley, explaining they would not arrive at Olde Gylda's by nightfall if they dallied in the stores. Ashley was confused when Robert glared at his sister like he wanted to clap a hand over her mouth to shut her up. What was that about?

Ashley struggled to take her eyes off an interesting small shop filled with curiosities, but nodded in agreement with Elena. Unexplored treasures beckoned to be found there, and perhaps one day she would get to search for them. For now, she knew they needed to move on.

As they strolled about town before they mounted to depart, Ashley noted people watched her more than they did Elena or Robert. Why? She didn't think she was doing anything they were not, so why were people watching *her*? Perhaps they were unused to strangers in their town and it was all her imagination.

"We shall eat and rest awhile at The Bramble and then be on our way," Robert said.

"ASAP," Elena added. When Robert frowned at his sister like she was speaking jibberish, Ashley giggled and explained the acronym.

"*Ah,* I should have known that came from you. You have always something new to share." Robert hugged her shoulders, savoring every touch and burning it into his memory. "'Tis why I want to keep you close." He gave the end of her nose a kiss and opened the rough-hewn door of the dilapidated inn, unleashing an odor that was hard to place. A mixture of dirt, sweat, food and ale whooshed up Ashley's nose, revolting and enticing at the same time.

It was dark inside even though the sun was shining brightly outside. Nonetheless, Ashley felt all the eyes of the patrons inside move to take stock of them the moment they entered. She was glad Robert was with them. The Hertford soldiers had chosen to dine at the tables placed in the inn yard under a shady oak near the front door. They would be well protected should anyone bother them.

As her eyes adjusted to the gloom, Ashley saw only a handful of other folks scattered around the room eating their midday fill. Most of them seemed to lose interest once they walked inside. Only a disheveled looking chap bent over a tankard in the back followed them with his droopy eyes as they found a place to sit. It was clear after a moment he was leering at Ashley and Elena.

Robert seated them so their backs were to the man, but Ashley saw Robert glare a challenge to the guy. A short time later, Robert winked at her and reported the man had wisely found his food more fascinating than ogling her and Elena.

Robert ordered a venison stew to be brought to the table. Soon, the serving wench, a haggard looking woman of indeterminate age, plopped a pot of stew in the middle of the table. She placed what Robert called a "bread trencher" and a tankard of ale in front of each of them, wiped her hands on her soiled apron and left.

Ashley picked up her rectangular slice of bread only to be disappointed and comment that it seemed quite stale. It was not until Elena showed her how the trencher was used like a spoon for the stew that she understood its purpose. As Elena explained it, the bread had to be hard or it would fall apart in the stew gravy. Once Ashley got the hang of it, it worked well enough. It was a tad sloppy, but did the job. They ate the surprisingly savory stew and were back on the road a short time later. Ashley was happy to be out in the sunshine once more, but Robert had grown quiet.

∞∞∞

Leaving the tiny town behind, they had traveled only a mile or two when Elena pulled her horse to a stop without warning. Everyone else had no choice but to do the same. Her action created a pileup that careened through the unit of men behind her causing the huge warhorses to neigh and stomp their annoyance.

"Robert?" Elena's voice held a mildly accusatory tone. "I believe we are headed in the wrong direction. This road goes to Stoke Poges and we want to go toward Kettering."

God's blood.

Must his little sister always know everything? Of course, she was right. He had followed the wrong road from the inn on purpose thinking perhaps it would be nice to wander for a while. He had made sure they had tents and plenty of food with them before they left Hertford. Now he wanted nothing more than a night with Ashley to himself before he had to give her up, mayhap forever.

Robert pretended to survey the road and the countryside before feigning to agree with his sister. "Right you are, Elena."

He turned to Ashley who had cocked her head and was eyeing him with a raised brow. "'Tis but a mistake, Lady Ashley. No need to stare at me in that manner." He was out of sorts and it showed despite his best efforts.

"I'm sure it's an accident, Robert. I was just waggling an eye at you to get your attention." Ashley delivered an exaggerated eye waggle that made him burst out laughing.

"Aye, so you were, sweeting! My attention is all yours now." Robert leaned over and gave her a quick kiss on the cheek, making her mare skitter sideways and Lucifer dance. Elena guffawed at their antics and the unit turned around rather unceremoniously amidst nudges and nickers, before heading back to Rickmansworth.

Once back on the right road, the day moved on much faster than he wished. After only a short time, Ashley declared, "Meggie and Alice's rickety old cart seems like a better option than this mare." When she tried to stretch her legs, she whined, "Ow! I don't believe I'll be able to walk once we get to Gylda's place. My legs are numb." Catching Robert's eye, she batted her own at him, adding with false innocence, "Will you carry me then, my love?"

Robert happily took pity on her and pulled her onto his horse so she could ride sitting across his lap for a while. He tied Ashley's mare with a loose rein to his saddle and let the gray mare tag along behind the much larger stallion.

It was hard telling who enjoyed this interlude more. To his mind, Ashley reveled at being in his arms as much as he loved the feel of her in his. Elena teased the lovesick pair at every turn for their obvious delight with one other.

Entering Ravensthorpe at dusk, Robert halted their unit. They were still a few miles from Olde Gylda's cottage and it would be dark before they could get there. Perhaps his sidetracking of their party had done its job after all. He knew of a good inn nearby that could house them in comfort for the night.

The Hertford soldiers were left to camp outside the village and remain encamped until further orders. Robert did not want the men to accompany them to Gylda's place. He wanted no witnesses to what the wizards might do regarding Ashley's disappearance if it came to that.

Once their horses were cared for in the mews, he walked Ashley and Elena to the front of the Quiet Woman Inn. All was well until Elena and Ashley saw the sign swinging above the door to the place. The quiet woman pictured on the sign was quiet for a very good reason: she was carrying her own severed head.

"What kind of advertisement is that," Ashley cried in disbelief.

"What an odd name, brother. Are you sure this is an appropriate place to stay?"

Robert threw his head back and barked a laugh. "I had forgotten about the sign. As the story was told to me, the innkeeper had a shrew for a wife. When she passed on--of natural causes, they say--no one was left to argue with him over the sign."

"Well, we must be quiet then, indeed." Elena drew herself up to her full height with mock severity.

"As long as no headless female joins us in our beds, I guess it'll be okay," Ashley croaked, grasping her neck with both hands as if to prevent it from being lopped off.

"I shall insist on adjoining rooms so you ladies may sleep without fear. I will be on guard." Robert struck a pose for a moment, flexing his arm muscles in a twitchy dance to demonstrate his prowess.

Ashley fluttered her eyes and responded with a high, breathy voice, "Oh, thank you, Lord Robert. We shall be evah so safe." She grinned and retuned to her normal voice, "Besides, whatever it is they're roasting smells scrumptious."

Robert's eyes twinkled in amusement as he held the door for Ashley and Elena. "Lady Ashley, 'tis hard to imagine you afraid of anything."

Ashley scowled, her first thought of Abasi, but that was

back home. She scrunched one side of her face for a moment until she knew just what to say. Focusing a wicked grin on Elena, she said, "Rats. I'm not fond of rats." That sent Elena into giggles and Ashley soon joined her. They told Robert in fits and starts about the army of rats that scurried around on the escape stairs from Elena's room.

"And did you know, Robert, your stable rats are bigger than your foot?" Ashley relished Robert's horrified expression. "You didn't? Oh, your sister loved terrorizing me with that whopper."

Elena blinked her eyes in an attempt to play innocent which made Ashley snort.

Robert shook his head at their silliness. "Let us eat now and call it an early night." Then he touched the sore spot no one wanted to talk about. "We should arrive at Olde Gylda's cottage before noon tomorrow if we get an early start."

Somberness ruled after that. Robert discussed their room requirements with the innkeeper and handed the impatient Elena the key to the room she was to share with Ashley. He sidled up to his intended and whispered, "Our chambers do adjoin. Will you come to me once Elena falls asleep?"

Before Ashley could reply, Elena grabbed her hand and tugged her toward the stairs to their room. "Come, Ashley, I cannot wait to wash the dust from my face." She called to her brother over her shoulder, "We shall hurry and join you here for dinner ASAP."

∞∞∞

Ashley was not sorry Elena pulled her away. She needed time to think. Not about whether she loved Robert. That was not the issue; it was the problem. How could she control her emotions with Robert when she really wanted to love him heart, soul, and body?

That last was a giant step. Could she risk placing a baby in the mix if she weren't sure she could go home to Texas and return safely? Would it harm the child to be transported that way? Her insides had felt like they'd been whirled in a blender before. What would it do if she were carrying a child? Ashley turned and looked over her shoulder in time to catch the dark look on Robert's face. Her heart ached for him. None of this was easy for either of them. She vowed to go and at least re-assure him of her love after Elena fell asleep. How could she stay away?

Their room smelled of freshly waxed wood mixed with fresh linen. It was a soothing scent. As Ashley and Elena read-ied themselves for bed, Ashley asked the question that had bugged her all day. "Elena, did you notice when we were out and about the villages today, people watched me more than you or Robert?

Elena smiled, "As a matter of fact, I did. I wondered if *you* had noticed."

Interesting, Ashley thought. "Was I doing something wrong to make everyone's eyes follow me? I thought I blended in."

Elena laughed, "Well, dear Ashley, you are far too beautiful to blend in, as you put it."

"But you are more beautiful than I'll ever be, Elena, so why me?"

"*Ah,* thank you, Ashley, but 'tis more than that." She was thoughtful for a moment and then began as though she had finally selected the right thread to weave. "'Tis not only the fact you are a glowing, beautiful woman who happens to be in love. 'Tis more. You project an air of confidence for a woman such as I have never seen before and I suspect others have not either."

Ashley still looked puzzled.

"You stride about in steps I must run to match and you look men in the eye like you are their equal--something I was taught not to do." Ashley nodded her understanding as Elena added, "I think men are not quite sure what to make of you and women are fascinated by you."

"I see." Ashley understood now what Elena meant. "In the world I'm from, women have the same rights as men do. They vote, they can hold political office, own property, work pretty much any job a man works, and support themselves, if need be. Women are not considered the property of men."

Elena's mouth had dropped open, and her eyes darted about as if racing to comprehend this information. *"What kind of world that must be.* I cannot even dream of a life where I would be thought equal to Robert and Elric."

"Well, women are in my world, or at least they're supposed to be. I do consider myself equal to men, so I guess it shows in how I see the world."

"But who protects you?"

"For the most part we live in a law-abiding society. There are many more of us in our towns and cities than there are of you here in England. When needed, our police chase down the bad guys and keep us safe--men and women alike. The only real warriors are enlisted soldiers who fight for our country when necessary. The sad thing is unlike here, we don't even have to be in the same part of the world as our enemies to do them in. Over the ages mankind has developed all kinds of ways to attack their foes, but that story I'll save for another day."

The girls scrambled into bed, still thinking about their conversation. "Ashley? You do realize Robert will want to possess you, do you not?"

"Yeah, I know. I gotta admit, though, when Robert is doing the possessing, and not Damien, I rather like it."

"Oh my, why am I not surprised? You never do or say what I think you will. Goodnight, my friend."

"'Night, Elena. And thanks for the explanation. You've given me a lot to think about."

"You have given *me* much to think on. Women equal to men? Can it be?"

∞∞∞

"Robert?"

Hidden under the covers his body jerked at the sound of Ashley's whispered voice. Had he fallen asleep fearing she had decided not to come? Feeling shy, she had only smiled at him after dinner without committing to anything. When he again murmured in her ear his wish for her to come to him, her fears had vanished. Yet it had taken most of her nerve to come this far.

"Over here," he called through the dark room, returning her whisper with one of his own. He sat up in bed and held his hands out to her in invitation. Wearing but her thin chemise, Ashley scampered across the wood floor to Robert and let him enfold her in his arms. She shivered, so he tucked her under the covers next to his warm body. Was the shiver from cold or anticipation of being with him? She wasn't sure.

Ashley snuggled down next to him, fitting her body against his. She inhaled his distinctive, delicious scent of mint and the outdoors, when a sudden realization struck her.

"Robert! *You're naked!"* Her intended whisper bordered on a shriek.

"Shhh, Ashley, you will wake the dead, if you take not a care. Of course I am naked. Did you think I slept in a chemise too?" he snickered. "I must say, however, the thinness of *your* chemise pleases me." He pressed his hands over her breasts, shaping them for emphasis.

She tried to bring her voice down. "But that's not fair, Robert. You *knew* I would come to you."

"Hmm, I *hoped* you would come to me, Ashley, but I *knew* it not. Still, are you not happy here with me?" His breath blew puffs of air across her face as he smoothed a hand along her hip.

"That's just what I mean, you evil man. I can never resist

you, yet here you are, temptation in the flesh." Robert smirked his satisfaction with her answer.

"Have you forgotten, sir, we cannot risk satisfying our lustful selves right now?" Robert grimaced at the reminder, pulling her closer.

"How could I forget? I want to marry you, Ashley. *I love you. Is that so bad?*" he growled into her ear. "I want you to be mine, so we can be naked in my bed any time we choose."

Ashley's resistance melted into mush with his words. She clung to him, drawn like a bee to nectar, yet a niggling thought in her brain still persisted. Frantically, she searched for that thought hiding behind her desire and plucked it out. "Robert," she sighed, still stroking his arms as he trailed soft kisses over her neck and her breasts. "I love you, too, but we can't marry right now ... and until this little business of our being from two different worlds is settled ... "

Robert ignored her. Ashley was having great difficulty maintaining her thought as his lips reversed their path, moving back up her throat to her lips. She had so much more to say, but her thoughts floated away on the wings of Robert's butterfly kisses. Some time later she snatched the elusive thought as it drifted back. "We ... we can't let a child come of this. What if we are stuck in two different worlds?" He kissed both her eyelids, which seemed to make her thoughts disintegrate again into thin air. Breathing hard, she pulled the last thought together with a valiant effort. "We can't ... "

Robert covered her mouth with his and deepened the kiss. She surrendered to the moment until Robert pulled back and groaned. "You are right," he breathed. "But let me hold you. I must remember the feel and the smell and the taste of you." He let out a heartfelt sigh, gathered her in his arms, and stroked her hair. Ashley shared his pain and wanted to cry, hating the stress she was putting on their relationship.

Rising up on one elbow, Robert framed her face with strong but gentle hands. "If you must go away for a time and I cannot yet have you, I want to always recall what it is like to hold you this way."

Her words slipped out of her grasp like sand, so she reached up and pulled his lips down to hers and answered with her heart. It was torture, indeed, to be so close yet so unsatisfied.

"Ashley? Robert?"

Elena's frazzled voice drifted into the room. Abruptly, Robert and Ashley crashed back to earth. Struggling to comprehend the intrusion, they were mortified to be caught by Elena in the midst of such a heated moment.

"I do not wish to interrupt," Elena began, embarrassment making her voice quaver, "but there is a man banging on my door to the hallway. I will not open it, and he will not leave."

That got Robert's attention, so Elena ducked back into her room. Robert rolled his long body over Ashley in one graceful move, landing catlike on the cold wood floor. He paused to pull on breeches before soundlessly crossing the dark room to his sister's side. Ashley found her feet a moment later and joined them, any pretense over their previous activity forgotten.

Moving through the adjoining door and into the girls' room, they heard the persistent pounding and a harsh voice taunting them.

"Open up, little ladies, open up! Ye wants to, ye do. I 'ave somethin' *big* to share wit ye." A man's raspy voice cackled at his own vulgar joke.

Robert motioned to Elena and Ashley to stand back. Then he threw open the door to reveal a ragged, disheveled man with his grubby hand raised to bang on the door again. A moment passed before they all recognized him as the droopy-eyed man who had ogled Elena and Ashley back at The Bramble. All three were shocked to think this man had followed them from their lunch stop at the inn. In the torchlight of the hall he drunkenly swayed on his feet and turned a green color as Robert's powerful, half-naked body loomed over him.

In one swift move, Robert hooked the man's chin with an upper cut and sent him sprawling with a thud to the hall floor.

Robert grinned over his shoulder at the two ladies behind him who were still standing in the doorway gaping at the flattened intruder. "You can shut your mouths now, *little ladies*, and get some rest," he teased with a guffaw. "I think this one will bother you no more tonight." He hoisted the limp man over his shoulder and took off down the hall saying he would dispose of the fool by dumping him outside.

Elena and Ashley looked at each other wide-eyed and then burst into laughter.

"I told you people found you fascinating, dear friend. Now look what followed you home."

"Yeah, thanks a lot for that kind thought. He was following *you* home, too. After all, I think his words were addressed to some 'little ladies,' were they not?"

They jumped back into bed, still giggling over the ridiculous, drunken man.

"Who would have guessed he'd show up here in the middle of the night?"

"Oh, forgive me, Ashley. I am sorry I disturbed you and Robert earlier. I was afraid and unsure of what else to do."

Ashley loosed a shaky sigh, remembering that moment. "I'm glad you interrupted us. I don't know what would have happened had you not come when you did, but I believe I would have been unhappy about it in the morning."

"Truly?" Elena did not sound convinced.

"Truly. I love Robert with all my heart and soul, so how can I tell my body not to follow suit?" A hint of anguish rode the groan Ashley emitted. She ached for Robert's touch. "It's just not the right time. Our search for the stone is not over."

"*Ah,* the stone. Of course. And what thinks Robert of all this?"

"Robert just wants to be married and forget there ever was such a thing."

"Would that be so bad, Ashley?"

"Of course not! But I have to try to go back home. If I don't, I will always wonder if I should have. I don't want to suffer guilt the rest of my life for not trying to find my way back home. I miss my mother and my brother. I want to tell them all about my life here so they understand why I have to return."

Elena let that sink in. "You will try equally hard to come back, will you not?"

"I will, Elena. I have family I love in *both* places."

Chapter 31

The next morning spirits were as dreary as the day that dawned. A fine mist further dampened everyone's desire to dress, eat and be on the road to Olde Gylda's cottage. When Elena attempted to be cheerful, Ashley could not respond in kind, and Robert was all but mute, so she quieted and let him be.

With only a few miles to ride, and without the extra men along, they would make good time ... only no one wanted to make good time. With every glance at Robert, Ashley's determination to find the stone and go back home took another hit. Soon her wariness over finding Cedric and Olde Gylda almost matched Robert's.

They plodded along in silence, Elena in the lead followed by Ashley and Robert, riding side by side. Ashley knew Elena wanted to give them as much privacy as possible in their last hours together. Always the sweetheart, she kept her eyes trained on the road ahead.

Each held out some hope the stone had not been found, but all feared jinxing themselves if they talked of it. Having grown up with Olde Gylda at the castle, both Robert and Elena believed it would be akin to false hope to talk of never locating the stone. She might appear to be a harmless old crone, but Gylda's powerful magic far surpassed Cedric's abilities.

As early morning made way for mid-day, the mist burned off and cleared the sky for a bright yellow sun to shine against a sea of baby blue. Ashley's spirits rose with the sun and she began to feel sure of her plans. Her confidence built with each dainty hoof the mare placed on the narrow trail. By the time they neared Olde Gylda's cottage, a smile played in the corners of her mouth.

She worked to freeze-frame in her mind the sight of Robert riding beside her, but she reminded herself she could go one step better than that. She could take out her phone and snap a picture of him. She had never laid eyes on a man as handsome as Robert. She fumbled in her bag for the phone, unwilling to take her eyes off him to search for it properly. At that moment, he gave her a woeful frown and she smiled at him, "Aw, Robert, no need to be so down in the mouth. Nothing is gained by delaying the inevitable. The sooner I go home and talk to my family, the sooner I'll be back."

Robert tried to answer her chipper ribbing with a grin of his own, but his face was not up to the task. The overall result was more of a grimace than a grin. "'Tis what I keep telling myself, sweeting, but 'tis hard to make my head listen when my heart fears otherwise."

Thrusting her hand out for Robert to take, Ashley felt the strength of his grip as his hand grasped hers securely across the distance between their mounts. "Never fear, Robert. I will be back."

This time when their eyes met, he smiled that lopsided smile she so loved. "I believe you, my love. I believe you."

That tightness in her chest might just be her heart swelling. Could he be more beautiful? Her mare stepped too far away and Robert let go of her hand for a moment. Geez, there it was again. Robert flashed that adorable lopsided grin at her as she awkwardly regained her balance.

Wait. The camera.

She dug in the pouch tied at her waist and pulled out her phone.

Snap. Ha. She'd keep that to remember him by. Startled, Robert began to laugh when he understood what she had done. "Taking a bit of me with you, I see."

"I wish I could take *all* of you with me so I'd never have to leave you." She turned off the phone and tucked it back into her bag. "I promise I will look at it every day to remind myself how wonderful you are."

That pleased him. Robert reached over and plucked Ashley from her horse as easily as if she were a piece of low hanging fruit. He pulled her to him with the express purpose of taking a bite out of her. She giggled and sighed with happiness as Robert nuzzled the sensitive spot behind her ear. *This is exactly where I want to be.*

"Alright, 'tis sorry I am to break up you love birds, but I believe that little cottage there in the distance is Olde Gylda's, is it not, Robert?

Reluctantly, Robert let his eyes follow where Elena pointed and confirmed it was, indeed, Gylda's place. Ashley moved as if to return to her mare, but Robert stopped her with an iron grip on her waist. "No, love, I cannot let you go yet." His voice sounded firm, but gentle in her ear. "Not yet." Anxiety knifed its way through her body at the thought of the separation to come. Ashley said not a word, only nodded and snuggled tighter against his chest.

∞∞∞

Nestled into a valley not far from the road, Olde Gylda of Hampshire's cottage sat in an isolated but picturesque spot. A sharp, rocky rise on one side swooped into the valley with grasses in shades of green and beige covering the low treeless hills surrounding the cottage. Yellow wildflowers grew in thick patches like fat polka dots on the landscape. It was a happy place. Not the kind one would pick for a witch, Ashley thought.

As they approached the cottage, Ashley took a good look at the house and convinced herself she was not seeing it clearly. It seemed to be a ridiculously small stone cottage, despite its two stories. Multiple chimneys stuck out at weird angles atop the thatched roof as though many fireplaces were housed within. That struck Ashley as odd since the house didn't appear big enough for more than one room on each floor. The door was cocked at an angle with freeform windows on either side. The proportions of the cottage were severely off. It was like looking at something M.C. Escher would have drawn--an interesting but impossible structure, to be sure.

Elena's horse whinnied as if announcing their arrival, and moments later Olde Gylda stepped out of the crooked door with Cedric following. One glimpse told them Cedric was hale and hearty despite the crutch he leaned on and the white bandage wrapped haphazardly about his forehead. Elena cheered a hello when she saw Cedric and an ear-to-ear smile enlivened the old wizard's face as he spotted his favorite child. Elena slipped off her mare and dived into his arms, hugging the old man for all she was worth.

Ashley waved at the wizard, and Robert smoothly planted her on her feet to greet him with a warm hug, too. Dismounting, Robert staked the horses behind the cottage so they could graze on the tender grasses there. Instead of joining her beside Cedric, Ashley watched him scan the horizon as he completed a full turn. What was he doing? The scowl on his face worried her. Was he concerned about their safety?

She started to go to Robert to find out, but Cedric caught her arm and tugged her instead toward Olde Gylda. He wasted no time making the introduction so Ashley was forced to direct her attention to the face of the woman before her. As her eyes met the old crone's, she was stunned to see a pair of lively, ice blue eyes that should have belonged to a twenty-year-old. They examined her with surgical precision. True, the eyes inhabited a wizened and crinkled face, but they were *young*. Before Ashley recovered from her shock, the bent, old woman dressed all in voluminous black let out a loud whoop. "'Tis *ye*, my fine miss, 'tis *ye!* I hoped it would be *ye!*" She jumped up and down in her excitement and clutched Ashley's hands in both of hers. Then she led Ashley in an awkward jig, dancing in circles and singing a strange little tune.

Ashley's first instinct was to pull back in embarrassment and laugh at the peculiar, old woman's antics, but then something *was* familiar about her. She puzzled for a moment until the melody jolted her memory.

Naw, it couldn't be ... could it? Memories rushed into her consciousness like floodwaters through gaps in a door jam.

She had danced with this old woman before.

Ashley had been nine years old when her family joined Uncle Zeek in London for Christmas--a huge deal for the never-enough-money Duvall clan. In London for university research, Zeek had rented a flat in a lovely part of town for her family to share with him during the visit. They had had a marvelous time sightseeing around the city. Her uncle had contacts in all the right places to get them into museums and other tourist attractions, often with special treatment to boot. They were enjoying a balmy winter's day in Kensington Gardens examining the statue of Peter Pan near the Longwater area, when an old woman spied Ashley. Dressed in an antiquated black gown, she had been feeding the pigeons from her apron like a scene from an old movie. She shook the crumbs from her clothes and approached them. Much to everyone's surprise, the old woman seized Ashley's hands and the two of them danced a jig around the statue.

Uncle Zeek declared her a harmless old gypsy and chose to be amused, but her father glared thunderclouds. At last the old woman twirled his daughter around and deposited her in his embrace with nothing but a gap-toothed grin and a wink as an excuse for her behavior.

The family then beat a hasty retreat to another part of the park. Once there, her mother hugged her and anxiously asked if the old woman had hurt her in any way. Baffled, Ashley simply responded that the flute music made her want to dance. She would never forget the shocked faces of her mother and Uncle Zeek. Unsettled, her mother spit out, "But there was no music." Ashley told them she had heard it plainly and since the old lady did, too, they'd danced together until the music stopped.

This seemed to upset the adults again, although her father was strangely quiet. She was aware of her mother and Zeek talking in hushed tones the rest of the day about the incident. She had always wondered what was so remarkable about the episode. They may not have heard the music, but she had. Oddly, her little brother, who had watched the whole thing thinking Ashley was pretty funny, had changed the subject when asked if he could hear the music, too. It was a very curious encounter.

The same old woman danced with her now.

As they twirled Ashley became speechless, her brain swept clean of all words, but somehow her feet had no trouble moving in time with the old lady's.

∞∞∞

Noting the blood draining from his love's face, Robert became concerned and stepped into the path of the dancers, forcing them to stop. Ashley's eyes remained locked on the old woman's, unaware of his intrusion. Robert shot a glance at Elena and seeing his unease mirrored in her eyes waited no longer. He pushed between the two, forcing Ashley to look at him by blocking her view of the old lady. As he opened his mouth to question her, Ashley's vacant eyes fluttered and closed. She sank lifeless into his arms.

Elena shrieked.

Terrified, Robert scooped up Ashley and carried her into the tiny cottage, searching frantically for a soft place to lay her so he could examine her. He spun about the empty room looking for a bed, fearing he was in the midst of a nightmare. The room was enormous, like an empty great room. It made no sense. He hesitated for a moment, spying three doors facing him on the wall opposite the front door. *Which one?*

Olde Gylda answered his unspoken question when she marched to the center door, opened it for them, and stepped back to let them pass through. They entered a luxuriously draped and furnished bedroom fit for a king. Robert's head began to roll and he hastily laid Ashley on the bed before he lost his own balance.

What magic was this?

Furiously, he whirled to glare his question at Gylda who followed them into the bedchamber. She calmly placed a hand on the center of his back. It drained his body of the adrenaline pumping violently through him and dropped him to his knees.

"Ashley?" Robert choked on his words as he tried to catch his breath. "Wh-what happened?" Worried, Cedric and Elena joined them in the chamber, standing behind Gylda. To everyone's surprise, Olde Gylda loosed a raspy cackle that sent a chill through them. Three sets of eyes landed fiercely on Gylda's and she hurried to explain.

"All is right, my friends, all is right." Olde Gylda displayed her tooth-impaired smile to each of them. "I *know* this miss. I have danced with her before." She cackled again and her delight showed. The eyes on her now appeared thoroughly confused. "This young lady was but a child when I met her in London. She heard the music my magic played and we danced around Pan's statue in the park."

Still unsure, all were distracted from the tale as Ashley mumbled something as she tried to come around. She awoke to Robert's face inches from hers and smiled. Then, as memory returned, her smile fell into a grimace.

"Robert, I never, ever fainted, not once in my whole life until I came here." Ashley's eyes opened wide in wonder. "Every time I think I understand where I am and what's going on, something else freaks me out, and I'm out like a light." She tried to sit up, but Robert stilled her.

"Stay where you are a moment, sweeting." Concern mixed with relief in his eyes. "Regain your strength before you sit up or you may faint again."

Robert watched Ashley's eyes dart to the others in the room. Cedric stood behind a wide-eyed Elena and held her shoulders to steady her, but worry etched both faces. Gylda was grinning that tooth-challenged grin like she was a child of six. *What was going on?*

Gylda pushed Robert aside, much to his annoyance, and proceeded to pat Ashley's cheeks and place a hand on her forehead. Instantly, Ashley responded. She sat up and swung her legs around to sit on the side of the bed. Robert noted her cheeks had pinked and soon her color was normal again.

"I remember you. You are the old woman in Kensington Gardens I danced with as a child, aren't you?"

"Aha! Aha!" the old crone crowed. "I knew 'twas ye the minute I laid eyes on ye." Gylda rolled her eyes at each of the onlookers as if to say "told you so" and went on uninterrupted. "When Cedric came and told me of yer arrival at the castle, Lady Ashley, I hoped it was yer turn to travel."

"My turn? Thanks ... I guess." Ashley did not quite trust the old woman. "Why do you care? What difference does it make?"

For a moment, Gylda contemplated the audience witnessing this exchange while they waited for her explanation. "Ye all know by now our Lady Ashley is a time traveler, correct?" Everyone nodded. "What ye do not know is only a chosen few are Guardians of the Stones. I am one such being," she halted mid sentence to engage each of them, " ... and Lady Ashley is another."

Shocked silence ensued. Ashley's mind raced, however, as several bits of remembered conversation fell into place. She gained her tongue before anyone else. "So my uncovering the stone was not an accident?"

"Correct, m'darlin'." Those ice blue eyes danced and she grinned even bigger. "I knew ye were a quick one when I met ye."

Uncle Zeek flashed in Ashley's mind. He had invited her along on the dig and had moved her from group to group and place to place for no apparent reason. He had witnessed her meeting with Gylda years ago. Did he know about the stone?

"Where did this stone come from?" Ashley's mind ricocheted around her own experience, trying to piece it all together.

"*Ah,* the stone," Gylda rubbed her hands together with glee. "Time travelers have used stones to step through the universe since the beginning of time." Attention in the room was riveted to the old woman.

"There is more than one stone?"

"Yes, m'lord. The stones open portals to places separated by hundreds of years."

"Can you get lost using one?" Fear warped Elena's features as her eyes darted to Ashley.

"Nay, child, both ends of a portal move together in time, so a traveler steps out of one place and into the next in sync. If I spend a fortnight in one place, a fortnight hath passed in the other. See how 'tis?"

"Then it's been nine years for you, too, since we met." The witch confirmed with a nod. "So, can you tell me, Gylda, who created these stones? What's their purpose? Why do they exist?"

"My, my, child. Ye are a curious one, are ye not?" The old woman's pleased expression belied the gentle chiding. "The origin of the stones was lost long ago. Least-ways, 'tis what me ma said. She was a Guardian, too." Gylda's brow furrowed deep in thought. "The stones jest *are,*" she concluded. "To my way o' thinkin' they exist because humans have a knack for gittin' off track now and again. It takes a Guardian of the Stones to nudge 'em back on the right road."

"Who got off track, Gylda?" Elena asked what everyone else wanted to know as well.

Gylda smiled at the girl. "An example ye be needin', huh?" She squinted at the rest of her audience to be sure everyone was listening. "Well, most of ye are too young to remember the Black Plague that swept through the country with a vengeance not so very long ago." Cedric's face scrunched while Robert and Elena shuddered, well aware of the misery the plague had spread across their lands. Only Ashley knew the extent of it from her school days in history class. Olde Gylda forged ahead with her account. "'Twill one day be accepted by all that filth and fleas caused all the dyin'. 'Twas first learned by a time walker travelin' to the future, or we might all be restin' in our graves by now."

"You are correct regarding the cause, but how could one Guardian stop something as horrible and wide-spread as the plague?" Ashley's tone was doubtful as one eyebrow poked up.

"*Ah,* 'tis the rub, ain't it?" Gylda acknowledged. "Here, we will no' be rid of the plague fer years to come. But do no' mistake the power of a word whispered in an ear *here* and a hint dropped *there* to finally get the message across. 'Twill one day solve the problem. 'Tis all a Guardian can do, but in the end, 'tis enough." Gylda paused for emphasis. "Ye can be sure when an important discovery is made there is a Guardian behind it. Sometimes the one makin' the discovery *is* a Guardian."

"Maybe so," Ashley shrugged, not ready yet to accept the explanation, "but what am I doing here? What path am I correcting?"

"Why child, ye have no' figured that out?" Gylda gifted her with a toothless smirk. Ashley shook her head slowly, puzzling over what the old crone could be thinking.

"Why have ye not noticed women here have lost their way?"

Elena gasped and Ashley's eyes widened.

"I'm to show women they're equal to men?" Ashley blurted.

"Ye plant the seeds of rebellion," Gylda winked, her face dissolving into a mammoth grin.

"But I have done no such thing, Gylda. I've only stirred up trouble."

"Thus far ... " Gylda's head bobbed agreeably.

Now it was Ashley's turn to gasp as she grasped Gylda's meaning. Robert was one step ahead and grabbed Ashley's shoulders, spinning her to face him. Ashley beamed up at him, "There! You see, Robert? I *will* be back." Robert found her lips in reply.

∞ ∞ ∞

The rules for Guardians of the Stones, Ashley discovered, were few. First, she learned the stones only revealed themselves to Guardians. Anyone could activate the portals once unearthed by reading the inscription three times. Thus, it was up to the Guardians to protect the secret location of each stone to prevent unsuspecting souls from falling through the various holes in time.

When Ashley complained *she* had been an unsuspecting soul who had fallen through the hole, Gylda apologized for not meeting her.

"Ye arrived early according to my signs. Then this one," she indicated Cedric, "got himself knocked about by highwaymen when comin' to tell me ye were here. And, well, ye know the rest." Cedric managed to look a wee bit sheepish during this speech but said nothing.

This rule disturbed Ashley. What if the stone that showed itself to her on the dig near Stonehenge had been found in her absence by others searching for her? Had anyone else fallen through the hole in time? Gylda assured her this was not so, as the stone would have buried itself when the portal closed on that end. Others must be present to see where the stone buried itself. The rule referred to leaving the stone unguarded once it had appeared to a Guardian who did not immediately travel through the portal.

The only other rule was that a Guardian traveling back

in time or forward in time had an obligation to improve the lives of the people they met. This might be planting the seeds of social change in a previous time or sharing the knowledge gleaned from a visit to the future. It depended on what a Guardian discovered during the time walk. In addition, Guardians were taught they must do no harm, and they could stay on either end of a portal as long as they wished.

This was music to Ashley's ears. She would be able to travel back and forth between her home and here with impunity. Robert and Elena began to relax as Gylda explained the rules. Cedric was beside himself with excitement. He had so much to learn from Ashley, and he could not wait to begin.

One thing still troubled Ashley, however. She had been told Olde Gylda of Hampshire was dismissed from Hertford Castle for practicing the Dark Arts. Ashley had witnessed powers beyond that of the stone several times already here at Gylda's. Then there were the strange rooms inside the cottage where they were now. Were Guardians witches? Was she herself a witch and didn't know it?

"Gylda?" Ashley asked haltingly. "Are Guardians ... witches?"

"Why no, silly girl. Witches are an altogether different thing," Gylda chided. "Some witches are Guardians like me, 'tis true, but the two are not tied in any way. Cedric here is a wizard, but not a Guardian."

"Oh." Somewhat disappointed, Ashley thought having powers like Cedric and Gylda would have been pretty cool. "Then you do practice Dark Arts?"

Gylda's eyes narrowed and Cedric chuckled at the witch's consternation, replying for her, "That was an accident that was difficult to explain, Lady Ashley." He patted Gylda affectionately on the back. "The earl dismissed Gylda from the castle because he feared her powers. She knew from knowledge gained in a time walk he would likely lose hundreds of sheep to a sudden influx of marsh marigolds. Due to unusually heavy rains in their grazing pastures, the flowers were prolific. Gylda told the earl if he did not move his sheep to a different location, they would die from eating so many blooms. My lord did not heed her warning, as the flowers had never been a problem before. When the beasts keeled over as she predicted, the earl blamed the deaths of the animals on Gylda. He believed she had poisoned them herself by practicing Dark Arts. How else, he presumed, could she know 't'would happen?"

This was news to Robert and he shook his head disparagingly at his father's typical stubbornness.

"*Ah,* I see," Ashley nodded. "Fear of the unknown or the unexplained equals Dark Arts." She frowned for a moment and found the courage to ask the question she really wanted answered. "But magic does exist, doesn't it? I felt it myself when you touched my face and forehead today, didn't I?

Cedric and Gylda looked at one another and at each young person before blithely responding in unison, "Of course." Funny how the many questions poised on her lips drifted away on the afternoon breeze.

Chapter 32

It was time. Nothing was left to say that had not already been said, and the daylight would not last long, yet the unspoken need to prolong the inevitable persisted.

Ashley changed into her own clothes and tucked all her remaining possessions into the pockets of her pants. Then everyone piled out of the house at Cedric's command to gather in front of the cottage to watch Ashley's departure.

Olde Gylda ceremoniously presented the Guardian stone to Ashley. The old woman had summoned it in a spell when Cedric first told her about Ashley's arrival. In the meantime it had been hidden in full sight as a steppingstone to the well. Who would have thought?

Ashley flipped out about the spell part. "But Gylda, how can I summon a stone to appear to me? I don't know any spells."

"*Ah,* my child, 'tis simple. Ye need only be in the vicinity of a stone and 'twill find you." Gylda's face squished into a smile. "So calm yerself. Ye need not fear."

At the mention of the word fear, Ashley thought of the man on the other end she didn't want to see. "Gylda, do you know someone in my world named Abasi?"

A black look darkened the old woman's face, surprising Ashley with its intensity. "I do indeed. Our time travel was simple until he happened to catch me one day in the act of using a stone near Pan's statue in Hyde Park. Since then he and his men have chased me and other time travelers, getting closer to catching us each time. What do you know of him?"

Hearing this, Ashley didn't want to answer. "I'm afraid he followed Uncle Zeek and me from London and witnessed the stone taking me away." She cringed at Gylda's response.

"Damn and blast! The man will be the very death of me. He will not allow me to get close enough to make him forget what he has seen."

"Is he wanting to time travel or what is it he wants from you?"

"Oh, we know what he wants, the bugger." She stomped her foot and spit at the ground. "He believes my time travelers will make him rich if he blackmails 'em into bringing back articles from the past."

"Oh, like shopping by time traveler?" Ashley understood now why Abasi, the antiquities dealer, acted as he did. "He threatens me with exposure as a time traveler unless I bring him antiquities he can sell. What a way to make a fortune!"

"I told ye she was a smart one," Gylda said, nudging Cedric in the ribs with a sharp elbow. "You have the right of it, my girl." She turned a serious face to Ashley and continued, "I do not believe he will hurt you because he needs you, but avoid him, if at all you can. One day I will catch him unawares and erase his memory of time travelers. Until then, you will have to do your best to stay out of his clutches."

Ashley found herself tucked protectively under Robert's arm, the grim set of his face telling her he had not liked any part of this conversation.

"She's right, you know. He won't hurt me or he'd never get what he wants, Robert. It'll be okay."

"I understand, but I cannot be happy if a man in your world wants to threaten you and chase you about to make you work for him, now can I? Who will protect you?"

"Uncle Zeek won't let anyone hurt me, Robert, and once I'm out of England, Abasi won't know where I am, right Gylda?" The old woman stayed mum. That bothered Ashley. What territorial range did Abasi have, anyway? She was about to ask when Robert interrupted the thought with a whole new concern.

"What if Ashley finds a different stone and it opens a new portal? How would she get back home?" *Ah*, she thought, good question.

Olde Gylda was happy to change the subject from Abasi. "As long as the inscriptions are the same on either end, dearie, ye'll have no problem returning to where ye started."

At least that made Ashley feel a little better, but her anxiety about leaving, along with Abasi and all he entailed, kept her wired. Plus, Elena was so quiet and melancholy, Ashley had begun to worry about her.

Robert worried her even more. He kept muttering something about a dream and how this was just like it. What did that mean? His face had moved from worry to now the very picture of despair. No amount of reassurances from Gylda regarding time travel, Abasi, and Guardians of the Stones had changed his mind. He was heartsick to think she would be transported to a different world in a matter of minutes. In truth, she was pretty heartsick herself. Leaving here wasn't going to be easy.

Ashley stepped to him and took his hands, looking deep into his eyes, "You know I love you, Robert." He kissed her fingers and that prompted tears to run down her face. Thankfully, her voice was steady. "I promise not to be gone long, and when I come back I will not go traipsing about the world on stones, I can assure you."

Robert said nothing. He simply took Ashley in his arms and kissed her as if it were the last kiss they would ever share.

A wail rent the air, interrupting their goodbye. Ashley tracked it to Elena standing next to Cedric and Gylda. Her forlorn face made Ashley's heart ache. She ran to her and put her arms around her dear friend and kissed her cheek.

"It's okay, Elena. You've got to keep everyone in check until you see me again. Besides," she winked, "I'll be back ASAP." That got a smile through the tears from Elena and the two friends hugged hard before Robert pulled Ashley away.

"I cannot believe I am letting you go, sweeting. Have I lost my mind?" Tears welled in Robert's eyes, threatening to spill over and he quickly looked away, blinking hard to hold them back.

Ashley reached up and touched his cheek, memorizing that wonderful face. "Goodbye for now, Robert. Don't forget I love you!" Before Robert could stop her, Ashley dashed to the stone in front of Gylda and Cedric. With all the love in her heart, she gave them a blazing smile and repeated the inscription on the stone three times.

Twll yn amser.

Twll yn amser.

Twll yn amser.

Right on cue, the winds came, the dust swirled and *Ashley was gone.*

Chapter 33

This time Ashley knew what to expect and she let herself go willingly into the whirling, tempestuous storm, wrapping her arms tightly around herself to keep from flailing. She tried to stay alert, but her mind was no competition for the twirling funnel moving her through time. She was lost to it in a matter of moments.

When consciousness found her, Ashley had no idea how long she had been out, but the sun was lower in the sky. She knew immediately she was alone. She heard the solitary sounds of the wind whiffling through the grasses of the Salisbury plains before she even opened her eyes.

There's no place like home, huh?

She groaned, found her feet, dusted herself off, and noted she had only a few scrapes this time. *Hmm.* At least that was better.

Then without warning, panic slammed into her, making her stomach turn inside out and throwing everything she believed she knew in question. What had she done? Here she was by herself, stuck in this desolate place when she could have stayed with Robert. Why had she chosen to come back? Her chest tightened and she struggled to fill her lungs with air.

As if programmed, Gylda's warning flashed in her mind. *Abasi!* Was he here where she had left him? Spinning in circles, her heart thumped loudly in her ears as her eyes darted about the barren landscape checking to be sure the sly man was not in the shadows watching her. Finding no sign of him, she dropped to the ground in relief and put her head between her knees trying to get a grip on herself. *Just breathe.* What was done was done. She was here. She knew what she had to do and she'd better do it before it got darker or before Abasi did show up.

She struggled to her feet, brushed the tears from her eyes, took a deep breath, and reached into her back pocket for her phone. Turning it on she prayed it would have enough charge and bars to complete a call to her mother. The phone on the other end rang once, twice, three times, and then her mother answered. Tears flowed down her face at the sound of the voice she knew so well. She had believed she might never hear it again.

"Mom! Mom, it's me ... Yes, *Ashley* ... I know, Mom ... Don't cry. I'm fine!" As if talking to a child, Ashley explained to her astonished mother where she was standing.

"It's getting dark now and I'd rather not spend the night here alone ... I know, my phone battery is almost dead and I may not be able to get through to Uncle Zeek before it dies. Would you please call him and tell him to come pick me up? ... Thanks, Mom. He knows where to find me at the dig site ... Yeah, I'll have to tell you all about where I've been when I see you."

Her mom had been in England until yesterday looking for her and had just returned home. That narrow miss honestly hurt since Ashley wanted nothing more than to hug her mom right now. She would just have to wait.

"Hey, Mom, I need you to book me a ticket home, okay? ... I'm sure Uncle Zeek can get me to the airport, but I can do that, too ... I'm sure he *has* been worried ... I want to talk to him, too."

Static started to drown out her mother's voice so she frantically whirled around looking for better reception and *walked straight into a hard body.* Instantly, the hairs on the nape of her neck stood up announcing the owner of that body. Shocked, her knees wobbled and she swayed precariously.

"Robert? *Robert!*" Nothing else came out of her mouth because her addled brain melted and ran south. Robert scooped her up before she fainted and held her like a baby in his arms, kissing her until her mind was as empty as the land around them.

She finally pulled herself together and recovered a bit from the shock. Looking up into Robert's beloved face, peace replaced all panic. *This is exactly where I want to be.*

Ashley was pretty sure the dopey grin spreading from ear to ear on Robert's face matched the one on her own. "How did you get here?" she breathed, still not believing her good fortune.

"Remember Olde Gylda telling us anyone could use the stone by repeating the words inscribed if it were left exposed?" She nodded. "Well, I watched where it went and I used it." "You risked that for me?" Ashley whispered, supremely touched by this show of love.

"Someone must protect you," Robert replied, his grin now edging on smug.

"Ashley ... Ashley Marie Duvall, answer me ... Ashleeeey ... "

Abruptly, Ashley became aware of her mother yelling over the phone she had dropped in the grass. Not understanding where the noise was coming from, Robert hesitated before he let her go when she squirmed. Ashley jumped down to retrieve the device. "Oh my God, Mom, I'm so sorry ... Yes, yes ... I'm still here. Did you think I disappeared again?"

Ashley found a better spot a few steps away where the reception was clear and listened patiently to her mom. Her eyes, however, were fixed on Robert's perfect form silhouetted against the sunset. She was so overwhelmed by her love for him she thought it might spill out her pores. He watched her with that endearing, lopsided smile plastered across his face.

"Hey, Mom? Remember that ticket I asked you to book? ... Well, I'm gonna need you to book *two* tickets ... *Have I got a surprise for you!"*

Epilogue

1363 England

Restless, the enormous black stallion swished his tail in impatience and stomped an impressive hoof against the rocky ridge upon which his master held him. Damien Lundene, Baron of Bedford, might have blended as a shadow into the landscape dressed as he was from head to toe in dark clothing. A cape extended over the back of his horse and tussled with the wind along its edges to show an occasional glimpse of a white shirt underneath. The jaunty red feather in his cap set him apart from his surroundings. His attention was focused on the tiny cottage tucked into the valley below that belonged to Olde Gylda of Hampshire. He did not understand what he saw there.

He was here only because of the bizarre tale his blacksmith had told him. The man had shown up for work still drunk and sporting scrapes and bruises from an evening of debauchery. When questioned, the man told him of falling afoul of a lovely blonde woman he had followed to an inn. Much to his surprise, Bedford realized his smithy had described Lady Ashley Duvall, his former betrothed. She was an obsession he had yet to quit. Why was she not at Hertford Castle? Fearing for her safety, Bedford had promptly dropped everything to track her small party to Olde Gylda's cottage.

Pulling a spyglass from his saddlebag, he squinted into the device and blanched at what he saw. Robert Spycer, the Earl of Hertford's heir and his nemesis, stood out among the people below. He identified Robert's sister, Elena, standing between Olde Gylda and Cedric, the Hertford soothsayer. All were gathered around Lady Ashley in front of the old witch's house.

He was certain his friend Hertford had not given his children permission to visit Olde Gylda. The earl himself had banned the crone from his castle for practicing the Dark Arts, so why were the young people here and in the company of a witch and a wizard? Bedford shuddered and tried to shake off a premonition something evil was afoot.

The delectable Lady Ashley still occupied his foremost thoughts despite her wanting nothing to do with him. He would protect her at all cost if need arose. Even betrothed to another, she still drew him to her. He did not understand his own fixation, but like a bear to honey, he knew he would be stung, yet pursued her anyway.

Needing to make sense of what he watched below, he scanned the familiar faces. All were poised at the entrance to the cottage, ready for ... *what?*

He absently scratched the silver-haired side of his head as he pondered the question. Then Lady Ashley ran to Lady Elena and hugged her tightly. He grimaced, thinking they looked upset. What were they discussing that was so unsettling? Surely he was not at fault, was he? Both women had rejected his offer of marriage, but Hertford had not blamed him for that. Why would they? He sighed unhappily.

Still contemplating that notion, a sudden gust of wind whipped his hat off his head. He deftly snatched it before it soared over the ridge, but not before the red feather was sucked out of its nest in the cap. Startled, he watched the feather be inhaled by a larger twister that swirled, whirled, and then enfolded Lady Ashley in its winds. In a flash, the whirlwind was gone ... *and so was Lady Ashley.*

He was stunned. For a moment he could not breathe as if his lungs had been snatched along with his feather. Gasping, he shook his head and tried to locate his wits. Expecting pandemonium below, he searched the faces of the remaining four and was shocked by their responses. Their distress was apparent, yet they seemed to accept Ashley's disappearance. They hugged each other before entering the cottage in a somber single file.

The last to go inside, Robert hesitated in the doorway, turning around to peer at the spot where Ashley had vanished. A moment later, he strode to the exact place Ashley had stood and leaned down to dig out of the ground what appeared to be a paving stone.

The deep sound of Robert's voice reverberated in the now empty valley, as he intoned something Bedford could not quite make out, three times in quick succession.

How very odd.

The thought had only to form in his head when the mysterious twister was back, engulfing Robert in its winds. This time when its fury subsided, Robert was nowhere to be found. *He was gone.* Like Lady Ashley, the man had disappeared.

God's blood! Where did they go? What dreadful thing was this?

Cold shimmied down his spine as remnants of the whirlwind riffled and crackled through the dry grasses jutting out from the rock beneath him. His stallion sensed his unease. Threatening to bolt, he danced sideways, forcing Bedford to rein him in even tighter.

'Twas rumored Olde Gylda performed serious black magic, but no one had ever suspected her of making people disappear into thin air. This was outrageous. What should he do? What could he do?

Dismayed, he decided to investigate the cottage when no one else was around, thus avoiding Olde Gylda and her dark magic. He made a silent vow to find the stone Robert had held and get to the bottom of the mystery.

People do not simply disappear.

Lady Ashley had to be somewhere. Perhaps if he found and rescued her, she would return to him as his rightful betrothed and become his wife. The thought pleased him. Still, he had to contend with Lord Robert, did he not?

With much to think about, Bedford heaved a sigh, spun

his stallion around, and gave the big black his head. In seconds, they were engulfed by the swirling mists that settled in around them.

Acknowledgement

Special thanks to Hope Mason, Meredith Wise, Laurie Sauerbry, and Jim May for your time, guidance, and expertise in helping me create and edit *Time-Crossed Love*. Your love and support in slogging through early drafts and providing me with necessary feedback and advice has been invaluable.

About The Author

Jane Degray

Jane DeGray, known to family and friends as Jane May, lives with her husband Jim and her cat Toby (her boys) in the little Texas town of Friendswood, tucked between Houston and Galveston. As a casting director for independent film (Lifetime's The Preacher's Daughter and The Preacher's Mistress), she decided to write a screenplay that somehow morphed into a novel. Now she spends her time writing novels, reading all she can, and traveling the world, always with the next story in mind.

Books By This Author

Time-Crossed Wedding

Guardians of the Stones
Time Travel, Book 2

She's modern. He's medieval. Will they be stuck in time in between?

Time-crossed lovers Ashley Duvall and medieval Lord Robert Spycer plan to marry in modern day Texas but are interrupted and chased by an unscrupulous London antiquities dealer who hopes to catch a time traveler. Escaping through a Guardian stone, Robert and Ashley, along with her mother and brother, land in 1863 Lawrence, Kansas amid Civil War strife.

Will the foursome find their way back home? Not without the help of surprises from the past, a timely wedding, and a familiar witch.

Dear Reader

Time-Crossed Love was an adventure for me in researching the 1300s and the dress, customs, foods, falconing, and countless other intricacies of the time. As per historical fiction, I built a world for my characters based on historical accuracy where possible but with a lot of my own imagining in the process.

If a time traveler like Ashley really landed in 1363 England, her communication efforts would have been hampered by a language with many common words but a rather different sound and spelling we wouldn't recognize. I simplified their speech a great deal to make for easier reading.

The Earls of Hertford and Mowbray, Castle Hertford, and a Baron of Bedford did exist, but they bear little resemblance to mine in this novel.

The description of falconing is as accurate as I could make it. Please visit my website at *JaneDeGray.com* to see photos in the blog section of the gorgeous falcons from the novel.

The parts of the castle Ashley must navigate like uneven stairs, great hall, bailey, donjon, and the guarderobe are accurate for the time period. There really was a Quiet Woman Inn where the sign showed the body of a woman carrying her own head.

The medieval period gave me lots of fun things to play with for my time traveler, but on a more serious note, women had little power to speak of and were used and abused with great regularity by the men in their lives. Arranged marriages for daughters of the upper classes were the rule, so the marriage arrangements for my lovely ladies would not have been an exaggeration.

If you enjoyed *Time-Crossed Love,* please look for its sequel *Time-Crossed Wedding,* coming soon in 2020. More adventure awaits as Robert and Ashley are confronted with new complications as they step through time together in their travels.

Please consider writing a review wherever you purchased your book. Reviews help readers find books and help writers understand what you like to read.

Thank you! You can always find me as Jane DeGray Author on FaceBook, Twitter, and Instagram, email me at DeGray.Jane@gmail.com, or at *JaneDeGray.com.*

Jane DeGray

Made in the USA
Coppell, TX
05 July 2020